# Conclave

# Conclave

•••

*Tom Davis*

© Copyright 2016 Tom Davis

All rights reserved.

ISBN-13: 9781534706613
ISBN-10: 1534706615
Library of Congress Control Number: 2016909952
CreateSpace Independent Publishing Platform
North Charleston, South Carolina

PROLOGUE

# Sunday, April 27, 2014
# Rome, Italy

● ● ●

IT WAS SUPPOSED TO BE a gorgeous day, one resplendent with blue skies and wispy clouds, matching great weather with great ceremony. But it wasn't. The skies behind St. Peter's Basilica were thick and threatening. The great dome covering the mammoth church seemed to be waging a fight against the light but steady drizzle, doing its best to block the path of the dark clouds slowly forcing their way into St. Peter's Square. Nonetheless, the square's damp pavement and wet cobblestones showed that even the mightiest of man's monuments had limits when confronting the preferences and plans of the Almighty. God's timing could be mysterious, and on this day, it strangely was.

But despite the soft rain, few seemed concerned about the disappointing weather. Indifferent to the drizzle, a huge crowd was already present in the famous square, and thousands more continued to press into it from the surrounding streets and up the Via della Conciliazione, the broad avenue in front of the massive church leading into Rome. The mood was festive, the air filled with excitement and expectation. It seemed every face was glowing, covered with a broad smile, and even with the inevitable jostling that occurs when great gatherings of humanity get squeezed together in an enclosed space, everyone was courteous, greeting one another more as neighbors and friends than as the strangers they actually were. This crowd was polite, prayerful, playful, and in no small way, Polish.

The stone facade of St. Peter's was uncommonly adorned. Suspended from the space between the two huge columns on both sides of the immense church's main entrance were enormous banners showing the smiling faces of two giants of the Catholic faith, two men who had once ruled over this famous place and had delivered prayers and messages from the papal apartments overlooking the northern side of the square, whose influence had been—and still was—felt worldwide; two men who in some ways represented views that defined the poles of the church's doctrinal spectrum but who today shared one important thing in common: they were about to become saints.

It was an unprecedented event, the joint canonization of Popes John XXIII and John Paul II, who would from this day forward be forever linked by the grandeur of the moment. But for Bob Bishop, the chief Vatican correspondent for Cable News Network (CNN), it was proving to be a moment of major frustration. His white communications van was parked just outside the square, its large dish antenna one among the many creating something of an electronic forest, with each of the large saucers aimed to the heavens, pulsing invisible signals to invisible satellites orbiting far above. It was near 9:00 a.m., there was an hour to go before the actual ceremony was to begin, and CNN headquarters in Atlanta desperately wanted an interview with Americans who had made the long journey to witness the historic event.

Bishop's head hurt. For the past ten minutes, his earpiece had been blasting the same message from his producer, which was coming through in tones that were excited, harsh, and annoyingly loud. "Goddamn it, Bob! Get me an interview with some Americans! Any Americans! Hopefully literate Americans! An American couple, an American family, if you can find one! Hell, I'll take an American dog! But enough of all these foreigners…*I need some Americans!*"

Bishop grimaced, his face reflecting both the mental frustration in his brain and the physical pain in his right ear. "I'm trying, Jack!" he protested into the small microphone clipped to his collar. "But I just haven't seen any! Rome is in Italy, you know! And guess what, most of the people here are Italian! And those who aren't are Polish! And—*news flash*—Italians and Poles are foreigners, Jack!"

There was a slight delay as his words worked their way through the heavens and back to Atlanta, but the inevitable response was predictably harsh. "Don't BS me, Bob! There have got to be plenty of Americans there! Get off the goddamn van—and your goddamn ass—and go find some! Go find one! *Now, Goddamn it!*"

"Poor choice of words, Jack!" Bishop yelled back. *"Especially given where I am at the moment! I said I'm working on it!"*

Bishop had been walking around, looking for possible guests among the crowd swirling around near his van, but now he changed tactics and sprinted to the temporary camera platform that stood on the edge of the square facing St. Peter's. It had two levels to accommodate all the cameras and their crews, and he scurried to the ladder attached to the side and climbed briskly up to the topmost level. Since his days as a war correspondent in Iraq, he had taken to carrying a pair of military-style binoculars around his neck, complete with an artillery reticle pattern in one lens. He had found them abandoned in the desert while covering the American invasion in 2003. Wedging himself between a camera and one of the aluminum support poles, he raised the binos and looked out across the rapidly swelling crowd.

"Oh my God!" he mumbled to himself as he scanned the huge multitude, searching for anything that would suggest Americans. Maybe a homemade sign of some sort, maybe something saying: "Hi there, Omaha." Perhaps even a small American flag—one either sewn onto a jacket or being waved. Jack was right, there had to be some Americans in this growing mass of humanity. After all, Catholics comprised the single largest religious denomination in the United States, accounting for about a quarter of the American population. It would be a statistical impossibility that there weren't Americans in St. Peter's Square for such a momentous church event.

"Come on…Come on!" Bishop whispered to himself, as he rolled the binoculars' focusing wheel with his right index finger. He spotted someone. "There! He's gotta be American," he softly exclaimed to nobody, after spotting a fellow wearing a Chicago Cubs baseball cap. But that hope quickly vanished when this particular Cubs fan suddenly lifted a red-and-white Polish flag. Red-and-white Polish flags were flying everywhere around the square, but what Bishop needed was red, white, and blue. "That fellow probably supports the Cubs from Warsaw rather than Wrigley," he grumbled to himself.

He continued to slowly scan the crowd, sector by sector, using the scanning technique the Third Infantry Division artillery lieutenant had shown him on the road to Baghdad eleven years before. It was a simple yet effective method. He aimed the binos at the temporary red throne box in front of the basilica, the one Pope Francis would use to address the crowd during the ceremony on this misty Divine Mercy Sunday. He slowly scanned left and then back to the right, passing the temporary altar that had been constructed just in front of the pope's throne. The thought momentarily flashed through his head of the many ironies in the modern world. Here he was using a set of old Iraqi artillery binoculars, found outside of Fallujah in Iraq, to survey a huge crowd gathered in front of one of the holiest places in the Christian world.

"Bishop!" His earpiece was screaming at him again. "Bishop, Goddamnit! Are you there?" It was Atlanta again. He ignored it. He'd never find what they wanted if he kept talking to them. But this was like finding the famous needle in the famous…

"Ahhh," he mumbled to himself. "What have we here?" He quickly rolled the focus knob back and forth to sharpen the picture he was seeing through the old lenses. He had spied a tall couple, walking along one of the metal barricades, strolling casually through the crowd between him and the giant *witness* obelisk that marked the center of the great square. They could be American. They had that American look. They were both tall, and Americans were tall—usually taller than the Europeans—and this was obviously an overwhelmingly European crowd. They stopped, and the woman looked over in his direction, pointing to something. She had on a very stylish rain hat with a wide brim that slightly sagged over her glasses. Her raincoat was open, revealing a very nicely cut floral-print dress, also very stylish.

Now the man looked in Bishop's direction. The reporter's eyes widened. "Bingo," he said to himself. The man had on a red cotton shirt worn beneath a light jacket, its Nike swoosh logo clearly visible. And he wore a baby-blue baseball hat with gold lettering above the bill. Bishop squinted slightly as he looked through the binoculars. The letters were scripted and a bit hard to read, but he was certain that they said, "UCLA." Like the artillery lieutenant he had been embedded with in Iraq, Bishop now had a target.

He dropped the binoculars, and they fell down to his chest, their leather strap going taut around his neck. He dashed over to the edge of the camera platform, threw his legs on either side of the ladder attached to it, and slid down to the ground, using the speed technique he had learned during a week covering the New York City fire department. Immediately upon hitting the ground, he dashed to the bottom area of the platform where his cameraman was taking refuge from the annoying rain and enjoying a cup of coffee, his camera gear piled on the pavement beside him. "Curtis, grab your stuff! Follow me! Quickly!"

The cameraman dropped the coffee and lifted his bulky TV camera. He didn't ask any questions. His job was simply to follow Bishop and capture images of him asking questions. It was a very straightforward arrangement. And this gig in Rome was an especially good deal. No one was shooting at them for a change, and they were going to a great pasta place later that night.

"Jack!" Bishop shouted into the small microphone clipped to his shirt collar. "I think I've got an American couple! They're maybe a hundred and fifty yards away! Curtis and I are headed toward them now."

"About goddamn time!" the earpiece replied.

Bishop ignored it again. No time to be talking to Atlanta. By then, he and Curtis were in full stride, dashing through the crowd as quickly as they could, trying to avoid knocking anyone down. The media had a bad enough reputation without someone capturing an image of a

CNN reporter and his cameraman knocking an old Polish nun to the pavement.

They reached the low metal barricade that had been set up along the edge of the square. It more or less marked the dividing line between Italy and the Vatican city-state, in no small way demarcating the chaos of Rome from the highly organized, scripted life inside the epicenter of Catholicism. Bishop hopped onto one of the barricades, landing with his feet on its lower strut, giving him about an extra foot of height. He scanned the crowd, looking for the couple, a task made more difficult by the need to balance himself on the rickety barrier. He couldn't see them. His spirits sagged slightly.

"Shit!" he snarled, as his head quickly snapped to the left and right, feverishly trying to locate the UCLA baseball hat.

By now Curtis had caught up to him, lugging the awkward and bulky camera gear. "See what you're looking for, Bob?"

"Nah! I think I've lost them. Damn it!" Bishop was about to jump down and move further right, the direction in which the couple had been headed when he had last spotted them. But suddenly, the crowd parted a bit, something of a Red Sea moment, and there they were, standing about twenty yards away, the man pointing toward something of interest on the colonnade bordering the north side of the square, while the woman nodded in acknowledgment. They had to be American, and they would be perfect: middle-aged, tall, well dressed, attractive, and no doubt articulate. They should be a TV reporter's dream, especially when that pesky voice in Atlanta was trying to make it into a nightmare.

"There!" Bishop pointed the couple out to his cameraman as he hopped across the barrier. Curtis nodded, looking left and right to see if there was an opening in the barricade he could get through. He couldn't see one. Bishop could see his problem. "I'll go over to them! Get to me as fast as you can!" he barked.

Curtis nodded again and headed off to his right. He quickly found a place where two of the barriers had pulled apart, leaving a slight gap that he could squeeze through.

Bishop moved quickly through the crowd, his eyes fixed on the couple. He was standing beside them in a few seconds. "Excuse me," he said to the woman, reaching her first.

The two of them looked down into his face—down because they both towered above the reporter's five-feet-eight-inch frame.

Bishop didn't wait for them to ask questions. He was in a rush to ask his own. "Hi, I'm Bob Bishop with CNN. I'm covering the ceremony today. Are you from the United States?"

The couple exchanged a quick glance.

"Yes, we are," the man crisply replied, adding no additional information.

Bishop looked back and forth between the two faces in front of him. Maybe this wouldn't work so well. They were American, they were both quite telegenic, but they might not be very chatty. In the middle of all this excitement, they seemed rather calm, even a bit detached.

"OK, great," Bishop continued. "We want to get Americans on camera for our coverage. You know, just kind of a background setting thing. Who are you? Why are you here? What does all this mean to you? That sort of stuff. I'm sorry I'm being somewhat cryptic, but we're on deadline and my producer back in Atlanta has been giving me a lot of shit... Excuse my language."

The man and the woman briefly glanced at each other and then smiled at the reporter.

"Well, we understand pushy superiors," the man replied. He turned to the woman. "What do you think? You OK with a little scene-setting interview? I'm sure the kids will get a chuckle out of it."

"I don't think they watch CNN," she responded with a slight smile. "But...OK. Sure." She turned back to Bishop, who was fumbling with the power pack for his microphone. "How many questions will you likely be asking?"

Before the reporter could answer, Curtis showed up with his heavy camera and immediately began to look for the best angle to do the filming. If they played it just right, he should be able to get a good view of the couple in the foreground, along with the obelisk, the papal apartments, and probably most of Apostolic Palace itself in the background. Since the couple was tall, and he would be aiming the camera up slightly; it should work—be great in fact.

Bishop nodded to Curtis. He could see the angle his cameraman had developed. They had worked together so long they barely needed verbal communication. He turned back to the woman. "As I said, basic questions, ma'am. Just a few. The basic what, where, and why of journalism. As I said, it'll only take a minute. Maybe less. I don't know how they'll use it. It'll probably get included in final coverage tonight when we wrap it all up. Atlanta will make that decision. Sorry for all the haste, but I'm just the little foot soldier on the ground."

"Well, I understand being a foot soldier," the man answered. "My wife and I have had that sort of role once. I would prefer, however, that you not mention our names. Can we maybe just be 'an American couple'?"

Bishop thought this a bit odd. Most people wanted to be mentioned by name in these spots. But he didn't have time to debate it, and it was not a big deal for what would likely be thirty seconds of air. "Sure, no problem. We'll go with that—just identifying you as an 'American couple.' And the UCLA hat will drive the point home. As I said, this will be simple, unscripted, and—"

"*Bishop*!" The earpiece was screaming yet again. "I need Americans, and I need them *immediately*!"

"Jack, I've got an American couple with me right now. Right in the square."

"Great! Let me see 'em!"

Bishop motioned to Curtis to power up and start the camera feed. His cameraman positioned himself and framed the American couple in his lens. "Sir, can you move a bit closer to your wife and maybe the two of you move a bit to your left. A little more please…there! Right there." Curtis pulled his eye away from his lens protector and nodded at Bob.

Bishop's earpiece came to life again. "All right there, Bob! They look great. All-American. OK. Get set, and we'll be going live with them in about ninety seconds."

"Live?" Bishop exclaimed. "Did you say *live*?"

"Yes, butthead. We're going to do it live! You act like you've never done live TV before! Jesus, Bob…pull it out of your ass, OK?"

The couple stood by silently while Bishop's private conversation with Atlanta continued. He was glad they didn't have earpieces themselves to hear the discussion. Bob turned to the man. "OK, sir, we'll be on in about a minute, and we're going to try and do it live, OK?"

The man and the woman nodded. It made no difference to them. They struck Bishop as unusually cool and collected. He briefly wondered who they actually were and what they did, but his mind quickly shifted back to the questions he had to ask to make this into compelling and now *live* TV.

"Stand by," Atlanta instructed. "Five, four, three, two…You're on!"

"Good morning, ladies and gentlemen. This is Bob Bishop broadcasting live from St. Peter's Square in front of the Vatican where in about an hour Pope Francis will declare two of his predecessors, Popes John XXIII and John Paul II, to be Saints of the Catholic church. A large crowd has been building in the square since earlier this morning. I have no estimates on how big it is or how big it will become, but—believe me—it's big. I'm standing here in the square with an American couple who has come to witness today's historic event. Sir, where have you traveled from in the United States?"

"California."

"And when did you and your wife arrive?"

"Yesterday."

Bishop was suddenly quite uneasy. After all his crowd scanning to find Americans, he might have wound up with a couple so shy he was only going to get one-word answers. Riveting TV that would be! But, Atlanta wanted it now -- and wanted it live. He was stuck with what he had. "Have you been to Rome before?" He pushed the microphone toward the woman, hoping she would be chattier. She was.

"Oh yes, we have been here before. In fact, we were here, in this very square, thirty-six years ago when Pope John Paul walked out on that balcony and was presented as the new pope. It's so hard to believe. I mean… it seems like yesterday."

Bishop had just gone from rags to riches! What a coup! They were Americans! They were here! And they were here when John Paul first became pope! "How exciting for you!" he instinctively exclaimed. "You were *here* when John Paul became pope! And what were you doing here way back then?"

"We were on a business trip," the man quickly interjected. Bishop had hoped more details would follow, maybe what sort of business they were in, but nope, that was it.

"So, how does it feel to be here again? In a sense, you've made this journey with John Paul II, from cardinal of Kraków…to pope…to saint." He again pushed the microphone toward the woman, hoping to increase his odds of greater detail and color.

"It's just wonderful…absolutely wonderful. And yes, I do feel like we have made the journey with him, in a sense. Back then, no one expected him to be selected as pope since there hadn't been a non-Italian pope in centuries. So that alone…watching the surprise on the faces of the people and then, when he addressed them in Italian, watching them as they immediately embraced him. It was almost magical. Wouldn't you agree, dear?"

The woman turned to the man, and Bishop reluctantly shifted the microphone toward him, hoping it would not result in dead air. This time, it didn't.

"Oh yeah, I'd agree. It very much was close to magical. It was history being made, and, I think, even the Italians who were with us here in the square that night could recognize that. And it seemed after so many years of having a pope who was a bit proper and somewhat distant and, of course in his last years, aging, they were pleased to have a pope who was relatively young, energetic, in possession of a warm smile, and clearly charismatic."

"You're referring to Pope Paul there…being proper and distant? Rather than the first Pope John Paul?"

"Yes, of course. The first John Paul had many engaging qualities as well. He also was warm, connected well with people, and his smile was electric. It was a great shame that his reign only lasted a month, but sometimes history moves in unexpected ways. He might have been a great pope himself. Pope Benedict has commented in the past that he believes John Paul I was also a saint. But his successor had the qualities needed for the period of his reign, and…well, now he *is* a saint—or shortly will be!"

"Bob! *Great*! Really *great*! Just fucking *great*!" Atlanta was again torturing Bishop's eardrum, but he could tell they were thrilled. "That's enough, Bob. Thank them and then cut it and move on. We're going to the anchors at the platform."

Bishop immediately wrapped it up. "Let me thank the two of you for talking with us and sharing your unique perspective on today's canonization ceremony. Best wishes, enjoy the ceremony, and have a safe trip home."

The woman leaned in a bit to get closer to the microphone. "You're welcome, and best to you as well."

"We're off," Curtis barked, lowering the heavy camera from his increasingly aching shoulder.

By this time, the crowd around them had thickened, many hoping for the chance to have a brief moment on TV, even if just in the background. Bishop lowered his microphone and reached out to the Americans in front of him. He extended his hand to the man and then to the woman. "Thank you both very much. My goodness. I wish you had given me a little more advance warning that you were here when John Paul became pope. That would have been an interesting angle to develop further. I think we might even have done a segment on it. That's all so interesting—fascinating even."

The man briefly shook his head. "Not really. We were here then. We're here now. That's about all there is to it."

The woman smiled and nodded in agreement.

Bishop's eyes switched back and forth between the two of them. He was a journalist—and a good one. He had won prizes, professional recognition. Everyone expected that he would replace Wolf Blitzer at some point. He could smell a story a mile away. And he smelled one here. The aroma was unmistakable. But he had other things to do on this historic day, so at least for the time being, he knew he'd have to let it go. He didn't have time to trail them, and they had never offered their names. Nor had they once referred to one another by name. Somehow there was more to this, but he had to move on. He reached into his jacket pocket and pulled out a business card, handing it to the woman.

"Here. Send me a note, and let's keep in touch. It was wonderful meeting you both. Enjoy the day." With that, he and his cameraman scurried away, Atlanta already barking new instructions into their ears.

The man and woman watched them disappear and then turned their gazes to each other and enjoyed a quick, subtle laugh. The woman looked at Bishop's business card for a few seconds and then methodically tore it into small pieces and dropped them on the cobblestones. The man stretched upward on his toes to look over the sea of humanity in front of him and then dropped down a bit and turned to his companion.

"We obviously can't stand where we did then, but how about over there?" He pointed ahead and to his right. "That should be a similar angle, and it's rather close to where we were."

The woman shook her head. "Oh, it's not at all. And you know it," she playfully replied. "But let's go. I'm sure it will be fine."

He took her hand, and they moved through the crowd to the spot he had selected. It offered something of a view of the pope's throne, the temporary altar, the flowers arrayed all around it, and to their right rear, the Apostolic Palace. Suddenly the air was filled with the sounds of the singing the Litany of the Saints, and the cardinals of the church, clad in white vestments, slowly began to emerge from the great basilica, eventually followed by Pope Francis and his attendants. And there the American couple stood for the next two hours while the ceremony was conducted, enjoying it all immensely, feeling a swell of emotion, and rocking constantly back and forth on their increasingly aching middle-aged feet.

And then, seemingly in no time, it was over. Moments of great history tend to pass quickly, and this one was no different. There was some more singing among those gathered around them, some of it in Italian, some of it in Polish, some of it in tongues that were hard to interpret. But slowly, the great throng of which the couple was a part began to drift out of St. Peter's Square, and they shuffled out with them. Crossing the barricades, they turned left and headed north along the Via di Porta Angelica, the Roman street defining the eastern border between Italy and the Vatican city-state. Reaching the square's end, they turned left onto Via Leone IV, which also bordered the Vatican, and followed it to the intersection with Viale Vaticano, where they turned toward the area across from the entrance to the Vatican Museum.

Each scanned the route ahead, speaking little, looking for a location they had visited long ago, one they had decided to seek out, wondering if it was still there and if it was, after all these years, if they would recognize it. He was sure he would, and she was equally sure she wouldn't.

"I think I see it up ahead. Yeah, right over there, that's definitely it," he said, pointing.

"How can you tell?"

"Remember this walkway that headed down the slope between these two buildings? The one you slipped on?"

"Not really."

"Well, trust me. It was here then. And that, my dear, is the Café Vaticano. Right there on the corner. See the name on the awning? It's a bit hard to read from where you're standing."

The woman stepped around him. He was right. The lettering was a bit faded, but that was clearly what it said. She smiled at him, took his hand, and led him underneath the awning and out of the slight drizzle that continued to fall. She saw the table she wanted, and it was empty. He followed as she gently stepped toward a couple of metal chairs around a slightly wobbly table just outside the main entrance into this small, very typically Italian coffee shop. As they adjusted themselves into their only moderately comfortable seats, each scanned the scene surrounding them. Small Fiats moved along the street, usually at a somewhat faster pace than prudent, while people walked past, usually at a much slower pace than the Americans thought possible. The excitement of the occasion still lingered, but it was now after the noon hour and everyone was getting hungry. The scene was somehow identical to the one she remembered from long ago, yet in some ways, it was not at all the same.

"Can I get you something?"

The American couple looked up at the attractive young Italian waitress, who had obviously pegged them as Americans and rolled out her flawless English.

"What red wines would you have?" the woman asked.

The waitress immediately pulled a short wine list from her apron and handed it to her. The Americans located a light-bodied Tuscan vintage they were familiar with and—since it was a special day—ordered a bottle. They then returned to their own private reflections, watching the scene on the street but not speaking, awaiting the wine.

It arrived quickly. The waitress skillfully cut the wrapping and removed the cork. The woman tasted it, going through the usual ritual before declaring it suitable. The waitress poured them each a glass and quickly departed, sensing that the Americans wanted some quiet time, at least to the extent that quiet time was feasible in an early afternoon while sitting at a sidewalk café in Rome.

There was an audible sound that ended their moment of reflection. It was her cell phone, playing her "California Dreamin'" ringtone, signaling a call from their daughter. She dug into her purse for the iPhone and pushed the "answer" button. "Hi, Zoe. How are you? Did you see the ceremony? I'm sure it was covered, wasn't it?" She looked at her husband and whispered, "Zoe."

He nodded and took another sip of the wine, watching his wife as she suddenly became quite excited.

"Really! Seriously!" She pulled the phone away from her ear and looked across the table. "Zoe saw us on TV! She saw the interview we did with CNN!"

"She did! Already! Goodness. What—"

She waved him off. Discussions between a mother and daughter took on an immediacy that couldn't be interrupted. He smiled; leaned back in his shaky, unlevel metal chair; took another sip of the wine; and waited for the phone conversation to run its course.

After several minutes, the woman said good-bye to her daughter, stuffed the phone back in her purse, and turned to her companion. "Well, what are you thinking?"

He paused to gather his thoughts, as he usually did. "I'm thinking it was an amazing day—amazing that it has no precedent in history and amazing that we were here to witness it after so many years, and even more amazing that it would end this way. What an exclamation point to put at the end of a very complex sentence." He hesitated and turned toward the woman, reaching for her forearm with one hand while lifting his glass with the other. They exchanged smiles, softly clinked their glasses, and took a sip of the Tuscan red, which had been a very good choice.

Placing the glasses back on the small round table, they both glanced around again, calibrating what they were seeing now against what they remembered. The woman saw it first. She squinted her eyes a bit before reaching into her purse for her glasses. She placed them on her face and then squinted a bit more, searching for the right magnification in the progressive lenses. "Look," she said, pointing to an area on the limestone wall just above the corner of the café's large sliding door.

The man looked to where she was pointing, narrowed his eyes, and then got up from his chair to walk over to the doorway, using his height to get a good look at the streaked limestone. He reached up with his long arm and rubbed his fingers across a jagged hole. He smiled, slowly turned, and headed back to their table, lowering his large, tired frame rather heavily into his small chair.

The woman looked at him. "Is that it? Is it actually still there?"

"That's it," the man said, more exhaling than speaking. "I'm quite sure that's it. All these years and they've never bothered to fix it or fill it in. Italians! Thank goodness they have great food and wine."

The woman looked at him across the top of her glasses, softly smiling as she usually did. "Well, maybe they saved it for us, figuring someday we'd come back."

The man nodded, leaned back in his chair, folded his hands in front of his face, and rested his chin on them. "Or maybe they saved it for themselves."

Once more their hands grasped together, and they raised their wineglasses and shared another silent toast. It had been a great day. It had been a great story. And for them, it had been a great journey.

CHAPTER 1

# September 29, 1978
# Rome

• • •

Even for a commonly quiet place, it was an uncommonly quiet night. And for the couple slowly strolling into St. Peter's Square, the quiet was such that the echoing of their shoes on the old cobblestones seemed to be the only sound. They were coming from a lovely dinner in Rome, and with the night so still and pleasant, they had decided to walk back to the Vatican, the place where she occasionally visited and where he worked.

"It's always so fabulous here," Maria Bruhlmann said to her son, as she scanned the buildings around the square—all magnificent even when only dimly lit. "I so enjoy coming to see you whenever I can. But then again, what mother doesn't enjoy seeing her son?"

Sergeant Hans Bruhlmann smiled. He was a proud member of one of the world's most famous, if certainly smallest, armies: the Pontifical Swiss Guards. Although visitors to the Vatican, the historic city-state in the center of Rome, perceived the Swiss Guards—in their famously colorful outfits of blue, red, and orange—to be everywhere, such omnipotence was quite the illusion. In fact, the Swiss Guards only numbered 110 soldiers, barely a rifle company in most militaries. But all Swiss Guards were, like Bruhlmann, Swiss, male, Catholic, volunteers, educated, and committed solely to the safety of the pontiff of the Catholic church. To those outside the Vatican, their duties and responsibilities, like their largely dysfunctional uniforms, seemed much more ceremonial than tactical, but to those inside the Holy See, the Swiss Guards were highly valued and in some ways a metaphorical reminder of a strong commitment to the church.

Bruhlmann's mother traveled from Switzerland three times a year. It was easier for her to get to Rome than for him to get to Zurich. She enjoyed the visits, and so did he. They continued their leisurely evening stroll and in a few more steps were standing near the center of the open plaza that sprawled in front of St. Peter's Basilica, one of the world's most famous buildings and the literal and figurative center of both the Vatican city-state and the worldwide Catholic church.

St. Peter's square was elliptical with the magnificent Bernini colonnades facing each other across 250 meters of elaborate, polished cobblestone. In the center stood an ancient Egyptian obelisk, believed to have been present at the execution of Saint Peter, the first pope, and moved to its current location in front of the basilica by Pope Sixtus V in 1586, providing a physical reminder of historical continuity.

Bruhlmann and his mother stopped near the obelisk to gaze around the great square.

Maria scanned the scene admiringly and then turned inquisitively to her son. "I know you've told me before, Hans, but where's the pope's apartment?"

Bruhlmann took a moment to serve as tour guide. "The pope," he replied, pointing to the rightmost corner on the top floor of the Apostolic Palace, "lives right up there."

"You mean in that room with the light on?" his mother asked.

Bruhlmann looked up in surprise. This was odd. Pope John Paul had only been the supreme pontiff for a month, but everyone at the Vatican had learned his schedule, one dictating much of their own. The pontiff turned in every night precisely at 9:30 and rose in the morning at 4:30. Bruhlmann glanced at his watch. Its hands showed 10:45. "Yes, Mother... correct, the one with the light on." He checked his watch again, ensuring he had read it correctly. "Well, we should say good night, as I have duty this evening. I'm the commander of the watch starting at midnight. I'll be supervising the guards until dawn. Can we have lunch tomorrow before you leave?"

Maria smiled. "Of course. My train leaves at three in the afternoon. I'll do some shopping in the morning and call you."

"Great," Bruhlmann replied before leaning down to his mother and giving her a soft kiss on the forehead. They parted, and she headed off in the mist to her hotel, about two blocks down the Via della Conciliazione, the sprawling boulevard in front of St. Peter's. Bruhlmann turned his eyes back to the pope's bedroom window. "What's going on?" he wondered, thinking for a moment he'd call up to the guard at the papal apartment to see if anything was wrong. But he decided not to. He'd change into his uniform and then go to the guardroom and get some sleep. As the sergeant of the guard, he was allowed to rest, as long as he was physically present and making his prescribed rounds. After going to the guard barracks and changing into his uniform, he returned to the central guardroom and was soon stretched out on the cot reserved for the sergeant in charge.

As a few hours passed, he discovered that he couldn't get comfortable on his lumpy mattress. His body wanted to sleep, but his brain kept interrupting with lengthy lists of those things for which he was responsible, and he was still bothered by that light in the pope's window. He tried to dismiss it all, but his brain refused to shut down. He sensed something was wrong. The concerns of his brain slowly defeated the desires of his body. Such was the lot of all professional soldiers—duty first.

Bruhlmann got off the cot, deciding to abandon the sleep effort. There was no immediate alternative; he would pull on his uniform and take a brief walk around the historic domain over which he was—temporarily at least—the senior supervisor. He flipped on the small night-light on the table next to his bed and then reached down to the floor, grabbed his ankle-high black shoes, and slowly pulled them over the knee-high black stockings he had worn to bed along with his baggy blue trousers. He pulled on a matching blue shirt and buttoned it up to his chin before snapping into place a starched white collar that fit snuggly around his neck. Finally, he placed a black beret on his head and adjusted it to the precisely prescribed angle. After grabbing a pair of white gloves on the folding chair by the door, he stepped out into the cool morning air.

Bruhlmann strolled out of the guardhouse, turned to his left, and moved through a tight passageway allowing access into St. Peter's

Square. One of his sentries was standing there, as he was supposed to be, keeping a silent vigil on the small opening. Bruhlmann and the sentry nodded at each other as he walked by, but they exchanged no words. It was calm and quiet, and there was nothing that needed to be said.

The Swiss sergeant sauntered into the square and slowly walked about halfway to the obelisk. He checked his watch again; it now read 4:25 a.m., and the square was empty, as it always was at such an early hour. He looked up to the pope's bedroom window. The light was still on. But it was about time for His Holiness to arise, enjoy his morning coffee, and begin his meditations, so maybe things were normal after all. Perhaps last evening, John Paul had been plagued by the same strange restlessness that Bruhlmann himself had experienced. Perhaps there was just something in the autumn air. Bruhlmann looked around and then, satisfied that all was well, headed back to the guardhouse.

● ● ●

Several floors above in the papal apartment, Sister Vincenza Taffarel, the pope's primary personal assistant and cook, was going about her own early morning chores. Sister Vincenza was a dedicated servant of the church. She had become a nun at a young age, and service to the church and God were all she aspired to in life. She had risen to mother superior back in Venice, and her determined character and slender build allowed her to hustle those under her charge from chore to chore on the tight household schedule she had strictly enforced for Cardinal Albino Luciani.

Vincenza had served Luciani since his days as a bishop in Vittorio Veneto nineteen years earlier, and she knew his daily preferences and needs better than anyone. In the morning, upon waking, his most immediate need was for a cup of coffee. In addition to helping him accelerate through the normal human waking process, Luciani liked the coffee for a personal reason; it covered an unpleasant morning taste in his mouth, the lingering result of a sinus operation years before.

During their years in Venice, prior to his election as pope, Sister Vincenza had always taken the coffee straight into Luciani's bedroom. But in Rome, the always vigilant Vatican curia, the governing bureaucracy of the church, led by its authoritarian secretary of state, French cardinal Jean Villot, felt this violated some unknown historical protocol. Villot had instructed that the morning brew be left in an adjoining study outside the pope's bedroom, with its presence signaled to His Holiness by a knock on his bedroom door. John Paul did not see the need for this adjustment to his previous practice, but as he already had a lengthy catalogue of substantive issues he intended to raise with Villot and the curia, he had decided to yield on this minor demand. He evidently referenced the overall issue in a comment he made to a visitor following his papal election, noting that the two most difficult things to find in the Vatican were "honesty and a good cup of coffee."

Having brewed the coffee in the papal apartment's small kitchen, Sister Vincenza poured it into a silver flask, placed in on a round pewter tray along with a cup and saucer, and headed toward the study adjacent to the pope's bedroom. As she approached the open door of the study, she paused in surprise at seeing light beneath John Paul's bedroom door, suggesting he was already awake. She stood in place for a moment, puzzled, but positioned the coffee flask in its usual place, then walked over to knock gently on the bedroom door. "Good morning, Holy Father," she said softly. There was no reply. This was also unusual, but after a few moments Vincenza departed and headed back toward the kitchen to assemble the pope's simple breakfast.

Curious and somewhat concerned, Sister Vincenza returned fifteen minutes later to the pope's study only to find the coffee flask and tray untouched. The bedroom light still reflected on the floor below the doorsill. Sister Vincenza walked over to the door and lightly tapped on it again. In the two decades she had served Albino Luciani, he had never once overslept, nor had she known him to sleep with a light on.

"Holy Father?" she called again, a bit louder than before. "Are you up, Holy Father?" Still, there was no answer. The sister crossed herself, asking for forgiveness for her impending disobedience of Cardinal Villot's instructions. She opened the door and stepped into the room. Once she did, her eyes widened, and her hands instinctively shot up, nearly knocking the dark-rimmed glasses from her face. She stumbled backward against the door, gasping for air.

John Paul was sitting up in his bed, still clothed. His head was slightly canted and turned to the right, his glasses still in place. His face reflected the agony of death rather than the radiant smile of life for which he had become internationally famous during the thirty-three days since his election. In his hands, he held some papers that he had been studying. The light on his nightstand was illuminating a book and the small vile of the low blood pressure medication he took, which Sister Vincenza closely monitored.

Composing herself as quickly as she could, Vincenza dashed across the room and grabbed the Holy Father's wrist, desperately checking for a pulse. She detected nothing. She felt his forehead; it was not cold, but neither was it warm. She stepped back from the bed, quickly made the sign of the cross and ended it with her hand on her heart. She herself had suffered from heart issues in the past, and now she felt her heart beginning to pound in her chest. Fighting to take deep breaths, she reached across the nightstand and jabbed furiously at the wall, frantically trying to push a button that would ring a bell in the attic bedroom of the pope's secretaries, one floor up. After finally hitting the button, she darted from the room to get the other two nuns who worked with her. Their room was at the other end of the papal apartment.

"What in the world?" thought Father John Magee, one of the pope's two secretaries, as the bell by his bed rang annoyingly. Magee rolled his legs from under his covers, reached across his nightstand, and silenced the shrill alarm. He then flipped on a light, glanced at the time, and reached for his robe. "I hope I didn't overlook something His Holiness needed first thing this morning," he mumbled to himself. With that as his main concern, he fished around for the old worn slippers hiding under his bed, slipped his feet into them, opened his door, and trotted groggily toward the stairway leading to the floor below.

Magee's personal biorhythms did not match those of the Holy Father. He was usually left with several items to attend to after the pope went to bed, chores that inevitably pushed his own bedtime a couple of hours past the pontiff's. So, he compensated by sleeping in a bit longer in the morning, usually not joining the Holy Father until morning prayers just before breakfast. He was in no way an early-morning person. Today, that wouldn't matter.

● ● ●

Father Diego Lorenzi, John Paul's other secretary, was temporarily sleeping in a bedroom just down the hallway from the nuns. His attic quarters, adjacent to Magee's, were being repaired to stop annoying leaks from the roof. Lorenzi had been with Cardinal Luciani for two years, and the older man had become a true father figure. Like the new pope himself, Lorenzi was awed at his new station in life, but also like the new pope, he had little experience in Rome. Cardinal Luciani rarely came to Rome while a bishop or even later when a cardinal in Venice. He preferred the simpler surroundings of northeastern Italy. So did Lorenzi.

Lorenzi had copied Magee's schedule and usually slept in until about 6:00 a.m. But this was not a usual morning, brusquely signaled when his bedroom door flew open and Sister Vincenza darted across the room to his bed, grabbing his exposed shoulder. "Father Diego! Father Diego!" she quietly but firmly called. "Get up and come with me…*now*!"

Lorenzi was immediately awake and sitting up on his rickety cot, gazing with bewilderment at the unusually assertive Vincenza. "What's the matter, Sister?" he asked while reaching for his watch. "What's happening?"

"It's the Holy Father," Vincenza replied, the words spilling out of her mouth between heavy breaths. "It's…the…Holy Father," she repeated.

Lorenzi was immediately alarmed. He jumped from the cot, wearing only his nightshirt and worn white socks. "What about him, Sister? What's happened?"

Without answering, Vincenza put her hand over her mouth and quickly backed out of the small room, turning down the hall toward the bedroom of the other two nuns. Lorenzi heard her footsteps as they echoed away. He jumped toward the door and dashed the few steps toward the pope's bedroom, arriving there just ahead of Father Magee.

Lorenzi stepped into the room, encountering the same scene that had shocked Sister Vincenza a few minutes earlier. Magee entered right behind him. Lorenzi froze in place—unable to move, unsure what to do, as Father Magee gingerly stepped around him, staring intently at the pontiff before moving over to the bed where he paused to gaze back at his stunned colleague. He reached for the pope's hand, which was still grasping the papers he had been reading, and felt for a pulse—however weak. Like Sister Vincenza before him, he found none. Magee looked over to Lorenzi and slowly shook his head. The two of them made the sign of the cross as tears began to stream from Lorenzi's eyes.

"What should we do, Father Magee? What do we do?" Lorenzi pleaded, leaning unsteadily against the door.

"I'm not sure," Magee calmly replied, his mind only starting to consider the necessary actions.

"You must know!" Lorenzi responded. "You're supposed to know these things. You were secretary to Pope Paul. You were there with him when he died at Castel Gondolfo in August. That's why the Holy Father kept you here with us! You know Rome! You know the Vatican! You're supposed to know what to do. You're—"

Magee raised his hand, signaling for the younger man to calm himself. "Lorenzi, please. Pope Paul had been the pontiff for fifteen years. He was eighty years old. Yes, I was with him, along with many others. We knew he was dying, there were doctors present, we were issuing frequent messages about his condition, and we were already quietly thinking about the conclave. It wasn't like this, Lorenzi…It wasn't anything like this! Let me think!"

Lorenzi stared back at Magee, wide-eyed, his mind struggling to come to grips with the shock that John Paul was dead. "Tell me what to do, Father Magee. Just tell me what to do," he mumbled, the words barely understandable.

Magee took a deep breath before walking across the room to a phone in the corner, where he slowly dialed up the Vatican switchboard. When the operator answered, he addressed him in a calm, quiet voice. "Yes, this is Father Magee. I'm in the Holy Father's apartment. Please connect me to Cardinal Villot...right away."

● ● ●

A few floors below in the Apostolic Palace, the Vatican secretary of state had been up for several minutes. He had met with John Paul the evening before and had been given numerous action items that the new pope wanted dealt with quickly, although he was unhappy about more than a few of them. As the secretary of state of the Holy See, Cardinal Jean Villot was essentially the second-highest-ranking person in the Vatican. In addition to this powerful position, eight years earlier, Pope Paul had also named Villot the *camerlengo*, the chamberlain of the Catholic church, the first non-Italian to have the position in over five hundred years. As *camerlengo*, Villot was essentially in charge of the church during a papal vacancy, formally known as a period of *sede vacante*, and was, therefore, the official charged with preparing for and then executing the complex requirements of the conclave of cardinals that elected a new pope. Villot had just recently managed the conclave that had elected Cardinal Luciani as Pope John Paul, and it had been exhausting.

Although the management of the August conclave had gone well enough and met with few complaints from the participants, it had not resulted in the outcome Villot had wanted. Where Cardinal Villot had spent much of his career in the Vatican, Cardinal Luciani had minimized his exposure to the curia. Whereas Villot was bureaucratic, cold, and aloof, Luciani was pastoral, personable, warm, and always smiling. They were as different as two men of the church could be. But Luciani needed the experience of Villot, so after becoming pope, he had asked him to remain in his position—for the time being.

The two men had clear differences of opinion beyond style, and Villot was beginning to wrestle with how he would deal with their distinctions. Now, as he reached for the phone, while wiping shaving cream from his face, he was about to learn that such concerns were moot. Putting the telephone receiver to his ear, he uttered his normal, gruff greeting, "Cardinal Villot. To whom am I speaking?"

"Eminence, this is Father Magee in the Holy Father's apartment. I need you to come to the Holy Father's bedroom…quickly!"

"Why?" Villot asked.

"Your Eminence, I believe it would be best to discuss that when you get here," Magee firmly replied, glancing across the bedroom at Lorenzi, who was still frozen in place, his hands covering his face, continuing the struggle to calm himself. Magee silently stared at Lorenzi, slightly widening his eyes, sending a visual command to compose himself. His younger colleague got the message, straightened himself, and nodded, signaling that he would be ready when Villot arrived.

On the other end of the line, Villot paused, puzzled, but then replied, "All right. Let me get dressed, and I'll be right there." Villot was accustomed to tight schedules and to frequent changes of his official clothing. He could quickly go from one to another, especially when putting on his regular work clothes. He dressed hurriedly, affixed his red sash and hat, and headed to the pope's apartment, sensing something was badly amiss. He bounded up the back staircase as fast as his aging legs could take the steps, thereby avoiding a meeting with the Swiss Guard who was routinely stationed outside the apartment's front door.

When he reached the landing on the top floor, Villot opened the door and strode quickly down the hallway toward the pope's bedroom. As he rounded the corner, he could see the shadowy figure of Father Magee, standing in the hall, the light from the pope's bedroom illuminating his right side.

Villot walked briskly up to Magee. They did not speak. Magee gestured with his hand that Villot should step inside. The old cardinal did so slowly, stopping just inside the doorway. Father Lorenzi stood next to the pope's bed, his hands together, watching over his old mentor. The three nuns were kneeling in prayer at the foot of the bed. Villot crossed himself and then backed out of the bedroom, grabbing Magee's arm and pulling him into the hall.

"Do we know what happened?" he whispered to Magee, whose rumpled appearance was very much in contrast to the formal Villot's.

"Sister Vincenza brought him his coffee this morning as usual. After a few minutes, she returned and His Holiness had still not emerged from his room. She grew concerned and entered the bedroom. She found him just as you see him."

"She entered his bedroom?" Villot snarled, his eyes narrowing. "I believe I left clear instructions that she was not to enter the Holy Father's bedroom. Ever!"

"Eminence," Magee replied firmly, "clearly something was not right. Sister Vincenza has known the Holy Father many years and has served him faithfully for all of them. She did the right thing. Had she known what she would find, I'm quite certain she would have preferred that someone else make the discovery."

Villot did not like being challenged, but he knew Magee was right. He drew and then quickly exhaled a deep breath. His question about why Vincenza had entered the bedroom was a strong demonstration of where his thoughts were already racing. The primary issue here was to protect the church, and in Villot's view, protecting the church included controlling information about the scene he was viewing. Like Father Magee, he too had been present as Paul VI, his friend and patron, had traveled the road to his final rest. Everyone expected Paul to die shortly, still all sorts of stories emerged, speculating over the quality of care he had received from the chosen Vatican doctors. Now Villot had this to deal with. A supposedly healthy, sixty-five-year-old man, who had hiked the Italian Alps and who had been pope for only thirty-three days, dead in his bed? He had to take control.

But if Villot's instincts were correct, his immediate actions were not. Perhaps his decisions were too hasty, perhaps they were driven more by panic than reason. Perhaps the *camerlengo* himself, despite his many years near the pinnacle of the church, just did not fully appreciate the delicacy required by the moment or the inevitable international interest that such a tragic death would generate. In his desire to have no questions asked, Villot took steps that guaranteed they would be.

The cardinal walked across the room to the phone and called the switchboard, asking to be connected to the Swiss Guard commander of the relief.

● ● ●

Quickly the phone on the duty desk of Sergeant Bruhlmann rang, and he picked it up. "Swiss Guard post number one, Sergeant Hans Bruhlmann at your service." When he heard the voice at the other end of the line, Bruhlmann reflexively jumped to his feet.

"Sergeant, this is Cardinal Villot. I need you to come to the papal apartment as quickly as you can."

"Certainly, Your Eminence," Bruhlmann responded. "Might I ask why?"

"No, you may not!" Villot barked. "Just get up here immediately… and take the rear stairway."

"Of course, Your Eminence," Bruhlmann replied before quickly hanging up the phone, grabbing his beret, and dashing out of the guardhouse.

Villot gently lowered the phone back into its cradle. He slowly turned and walked over to the pontiff's bed. Looking at the three nuns, he waved his hand, motioning for them to leave. Sister Vincenza rose to her feet and slowly backed toward the door followed by the others. Following the departure of the nuns, Villot placed his hand on Father Lorenzi's shoulder.

"I know this is very hurtful for you," Villot whispered. "But I need you to leave and step outside. The guards will be here in a few minutes. Ask them to wait in the hall until I send for them. Do you understand?"

Lorenzi silently nodded and walked out of the room. Villot motioned for Father Magee to go with him. When the room was cleared, Villot closed the door. Returning to the pope's bed he too felt for a pulse, just to be sure, but as with the others, he felt nothing. He sensed the onset of rigor mortis in the pope's hands. Villot leaned in to see the papers Luciani was holding. They were notes from his discussion with the pope the previous evening, before both had called it a day and prepared for bed. There were some comments scribbled by the pope in the margins of the papers. Villot scanned them quickly, deciding that they might be open to misinterpretation. They directed specific instructions that would now have to await the election of a new pope, so they no longer served any purpose. The cardinal pulled the papers from the pope's hands, folded them, and placed them inside his tunic. He next reached for the medication on the pope's nightstand. He examined the small vile briefly and then placed it in an inside pocket. He then gently removed the glasses from the pope's face. They were sitting awkwardly on Luciani's face and combined with the contorted expression, gave the late pontiff something of an evil look.

There was a light knock at the door. Villot stepped over and opened it. In the small study outside the bedroom stood Magee and Lorenzi with Sergeant Bruhlmann. They nodded to the cardinal as he approached them.

"Father Magee, Father Lorenzi," Villot said, looking at each man in turn, "the Holy Father is dead. I need the two of you to go directly to your rooms and pack all your belongings. You will leave the Vatican immediately along with the three sisters."

Magee and Lorenzi looked at each other, baffled. "Where are we to go?" Lorenzi asked.

"My office will make the arrangements and tell you shortly. It will be out of Rome, probably up north," Villot replied. "The sisters will go to a nunnery. Please move quickly, as time is of the essence."

"Why…is time of the essence?" Magee asked, suddenly suspicious of what was unfolding.

"Largely, Father Magee, because I said it was," Villot shot back.

The two priests delayed momentarily but then stepped into the hallway and headed to their rooms to do as asked. Their departure left Villot standing alone with Sergeant Bruhlmann. The older man stepped toward the blue-clad guard and leaned in close to his face.

"Sergeant," Villot began in a low voice, "go summon as many of your men as you can and seal off the Holy Father's residence. Allow no one in without specific authorization from me. Give the two secretaries and the sisters about an hour to pack their things. That should be more than sufficient. Get them boxes or additional suitcases if needed, but they need to be out within the hour. I'll send up a cleaning team from the facilities office. They'll thoroughly clean the apartment, and when this is finished, as is customary, it will be sealed, pending the election of the new pontiff. I'll go to my office and contact a doctor and an embalmer to tend to the Holy Father's remains. Assist them as needed, but ensure nothing is taken from the Holy Father's room until his body is removed. Is that clear?"

"Yes, Eminence," Bruhlmann answered, with a sharp nod of the head.

"Thank you, my son," Villot replied and then added, "Also, I am imposing upon you and the others a vow of silence about everything you have observed and heard this evening. Is that also clear?"

"Yes, Eminence," Bruhlmann replied again.

With that, Cardinal Jean Villot, Vatican secretary of state and camerlengo of the church, left the papal apartment and headed toward his office. He had a million things to do, involving the funeral and internment of John Paul and the conclave that would have to meet to elect his successor. The sheer amount of detail was daunting, and it was all going to be greatly complicated by the need to manage the shocking circumstances of the pope's death. In that regard, Villot, with his early actions, was already starting in the hole. There would be questions, and a large number of them about what had happened during the hours after the bedroom light was first seen shining into St. Peter's Square.

As for the conclave, in that, Villot was experienced. There was very detailed and specific guidance on the conduct of papal elections that had been passed down from pope to pope for hundreds of years, and Pope Paul had added considerably more. Plus, Villot had just orchestrated a conclave the month before, so he was now quite familiar with the drill. And this time, having mastered the details of the process, he would use his familiarity with it to try to shape an outcome that would be more to his preference than the one six weeks earlier.

● ● ●

## Weimar, East Germany

The siren was wailing—loudly. Pasha Petrov jumped from his bed. Despite his years in the Soviet Red Army, he had never learned to respond to the alert siren in a calm way, and it was a constant irritant to his wife of five years, who rolled over and glared at him. She didn't say anything. She just glared. Petrov was thankful for just the glare. His feet hit the cold floor, and he tiptoed across the small bedroom to the door of the adjoining room, where their three-year-old son was, luckily, still asleep. He slowly pulled the door shut, hoping that would keep the child from waking. It did.

Pasha Petrov was a sergeant in a tank battalion of the Soviet Union's Eighth Guards Tank Army. He was being summoned to work. His regiment's tanks were neatly parked in a large motor park just down the hill from the housing area where he and other married soldiers lived in shoddy two-bedroom apartments. His immediate job was to put on his tank commander's uniform, slip into the small living room as quietly as possible, pull his two duffel bags from the space above the worn and unstable wooden closet that doubled as a place for his old radio set, and rush to his vehicle.

Petrov had done this drill many times before. Sometimes the captain in charge of his company just took roll and they headed back home for breakfast. Sometimes they actually mounted their powerful T-72 tanks, fired up the engines, and stormed out of the base to a dispersal area about ten kilometers away, on the west side of the hill above the base, a hill that had once been the site of the Nazis' notorious Buchenwald concentration camp. Buchenwald was one of the many camps where the Nazi capitalist regime of Adolph Hitler had executed thousands of people, many of them committed socialists and communists—or so he had been told. He had never actually walked up the hill to the camp itself. He didn't care to see it.

Pasha snapped the two duffel bags together and threw them over his shoulder as he tiptoed through the apartment door as quickly and quietly as possible. He closed it behind him and began running toward the base. Although they were Red Army tankers, his unit did a lot of running to stay fit. They had to. You never knew when the large American army stationed across the border in West Germany might attack in an effort to drive the Soviet Union from East Germany, reunite it with West Germany, and then continue on into Russia, just as Hitler had done. Mother Russia must be protected, and East Germany provided the first line of defense against the designs of the Western capitalists.

Within five minutes, Pasha arrived at the entrance to his regiment's motor park. A guard was standing at the gate, waving the soldiers through. Pasha stepped through the gate and immediately found himself facing his tank's driver, Private Igor Rostov, whose appearance suggested he had been out late enjoying the local German beer—again.

Pasha reached over and grabbed Rostov, shaking him. "Igor, are you drunk?"

The private shook his head.

Pasha thought otherwise and gave Rostov a sharp slap to the face. "Are you sure? Can you drive?"

Rostov nodded. "I'm fine, sergeant. How long do you think this drill will last? We just had a drill last week. How many of these does the colonel need?"

Pasha grabbed Rostov by his tunic and began to basically drag him toward their tank, the one parked near the end of the row of the ten tanks comprising their company. Theirs was marked with large white stenciling on the turret, identifying it as number "C-12."

"Not sure how long we'll be this morning," the sergeant replied. "We rolled out to the woods last week, so I doubt we'll do that again. It burns too much fuel. I'm sure we'll count who's here, the captain will check to see we all brought our bags, and we'll go home for breakfast."

"*Korosho*," Rostov replied. "Good…because I feel sick. And if I have to cram myself into that driver's seat and start smelling that awful fuel—I'll puke."

Pasha tightened his grip on his driver's collar as he continued to drag him along. "If you puke, you'll clean it up."

"What do you care?" Rostov answered, turning his red eyes toward his superior. "You get to ride with your head outside the turret. You don't have to smell that awful shit coming from the engine."

"Private, I was a driver once," Pasha sharply replied as they arrived at tank C-12, "and believe me, the old T-62s smelled worse. Now stow away your bags and get inside the hatch."

"Sergeant Petrov!"

Pasha turned to see his company commander, Captain Belikov, calling to him. He dropped his bags next to the tank and scurried over to the young officer. He didn't much care for Belikov; he struck Pasha as an arrogant ass. He didn't know for certain, of course, as most things in the Red Army were secret, but he had heard from others that Belikov's father was a senior officer at the headquarters for all Soviet forces in Germany, located at Zossen about a hundred kilometers away. Pasha felt it was probably true, as Belikov seemed to get special treatment from the colonel.

"Yes, Captain," Pasha reported as he reached the officer and stopped to salute.

"We're moving out right away," Belikov replied, giving Pasha a stern look as he handed him a simple strip map, hand-drawn on paper, as the Red Army did not issue real maps to its enlisted men. Maps were considered secret. "Here's the route we're following this morning. No lights on. Keep your three tanks close together on the road."

"Yes, Comrade Captain," Pasha answered as he scanned the strip map. Something was wrong. He turned his eyes back to Belikov. "Comrade Captain, this map can't be right. It shows us leaving the base and turning left. Isn't that heading east? Our dispersal area is west, toward the border—toward the Americans. Why would we be heading east?"

Belikov's eyes narrowed. "Because, Sergeant, those are our orders. We move east as the map shows."

"But why? We have no prepared battle positions to the east. So, why are we going that way?"

"Sergeant, you are going east because I am going east. And I am going east because our orders are to go east. That is all I know, and that is all either of us needs to know. Maybe tomorrow we'll turn and head west. Now go start your engines. We move out in fifteen minutes."

The two Soviet soldiers saluted, and Pasha headed back to his tank. Before he arrived, he could hear Private Rostov throwing up in the driver's compartment. "This is going to be a shitty few days," he thought. "I'm assigned to a captain who's an asshole, I have a driver who's a drunk, I have a wife who'll be pissed when I don't come home, and we're going the wrong way. *Korosho! Ochen, ochen korosho!*"

Fifteen minutes later, the ninety-four tanks in Sergeant Petrov's tank regiment were clanking through the gate of their motor pool and headed to the main highway, where they turned left and headed east, fouling the morning air with clouds of smelly black exhaust as they roared down the pockmarked East German autobahn.

CHAPTER 2

# September 29, 1978
# Washington, DC

• • •

CARTER CALDWELL WAS SOUND ASLEEP in the upstairs bedroom of his tidy Washington, DC, row house. But that was about to change and change in many ways. For now, as his small alarm clock reached 5:00 a.m., its unpleasant buzzer erupted in noise and the clock itself, being far from Rolex quality, began to vibrate across his antique nightstand. Numbly, Carter slapped at the clock several times until he succeeded in squarely hitting the dysfunctionally small button on its top.

Unlike so many who suffered this morning ritual, Carter never made any effort to roll over and capture a few more minutes of sleep. If he did, he was toast. A few more minutes would inevitably become another hour, and he could hardly afford another hour. It would mean getting to the office late, thereby missing the vital time window needed to read the morning reports before his boss arrived and started asking questions. So, after running his hands across his face and up into his scalp, he rolled to a sitting position on the side of his bed and, without pausing, rotated straight to the vertical while robotically slipping his feet into the gray slippers strategically placed on a small throw rug.

Carter led a very organized life with a very structured schedule. This was the result of his mother, his past training, a natural preference for order, impressive self-discipline, and in no minor way, his current vocation. He enjoyed what he did at work, and whenever he could, he enjoyed the social life in Washington with his numerous friends in the thirty-something age group. His life did not actually allow for wasted time, and to him, that fit his personal style and general preferences just fine.

He walked across his small bedroom and into the shower. Five minutes later, he was done, dried, and in front of the sink to carefully and closely shave his face—closely because his day would be at least twelve hours long and the morning shave had to last, as there would certainly be no time for an afternoon touchup. Putting down the same Gillette razor he had loyally used for many years, he quickly brushed his thick brown hair into place. He was fortunate in having hair with a wirelike texture, which once brushed into place almost never moved. He took a step back and quickly checked himself in the mirror; then he strolled over toward the bedroom closet where his suit, shirt, and tie had been prehung the evening before.

The suit was well tailored by Britches of Georgetown for his six-foot-four-inch, muscular, long-legged frame—the build of the college basketball power forward he once was. Below the suit was a recently purchased, highly polished pair of cap-toed shoes. In less than twenty minutes after waking, Carter was dressed, groomed, and headed for the stairs leading down to the front door. As he quickly descended, he passed a collage of pictures carefully arranged on the stairwell wall, pictures showing young men in gray uniforms, white hats flying into a clear blue sky, two generations of family, and a young basketball star forever suspended in midair, about to release a shot toward an unseen iron hoop, his coach shouting in the background. He almost never looked at the photos, but his mother had selected, framed, and arranged them so he deeply appreciated what they depicted and represented.

Pushing through his front door, he stepped out onto DC's Fourth Street Southeast and turned left toward the Eastern Market metro stop about three short blocks away. The weather was wonderful, and he walked quickly, carrying the black briefcase he had grabbed by the front door. Upon reaching the metro, he dropped a quarter into the *Washington Post* news rack anchored by the entrance, pulled out a paper, folded it, and tucked it under his arm. He then hopped on the escalator and descended to the train platform. If all went well, he would hit the platform just as a train arrived to take him on his twelve-minute ride to his exit at the Farragut West station. This allowed enough time for him to scan the paper for anything relevant to his job.

Carter arrived on the platform just as an orange line train pulled up. "Perfect timing," he thought. He waited as the doors opened and then stepped into a half-filled car, taking a seat next to the door. He made himself comfortable, placed the briefcase by his feet, and opened his paper. His eyes immediately confronted a large, screaming headline, and he reflexively uttered a sophisticated assessment: "Holy *shit*!"

Carter read the article quickly, and as the train rolled into Farragut West, he folded up the paper and stuffed it into his briefcase. When the train doors opened, he darted onto the platform and charged up the escalator, taking four steps at a time. He fumbled while stuffing his fare card into the exit gate but finally succeeded and rushed through. He bounded up the escalator and exited the station, turning south onto Seventeenth Street, and then sprinted toward Pennsylvania Avenue two blocks away. Normally he would stop by one of the street venders and get a cup of coffee and a doughnut, but this morning, he rushed by them in his haste to get to the office.

Rounding the corner of Seventeenth and Pennsylvania, he looked across the street at his destination: a huge, ornate—and many felt architecturally disastrous—building sitting on the western side of the White House. It was the Old Executive Office Building, the EOB in Washington parlance, and it primarily housed the numerous offices of the Executive Office of the President of the United States. Carter downshifted to a brisk walk, crossed the famous avenue with the world's most famous address, bounded up the steps, and pushed through the EOB's revolving front doors.

Mr. Lewis, the guard at the EOB entry desk, knew Carter well, and they usually exchanged some friendly banter but not today. "Good morning, Mr. Caldwell," Lewis said, greeting Carter as he came through the door, reaching into his coat to pull out the access badge suspended around his neck on a thin chain.

Carter waved the badge, a poor substitute for his usual morning chit-chat with Lewis, and then bolted through the turnstile, turned hard left, and headed toward the stairwell in the corner of the building. The EOB was an immense structure, with polished marble floors and incredibly high ceilings, making his shoes echo as he dashed down the hall.

Mr. Lewis looked after him, slowly shaking his head. "Must be sumptin' going on," he mumbled to himself. He had stood guard at the front door of the EOB for many years, and during that time, he had seen many days with "sumptin' going on." He recognized the signs.

● ● ●

Carter's office was in the corner on the third floor, but he always used the stairs to get a little early-morning exercise. The old elevators were far too slow and creaky for his taste, and with his long legs, he could beat them to the third floor without even breaking a sweat. Arriving at room 303, he briefly glanced at the nameplate beside the door as he dashed inside: "Carter Caldwell, Deputy Director, European and NATO Affairs." Good—the nameplate was still there, clear evidence that he had not been fired overnight. It was never a sure thing.

The office was already open, and the lights were on. Coffee was percolating in the antique pot that sat on a battered old table in the corner, and his secretary, Pat Meyers, was at her desk. No matter how early Carter came to the office or on what day of the week, Pat Meyers was always there. Somehow, she always knew when to be sitting there at her desk, even when Carter had not informed her of any particular reason for her presence. It was a bit uncanny—and slightly unnerving. On occasion, he was concerned that Pat had his home bugged, and given her days with the intelligence community, he was certain she had access to someone who could do it.

Meyers was one of those classic Washington secretaries, or "executive assistants," as they were increasingly called. She was midfifties with short red hair and a slim and attractive figure for her age, and she seemed to have worked for everyone of importance at one time or another. She had logged several years on the Hill, working for senior senators, had spent some time in the secretary of the army's office, and another period with the Central Intelligence Agency, followed by a stint with the deputy secretary of state. She could get anybody on the phone with her natural charm and the slight Southern accent that had survived her many years in the capital. And she could politely but firmly brush off anyone she felt would waste her boss's time, somehow having an unerring sixth sense about who was important and who wasn't.

She liked Carter, but she was still not quite sure he was the right fellow for the job. After all, he was young, just ten years out of college, and she—by comparison—was actually old enough to be his mother. Indeed, much to her disgust, she had recently seen a birthday card on his desk meant for his mother, and it confirmed she and Carter's mother were, distressingly enough, the same age.

As he entered his office, Carter stopped in front of Pat's desk, reached under his arm, and pulled out the folded *Washington Post*, dangling it by the top edge and allowing the front page to fall open. The headline filled most of the page: "Pope John Paul Dies of Heart Attack."

"Heard about this?" he asked the always unflappable secretary.

Pat calmly took a sip of the coffee she had just poured and then nodded her head in the direction of his office. "The preliminary report is on your desk," she replied. "Along with that special report you asked the CIA to prepare last week."

"Great. Thanks," Carter answered, somewhat haltingly, as he spun away and headed toward his desk. It was shaping up as an exciting day on the president's National Security Council staff, and for the first time in weeks, it would involve something from his European beat rather than the Middle East.

Carter marched quickly toward his office door, stopping briefly to hang his coat on a rack just inside. Stepping behind his desk, he looked down to the middle of his desk pad at two envelopes with striped borders, both stamped "Top Secret." One envelope was marked "IT

Immediate," the other "PL Report." The IT would stand for "Italy," so he opened that one first and pulled out a three-page, double-spaced memo from the CIA. The subject line on the front page tersely read: "Pope John Paul Found Dead." He leaned back in his chair and started to read, quickly concluding that the report was more descriptive than analytical. Although it was classified as "top secret," much of the information it contained closely paralleled what was already in the *Post* story. Nonetheless, it was highly classified because it had some other information to which the media would not be privy, and the Agency could only know because of the sources it had within the Vatican.

The Agency was reporting that there was some dispute as to the time of the pope's death. Both the Vatican and the media were reporting it as having happened the previous evening, but there was reason to believe it might have been in the early morning. Moreover, there seemed to be further dispute over exactly who had found the body and where it was in the papal apartment. The Vatican was saying it had been discovered by one of the pope's secretaries, but there were indications the discovery had actually been made by one of the nuns on the pontiff's household staff, who had shortly thereafter been whisked away from the Vatican to an unknown location.

Caldwell did not find any of this to be significant—interesting, perhaps, and maybe a bit puzzling, but not significant in the broader sense. But other information toward the back of the Agency report did catch his eye and capture his attention. Langley, the area in the Virginia suburbs outside DC where the CIA headquarters was located and the label by which the CIA was frequently referenced in nonsecure discussion, was reporting that the Vatican secretary of state was busily notifying the other voting members of the College of Cardinals and that he had spent considerable time on the phone with two of the Italian cardinals: Cardinal Giovanni Benelli of Florence and Cardinal Giuseppe Siri of Genoa. Both cardinals were believed to be serious candidates for the papacy, and both had rather different views about the recent policies of the church flowing from the Second Vatican Council. Whereas Benelli was described as an "energetic moderate" regarding the Vatican Council reforms, who had embraced them and had assisted Pope Paul VI in promulgating them, Siri was "aggressively conservative," known to be hostile to the changes made to the church's liturgical practices, changes originating in the papacy of John XXIII.

Carter paused for a moment and pondered what he had just read. The Agency had no firm idea what was actually said in Villot's two conversations, but they knew they were lengthy, much lengthier than the other calls he had made. Many of the voting cardinals outside of Italy in specific and Europe in general were evidently being notified either by telex or by lower-ranking curia officials. Was this just the common practice? Or was something else going on? Was there something Villot was trying to orchestrate…or prevent?

Carter recalled seeing a brief Agency report during the August conclave, suggesting that Cardinal Benelli was actively campaigning to be elected. Given the secretive nature of a papal election and the oath taken by the electors themselves not to discuss it, he recalled paying little attention. Trying to prepare a presidential position for the next Strategic Arms Limitation Talks with the Soviets, commonly called "SALT," was much more in line with his past, his interests, and his actual expertise. For Carter, SALT had easily trumped anything happening inside the Sistine Chapel.

But now the recently elected pope had suddenly and unexpectedly died, and the whole thing was going to be done again. So, why the long calls from the Vatican to Benelli and Siri? Suddenly, for reasons he couldn't explain, Carter was interested—oddly enough, more interested in black and white smoke than in missile throw weight.

The Agency memo ended quickly after reporting on the calls to Florence and Genoa. Carter was about to seal the paper back in its envelope when he noticed that the last page of the memo was a table showing a breakdown of the cardinal electors—by nationality. Evidently there would be 111 eligible to vote in the coming election, the same number that had voted in August to elect Albino Luciani. And of these twenty-five were Italian, with the next largest national contingent being the United States with nine, followed by France with seven. In the tier below that, Brazil had six, Germany five, Spain four, and Argentina and Canada three each. There were then nine countries that would have two cardinals in the conclave, and thirty-two—mostly from the third world—who would have one. This was getting interesting.

All CIA papers that came to the White House had the name of the Langley analyst who had prepared the report in the bottom left corner of the last page, along with their phone number. Technically, the report was the product of the department director where the report originated, but the analyst who actually wrote the paper and did the work was on that last page—on the "blame line" as it was called. If you had a question, it was best to call the person on the blame line. Carter grabbed the notepad on his desk and copied down the name and number on this blame line: "K. O'Connor, 703-866-9503." He might need to speak with this fellow at some point.

Leaning back in his chair, Carter recalled that for the August conclave he had heard from someone that to be chosen as pope, under rules that had been written by Pope Paul VI—evidently in an effort to influence the selection of his successor—one had to receive seventy-five votes from the cardinal electors. This was a formula that required a consensus among the voting cardinals amounting to two-thirds plus one majority of this very select electorate. In other words, even if the Italians voted as a block, they would need to secure the votes of fifty non-Italian cardinals representing Catholic churches scattered around the world. Based upon his quick scan of the CIA memo, that seemed to be an increasingly daunting task.

"Is it possible," Carter thought, "that the Italian cardinals are divided in some way between conservatives led by Siri and moderates led by Benelli?" If that was true, then how deep was the divide? What were the numbers? Whatever they were, it meant that there would have to be considerable non-Italian support if the Italian cardinals hoped to keep one of their own on the papal throne.

But Secretary of State Villot was French. So what was he trying to do? That was certainly a puzzle, but perhaps it came back to the simple fact that he was believed to be conservative himself and a man of the curia, so maybe he was simply accustomed to having an Italian to deal with, knew them all well from his many years in Rome, and would be more comfortable with another Italian pope than the unknown personality, perspectives, and interests of someone from far away. Perhaps he was trying to encourage Siri and Benelli to reconcile their differences and work together to get behind a single candidate, as they evidently had done with the August election of Cardinal Luciani.

If that were the case, it all made sense, but it was also complete speculation based on a single three-page memo. He needed to think about it some more. Maybe there was an opportunity here that could be quite positive for American interests. He looked down at his notepad again. K. O'Connor—he'd need to remember that name.

Putting the CIA memo back into its envelope, he opened the other one. Weeks before Carter had requested that the CIA's economic analysis section do an assessment of the economies of the Eastern European countries, with a focus on Poland. There had been numerous reports coming in from the US embassies in Eastern Europe, backed up by studies from several major American universities, most notably the centers for international studies at Columbia and Penn State, indicating that there were serious economic problems developing along the whole arc from the Baltic to the Adriatic, behind what Churchill had described as the "Iron Curtain."

The East European economies were all tied closely to the Soviet Union, and as the Soviet centrally planned economic model began to fray, so did the economies of the satellite nations along its western border. Adding to this stress, the oil crisis following the 1973 Arab-Israeli War had resulted in a general increase of global oil prices. As badly hurt as the Western economies were by the rapid rise of the energy price structure, it was worse for the East European states. Their own energy sources in the Soviet Union became more expensive overnight and then, because of Soviet mismanagement of its energy infrastructure, gradually but steadily, even more expensive afterward as supplies tightened. In addition, Western banks that had been willing to loan to the centrally planned economies, seeing them as low-risk, began to restrict credit and raise interest rates. By the mid-1970s, economic growth had all but stopped, debt repayment and credit became a significant challenge, and public unrest began to bubble beneath the surface.

In Poland, the economy began to fall into depression as foreign debt mounted. Worse still, workers were growing restive. In June 1976, there had been reports that a series of strikes had broken out in Plock, Ursus, and Radom that were quickly quelled by the government. There were other reports coming in about workers' organizations and unions forming across Poland, a clear theoretical affront to the entire Communist philosophy built around the fiction of workers controlling a workers' state.

Carter had asked for a report on Poland because it was the center of gravity of the Soviet sphere. In Eastern Europe, it was the biggest country in population, had the richest history, sat astride the major access routes into Russia, and was the major supply channel for nearly twenty Red Army divisions stationed in East Germany, watching the border with NATO. Without a controlled and controllable Poland, Moscow's domination of Eastern Europe would become tenuous.

Carter's scan of the executive summary of the CIA report said that the full report would substantiate the perception that the Polish economy was on a glide path from bad to worse. All economic indicators were negative, or so it seemed. Getting reliable data from a Soviet satellite state was far from easy, and even with its credible sources scattered all around Poland, the Agency was largely trying to piece together a jigsaw puzzle in the dark. By comparison, counting Soviet army divisions, rockets, and strategic missiles was relatively easy—and the Agency's track record was much better regarding military as opposed to economic analysis. But the bottom line was clear: Poland was in economic distress, and this would soon be reflected in increasing social unrest. What Warsaw and Moscow might do about it was the great question that the report, frustratingly, left unanswered. What Washington might do about it wasn't even implied.

The Agency had been promising this report for weeks, and Carter had impatiently asked about it on several occasions. But now that he had it, his attention was far more focused on the three-page papal memo from the faceless "K. O'Connor." He leaned back in his chair and pondered both reports, placing his hands together in front of his face, as was his habit when deep in thought.

"Villot was calling Benelli and Siri?" He kept pondering what those discussions could have been about. Was there something else, something reasonable, something simple, perhaps personal, that wasn't obvious? He ran it in his head over and over, even while his eyes dropped back to his desk, gazing at Langley's economics report.

Suddenly his eyes widened. He snapped forward in his chair and reached for the complex phone across his desk. Having not called this number very often, he looked at the NSC phone locator under his desk glass, found the extension he wanted, and dialed it. As soon as he did and heard the phone ringing on the other end, he regretted making the call. It was premature and impulsive. He started to hang up, but it was too late.

"Good morning. Dr. Brzezinski's office. This is Margaret. May I help you?"

It was Margaret Burrows, the long-serving secretary to Carter's boss, Dr. Zbigniew Brzezinski, the national security advisor to President Jimmy Carter.

"Good morning, Margaret. This is Mr. Caldwell over in the EOB," Carter replied, always careful not to leave Margaret thinking that "Carter" was "President Carter," which she was prone to do. "Margaret, I was wondering if Dr. Brzezinski was in this morning and might have fifteen or twenty minutes for a discussion," Carter asked meekly, hoping the answer would be "no."

"He will not be in this morning, Mr. Caldwell," Margaret flatly replied, her voice showing no emotion while somehow transmitting that she would have been unreceptive even if the security advisor were present. "How about next Tuesday…for ten minutes?"

"No, that won't work, Margaret. Let me think about it and get back to you. Thanks." Carter hung up the phone and let out a quick sigh of relief. That was close, but Margaret's tenacious protection of her boss's time had protected Carter from himself. He was nowhere near ready to see Dr. Brzezinski.

Within American foreign policy circles, Zbigniew Brzezinski was something of a legend. Many regarded Brzezinski as the Democratic Party's equivalent of Henry Kissinger, although Brzezinski himself considered Kissinger to be the Republican Party's equivalent of Brzezinski. The two men had much in common; both had been born in Europe—Kissinger in Germany and Brzezinski in Poland—both came from families that had immigrated to the United States during the 1930s, both had earned doctorates in international affairs at Harvard in the early 1950s, both had captured the ears of the powerful and prominent in their respective political circles, and both were strong personalities who powerfully articulated their views with vigor and certitude. Both Kissinger and Brzezinski were strongly anti-Communist, and both had personally seen the devastating results of totalitarian government, modern war, and political subjugation.

But there were significant philosophical differences between the two men. Whereas Kissinger felt international affairs were essentially an exercise in balancing the power and spheres of influence of the major global actors, Brzezinski believed there were other forces that also needed to be recognized and used to advantage, such as human rights. Brzezinski tended to believe there was merit in establishing institutions of world order and using them to one's benefit; Kissinger tended to believe that such institutions were obstacles to the exercise of power and that international rules of the road were inevitably going to be violated when it suited the interests of one power or the other.

Ironically, although both had made their early reputations as experts on Europe and American-Soviet relations, while serving their respective presidents, it was the Middle East and China that had consumed most of their intellectual energy and personal time. Kissinger's shuttle diplomacy had helped contain and then end the 1973 Arab-Israeli War, but President Carter and Brzezinski had been the ones who had gathered the Egyptian and Israeli leaders together and crafted a peace agreement. Kissinger had opened a dialogue with the People's Republic of China with his famous secret trip in 1971, but it was now left to Brzezinski to determine where to go from there.

But one major quality both men shared in abundance: they did not suffer fools well or long. Both were walking encyclopedias of historical facts, diplomatic feats, and anecdotal events. Before seeing them, you had best be prepared—well and fully prepared. And Carter Caldwell, a young army major on loan to the NSC, with a master's degree but not a doctorate, was not ready to see Zbigniew Brzezinski on the implications of the death of Pope John Paul, much less articulate the harebrained idea that was only partially formed in his head.

The EOB, when first constructed, had housed what was in the late 1800s the majority of the executive branch: the State Department, the War Department, and the Navy Department. All were long departed and displaced by the various offices of the Executive Office of the President. The military departments had moved across the Potomac to the Pentagon and the State Department to its own architecturally challenged building about four blocks away at Foggy Bottom near the Lincoln Memorial. But among the things left behind, beyond the ornate old doorknobs having an S, W, or N on them, corresponding to the departments that had once occupied those offices, was a four-story library originally used by State's diplomats and staff.

Carter popped up from his chair, grabbed a pencil and pad of paper, and strode out of his office.

"Headed to the library?" Pat asked as he passed her desk.

"Yup," Carter replied as he pulled open the door.

"Good idea," Pat responded, resting her chin on her hands. "I would certainly not be seeing Dr. Brzezinski unless I was awfully sure what the hell I was talking about."

"Agreed." Carter nodded. "Anything else for today? I may be down there awhile."

"Well, the army called again. They still say you need to get your annual medical physical. And they said get it or be reassigned to some place called Ft. Polk—wherever that is."

"It's in the Louisiana swamps," Carter answered, slightly shrugging his shoulders. "OK, do you have a number for the office at Walter Reed that schedules physicals? Call them and see if you can schedule one around the end of the month."

"I have the number somewhere," Pat answered. "I had to schedule one for Colonel Bell down in security policy while his EA was on vacation. The doctor who handles them for NSC staffers is a Major Harkins."

Carter stepped back inside the door. "Major Jack Harkins?" he inquired. "I think I know him. He was two years ahead of me at the academy. I think he was the heavyweight on the wrestling team."

"Sounds like the same man," Pat replied with a bemused smile as she reached for the phone. "Colonel Bell said he had the fattest fingers he had ever seen on a human being. Enjoy!"

Carter scowled. Nothing like a smart-mouthed EA to brighten your day. He stepped into the hall and headed for the library.

# Moscow

As Carter headed off to explore the EOB library stacks, Dimitry Zhukov was walking toward a massive yellow brick building on Lubyanka Square, about five blocks from Red Square in central Moscow. The building had a cold and forbidding facade that most Muscovites found quite appropriate. Originally built as the headquarters of the All Russia Insurance Company in 1898, following the 1917 Bolshevik Revolution, the building was seized by the new Soviet government and transformed into the headquarters of the secret police, then known as the *Cheka*. Although the name of the Soviet secret police had changed many times down through the years, the headquarters had always remained in this huge, Neo-Baroque building with its central loggia and seemingly endless windows arrayed in three horizontal layers. Now, the building served as both the headquarters of the Committee for State Security, commonly known as the KGB, the spy and internal security agency of the Soviet Union—and the counterpart to the American CIA. Lubyanka was also, fittingly, Moscow's central prison.

A statue of Felix Dzerzhinsky, the founder of the *Cheka*, dominated the center of Lubyanka Square. As Dimitry rushed past it, he looked up at the scowling figure. Although it was just a lifeless piece of bronze, it always made him feel uncomfortable, and this afternoon, he was more uncomfortable than usual. He had left work just before lunch to go do some grocery shopping and then clean and prepare his apartment. It was his girlfriend's birthday, and he had big plans. He was going to make her a great dinner, complemented with a wonderful bottle of Chianti sent to him in a diplomatic pouch by a colleague in Italy, and when the moment was right, he planned to propose marriage. But before he had even started on the dinner, the phone rang.

"*Zdravsveetya*, Zhukov here," Dimitry answered, unsure whose voice he would hear and hoping it would be his girlfriend's. He was disappointed.

"*Da*, Zhukov. This is Kornilov. I need you to come back to the office right away." It was his boss, Sergei Kornilov, the KGB deputy director for Western Europe within the KGB's First Chief Directorate, the organization that handled foreign intelligence.

"Certainly, Comrade Kornilov. I'll be there in about twenty minutes."

The phone on the other end immediately clicked off. Senior KGB officers were men of few words.

Dimitry exhaled, and briefly considered calling back to protest, explaining he had very special plans for the evening, but he decided against it, knowing it would be futile. Besides, he was the grandson of the legendary Red Army commander Marshal Georgy Zhukov, one of the Soviet Union's most famous generals of World War II. Dimitry Zhukov, therefore, had a family name and heritage to consider, a burden magnified by the frequent observation that his stout physique and bulldog appearance were identical to his grandfather's.

The Zhukov name, while certainly not despised in official Soviet circles, still carried an aroma of suspicion for some, perhaps somewhat more at KGB headquarters than elsewhere. The old soldier had been involved in the trial of Levrentiy Beria, one of the old guard Bolsheviks who had a long tenure leading the NKVD, another of the predecessor organizations to the KGB. Beria had been executed in the Lubyanka headquarters building, and some old KGB veterans still believed Marshal Zhukov had carried out the execution himself. Although that was all speculation from a quarter century ago, in some organizations, memories could be long.

Dimitry was determined to remove any lingering distrust and dislike from the past. This was a new era after all. Instead of protesting to his boss, he instead placed a brief call to his prospective fiancée, cancelling their evening dinner, grabbed his overcoat from its hook by the apartment door, and walked the ten blocks from his high-rise neighborhood back to Lubyanka.

Entering the headquarters, he turned left and headed toward his first-floor office. The inside of the building was strangely inconsistent with the building's primary occupants and main purpose. It was wonderfully ornate with a magnificent parquet floor and pale-green walls. It even had some expensive artwork scattered along the wide hallways. Dimitry's office area was in the corner, and he reached its door quickly only to be met by his secretary Elena Karkova, who was holding a large envelope. Her red face showed that she was agitated and uneasy.

"Dimitry," she whispered, looking left and right from the corner intersection of the two hallways, "you must go immediately to Comrade Andropov's office. He wants to discuss this report. Hurry! He called nearly an hour ago!"

Dimitry looked past Elena and into the office. "Is Sergei coming as well? He was the one who called me."

Elena nervously shook her head. "No, Comrade Andropov only asked for you."

Dimitry nodded, silently took the envelope, and turned toward the stairs. As he walked, he opened the envelope and noted that it only contained a very brief message from the KGB section within the Soviet embassy in Rome. The message was clear, but the details were few; in fact, there were none. Dimitry stopped at the bottom of the stairs and read the message: "Pope John Paul has died. Reasons unclear. Cardinals being summoned back to Rome. More to follow."

Dimitry was stunned. He had prepared a detailed report on John Paul's election that had gone to KGB Chairman Yuri Andropov the month before. He had been informed that the chairman had found it very useful, thorough, and professional. But it had been the result of some detailed study assisted by the KGB staff on the ground in Rome, who had some very knowledgeable sources around the Italian government—and within the Vatican itself. Dimitry was uneasy simply going up to Andropov's office with only a short dispatch containing no more information than he held in his hands, and this was certainly no basis for any in-depth discussion with the KGB chief. Yet, there must be some reason he had been summoned back from his planned evening, so perhaps the chairman wanted to brainstorm a bit—as he was known to do.

Dimitry was the KGB headquarters expert on the southern European countries, particularly Italy. He had studied in Rome for a year a decade earlier and then subsequently served two years as a "diplomat" in the Soviet embassy. He knew Italy, Rome, and the Vatican as well as anyone in Moscow, and he was among the few who spoke fluent Italian. He hoped that would be enough to meet Andropov's needs. Armed with that positive hope for his future, he quickly walked up the stairs to the chairman's third-floor office in the very center of the building, one with a clear view of Lubyanka Square—and the menacing Felix Dzerzhinsky.

Andropov's office was distinguished by the hallway presence of two uniformed KGB security officers on either side of its massive oaken door. In addition to intelligence, the KGB also provided border security for the Soviet Union and personal security for its high-ranking officials, such as Yuri Andropov and his fellow members of the Politburo, the highest governing body of the Soviet Communist Party and hence of the Soviet Union itself. Zhukov reached into his pocket and pulled out his KGB ID card, which he held up for the guards. Having seen him before, both guards gave the card only a cursory glance followed by a slight nod. Their expressionless faces did not change as he pushed open the door and stepped inside the chairman's large reception room, coming immediately face to face with KGB General Pavel Korilenko, Andropov's highly efficient senior aide and doorkeeper. Around the building, Korilenko was somewhat derisively called "CCO," standing for "Comrade Carbon Monoxide," as he was considered to be both colorless and odorless, the perfect KGB man.

Dispensing with any greetings or pleasantries, which he considered to be fully frivolous, Korilenko raised his hand with his palm facing Dimitry, a clear signal to stop in place and wait. Dimitry immediately complied. The general's large desk contained about fifteen telephones lined up along the left side. For some reason, despite all the technology they had developed for space flight and military prowess, the Soviets had never mastered multiple line phones. Korilenko reached for the one farthest to his left and picked it up while turning to face the wall behind him and away from the young KGB officer, waiting across the room. He uttered a couple of indistinguishable words, hung up the phone, and turned back toward Dimitry. "The chairman will see you now."

Korilenko remained at his desk and merely pointed toward the door. Dimitry slowly crossed the room, nodded to the general as he passed him, pulled down on the door latch, and walked carefully into the massive office of Yuri Andropov.

The office was dark, illuminated by only the large lamp on the chairman's desk and a few smaller lamps on the end tables between the couches arrayed on both sides of the room, creating two distinct, and widely separated, conversation areas, both facing large ornate fireplaces on the side walls. The large window behind the chairman's desk was aglow with the lights from the square outside, and standing in the window, looking out into the square, Dimitry could see the silhouette of Yuri Andropov, his hands clasped behind his back, seemingly deep in thought.

"Come in, Comrade Zhukov."

Dimitry only faintly heard the low, flat voice of the chairman, who still faced the darkening world outside the window. Dimitry moved over to one of the two chairs in front of the chairman's desk and stopped in front of it, waiting for the next order or motion from the KGB chief. After a few seconds, Andropov turned slowly around, walked over to his desk, and fell heavily into its large leather chair, motioning for his young guest to also take a seat.

Yuri Vladimirovich Andropov was by most accounts the second most powerful man in the Soviet Union behind Communist Party General Secretary Leonid Brezhnev. It was always difficult to calibrate the relative power of the fifteen members of the Soviet Politburo, as those with the obvious titles might in fact lack the authority their position implied. But clearly, the head of the KGB, in charge of international espionage as well as domestic security, was a powerful person. And Andropov wore his power well, visibly yet somehow subtly.

Andropov was sixty-four years old, tall and lean, with a hairline receded well back on his head, leaving his remaining gray hair circling from ear to ear. He always wore a simple pair of glasses with plain black frames extending across the top of the lens and the bottom secured by thin metal strips. His face was angular with a prominent nose having a sharp ridge ending in more rounded than normal nostrils. He was always well dressed and well accessorized with an expensive watch and elegant cuff links. His parents were both from upper-class families of the Czarist era, and although Andropov had joined the Communist Party just prior to World War II, outwardly he still retained something of a courtly aura. But inwardly, he was a dedicated Communist who believed that stern measures in the defense of the Soviet Union should be used without hesitation. And if stern measures did not work, then harsh measures should follow, and harsh should escalate to brutal if needed.

Andropov's managerial style for the KGB was similar—stern to brutal when needed. He was efficient, crisp, and humorless. He always got straight to the point of any issue and expected his chief deputies to do the same. He did not suffer fools, but the fools who came before him did suffer, as he was most quick to replace those he saw as incompetent. He had run the KGB for over a decade, and it now reflected him and his decisive, disciplined style more than it ever had for any of his predecessors, many of whom had been more zealous than capable. The Western intelligence services viewed the KGB as a worthy adversary, and most of the smaller, developing countries simply viewed it with fear. Andropov was well aware of those perceptions—he liked them, and he encouraged them.

Dimitry had only been in the chairman's office twice before, both times as part of a larger briefing group. This was his first visit alone, and his mind raced as he tried to determine if this was an effort to solicit his informed views or to punish some unknown oversight in his analysis.

"Zhukov, I found the report you did following the last papal election very useful and insightful," Andropov said with his usual flat delivery.

Dimitry began to relax, as it seemed this was a meeting to solicit his views rather than dissect some predictive error.

After a short pause, Andropov continued, "As I recall, most in the West who follow such things were predicting the election of one of the two more prominent Italian cardinals. What were their names?"

"Cardinals Siri and Benelli, Comrade Chairman."

"Yes, those two. But you predicted Cardinal Luciani. And you were right. What did you see that all the others, who supposedly have learned insights on such things, missed?"

"Comrade Chairman, it was a combination of historical analysis, insights on the personalities involved, some study of the more immediate issues facing the Vatican, and—I must say—a little bit of luck. At some point, you have to guess."

Andropov stared at his young subordinate for a few moments before slouching a bit deeper into his leather chair. "Yes, Zhukov, but you guessed right. The others guessed wrong. I sense in you that you have an instinct for accurately assessing the flow of events and the force of particular personalities…as did your grandfather."

Dimitry smiled slightly. "Thank you, Comrade Chairman. I appreciate your compliments…of both my grandfather and me."

Andropov's face maintained its stony stare. "Zhukov," he continued after a brief pause, "as I recall, your grandfather had only daughters. So, why is your surname Zhukov?"

Dimitry shifted slightly in his chair, whose legs he noted must have been cut in a way to make the seat shorter, forcing you to look slightly up at the chairman. "That is simple, Comrade Chairman. My mother happened to marry a man who was also named Zhukov and no relation. But had that not been the case, I am sure I would have chosen to use the name in any event. My grandfather was a great man who served the Soviet Union and Party with great distinction. Not many Soviet children have a grandfather who received the Order of Lenin and was named a Hero of the Soviet Union." Not knowing what Andropov actually thought about his grandfather, Dimitry knew he was taking a risk.

"I don't blame you, Zhukov," Andropov replied. "He was a great man. And he was tough…sometimes very tough. I liked that about him. In many ways, I have tried to run the KGB as he ran the Red Army during the drive to Berlin in 1945."

Andropov was not one for pleasantries, and the discussion of Marshal Zhukov with his grandson was brief but considerably lengthier than was his usual manner. Having gotten it out of the way or, perhaps more accurately, having worked his way through it, he returned to form and got to the point.

"Zhukov, I am concerned about what happens next in Rome after the pope's sudden death."

"Are you concerned some in the West will accuse us of his sudden death?" Dimitry asked.

"No, of course not," the chairman brusquely responded. "We had nothing to do with it. If I wanted to eliminate him, I would have done so and made it look like someone else did it. But I liked having Luciani there; it served our purposes. You laid it out in your report to me before his election."

Dimitry's mind raced. He did not recall addressing why Cardinal Luciani's election would be in the interest of the Soviet Union. His report had focused on the issues that would most likely be debated within the conclave. He was reluctant to ask the chairman to elaborate but decided it was best to take that route rather than strike out in some erroneous direction and be dismissed as a fool. "Comrade Chairman," he said, trying to come across as forceful and confident, even though at the moment he was neither, "as a member of the Politburo, how had you yourself concluded that Luciani's election was favorable to the Soviet Union?"

The phrasing of the question worked well, as it referenced Andropov's superior position and implied his superior knowledge, which both Dimitry and the chairman understood to be the case. Andropov went silent for a few moments, organizing his thoughts and structuring his reply.

"Zhukov, as you mentioned in your report, the Catholic church is currently consumed with its own internal issues, issues which—quite frankly—are of no relevance to us in Moscow. There have been ongoing concerns about what seems to be corruption or perhaps simple mismanagement of the Vatican Bank. A church and a bank don't mix well, and I have no idea why Pope Paul did not address this incompetence, but he didn't and, as I said, that is their concern.

"Then they have this major debate about the so-called reforms from John XXIII's Vatican Council. Do we in Moscow care what language the Catholic church uses in its countless rituals? Of course we don't. Do we care how many cardinals they want to appoint from Africa or elsewhere in the third world? Perhaps we do a bit, as it might impact on our own activities in certain places. But even that is only a secondary concern.

"Then they have this problem they have made for themselves over the birth-control pill. Why they would want to place themselves in such an awkward place is a mystery to me, but they have and it has put them at odds with the decadent habits of the West. They might as well try and change the orbit of the moon rather than order a change in basic human behavior. As Marx informed us, the wheels of history are turning in our direction, in our favor. The Catholic church does not recognize this. But the popes themselves seem to sense it, which is why they always go out of their way to criticize us, to confront us."

Andropov paused for a moment before moving on to his concluding thoughts. He leaned forward and placed his elbows on his desk. "Do you know where I was in 1956, Zhukov?" he asked, looking at Dimitry across the top edge of his glasses.

Dimitry, like all smart KGB officials, had committed Andropov's résumé to memory, for obvious reasons. He nodded his head and answered, "Yes, Comrade Chairman. You were the Soviet ambassador to Hungary. You were the senior Soviet official in Budapest during the revolt against us."

Andropov nodded sharply, reflecting both agreement and approval. "Correct. I was the Soviet ambassador in Hungary. And from the Soviet embassy, I could see the counterrevolutionaries—the 'partisans' as the Western propaganda machines called them—running wildly through the streets. They murdered loyal Hungarian soldiers and police—loyal to communism and the Soviet Union, which had delivered Hungary from the Nazi occupation only a decade before. I saw good men, some of them men we had trained and worked with, shot and their bodies strung up on light poles. I could see it from the embassy. Do you know what lesson I learned from that, Zhukov?"

Dimitry could imagine several lessons that the chairman might have taken from these events, but he wanted to hear the answer directly so he silently shook his head.

"I learned," Andropov continued with little pause, "that even in a place where one-party, communist rule seems to be well established, where the wheels of history seem to be turning as predicted by Marx, subversive elements can unravel things very quickly. And do you know who led—who inspired—this revolt in Hungary, Zhukov?"

"Yes, I do, Comrade Chairman," Dimitry replied. "Several elements but primarily it was the Hungarian Catholic prelate, Cardinal Mindszinty."

Showing a momentary burst of energy, Andropov slapped his hand hard on his desk. "Correct, Zhukov! It was Mindszinty! A man we had tried in court and put in prison for nearly eight years, and when released by the counterrevolutionaries, he still spoke out against us! Rallied support against us! I called Comrade Khrushchev and told him we had to invade and regain power. He was reluctant to do so, but there was no choice. So we used the might of the Red Army to crush the revolt. Unfortunately, Mindszinty escaped into the American embassy where he stayed for the next fifteen years under American protection, the whole time continuing to scheme against us!"

Andropov calmed himself after sharing this harsh piece of personal history and again leaned back into his big leather chair, shifting his emotions from the personal to the analytical, before continuing, "Do you know the percentage of the Hungarian population that is Catholic, Zhukov?"

"I do, Comrade Chairman," Dimitry replied, comfortable that he had seen the figure recently. "In Hungary, as I recall, a bit less than 40 percent of the population is Catholic. It has been a rather constant figure for many years."

"Very good, Zhukov. That is correct. So you see, a religious group comprising less than half the population caused us much trouble. The Catholic church is dangerous when it involves itself in such things as social justice, and this recently preferred phrase they now use, *human rights*. Human rights is nothing but a tool the Catholics and the Americans use to try and place us on the ideological defensive, which they must do because they are the past and we are the future."

Andropov fell silent for the moment and seemed to slip into deep thought. Dimitry sat quietly in his chair and pondered the thrust of this discussion. He could see where the chairman was going with this reflection on the past—or at least he thought he could. Mentally, he began to race through an outline of what to say when Andropov restarted the conversation. He did not have long to wait.

"So, Zhukov, you are clearly a smart young man. What outcome from this next election meeting of the cardinals…what is it called again?"

"They are called conclaves, Comrade Chairman. It is Latin for 'with a key,' meaning the cardinal electors are locked in a room to deliberate their decision."

"Yes, a conclave. What outcome for this next conclave would you say best serves the interest of the Soviet Union?"

Zhukov was ready with an answer. "The best outcome for us would be the election of yet another Italian cardinal."

"Agreed," Andropov immediately replied. "That is exactly my opinion. But tell me your reasoning?"

Dimitry drew a deep breath. "Well, Comrade Chairman, there are three obvious reasons for this view. First, the Italians tend to dominate the curia—the Vatican bureaucracy—and they are by nature the most conservative and always focused on narrow church issues. The Italians who are not in the curia tend to concentrate more on broad theological issues, but they are also very inwardly focused. So, another Italian will have to deal with the practical issues involving the bank, which you referred to, and the usual personal issues. Second, the theological friction involving such issues as the Vatican Council reforms and *Humanae Vitae*, which—"

"*Humanae* what?" Andropov interrupted.

"*Humanae Vitae*, the official document issued by Pope Paul VI regarding birth control."

"Oh, yes," Andropov replied with a nod of his head. "Continue."

"Yes, Comrade. An Italian will be more inclined to focus on the theological as the church has continual difficulty reconciling modern life and modern science with certain religious views from the past. This issue of birth control is the most obvious and pressing, but there are others—the role of women in the church, for example, as well as other members of their laity. Lastly, as the bishop of Rome, an Italian pope tends to spend considerable time dealing with certain pastoral responsibilities, at least to a degree. And this would include managing relations with the local Roman government, where the mayor is a communist, as well as the Italian government, where there remains some friction regarding the Lateran Treaty of 1929 that resolved the status of the papal states and established the Vatican as a separate political entity within Italy."

"And if we got a non-Italian?" Andropov asked.

"Much the opposite, Comrade Chairman. Less interest on the internal and theological and more interest on broader, global issues."

"Agreed," Andropov replied. "And thinking back to your analysis in August, I am losing sleep over the possibility of the election of either Cardinal Koenig of Austria or—God forbid, if I may use that phrase—that bastard Wyszynski in Warsaw. And both got votes in the last…what was it called again? Yes, conclave."

A quizzical expression crossed Dimitry's face. He had never provided any details of the votes cast in the last conclave that elected Cardinal Luciani, mainly because he didn't have any. "Comrade Chairman," he asked, "how could you know who got votes? The conclave is secret and all records are burned afterward. The burning makes the *fumata*, the smoke coming from the Sistine Chapel chimney after a vote."

Andropov's face showed a rare, brief smile—actually more of a smirk. "Zhukov," he replied in a low, calm voice, "we're the KGB. We have many ways to get information important to the Soviet Union."

Dimitry nodded but said nothing. Andropov sighed, leaned forward, and looked straight into his young colleague's eyes. "Zhukov, there have been Italian popes for nearly five hundred years. I would call that a trend. Your job is to make sure that the trend continues. Get the cardinals to elect an Italian. I don't care who it is, but I want another Italian. Do whatever you must to discredit Koenig, Wyszynski, the Americans, or anyone else who could be a threat. We have many problems brewing in Eastern Europe that we will have to deal with, and we may have to deal with them harshly, as we did in Hungary and Czechoslovakia. And if it comes to that, I don't want any additional complications caused by having a pope who excites resistance to us as Mindszinty did to me in 1956. Understand my concerns, Zhukov?"

Dimitry swallowed hard. "Comrade Chairman, the pope will be elected by 110 or so very committed, selected, and secretive people. They will meet in about two weeks. I don't see how we can get to them and influence a decision."

Andropov glared at Dimitry but paused before responding. "Zhukov, any voting body, even this one, is made up of human beings. All human beings have likes, dislikes, interests, things they cherish, things they despise, secrets they hope will never be known. This is a small number, 110. That should make it easy. Now, as described in your August memo, there are basically two Italian cardinals around which the others are likely to gather. The two you mentioned earlier, who are they again?"

"Comrade Chairman, those two would be Cardinal Siri of Genoa and Cardinal Benelli of Florence. Siri is a powerful personality and a leader of the conservative forces who have many objections to the reforms of the Vatican Council advocated by the last two popes. Benelli was an acolyte of Pope Paul, has considerable experience in the curia, and is a seasoned diplomat but also has a strong personality that many of the other cardinals in the curia dislike. Siri is stridently anticommunist, Benelli less so given his diplomatic background. So, Benelli would probably be the better choice for us."

Andropov was listening carefully, his brain recalling the details from Dimitry's August assessment. "Zhukov," he responded after mentally sorting the details, "I don't think it matters if they elect Siri or Benelli. If Siri is vocally anticommunist, then that means he has to invest considerable time dealing with the Italian Communist party and his own Italian Catholics, who have been voting for them, heavily in the case of Rome where, as you said, he would be bishop. And if he wants to take Catholic Mass back to being conducted in Latin, why should we care? We don't attend anyway. They are trying to expand the church into the third world, so I wish them well finding someone in Ethiopia who understands Latin. Benelli, the diplomat, may be more likely to pay attention to us, but if he wants to pursue these so-called reforms, then he will have to deal with those who supported Siri. Either one is fine with me, as, for somewhat different reasons, neither will find himself with much time to focus on us. Do you agree?"

"Yes…yes, I do," Zhukov replied.

"Fine," Andropov energetically replied. "So, go back to your office and draft up a plan that elects one of these two Italians. I don't care which one. Go with whichever you think can get enough votes to win, and then determine how we *encourage* the voters. Come brief me on it tomorrow evening. We need to plan, as the ball is rolling. Good evening."

With that, Andropov rose from his desk and stepped back over to the window to gaze out at Lubyanka Square, becoming once again what he had been when Dimitry arrived, more silhouette than man. Dimitry stood and slowly backed away from Andropov's desk and then turned and walked briskly to the door. As he stepped outside, he saw that CCO was still standing behind his desk, showing no signs of any movement since Dimitry had entered the chairman's office. He wondered if CCO was really a robot. Neither of them acknowledged the other. Dimitry stepped out into the hall and headed toward the stairs. He had a lot of work to do. Repeating something that had been happening on its own for half of a millennium would not seem to be a major challenge, but something told him this might be harder than it appeared. And what did Andropov mean when he said, "the ball is rolling"?

CHAPTER 3

# Saturday, September 30, 1978
# Florence, Italy

● ● ●

It was very quiet in the Basilica di Santa Maria del Fiore in the center of Florence, about three hours north of Rome. The archbishop of Florence, Cardinal Giovanni Benelli, was walking back and forth along the center of the magnificent old church with its enormous brick dome that dominated the Florentine skyline. The events of the previous day had taken a physical toll on Benelli, and as he often did, he had walked from his quarters in the nearby rectory to take refuge in the solitude of this historic old building. It was just after 4:00 a.m., and he had not been able to sleep, so he had donned a simple black suit and walked over to the nearly empty basilica, strolling slowly from the front facade to the area of the high altar, a distance of over 250 feet, a trip he always found relaxing and inspirational. And at this very moment, he was sorely in need of physical relaxation and intellectual inspiration.

The word had spread across Italy and the world about the unexpected death of Pope John Paul, and even in this early hour, there were a few worshipers scattered around the great building, lighting candles or kneeling in quiet prayer. None seemed to take notice of the prince of the church in their midst, perhaps because of the simple black suit that was momentarily replacing the black robes, red sash, and red cap that would have displayed his actual rank. Or it may have been that Benelli had only been a cardinal and the archbishop of Florence for a little over a year and many were still more familiar with his reputation than his appearance.

For an archbishop, such anonymity was a rare thing, and at this early morning moment, Benelli appreciated it.

"I thought I might find you here, Giovanni."

The words startled Benelli, and he looked away from the church's altar to see the smiling, familiar face of Angelo Sardi, a wealthy member of the Florentine business community, who had become a close friend and advisor over the past year.

"Did you? And why?" the cardinal replied.

Sardi grinned. "Well, Your Eminence, you've been a priest since 1943, you've spent many years in Rome, served as the Vatican secretary of state—"

"Deputy secretary of state," Benelli interrupted. "Cardinal Cicognani was the secretary of state. I was never more than the deputy."

Sardi grinned again and slightly shook his head. "A technicality, Giovanni. Everyone knows that you were the real secretary of state since Cicognani had many other duties and was quite old. Besides, he never had the relationship you had with Pope Paul. You served Paul for many years, even when he was the secretary of state—"

"Deputy secretary of state," Benelli interrupted again. "Paul was, like me, the deputy—never the secretary of state before he was sent to be archbishop of Milan."

"Yes, just as you were sent here by him. So, I must believe that your time has come, as Pope Paul's did in 1963. I know you sense it is time for you to fulfill your destiny and shoulder the heavy burdens that go with it, which is why I expected I would find you here…and in need of some close company."

Benelli smiled, reached over, and placed his hand on Sardi's shoulder. "You are a good friend, Angelo. And I appreciate your thoughts and the support they convey. But I am not the man. If I were, I would have been elected in August. But it was clear that during my years in the curia, I earned large contingents of both friends and enemies, and both were satisfied when His Holiness made me a cardinal and sent me here."

"They all admired your efficiency," Sardi replied.

"Perhaps, but most resented what was called my 'authoritarian style.' There were many times when I had to be tough on many senior curia members, most quite senior to me. Memories can be long in Rome."

"Your Eminence," Sardi continued after a brief pause, "what is past is past. And right now, what is past is the reign of Luciani as John Paul. We have discussed this before. You organized the group supporting him in the last conclave, as you had determined that if you could not be elected, then Luciani was the best prepared to carry on the reforms of John and Paul. But now there is no Luciani. The responsibility will fall to you…has already fallen to you. The only question is, will you accept it and take the steps that must be taken. If you do not, I believe we agree, someone else will."

Benelli gazed back at the altar. "I am sure, Angelo, that Pope Paul would have been pleased with the selection of Luciani. But now, after thirty-three days, it's over. We're back at square one, only without another obvious Luciani. And you are right; Siri and those behind him will be more watchful and organized this time. So, now what? I know I need to do something, but what? I'm the same man with the same issues I had six weeks ago. I'm still no Luciani."

"I believe you are selling yourself short, Giovanni. The church needs you. Think about it." With that, Sardi turned and headed toward the array of candles flickering in the corner, lit one, and then headed back down the long center aisle toward the door, leaving his friend to slip back into his own deep thoughts.

"Your Eminence?"

Benelli was startled back to reality from his deep introspection. He looked down to see an old woman, wearing a lace shawl. She was short, with one of those classical weathered faces reflecting many years of hard work in one of the many professions in central Italy where women worked hard and grew prematurely old. Benelli focused his eyes and looked into hers. "Yes, sister. How are you this very early morning?" He extended his hand, and she gently kissed his ring.

"We are very saddened by this horrible news, Eminence. But it must be even sadder for you, as I'm sure you knew the pope very well."

Benelli nodded without replying.

"Well, Your Eminence, we will pray for you in your next meeting in Rome. May God guide you to another selection worthy of Pope John Paul."

Benelli nodded again, and the old woman departed. He wished he had spoken more to her, been more comforting, but therein laid his major limitation—his demeanor was still more that of a politician than a priest, a shortcoming he fully recognized. He looked around and saw more people entering the basilica. He was in no mood to have any further encounters, so he headed toward a small door in a dark corner of the nave. Reaching it, he withdrew a key, opened it, and began the long climb that would lead him from the basilica floor to a narrow space between the inner and outer walls of the great dome far above. From there, he followed the stairs leading upward to the dome's observation platform, one providing a magnificent view of Florence and, in daytime, of the magnificent Tuscan countryside beyond. This was the place, in those hours when the dome was not open to the public, where he often went to ponder thorny issues. And he now faced a very thorny issue—indeed the thorniest of his life.

Although it was over 350 feet from the floor to the viewing platform at the top of the dome, Benelli made the journey in just a few minutes, something of a surprise, as he had recently been bothered because the climb had become increasingly difficult for him, a nagging worry, as he was only fifty-seven years old. Reaching the top of the dome, he stepped out onto the open viewing platform and leaned against an iron rail on the north side, looking out at the dark, sleeping city. The baptistery and the tall bell tower next to it, the *campanile*, were bathed in bright light, giving them the attention that they richly deserved as the architecturally famous companions of the basilica. Benelli could see the roof of a museum not far from the basilica that housed Michelangelo's sculpture of David, perhaps the most famous and celebrated piece of sculpted art in the world. For its history and beauty, Florence was a wonder, and Benelli always enjoyed the solitude at the top of the dome. This morning, it was more a refuge than a perch.

"How could this have happened?" he asked himself silently. "After all the work, all of the meetings, all of the cajoling and convincing to get Luciani elected, and now he is gone after only thirty-three days! How could the Lord have let this happen? What greater scheme or greater good could this possibly serve?"

Benelli twisted his hands together, continuing his silent reflections on the not very subtle encouragement of Angelo Sardi. "All of the great reforms—the needed reforms—of Popes John and Paul are now at risk," he thought. "With Luciani, they were secure, and more would have come, and now they will all be attacked again, and much of what I worked for all those years in the Vatican could be wiped away, discarded as if it had never existed."

Benelli looked up at the clear, starry sky and whispered to himself, "In August, they thought I was working to make myself pope. But I was actually working to make Luciani pope. And I did. And he was the right choice. He had the personal touch…the soul of a priest. There was great charisma behind that electric smile. He was humble. And I am none of those things. I have no personal touch, no great smile, little charisma. What I have are enemies who wanted the Holy Father to send me here, just as they had conspired to have John send Montini to Milan twenty years ago."

Benelli's thoughts turned to the call he had received the previous day from Cardinal Villot. "Villot wants Siri and me to come together and back a single Italian candidate," Benelli muttered to himself. "But Siri and I are oil and water—only oil and water mix better than we do. And Siri's candidate will be Siri himself, as it has been in every conclave since 1958 when he felt he was the best successor to Pius. He was nothing but trouble to both John and Paul. Yet he has an ardent following. So where do I go now? Who do I support and advocate for this time? How do we stop Siri again?"

Benelli began running down the possibilities, much as he had done back in August before deciding that Cardinal Luciani was the only reasonable choice and the only one likely to have enough appeal to thwart the election of Siri. "Perhaps Cardinal Colombo? No, he is too old and age will be a bigger issue now. Cardinal Poletti? Far too many suspicions about far too many things—real baggage. Baggio? No real appeal as either an administrator or a priest—neither fish nor fowl. Pignedoli? Not nearly enough clout. Even I could push him around the curia, before I was even a cardinal."

Benelli's head dropped. It was obvious, at least to him, that Villot was correct; the only viable candidates with a realistic chance were Siri and himself. He had thrown his weight behind Luciani in August, feeling his own time had not come, that he was still too young. But his fifty-seven years, which were a demerit a month ago, might be a merit now, maybe even a real plus. The church needed someone who would be around, who could outlast the archconservatives and, when necessary, stare them down. And Giovanni Benelli now knew who that man was. It was Giovanni Benelli.

Clasping his hands together, he turned and headed toward the stairs leading down to the interior of the dome. He had a lot of work to do.

## Genoa, Italy

As Benelli descended from the dome, 125 miles away in Genoa, Cardinal Giuseppe Siri was just rising for his morning prayers. He lived in a modest room in the Cardinal's Palace near the Cattedrale di San Lorenzo, the Cathedral of St. Lawrence, the seat of the archbishop of Genoa. San Lorenzo was originally consecrated in 1118, badly damaged by fire in 1296, and rebuilt during the early 1300s. It had survived numerous potentially destructive events through the years, including the chaos that engulfed Italy during and after World War II. Through it all, the old church had stood guard over the city, steady and strong. In that regard, it very much reflected the personality of its archbishop—old, steady, and strong.

Cardinal Siri was a native of Genoa, born in the city seventy-two years before. Something of a child prodigy, he had entered seminary at the mere age of eleven. He was a good and eager student, and following completion of his major seminary studies in Genoa, he had entered the Pontifical Gregorian University in Rome. He was ordained a priest in 1928 and earned a doctorate in theology the following year before returning to Genoa for pastoral work. In March 1944, Pope Pius XII named Siri the auxiliary bishop of Genoa, and he performed courageously in the latter days of World War II, working with the Italian resistance and eventually playing a role in negotiating an early surrender of the German army in the region, an effort that spared the historic city further damage as the war stumbled to a close. There was little surprise, therefore, that Siri was named the new archbishop of Genoa after his superior, Cardinal Boetto, died in 1946. In 1953, he was elevated to the College of Cardinals, becoming, at the time, its youngest member.

But now, he was among the college's oldest members and had participated in three papal conclaves, that of 1958, which elected John XXIII, that of 1963, which elected Paul VI, and the one this past August that chose John Paul. In all of these past elections, Siri was considered to be a *papabili*, and more than a few had predicted he would be the one sitting on the Throne of St. Peter. But it was never Siri who had emerged wearing the white robes.

Siri was an unusual combination of pastoral, intellectual, academic, and managerial experience and expertise, and although he had never held a senior position in the curia, he was well known throughout the Vatican for his stridently conservative views, views that had won him the solid support of many in Rome. Meanwhile, in Genoa, he was an active pastoral presence among the people of his native city. At one point, because of his frequent presence in soup kitchens, he carried the name of the "Minestrone Cardinal."

For those in the College of Cardinals who favored a pope with a pastoral background, Siri was appealing. For those who wanted an accomplished theological scholar, Siri was appealing. For those who sought a conservative who was cautious about yielding to the changing trends of modern times, Siri was appealing. And for those who wanted a strong, forceful personality unafraid of expressing contrarian views, Siri was appealing.

And, in addition to all those qualities, Siri was a master at cultivating a following and had done so throughout his quarter century wearing a red hat. There was a recurring rumor, having some ardent adherents, that Siri had, in fact, been elected pope in both 1958 and 1963. According to the story, he had accepted the vote and selected the name of Pope Gregory XVII. But, for reasons that were always vague and always heavily dependent on conspiracy theory, some in the College of Cardinals supposedly had asked for another vote, resulting in Siri being "unseated" by Cardinal Roncalli in 1958 and then Cardinal Montini in 1963. Siri never associated himself with any of these strange theories, never charged that either John or Paul were illegitimate pontiffs, and attached his signature to the formal documentation of many of the Vatican Council reforms. Nonetheless, at times, he could be coy and evasive when questioned about his alleged papal election. If the story worked to his advantage, he knew how to use it; if it worked against his interests, he knew how to trash it.

After attending to his normal daily rituals—bathing and shaving—Siri walked into his small sitting area where his private secretary and personal assistant, Monsignor Mario Grone, had laid out his clothing the night before. Since it was a normal day, despite following a most abnormal one, Siri would be wearing work clothes—a black wool cassock with black silk trim, a scarlet silk sash, a pectoral cross suspended from a thin chain, and the small scarlet skullcap that was the signature headgear of a cardinal. As he began to dress, there was a soft knock at the door. "Your Eminence, are you dressed?"

Siri recognized Grone's voice. "Almost, Mario. Please come in."

Grone entered the room and, as he did almost every morning, walked over to his superior and helped him adjust the scarlet sash around his waist. It was an awkward garment to put on, and after all these years, it still presented Siri with a daily challenge.

"Thank you…as always," Siri said, grinning at his young aide. "I don't know what I would do without your expert help regarding such pressing things," he added with a wide grin. "Man's relationship to God I can conceive. How to snap the fasteners on this sash remains a mystery."

Grone laughed. Despite Siri's reputation as a demanding taskmaster and the general view that a conservative theological outlook required a dour attitude, Siri had a great sense of humor, which was often on display. He certainly could be brusque when he felt the need, even brutal on occasion, but he could quickly pivot to a softer, more humorous side.

Siri walked to the mirror by the door, checked himself to ensure all was in order, and nodded toward Grone. "Very well," he said to the young priest. "Let's go to the office."

As they walked out of the apartment and headed down the stairs, Grone restarted the conversation they had ended the night before following the phone call from Rome. "Your Eminence, have you had the opportunity to reflect further on your discussion last evening with Cardinal Villot?" Grone had taken the initial call when the phone rang and knew its general content, as he had listened to Siri's side of the discussion until the cardinal had waved his hand, signaling for his young aide to leave the room. He knew it was a weighty matter that would be very much on his archbishop's mind.

"Yes, I have thought much about it—and prayed much about it," Siri replied, casting a slight smile toward Grone from across the top of his glasses. "Cardinal Villot knows well the difficulties of the last conclave and wants this one to go smoothly…and because of the costs, quickly."

"Will it likely go quickly, Your Eminence?" Grone cautiously asked, unsure as to whether he might be probing a bit too deeply into the internal dynamics of a very select group of which he was not a member.

"Difficult to say," Siri replied, with a slight shrug of his shoulders but without any indication that Grone should stay clear of the subject. "Villot is concerned that this may be a collision of the famous 'indestructible force colliding with the immovable object,' and he wants to avoid that if possible."

"What are the force and the object you refer to, Eminence?"

Siri stopped in place on the stairs and grinned again at his young secretary. "Grone, don't play dumb with me. You have been with me for how long now? Four years?"

"Actually six, Your Eminence?"

"Six! Really! Goodness I am getting old. But in those six years, I have learned that you are a very clever and astute young priest, and you have certainly learned that I am a very clever and cunning old priest. So, let's not be coy with one another. You know very well that Benelli is the force, and I am the object. Don't suggest to me that you don't?"

"I know, Your Eminence, but I felt it better to let you say it…in your own terms."

Siri smiled again. "As I said, Grone, you are a clever young man."

"Is there anything you need done right away, Your Eminence?"

By then, they had reached the exit to the street at the bottom of the stairs. Siri stopped and raised his hand to his chin. "Oh, yes, Grone. Several things. First, bring me the list of all the voting-age, Italian members of the conclave. I reviewed them last month, but let's go over them again. And be sure to add their phone numbers. I will have to make a considerable number of calls. Second, let's discuss when I should go to Rome. Back in 1963, Montini delayed his arrival for several days so he could build support without appearing to be doing so. Then he appeared when he felt he was in a strong position. He never had my support, as you know, but it was a clever ploy on his part—and effective. It worked well for him. We should consider it."

Grone reached into the pocket of his own cassock and pulled out a notepad and pen. It was now clear that following the discussion with Villot, his old mentor had given great thought to the conclave, had detailed directions in mind, and would expect Grone to address them right away. As he scribbled, he asked for one clarification. "Your

Eminence, did you say the names and numbers of only the Italian cardinals? Should you not be having discussions with others?"

"That will, of course, be required. But Villot is quite correct. We need to build a coalition to ensure the next pontiff is Italian. No easy task when only twenty-five of the electors are Italian at this point. But they need to be convinced to unite behind an Italian."

"Why, Your Eminence? Why another of us Italians?"

"Because, Grone, we have many issues that are very difficult and require considerable interaction with the Italian secular state. An Italian can best address such things. And besides, for our somewhat unfortunate country, there are only two Italians in today's world who have any international standing and recognition: the pope and Sophia Loren."

Grone lowered his head to mask the broad smile on his face. "Your Eminence, I had no idea you had any familiarity with Sophia Loren."

Siri looked at Grone so that his young colleague could see that he also wore a large smile. "Well, Grone," he said through the wide grin, "over the years, I have heard much about her during confessions."

"From men confessing lust, I assume."

"Yes…and from women confessing jealousy."

Siri and Grone laughed, and the old Cardinal placed his arm across his young secretary's shoulder and continued with his immediate list of needs. "So, therefore, the third task, Grone, get me the names and the numbers of all the European cardinals and those from Latin America. Given what I am certain Benelli is already planning, he will be communicating with this same group, and I will need to do so as well. See if you can call those who serve as their secretaries—your counterparts—and determine if they have spoken with Benelli and when. I would prefer to contact them after he has and certainly before they depart for Rome. So, timing is important, perhaps of the essence."

"Yes, Eminence. I understand. That makes sense."

Siri nodded, pleased that Grone was following his approach. "Fourth, call Villot's secretary and tell him that during the conclave, I want my temporary cell assigned so that it is close to a window, close to a bathroom, and, most important, close to a hallway so that I have easy access to the other cardinals as they pass back and forth."

Grone looked up from his notepad. "Your Eminence, I understand the procedure for assigning the temporary living quarters is that it is done strictly by lot. I doubt Cardinal Villot will be amenable to giving you such a preference."

"Grone, please, just make the call. Villot will be, as you say, 'amenable.' This will be my fourth conclave and that should certainly allow for some degree of, shall I say, *privilege*. Besides, even the best of Villot's, 'temporary living quarters,' as you call them, are uncomfortable. They are small, cramped, poorly ventilated, and in most cases, far from providing the privacy I'll need. And Villot knows this. It will not be resisted, trust me. Remember, last night, Villot called me, not the other way around."

Grone nodded, quickly yielding the point, and scribbled it down on his pad.

"Finally," Siri concluded, "call Gianni Licheri and set up a time for an interview."

Grone looked up in surprise. "Your Eminence, you mean Licheri the newspaper reporter from *Gazzetta del Popolo*? The one who covers the church? For an interview here in Genoa?"

"Yes, that would be the one I mean," Siri replied. "I think restating some of my theological and practical views about the church in today's world might be of interest to him and, in the long term, useful to me."

"Your Eminence, might that not seem a bit forward?" Grone meekly protested. "You mustn't be seen as advocating yourself for the papacy."

"Grone, the idea is to have these views published after the conclave begins, so they set a tone and identify an agenda…explaining it to the church."

"So you want an agenda of action for after your election?"

"I did not say anything about anyone's election," Siri inserted. "I said for after the conclave."

Grone nodded again. He could see this was an aggressive approach for a conclave that would almost certainly be Siri's last. Obviously, the wily old cardinal was going to approach this one in a very methodical and targeted way, hoping for a different outcome. "I have it all, Your Eminence. Is there anything further? If not, I had best get to work."

Siri reached across and again placed his hand on his young assistant's shoulder. "I think that will be enough for now, Grone. I need to invest some more time right now in thought and in prayer. Who knows what future lies ahead of us?"

Grone grinned at the old cardinal. "Yes, Your Eminence. Perhaps we are on the verge of finally electing Pope Gregory XVII."

Siri smiled. "I have no idea what you are talking about, Grone," he said as he opened the door to his office and stepped inside.

## Vienna, Austria

While Grone began to gather names and phone numbers, further to the north in Vienna, Cardinal Franz Koenig was entering his small study inside St. Stephen's Cathedral. He sat down heavily into the large leather chair behind an expansive, wood-carved desk. Reaching under his cassock, he withdrew the ornate letter he had just received from Rome, announcing the death of John Paul. He had already opened and read it; now he gently tossed it into the center of his desk. Slipping into deep thought, he unconsciously grabbed the letter and began to slowly rotate it, with each corner gently touching his desk pad as it went around in his fingers again and again.

"This is such a great misfortune," he thought, saddened as he was by the unexpected death of his old friend Albino Luciani, the now deceased Pope John Paul, in whose election he had played such a key role just over a month before. Among the non-Italian cardinals, Koenig was perhaps the most respected. He was now seventy-three years old and had been a prince of the church since being elevated to cardinal by John XXIII in 1958, and he had served as archbishop of Vienna since 1956. He was seen by many as being a prominent member of the *papabili* himself and was rumored to have received many votes in earlier conclaves. But during those earlier conclaves, the cardinals had clearly not been ready to select a non-Italian, and now, although in excellent health, he considered himself too old to be a serious candidate. He was, after all, seven years older than Luciani, and the age of the next pope was clearly going to be more important than it had been previously.

Koenig had been a priest since 1933 and had earned doctorates in both philosophy and theology from the Pontifical Gregorian University in Rome. He had also studied at Pontifical German-Hungarian College where he specialized in old Persian languages. This pursuit seemed unusual to many, but it combined two items of great interest to Koenig: other religions and other languages. Indeed, his gift for language was so great that he was fluent in seven, all of the Romance languages plus English, Russian, and his native German.

During the Cold War years, Austria, like some other European countries whose connections to the West were less concrete than their geographical proximity to the Soviet Bloc, had tried to take a path of neutrality between the two superpowers and their allies. Being Austrian, speaking seven languages, and having studied in Eastern Europe as a younger man, Koenig became a natural selection for Popes John XXIII and Paul VI to send on diplomatic missions to Moscow and other East European capitals. Koenig made it a major focus of his efforts to try to still the frequently stormy waters between the East and West, and between the church and Communism. "Reconciliation of our faith with Communism is not feasible," he had said on more than one occasion, "but conflict with Communism is not desirable." He still felt the church had a major role to play in preventing an East-West confrontation.

"Your Eminence. Coffee?" Koenig turned to see the door to his study opening and his assistant, Father Manfred Kühr, pushing a small teacart through it. "I saw that you skipped breakfast, but I thought some coffee might be needed," Kühr continued as he rolled the cart forward. "You are obviously deep in thought, Eminence. Might I ask about what?"

Koenig smiled. He enjoyed his morning coffee and always found Kühr's inquisitive mind a useful foil for checking his thoughts. "Yes, I was thinking about Cardinal Mindsvinty, actually."

"Mindsvinty? Why Mindsvinty?" Kühr asked as he handed his superior a large cup and then poured one for himself.

"I admired him greatly, Manfred. He was the most courageous—and stubborn—man I ever met. He's been dead three years now, and I think of him often. I'm increasingly concerned that we may be headed toward another confrontation between one of the Soviet satellites and NATO. Do you remember how long Mindsvinty was confined in the American embassy in Budapest after the Hungarian revolt?"

"Ten years, wasn't it?" Kühr replied, taking the seat next to the cardinal's desk.

"No, fifteen—1956 to 1971. Imagine spending fifteen years confined to a building, as a guest—although not a particularly welcome one, unable to meet with your worshippers, and the whole time knowing that your very presence was placing a hardship on them. I think for him it was worse than the years he actually spent in prison."

"So why did you involve yourself so heavily in getting him out, Eminence? Because of the church or because of him?"

"Oh, a bit of both. Plus the Holy Father asked me to, feeling I might be able to end this awkward standoff between Washington, Moscow, and Rome. I never thought I would succeed, but it taught me several things."

"Such as?"

"Such as there is a delicate balance between the two superpowers, and should it alter quickly there might be a global disaster. So, we must do what we can to allow it to alter slowly and gently. And I believe the church can play a major role in encouraging such an alteration. And I learned that the church has real leverage with the communist regimes. They think their ideology is superior to the church's theology, but they aren't really sure. And they don't really want to find out who actually is playing with the better hand."

Kühr leaned back in his chair, taking a sip from his cup. "And what of our theology, Your Eminence? We both know you've had your own issues with some of the recent edicts and encyclicals."

Koenig sat quietly for a few minutes, pondering how to phrase an answer. Theologically, Koenig was seen as quite moderate, and he carefully measured his words, like the scholar and diplomat he was. "As you know, Manfred, I have clashed with the Austrian government over its legalization of abortion, which I strongly opposed, but in other areas, I feel we must be more moderate, understanding, and flexible."

"Such as with birth control?" Kühr courageously asked.

Koenig could have ducked the question, but he didn't. "I have largely kept my own counsel on *Humanae Vitae* but believe the church must be more flexible on birth control. I once shared with some fellow cardinals that I thought *Humanae Vitae* was a tragic event. I believe my old friend, the archbishop of Venice, shared my view and was prepared to address it. But…we'll never know now, will we?"

"No, I suppose we won't," Kühr replied, awaiting further elaboration by Koenig, but there was none. "Well, Eminence, I'll leave you to your thoughts. I have several things to attend to. I know you need some time for prayer and reflection."

Koenig nodded in agreement, and Kühr departed.

Koenig had played a key role, along with several others, in the elevation of Luciani to the papal throne, but now, like Benelli, he faced the decision of what next, and he sat alone, fretting over what he considered to be disturbing possibilities. "I would never be comfortable with Siri," Koenig thought to himself. "He is certain to be the early favorite of the curia, but he is so conservative and inflexible and has been too open and strident with his anticommunist views. Communism is a problem that the church must address through reason and persuasion. Confrontation and public denunciation will bear us no fruit. Benelli is a good man, but he has many enemies in Rome, and he's unlikely to garner the necessary votes from outside the curia. And we can be certain that the curial cardinals who oppose him will oppose him strongly. So, who's left?"

Koenig mentally ran through the Italians in the college. His thoughts turned to Cardinal Poletti. "He is the vicar general of Rome. Only sixty-four years old, which will be a plus. Not a lot younger than Luciani, but still younger. He is in the curia and as vicar of Rome oversees the pope's pastoral work. He lacks the easy style and charisma of Luciani, but he could be a possibility. Then there is Pignedoli. He is older than Luciani and, like Poletti, has been in the curia for several years and works issues involving our relations with other faiths—which I feel is important. But he is neither an experienced priest nor a noted scholar. Not a bad one, but not notable. And he only speaks Italian and English, perhaps French as well—I'm not sure. But no Spanish and certainly no Slavic languages."

Koenig leaned back in his chair, rubbed his forehead, and began to think of a break with the past. "Perhaps the time has now come to choose a non-Italian," he whispered aloud. When this thought had occurred to him in the past, he had always felt that the well-regarded Dutch cardinal, Johannes Willebrands, the archbishop of Utrecht, was the best positioned. Willebrands was committed to ecumenism and had played a major role in getting other faiths to attend the Vatican Councils as observers. He was fluent in six languages, had both curial and pastoral experience, and had just turned sixty-nine—also older than Luciani—but he seemed rather fit and was quite active. "Willebrands, might work," thought Koenig. "He is well liked, is focused on the right issues, and, besides, for an organization that so likes tradition, the last non-Italian pope was also a Dutchman."

Koenig rotated in his chair and looked out the window of his small study. It faced east, and the morning sun was rising, its bright rays streaking the sky through some thin high-level clouds. The Austrian's thoughts fixed on the bright morning scene unfolding outside. "Or maybe," he thought, "it's time to look east."

## Warsaw, Poland

Cardinal Stefan Wyszynski sat alone in his office within St. John's Archcathedral in Warsaw. He also was slowly fingering his official notification letter from the Vatican. He saw the coming conclave as offering little opportunity for a change in direction and even less opportunity for a break with recent precedent. His immediate concerns were more personal. For him, the whole conclave experience was an ordeal, plain and simple. Despite his advanced age and notable position, he would once again have to wrestle with the Polish government over his travel arrangements, make the long flight to Rome, spend several days listening to the views of his fellow cardinals regarding matters that were of little relevance to him in his ongoing confrontation with the Polish Communist Party, sleep on a hard bed with a thin mattress, and eat God knows what for several days while he was a virtual captive within the walls of the Holy See.

Being a captive did not bother Stefan Wyszynski. A few months after Pope Pius XII had elevated him to cardinal in early 1953 and named him prelate of Poland, the Polish government had arrested and imprisoned him for three years because of his opposition to communist rule and Soviet domination. While in prison, he had seen others tortured and some executed. It was a searing experience, and it had made Wyszynski tough…very tough. He was even now, late in life, equal parts primate and prizefighter, and everyone recognized that he fought above his weight.

The Soviets were wary of him. Poland was the most populous country along its western security zone, and the population was nearly 90 percent Catholic. It was assumed in Moscow that this math meant that less than 10 percent of the population were committed communists, and it was never clear whose side the Polish people would select in the event of a serious showdown with the church. And with the events in Hungary in 1956, Czechoslovakia in 1968, and now the evident rise of a widely supported workers movement in Poland, Moscow was increasingly unhappy and uneasy. Accordingly, Moscow had grown quite cautious in its dealings with the always blunt, often sarcastic, and inevitably troublesome Cardinal Wyszynski.

Such complexities and confrontations were the daily diet of Wyszynski's life. But this next conclave was another wrinkle and he knew he had to give it some thought. The Italian cardinals would no doubt be colluding on how to elect another one of them to the papacy. And in that regard, Wyszynski was largely indifferent. Ever since Pope Paul had essentially buried the hatchet with the Hungarian government following the departure of Mindsvinty in 1971, Wyszynski had concluded there was little the Vatican could, or would, do for him and others in the Catholic church leadership who lived behind Churchill's

Iron Curtain. But if the Vatican could not make his condition easier, Wyszynski very much preferred that it not make it worse.

His thoughts turned to Cardinal Koenig. The Austrian had several times raised the issue of electing a non-Italian pope and seemed to feel that such a selection could be used to put additional pressure on the communist regimes and provide a lever to loosen Russian control of Eastern Europe. Koenig believed you had to be always direct but simultaneously subtle in dealing with the Soviets and their puppet regimes. But Koenig had never spent time in a communist prison. Wyszynski had. He also favored a direct approach, but saw little use for subtlety.

Despite this difference in views, Koenig in the past had explored with Wyszynski the possibility of advocating the Pole for pontiff. Wyszynski had never been in favor and had gone out of his way to discourage such thought. That was far *too* direct, even for him. His election to pope would certainly be seen in Moscow as a direct challenge of their authority, and who knew what steps they would take to ensure a compliant Poland, one safeguarding their lines of supply to their large Red Army force in East Germany. Wyszynski had never seen the Soviets at their best, but he had seen them at their worst—up close and personally.

Besides, he was now seventy-seven years old. He had been a cardinal for a quarter century and had spent much of it dancing in a Polish bottle with a Soviet scorpion. His issues had been near-term, immediate. He was not sure he was adequately in touch with global issues, much less the contentious theological issues that were so much at the front of the church's agenda. Throughout Poland, there was talk of a general strike, and concern that the Polish military would be called in to quell it. It could be civil war and could initiate another Soviet intervention, which was just a softer word for *invasion*. Wyszynski had that possibility weighing heavily on his mind at the moment, much more heavily than the coming conclave.

If Koenig approached him, he would tell him to look elsewhere. Willebrands had always been a clear *papabili*. Perhaps the old Pole would throw his weight and considerable prestige to the Dutchman—or even to Suenens of Belgium. He would have to wait and see. But of one thing he was clear: the next pontiff would not be Cardinal Wyszynski from Poland.

## Outside Jena, East Germany

Sergeant Pasha Petrov was tired. They had only been in the field for two days, but he was already very tired. Even for Germany, it was unusually damp and cold, and the field kitchen had served them a breakfast that was terrible even by Red Army standards. They had gotten on the road early from their dispersal area east of Weimar. He was riding at the top of his T-72 number C-12 with his upper torso outside the turret. His ribs were already very sore. No matter how often you rode in a T-72 as a tank commander, the constant motion as the tank turned, slowed, and accelerated bounced your body against the thick armor of the hatch. Like all Soviet equipment, a T-72 was not built for crew comfort. The rubber padding around the hatch was thin, with most of it peeled away on tank C-12. In addition, Captain Belikov had gotten them up extra early that morning to tell them they were moving. He hadn't said to where, just to follow Route 7 until told to stop.

The T-72 lurched hard to the right, bouncing Petrov around in the hatch again. "Rostov," he yelled into the intercom connecting him to the driver, "what are you doing?" There was no answer. "Rostov!" he yelled louder, pushing down hard on the intercom button.

"Sorry, Pasha," came the scratchy voice through the earpiece in his padded headset. "I'm getting tired driving this thing. The laterals are hard to control. My arms are exhausted. When can we stop and take a break?"

"When Belikov says we can," Pasha replied.

Driving a Soviet tank was no easy task. It didn't have a steering wheel, just two levers called laterals that controlled the two dead tracks on both sides of the tank. The T-72 was more like a bulldozer with armor than anything else, and constantly pulling the laterals to steer it was tiring. It never took long for the shoulders and arms to start going limp.

Pasha turned around in his turret to look behind him to tank C-13, the trailing tank of his three-tank platoon. It seemed to be doing well and was holding the right interval, acrid smoke bellowing behind it. As he turned back to the front, he heard a loud rumbling, crushing sound. He looked ahead as C-11, his lead tank, careened off the roadway and crashed into the stone buttress of an old bridge crossing the Saale River, a small waterway running through Jena.

Pasha saw the tank commander duck inside as the fifty-ton vehicle spun partway around, stopped, balanced momentarily on the slope leading to the water, and then slowly began sliding down the riverbank.

"Halt!" Pasha yelled into the intercom, as he instinctively held his hands high, crossing his arms, a signal to C-13 behind him to stop.

"It's going to flip over!" he heard Igor yelling as he pulled back hard on both steering laterals, bringing C-12 to a rough stop. "Oh, my God! It's going to flip upside down! They'll drown in the river!"

Pasha pulled his helmet off and jumped from the turret. He quickly ran across the front slope of his tank and leaped to the ground. He dashed to the bridge, arriving just as C-11 hit the water nose first, after about a ten-foot drop. The tank commander jumped out of the hatch, landing in about a foot of water. Pasha watched, waiting to see if the driver had managed to crawl from the front hatch before his compartment filled with water. It seemed like a long wait, but it was probably only seconds before the driver emerged from the river, dripping wet but alive.

"This is going to be dangerous," Pasha thought, relieved that his comrades had survived the accident. "Taking these tanks to places where we've never been before, over these narrow German roads…It's dangerous. Especially over these crappy old bridges. Who knows if they are wide enough and can carry fifty-tons? And heading east…why are we still heading east?"

The questions bounced around in his head, until out of the corner of his eye, he saw Captain Belikov running down the road toward him. He took a deep breath. It was certain to be a nasty conversation when Belikov arrived. And it was.

CHAPTER 4

# Saturday, September 30, 1978
# Washington, DC

• • •

It was quiet when Carter Caldwell arrived at the EOB. It was supposed to be. It was, after all, a Saturday morning. Carter had no idea how the Executive Office of the President handled its duty assignments—he assumed differently, if not necessarily better than the army. It was a bit mysterious why Mr. Lewis always seemed to be manning the front entrance to the building. But there he was, just as if it were a regular weekday.

"Good Saturday morning to you, Mr. Caldwell," the always jovial security guard said to Carter as he came through the door.

Carter instinctively pulled the ID badge from under his windbreaker and held it up. "Good morning, Mr. Lewis. How are you doing today?"

"I'm fine, Mr. Caldwell." Lewis looked around, checking to see if anyone was listening to their conversation before turning his attention back to the young official. "Seems like it's just us here, so I can just call you Carter, right?"

Carter shrugged his shoulders and smiled. "Mr. Lewis, of course you can. I thought we had settled that long ago. You're old enough to be my father…you admitted it! And guess what? My father calls me Carter."

Lewis laughed. "OK then, Carter. Just checking. This place is real heavy on protocol, you know? So, you all fired up for the big Redskins game against Dallas on Monday night?"

"Monday?" Carter replied. "I thought it was tomorrow."

"Nope. Monday. The Monday night game with Howard, Frank, and Dandy Don. Can hardly wait. We're 4–0 and the pokes are ready to be plucked. Meredith will try to cover for them, of course, being an old Cowboy hisself, but we're going to flatten 'em. I have tickets. I'll be able to see it at RFK in person."

Carter laughed. "Well, let me know how it goes."

"Who's Army playing today?"

"Washington State," Carter answered. "And they're at home. So, I think they have a chance."

"Well, Carter, as you know, this is definitely a navy town. Annapolis is just thirty miles away so they're almost like the local college. And the *Washington Post* certainly treats 'em like they are. But I'm an army man like you. So, I'll be rootin' for you guys."

"Thanks." Carter grinned, combining it with a slight grimace. "Army football needs all the help it can get these days." With that, he waved to Lewis, pushed through the turnstile, headed for the stairwell in the northeast corner, and, as usual, bounded up the three floors to his office. As he hit the third floor, he reached into his pocket for his office keys, but before he could pull them out, he saw light streaming into the hallway from the office's open door. Obviously, Pat Meyers was already there and the coffee was already brewing. Why was he not surprised?

"Morning, Pat," he said as he strolled through the door.

"Carter," she acknowledged as she stared into her steaming coffee. "Need a cup?"

"No, thanks," Carter replied. "Not today."

"Oh, I'd get one if I were you. I think you'll need it."

Carter stopped at the door of his office and turned toward his EA. "Might I ask why?"

"Sure. You have a meeting with Dr. Brzezinski in his office in thirty minutes. If I were you, I'd want to be fully alert and—shall I say—stimulated."

"In thirty minutes? As in thirty minutes from now!"

"Well, you did ask for the meeting."

"Shit," Carter reflexively exclaimed, as he darted into his office to quickly review the large stack of notes he had taken during his hours in the EOB library. Fortunately, unlike some highly intelligent people, Carter was also highly organized, took copious notes, and meticulously organized them. It was a useful habit, partly natural, consistent with his personality, and partly necessitated by his undergraduate experience. He jumped into the chair behind his desk and began quickly flipping through the folder he had prepared. Names, dates, history, procedures, facts, figures, rumors, suppositions, predictions…he quickly poured over the pages for twenty-five minutes, closed the folder, tucked it under his arm, and then tried to casually walk past Pat and out of their office.

"All ready, Carter?" she asked in her low, slightly gravelly voice.

"Absolutely," Carter replied, hoping he was not wildly exaggerating. He walked through the office door, quickly descended the stairs to the basement and dashed down the hallway to the doors in the middle of the building leading to the small parking lot that separated the EOB from the White House. As he approached the West Wing, the marine sentry on duty snapped to attention, saluted, and opened the door. Carter returned the salute, stepped inside, and bounded up the stairs to Dr. Brzezinski's office, on the main level in the corner facing Pennsylvania Avenue.

Hitting the top of the stairs, he found himself looking directly at the desk of Margaret Burrows, which occupied a space that resembled a closet as much as an office. But that was not unusual. All offices in the West Wing were small, as there were more people desiring to be close to the president than the square footage of the old White House auxiliary building allowed. Margaret held up her hand, signaling for Carter to stop and reached for the phone. "Mr. Caldwell is here," she said into the receiver and then placed it back on its cradle. "Go in," she instructed, motioning toward the door. Carter nodded, stepped to his left, and turned the doorknob.

"Come in, Mr. Caldwell. Sit over there." The voice of Zbigniew Brzezinski was distinctive. In addition to being clear and crisp, it still reflected slightly more than a trace of a Polish accent, reminding everyone of Brzezinski's interesting life.

Carter had no trouble getting to the right chair. There were only two, and one was filled with bulging intelligence reports. Brzezinski straightened a few things on his desk. Carter thought he looked tired, not surprising given that the national security advisor had been working hard over the past few weeks helping President Carter design the peace agreement between Israel and Egypt reached at Camp David. Brzezinski had done many things to keep the talks going: encouraging all three leaders, generating ideas, and even playing chess with Prime Minister Begin in an effort to help the Israeli relax.

Carter heard the old professor let out a big sigh as he cleared a space from his desk, placed his elbows on it, and turned his attention to his young guest. "I heard you wanted to see me," Brzezinski stated in his usual direct manner. "I have a meeting with the president in fifteen minutes. What do you have for me? Something from Moscow on the next SALT round, I hope?"

Carter had expected more than fifteen minutes. He would have to cram considerable information into a short time. "No, Dr. Brzezinski, nothing on SALT. I wanted to talk with you about the death of the pope and the next conclave."

"Why?" Brzezinski curtly responded. "They'll have a conclave. The cardinals will elect the Italian among them who is the most broadly liked and least controversial. White smoke will come out of the chimney in the Sistine Chapel. All of us who are Catholic will learn a new name with another number affixed to it, and we'll move on." Brzezinski clasped his hands together and paused briefly before emitting another deep sigh. "I met Cardinal Luciani once and found him enormously appealing. He was certainly off to a tremendous start. And he was one of those who had been granted that most precious, indefinable, and indispensable gift of leadership—enormous charisma. His death is such a shame. But I am well versed on the Catholic church and its ways. Are you Catholic?"

"No. Presbyterian. More or less."

"Well, I am Catholic…more than less. I see no need to invest much time in this, even though I am a Catholic, so why would I need to discuss it with you, a 'more or less' Presbyterian? As I said, it's a heavily scripted event. The seventy cardinals will gather, attend the funeral of John Paul, have some meetings, line up, and march into the Sistine Chapel signing their favorite hymns, close the door, and then choose one from among them."

"It's actually 111, sir," Carter responded very matter-of-factly.

"What is actually 111?"

"The number of cardinals. There are about 130 total, and we believe 111 will be voting. That being the number who are under eighty years of age and who we feel are healthy enough to make the trip and go through the election."

Brzezinski's eyes narrowed. "I thought a papal edict many years back capped the membership of the college at seventy cardinals."

"That is correct, sir. But it was indeed many years back—1586 to be precise in a papal bull issued by Pope Sixtus V. It remained at roughly that number until after World War II when Pope Pius XII, recognizing the growing international nature of the church, began raising the number. Popes John XXIII and Paul VI further increased the number, so now we have about 130."

"So how does a seemingly casual Presbyterian so precisely know all this?"

"It's in the intelligence analysis sent over yesterday by the Agency."

"What intelligence analysis?" Brzezinski asked, with an edge of irritation in his voice. "I've seen no such analysis."

"I think that's it over there," Carter replied, pointing at the pile of reports stacked in the other chair. "That looks like it on the top of the pile."

"Well," Brzezinski shot back, "whatever the number is doesn't alter either the calculation or the calculus. This is still a gathering of highly homogenous intellects who are largely immune from persuasion—as you and I practice the concept. Most feel they have been to the mountaintop and seen the tablets of stone."

Carter knew the shot clock was running on this meeting, so he decided to jump straight to the point. "Dr. Brzezinski, I won't dispute your characterization of the cardinal electors, but I still believe we should consider ways in which we might want to influence the outcome this time. I think we need to give some thought as to what sort of pope, with what background, would best serve American interests."

"Well, that would be easy enough to deduce," Brzezinski interrupted. "Obviously American interests would be best served by the selection of an American pope, one who was willing to support us unreservedly on our nuclear weapons posture, who would condemn communist insurrections in Africa and Latin America, and who would declare democracy to be consistent with the teachings of the Bible and communism fully inconsistent with Christianity, and all other faiths. Unfortunately, even if we had an American candidate who had fully embraced all these views—and I don't know that we do—getting him selected by this very unusual electoral body, which has been carefully populated over the past four decades, as you point out, by only three people, named Pius, John, and Paul, would be most unlikely. Or are we talking about some other Catholic church with some other selection process?"

Dr. Brzezinski's cutting wit was well known, and he could use it to both arm himself and disarm others. But a man who was close to Brzezinski had coached Carter on how to deal with it. "Dr. Brzezinski," Carter replied, summoning as much presence and calm as he could and trying to appear calmer than he actually was, "you and I both know that an American pope is unrealistic. But I believe the conditions may exist, in this coming conclave, for the election of a non-Italian. And I believe a non-Italian pope, perhaps one from elsewhere in Europe, one who has in the past been interested in East-West relations, who has seen the social and economic pain associated with communism, and who believes he could use faith to challenge Soviet rule—and their aspirations around the world—would clearly serve American interests. Wouldn't you agree?"

"Probably so," Brzezinski quickly responded, "but there has not been a non-Italian pope since 1622. So why would a non-Italian be appealing now when one was not appealing enough during the French Revolution, the Napoleonic period, the colonial period, the naval races of the late 1800s, World War I, World War II, and the current Cold War?"

"Actually, Dr. Brzezinski, it's worse than you think. The last non-Italian pope was in 1522. Hadrian VI. He died after a reign on one year. He was Dutch."

"Very good, Mr. Caldwell. So your young memory has trumped my old one. Or was that also in the CIA report?"

"No, I just happen to know that."

"Ah, so the Presbyterian has done some research. I knew it was Hadrian, so forgive me for being off by a century. My point is that this is a highly selective and very secretive body that elects a Pope. The Pope selects them while he is on the throne, and they heavily reflect his own infallible rules and perspectives. The perspectives of this electorate, developed over a lifetime, cannot be changed in a couple of weeks, which I believe is the time we would have before the conclave. And there is the tiny detail that they are, understandably, quite resistant to secular interventions. By us or anyone else."

Carter saw he was being unpersuasive. He tried another approach. "Dr. Brzezinski, there is no guarantee we will succeed. And the odds—and the history of the past five centuries—are certainly not in our favor. But I believe we should try. We should decide what outcome would be the most favorable for us and try to influence events to, let me say, *encourage* it. If you fully believed that past history and personal perspectives make positive change impossible, you would never have gone to Camp David for ten days with Begin and Sadat, would you?"

Brzezinski paused, but just for a moment. Carter had made a good point, but the national security advisor remained outwardly unconvinced. "Mr. Caldwell, the Arab-Israeli problem has been as it is for thirty years. The nationality of the pope has been as it is for a half millennium. The selection process as it has evolved favors incrementalism, conservatism, and caution. I don't see that changing in the next two weeks, and I don't see any realistic way to change it even in the next two centuries. I am surprised you would take my time on it."

Carter could see that he had exhausted Brzezinski's patience, but he was not ready to abandon his effort. "Dr. Brzezinski, I believe there must be a way we can influence this process. Maybe it's less calcified than you think. Maybe it just needs a slight nudge. Let me develop a plan for it."

Brzezinski did not reply. He stared at Carter for several seconds as he gathered the briefing material needed for his meeting with the president. Putting them under his arm, he stood up from his chair. Carter did the same.

"I have to go," Brzezinski said rather coldly. "Caldwell, do you know why I allowed you to serve here on my team?"

Caldwell knew the answer but decided not to indicate that he did. "No, sir, I really don't. Obviously, being Zbigniew Brzezinski, you don't really need a director of European and NATO affairs."

"True. I don't. But I took you because Brent Scowcroft, my predecessor with President Ford, strongly recommended you to me. He told me that among the nonpermanent faculty at West Point's Department of Social Sciences you were, he thought, the best—and the one with the most promise. I may not listen well to others, but I have learned to always listen to Brent Scowcroft. In fact, I first met him at West Point—at the SCUSA Conference run by the same Department of Social Sciences—back in 1954. He was a very sharp young air force captain, and I was a young academic at Columbia just gaining some note. We cochaired the European affairs panel. Did you know that?"

Carter shook his head. He actually was unaware that was the origin of the connection between Scowcroft and Brzezinski.

"I was reluctant," Brzezinski continued, "to take a fellow so young. You graduated from West Point when?"

"In 1968, Dr. Brzezinski."

"Only ten years ago. And you have stepped away from the mainstream army…why?"

"We discovered I have asthma. I am not deployable to combat zones. The army doesn't like its infantry officers sneezing while they try to sneak up on the enemy."

"Well, the asthma must have affected more than your sinus cavities. Refocus your thoughts on SALT, and let's not invest more time trying to influence a process over which we have—almost by definition—no influence."

With that, Brzezinski quickly departed the room and headed toward the Oval Office on the opposite side of the West Wing. Carter departed as well and headed back to the EOB. He had to work on a plan. General Scowcroft had told him that Brzezinski often tortured his graduate students by attacking their basic premise only to return to it later and help them refine it, smoothing and polishing an often rough stone. Maybe this would be one of those times.

## The Vatican, Rome

Cardinal Jean Villot was still trying to catch up on the myriad of details that had to be addressed for the conclave. Both he and his staff had been working nonstop ever since he was summoned to the pope's apartment early the previous morning, and all had not gone smoothly. The early releases from the Vatican press office were already causing him major headaches. Although he was Vatican secretary of state and camerlengo, Villot was not fully aware that the old rules of media relations no longer existed. Even the relatively trusting Vatican press reporters were asking very intrusive questions, digging for all kinds of minute detail and snooping around for "background" sources to verify everything imaginable.

Sitting in his large office overlooking St. Peter's Square, Villot was venting his frustrations to his key assistant and personal secretary, Monsignor Petar Sarac, a quiet, intense, and efficient Belgian who was among the few who had demonstrated an enduring capacity for dealing with the cardinal's temperamental emotions. Many felt that Sarac filled his current role with ease precisely because he apparently had few emotions of his own. Around the curia, Sarac was seen as quite the frigid fish—efficient, effective, meticulous, but distant and cold.

"Why is this such a mess?" Villot barked in French, referring to the press office problems. "Has the staff down there had a complete mental collapse?"

Sarac waited for the cardinal to calm down. Being Belgian, he was fluent in French as well as Flemish and Romanian. His family had fled from Romania to Vienna and later to Brussels in the closing months of World War II. Sarac remained in touch with relatives in Bucharest and had traveled there frequently to maintain contacts between the Vatican and the Romanian communist regime of President Nicolae Ceausescu. His efforts had been quite successful in protecting the small Catholic community in Romania and had caught the eye of the sometimes fiery Vatican secretary of state.

As Sarac had learned, Villot tended to vent in French, although he generally conducted daily business in Italian. "Your Eminence," Sarac replied after a lengthy moment of calm, "I think they are as stunned as the rest of us. They reported originally that the Holy Father died late in the evening of the twenty-eighth, then having no certainty of the actual time of death issued a second release saying it was on the morning of the twenty-ninth. It was a horrible mistake. The press became confused and then suspicious. Unfortunately, Your Eminence, we live in an age of suspicion. The media sees a conspiracy in every major story."

"For Christ's sake!" Villot billowed, his choice of expression showing the degree of his frustration. He quickly placed his hands together, turned his eyes skyward, and whispered a request for divine forgiveness for his pressure-driven outburst. "What difference does it make? He was alive when he went to bed. He was dead when he woke up."

Sarac lowered his head and rolled his eyes. "Your Eminence, no one wakes up dead."

"For Christ's sake...my goodness, there I go again! Forgive me, Almighty Father. Sarac, you know perfectly well what I mean!"

"I do know what you mean, Eminence. But your comments show that you are under great stress after suffering such a great shock. You are misspeaking as a result, just as they are in the press office. They are also in shock. We are all in shock. One can have a whole career in the press office and never cover a papal election. And many have. They now have to deal with two in five weeks—and, of course, the unexpected death of the Holy Father. I will meet with them, have them take a deep breath, and get them to clear their heads, and regroup."

"What are the other stories that have the press all up in arms? I heard there were other so-called 'discrepancies' they are asking about. Like the herd of jackals they are."

"There are two others, Your Eminence. The first involves who found the Holy Father in bed, the second involves what he was reading...what was he actually holding in his hands?"

"What!" Villot caught himself before uttering a third outburst requiring divine forgiveness. "All right. I understand the problem that has arisen about who discovered the Holy Father's body. It was clearly Sister Vincenza. She entered his bedroom when he did not respond to her calls about why he had not retrieved his morning coffee. Her entering was contrary to my instructions, and everyone knows what I had instructed, do they not?"

"Of course they do, Your Eminence. But the sister had been with the Holy Father many years. She was concerned—rightfully as it turned out. She did what was her custom from the past and went in to check on him. That is quite understandable, don't you agree?"

"Yes! Understandable! But against my directions! And everyone in the Vatican knows it. So I instructed the press office to say Father Magee made the terrible discovery. Who told the media it was Sister Vincenza anyway!"

"I don't know the answer to that, Eminence. Perhaps one of the Swiss Guards. One would presume it was not anyone from the Holy Father's household, who are no longer here anyway. I guess we could question them about it, but I don't feel that would be in good taste, given their own state of mind. And it may well have been someone in the Holy Father's family. Perhaps the niece he was so close to. But all we can do now is correct the error and try to avoid others. If it was Sister Vincenza, then we must say it was Sister Vincenza. Otherwise, it becomes a bigger issue than it already is…and it's already big and getting bigger."

Villot glared at his young secretary. He knew Sarac was right and hated admitting that he, Villot, had been wrong. "Very well." He sighed. "Let's get out a confirmation that the horrible discovery was made by Sister Vincenza. What is the other problem again?"

"The press office released a statement saying the Holy Father was discovered sitting upright and holding in his hands a copy of the book *The Imitation of Christ*. But it appears someone has now reported that he was actually holding church documents on some unknown subjects, which are now unaccounted for."

"They are not unaccounted for!" Villot exclaimed, his face suddenly covered by a glowing red hue. He opened the top drawer of his desk and pulled out four sheets of paper. "They are right here…in my desk. I have them. They are of no concern to anyone, so why does the press care?"

"If they are of no concern, Eminence, then why have we not simply acknowledged what they were? And what they were about?"

"Because they are internal church issues that the Holy Father was considering! They were not intended for public review where they might be misrepresented or misconstrued!"

"Misconstrued how?"

"Who knows, Sarac? But I am not willing to take such a risk given they cover numerous issues and contain some marginal notes from the Holy Father himself! So they stay here…in my desk, until I have the time to personally destroy them." Villot took a deep breath and forcefully exhaled it. "What else? Did I hear that they are also suspicious that we cleaned and locked the Holy Father's residence?"

Sarac was not doing well answering these rapid-fire questions in a manner calming to his excitable superior, but he had no choice other than to press forward. "Yes, Your Eminence. There have been questions raised about the sealing of the residence."

"Why?" Villot roared, his blood pressure now rising rapidly. "What could be suspicious about that? That is normal practice. It is what we do when the pope dies, whether he dies in his residence or elsewhere. Do these excessively inquisitive idiots think we should just leave the place as it was, and expect the new pontiff to sleep on his dead predecessor's wrinkled sheets? This is foolishness!"

"Very well, Your Eminence. We will just emphasize that it is normal practice. I am sure, except for the August conclave, that very few of the media covering the death of the Holy Father have ever covered one before and therefore are unfamiliar with our practices—usual to us, but perhaps unusual to them."

"Obviously!" Villot loudly replied, clasping his hands in front of him, leaning forward on his elbows, and rocking slightly in his chair. "Enough of this press lunacy. Please sit down with the leaders of the press office and get the story corrected in such a way that the reporters will drop all of this unimportant nonsense and focus on the serious task at hand. They act like this is Dallas after the murder of President Kennedy…colorful characters and conspiracy hiding behind every tree. This is not Texas; this is Rome!"

Villot turned in his chair and reached toward the outsized window behind him. A large, brown leather briefcase was resting on the windowsill. The cardinal grabbed it and lifted it to his desk, where it made a noticeable thud as it landed heavily on his desk pad. The top of the briefcase had small embossed, golden papal seals on either side of the thick leather handle. Villot pulled a small key from his pocket, inserted it into the locks on the top of the briefcase, and popped it open. He reached across the table to Sarac. "Do you have the files with the position papers I asked you to have prepared?"

"Yes, Your Eminence." Sarac reached down beside the chair where he had previously placed a pile of file folders, arranged in alphabetical order by topic. He lifted them with both hands, being careful not to drop any of the contents onto the floor, and handed them all to Villot.

"Is that all?" the old Cardinal asked. "It seems like it should be."

"No, Your Eminence, I still have a few items coming from the bank."

"Of course, I could have guessed. The bank. They are probably still trying to come up with a story that will prevent the new pontiff from excommunicating them all. Well…get those items to me when they're delivered and I'll add them to this growing pile in the Holy Father's briefcase. Just after the selection is made, I'll want you to get the briefcase, carry it up to the papal apartment, and place it in the new Holy Father's study next to his bedroom. There are several things in here he'll have to address immediately."

"Yes, Eminence. Certainly. I'll ensure it gets there—personally as you have asked."

Villot put the files in the briefcase, slammed it shut, relocked the clasps, and swung the increasingly heavy bag back to the windowsill. He then reached across his desk to grab a glass of water, took a quick drink, and turned back to Sarac. "Food? What about food?"

Sarac glanced down at his notes, flipped a few pages, and then returned his gaze to the cardinal. "The sisters we brought in to prepare the meals for the August conclave are being notified and asked to return. I see no problems there. We will just reestablish and reuse the same accommodations for them as we did last time. And, they will be preparing the food in the same kitchens."

Villot grimaced at the mention of food. "The meals," the old cardinal mumbled to himself, as if recalling a bad dream. "It's just hopeless. There is no way to win…absolutely no way. Providing food that Cardinals Ratzinger of Germany and Ekandem of Nigeria will both enjoy is impossible. Throw in the nine Americans who evidently only want hamburgers and…well, it's just impossible. Have the nuns do the best they can. I'll just have to smile and absorb the comments."

"Can you do that, Your Eminence?" Sarac asked, his face covered with an impassive stare, his mind filled with concern, knowing that quiet humility was not normally part of the camerlengo's personality. "You know, Your Eminence, we could simply ask a local hotel or restaurant to cater for us. That would certainly be a delight for the majority of the cardinals."

"Until they saw the bill!" Villot quickly countered, before calming himself and slipping into some momentary reflection of the clear irony before him. "How absurd. This is Italy. We are famous for our wonderful food. People come on holiday just to eat! Yet when you combine a conclave, a hundred cardinals, and food, for me, it becomes a pain in the…shall I say, stomach?" Villot slowly shook his head. "Very well… enough on the food. How about the living quarters?"

"They'll be a challenge again, Eminence. After August, we looked at the square footage to see if—in the future, and we assumed the far future—we might make adjustments and add extra comfort, but for the moment, it does not seem feasible. Fortunately, we have the raw material and the furnishings, if we can call them that, still available. This will, I would say, be more an effort at reconstruction than construction."

By far, Villot's biggest headache was the living quarters for the visiting cardinals. Although they were nearly all—but not all—humble men, they were nonetheless highly accomplished within the church, had firm opinions, and most worked hard to conceal well-developed egos. Constructing the temporary living quarters, or cells, as they were commonly called, for nearly one hundred temporary guests was no easy task and one that had frustrated and bedeviled Vatican secretaries of state for years.

When Paul VI died, Villot had great difficulty finding the workmen to construct the cardinals' temporary wooden rooms because August was the traditional vacation month for most Italians. Locating carpenters to augment those in the Vatican's small facilities office became a major headache. That would be less of a problem this time, as the summer season had passed. But the fundamental problem remained: while the College of Cardinals had grown significantly in size over the past twenty years following the election of Pope John XXIII, the acreage within the Vatican walls had not. The cells had to be wedged into whatever space could be found throughout the small city-state and done in a way that made each room as similar in size and configuration as possible. All would be small and identically outfitted with a hospital bed sporting a thin mattress, one simple wooden chair, a kneeler for prayer, and some basic toiletries.

"Have we had a phone call from Cardinal Siri, asking for a particular room or location?" Villot asked Sarac.

"No, Your Eminence. I've heard nothing from Monsignor Grone."

"You will," the camerlengo replied. "And give him whatever he wants."

"But, Your Eminence," Sarac started to protest, "our procedure for assignment of the rooms does not—"

Villot cut the young monsignor off. "Sarac, give him what he wants!"

Villot fell briefly quiet, taking a couple of deep breaths to lower his blood pressure and overall intensity. "Do the best you can, Sarac. This is another no-win situation. At least it is October and we will not have the August heat. Did you hear what Cardinal Oddi did last time?"

"No, Your Eminence. I did not."

"He said that with the windows sealed—in conformity to the instructions of Pope Paul, mind you, that he was being suffocated. So, being on the conclave organizing committee, he had workers come in and remove the seals and open his windows. Can you believe that?"

The two men stared at each other for a few moments. There was nothing else to be done on these matters, and both Villot and Sarac had an enormously long list of other items to deal with: the extensive details of the late pope's funeral, the preparation of his burial crypt under the basilica, the countless decisions about television coverage, security details for hundreds of dignitaries, and a protocol-proper seating plan—which was certain to be a huge challenge.

"Well," Villot said after a few moments, "let's get on with it. We both have much to do in the next few days. There will be things to decide that we can't even imagine at the moment. And when we have a new pope, who knows what he will want done?" Villot leaned forward on his desk and cupped his head between his large hands. "You know, Sarac, much of this stress and discomfort is by design. The Holy Father devised election procedures to give the Holy Spirit ample chance to reveal itself to the cardinals of the church, but he also wanted to create sufficient discomfort to encourage a relatively quick decision. And there is a reason for it: nothing would be as difficult for the church as a lengthy conclave, one whose very duration would suggest doubt and dissent at the top of the church. So we walk a fine line between being good hosts and providing as much comfort as possible, but…not too much. Does that make sense to you?"

"Yes, Your Eminence," Sarac replied, "it does. And it will all go well. We will not let you down. The only uncertainty that I cannot address for you is who will be the next Holy Father."

Villot looked up from his desk, turning his gaze to his young aide. "Well, one thing that is a certainty, Monsignor Sarac. After they all arrive, see the rooms and eat a meal, I assure you, it won't be me."

## Moscow

It was already dark in Moscow as Dimitry Zhukov and his immediate superior, Sergei Kornilov, began to climb the stairs toward KGB Chief Andropov's office. Kornilov had been with the KGB his entire professional life, joining right after graduation from the Moscow Power Engineering Institute.

The Soviets were world famous for constructing huge electrical generation plants, mainly dams on the numerous rivers that flowed through their country, and Kornilov had demonstrated a clear skill at devising innovative new approaches for generating hydroelectric power. As he was about to graduate with honors from the institute, he had been summoned to a meeting with a man he had never met who turned out to be the KGB intelligence chief for the Middle East. Kornilov was to join the spy agency and go to Egypt as a senior engineer working on President Abdul Gamal Nasser's prized project, the high dam across the Nile River at Aswan. It wasn't exactly what Kornilov had in mind for a career, and he had not been eager to move to such a hot, inhospitable climate. But, as it turned out, he had enjoyed the Egyptian assignment thoroughly and, over the years, went on to several similar postings in Syria, Iraq, Turkey, and even in China. Now, he had been with the KGB for twenty-five years, had become more spy than engineer, and had been promoted to head the First Chief Directorate, the one that handled foreign intelligence.

Kornilov was far from comfortable with this meeting. He had gone over the material they were to present to Chairman Andropov, but he felt it was highly speculative and advocated a plan of action that was far from executable. Failures were not welcomed in the KGB, and the way to avoid them was to have clear intelligence leading to clear action to achieve a clear outcome. That was Kornilov's trilogy: intelligence, action, outcome. That he had none of the three after a mere day of working on this strange Catholic project bothered him greatly as he and his young analyst passed by the door guards and stepped into Andropov's receiving room and into the always emotionless gaze of General Korilenko, CCO himself.

Dimitry was curious as to whether Korilenko would instruct them to stop as he had with him the night before. After all, within the structure of the KGB Sergei outranked CCO, who was nothing more than a high-ranking doorkeeper. That question was quickly answered. Korilenko silently raised his hand, signaling for them to halt where they were. Sergei did so immediately, and Dimitry followed his boss's example. As the previous evening, Korilenko picked up a phone, turned his back to the two guests, and spoke in a hushed tone. Placing the phone down, he turned and motioned for Sergei and Dimitry to enter Andropov's office. Sergei led the two across the room, pulled down the latch on the door, and stepped inside.

Dimitry was struck by how little had changed in Andropov's office from twenty-four hours earlier, including the chairman's position, standing in front of the large window, his figure again outlined by the lights of Lubyanka Square, his hands behind his back, still deep in thought.

"Come in, gentlemen. Please be seated." Hearing Andropov's low voice, Sergei and Dimitry crossed the room and sat in the two chairs in front of Andropov's desk. As the KGB chief moved to his own chair, his two subordinates pulled identical briefing papers and notes from the folders they had carried in, and placed them on their laps. Andropov again fell heavily into his seat, which creaked under his weight. There were no pleasantries; he got straight to the point. "So, gentlemen, what have we determined about this problem in Rome?"

Kornilov knew that his boss did not like to waste time, so he immediately initiated the discussion. "Comrade Chairman, there are two ways to look at this. The first way suggests we may not have a problem in Rome. Zhukov pointed out last night, as I understand it…" Kornilov paused briefly, having used this phrasing to signal his displeasure at not being part of the discussion the previous evening. "That the church has elected Italians as popes for nearly five hundred years. So, we may need to take no action at all and just watch them as they do what they're likely to do anyway."

Andropov's hand cut across in front of his face, signaling a dismissal of such passive reasoning. "Kornilov, the Soviet Union has existed since 1917. During that period, there have been four popes—five, if we count this fellow who just died in his sleep. What was once a European church that drew much of its following and wealth from Europe, particularly the papal states, is greatly changed. Catholics are now very prevalent in Latin America and even Asia and Africa, areas where we have been trying to expand the influence of local communist movements. People in Western Europe are attending church less; people in these other areas are attending more. And right in our own Eastern Europe backyard—or as I prefer to call it, our own *front door*—the church is a major force of opposition to us. I am, therefore, not content to just assume nature will take its course. Does anybody seriously think that God feels popes must be born eating spaghetti?"

Kornilov had not risen to his current position by being a shrinking violet. And with his own assignments over the past quarter century, he knew a considerable amount about the history and cultures of these regions Andropov had just mentioned. "Comrade Chairman, we are merely pointing out that past practice has been to select Italians, the most obvious contenders are Italian, the largest voting bloc is Italian, and the election occurs in Italy. So, there may be no need to do more than monitor this."

Andropov grimaced and shook his head. "The place they have this silly ritual is irrelevant. And I believe in that old statement 'familiarity breeds contempt.' The fact that the largest voting bloc is Italian and they are mostly my age tells me there is most likely a high level of mutual contempt and dislike for one another, just as I have for many in the Politburo."

Sergei and Dimitry quickly glanced at one another. They were surprised by this most candid comment about the Politburo, and both knew the only safe action was to pretend they had not heard anything and move along. "I understand your point of view, Comrade Chairman," Sergei said, picking up the discussion where he had planned to take it before Andropov had interrupted, "and we do have some thoughts on what we should do. I'll have Dimitry detail them."

Sergei nodded to Dimitry who was ready to move to the action concept. The younger analyst cleared his throat quickly. "Comrade Chairman, for many reasons, there are, we believe, just six of the twenty-five Italian cardinals who can be considered serious *papabili*."

"Papa what?" Andropov sharply inquired.

"*Papabili*. It's the Italian word for a possible pope."

"Ah," Andropov grunted, gesturing for Dimitry to continue.

"The six we see as feasible are Siri and Benelli, whom we discussed last night, and then we see Cardinal Baggio, Cardinal Pignedoli, Cardinal Poletti, and Cardinal Colombo."

"So, Zhukov, given your powers of prediction, how will this play out and who is the most likely?"

"Comrade Chairman, last night, we discussed only Siri and Benelli, and you asked me to come up with a plan to elect one of them. But after further study and analysis, I believe neither can win, nor can we—as you say—influence the proceedings in such a way that one of them will. They are personally opposed to each other, both have clear opposition among the Italian cardinals, and so I think they will largely cancel each other out, forcing the voters to look for a compromise."

"And who would be the likely compromise?"

"I feel that would be Poletti, currently the vicar of Rome."

"Why?"

"Comrade Chairman, he is not known to be aligned closely with either Siri or Benelli. He serves essentially as the local pastor for Rome itself, in the name of the pope, and is well regarded in the city. He is sixty-three years old, so ten years younger than Siri, six years older than Benelli, but three years younger than Luciani. Given the recent death, they will be looking for someone young—but not too young. Living in Rome as he does, Poletti is well known to the curial cardinals, and we understand he has very good relations with them. His focus has been on the church rather than anything international, and he is clearly a man of Rome at this point, so I believe he is the one they'll turn to if Siri and Benelli falter."

Andropov rubbed his chin. "So what do we do to encourage this?"

At this point, Kornilov took over. Dimitry was basically an academic and analyst; Sergei was the engineer and operator. Dimitry, and those like him in foreign intelligence worked the what; Sergei and those like him worked the how. "Comrade Chairman, in Genoa, Florence, and Rome, we'll have many people, loyal to us, going to the various churches and advocating with the priests and other church members for Siri, Benelli, and Poletti respectively. We will then use local media to emphasize the enthusiasm that exists for them and begin to build a sentiment that the choice is actually only among these three. Conversely, we have local agents who will be delivering…shall I say…*messages* to other Italian cardinals, hinting that they either support one of the three we have discussed or else risk some unflattering information being released about them."

"Do we have such unflattering information?" Andropov asked, following all of the details closely.

"We do," Kornilov replied. "Some of it is personal, but the large majority is information we have about their families. Italian Catholics have large families, and large families always have someone involved in something they desperately want kept secret. And, after all, this is Italy. There are so many illegal things going on, and the Italian government is so incapable of stopping them, that *digging up dirt*, as they say in the West, is quite easy."

Dimitry watched this exchange without comment. He knew the KGB operational setup in Rome rather well and knew about many of the specifics that his boss referred to. Sergei was correct. All Italians were protective of their families, and nearly all knew of something hidden in the closet of a distant uncle or cousin that needed to stay there. He had no idea what that might be specifically regarding any of the cardinals, but he was sure there would be something. But he was skeptical nonetheless. The Italian cardinals, as he had just told Andropov, were badly divided, so focusing on them was unlikely to be decisive.

Andropov nodded to Sergei. "And we have the means to create news and deliver messages as needed, Kornilov?"

"We do, Comrade Chairman."

"And what about the non-Italians. How do we deal with them?"

Kornilov quickly shifted gears. "I believe we might have to play more roughly with them. They do not come from families so large and with so much to hide, and many are accustomed to dealing with us, if I can put it that way. They act primarily on principle, and a major principle is opposing the Soviet Union and all that it represents."

"I presume we are talking about Cardinal Koenig of Austria and that bastard Wyszynski in Warsaw?" Andropov growled.

"Certainly them and a couple of others, such as Willebrands in Holland, Suenens in Beligium, and Lorscheider in Brazil."

"Brazil?" Andropov asked, his eyes narrowing slightly.

"Yes," Dimitry inserted, as this was more his area. "Cardinal Lorscheider is a strong advocate of what is being called in some quarters 'liberation theology,' a challenge to the church and the moneyed class in the West to do more for the poor. There are those who have denounced Lorscheider's views as being akin to 'theological Marxism.' I find the assertion ridiculous, as the church has firmly rejected Marxism. However, Lorscheider has followers and passionate advocates who have spoken favorably of his views, such as Cardinal Wojtyla."

"Cardinal who? Who's this last fellow Wojtyla?" Andropov asked, hearing a name Dimitry had thought he would be familiar with.

"Cardinal Wojtyla," Dimitry crisply replied, slowly pronouncing the name. "The archbishop of Kraków. He's the one most observers of the church routinely describe as the 'other Polish cardinal.'"

"I am not familiar with him," Andropov replied. "Is he a possibility?"

Kornilov jumped back in before Dimitry could reply. "We don't think so. He's too young for one thing—fifty-seven or fifty-eight, I believe." Dimitry nodded to his boss, who then continued, "If they were to go with a non-Italian pope, they would certainly go with an older one, giving them a chance to switch back in a few years if it didn't work out. And besides, he always defers to Wyszynski."

"So, am I to take it that Koenig and Wyszynski are the real threats?" Andropov asked, rotating in his chair and looking at the window facing the square.

"Yes, we believe so," Sergei answered. "So we will be watching to see if either gains any traction."

"Watching?" Andropov swung back to face Kornilov. "Do we still have that source we have had in the past? I should have asked that earlier."

"We do," Sergei answered, as Dimitry turned to look at him, his face masking enormous surprise.

"We have a source within the College of Cardinals?" Dimitry thought. He was unaware of this, and Kornilov had never mentioned it in previous discussions.

Kornilov continued, speaking directly to Andropov as if Dimitry was no longer even in the room. "We have that source whom we code-named 'Omega.' And, of course, we have several other operatives within the Italian and Roman governments, the local media, and the Vatican itself. Some are highly placed, some less so but still available. Should we conclude that any of the non-Italians are gathering a following, we'll take direct action against them."

"Meaning you will simply kill them…somehow?" Andropov asked in a matter-of-fact voice, one so cold that it made Dimitry uncomfortable.

"Yes," replied Kornilov, with a nonchalance matching that of his superior. Kornilov was well aware that within the KGB, there was an office that specialized in poisons and other techniques for evoking a "natural" death. He had been a customer in the past and knew he would undoubtedly be one in the future. If the need arose, Koenig and Wyszynski would simply die before being elected to the papal throne. Both were in their seventies, and men in their seventies could die quickly. John Paul had just died quickly, and he was only sixty-six.

Andropov thought for a few moments and then turned back to his two colleagues. "Very well," he said. "I think we are all in agreement on what has to be done. Go work on the details and put the plan in motion. We don't have a lot of time. And if I have to send someone from the Politburo to Wyszynski's funeral, we'll be drawing straws to see who gets the pleasure of attending. Let's try to do this quietly, as you have discussed, with rumor and innuendo, but if we have to use more extreme measures, so be it. But I, of course, will make that call."

Kornilov stiffened slightly in his seat. "You mean, you would make that call together with the other members of the Politburo?" he asked, somewhat nervously seeking an important clarification.

"No, Comrade Kornilov," Andropov replied, as coldly as Sergei had ever heard him. "I mean I personally will make that call. Good evening, gentlemen."

With that, Andropov stood up and slowly strolled back to the window, becoming once more an illuminated silhouette, and Sergei and Dimitry headed toward the door. As they stepped outside, they quietly closed it, nodded slightly to CCO, walked out into the hall, and started down the stairs back to the first floor.

Just before they reached the bottom landing, Dimitry firmly grabbed his boss's elbow. "Comrade Kornilov, do we really have a source among the church's cardinals?"

"Of course we do," Kornilov replied. "We're the KGB. We have sources everywhere."

Dimitry was truly surprised, despite his own position within this most secretive of organizations. But, he recalled the comment Andropov had made the previous evening about the voting in August, so he should have realized that a source was available. Dimitry paused for a moment, trying to decide how to word what he was about to ask next. "Comrade," he whispered to Sergei, "given what I do and have been charged with organizing by the chairman, is it too much to ask who this source is?"

Kornilov smiled. "Yes, it is, as you say, too much to ask. When and if you need to know, well…then I'll let you know. Perhaps." With that, the director of foreign intelligence turned and headed down the hall, leaving Dimitry standing alone, his head filled with more questions than answers.

CHAPTER 5

# Sunday, October 1, 1978
# Washington, DC

● ● ●

CARTER HAD RISEN EARLY. It was a beautiful Sunday morning, and it was quiet in his Capitol Hill neighborhood. He had enjoyed dinner in Georgetown the night before with some West Point classmates, and they had all been irritated about the accuracy of Mr. Lewis's observation when it came to the local coverage of Army football. There was none. For Navy, there was plenty; for Army, there was zero. No one knew who had won the game Saturday afternoon, so Carter had crawled out of bed a bit earlier than normal for a Sunday morning to see if he could catch the score on the *College Football Roundup*. And he had been rewarded, more or less: Army and Washington State had played to a twenty-one to twenty-one tie. As the old saying went, it was "the thrill of kissing your sister." But at least they didn't lose. Carter hated losing.

As he was scrambling some eggs picked up the day before at the Eastern Market, just down the street from his home, the phone rang. "Uh-oh, that's not normal," he thought. "Not unprecedented, but not normal—and probably not good." He walked over to the small phone table and lifted the receiver. "Good morning, Carter Caldwell."

The voice on the other end was the one he expected. "Good morning, Carter. It's Pat. You need to get down to the office as soon as you can."

"Why?" Carter inquired, even as he was reaching across the small kitchen to turn the gas burners off beneath his eggs.

"Dr. Brzczinski wants to see you right away."

"Did he say why?"

"Nope. Margaret just called and said he wanted to see you as soon as you can get here. I'll alert security and get you a pass to park in Jackson Place. Just drive. On Sunday morning, the metro will take too long. I'll see if I can get the subject before you get here."

"Thanks, Pat," Carter said. "See you in about thirty minutes…or less!" He hung up the phone and raced upstairs to get dressed. Pat could be brusque, even rude at times, but the truth was she really covered his ass. And Carter knew it—as did Pat.

He dressed quickly. To be ready for events such as this, he had prepared what he called his "QRF" outfit, an army acronym standing for "quick reaction force," meaning he always had a nicely matched set of clothes hanging in his closet. Although President Carter was comfortable going around the West Wing in jeans, Major Caldwell was not. He preferred to look at least casually professional, as did Brzezinski. Very quickly, he was outfitted in a blue button-down shirt and khaki pants with brown loafers and was headed out the back door to the small garage behind his town house. He jerked up hard on the old garage door to get its creaky roller system to function, but he still had to get beneath it to provide the final push.

That exposed the only thing housed in his garage, his most prized possession, a 1968 dark-blue Corvette, the car he had purchased when he graduated ten years earlier. Corvettes were the preferred car of graduating cadets in the late sixties, and the Chevrolet dealership just down the road from West Point in Fort Montgomery offered a good price, along with several banks that catered to the young academy graduates, each offering incredibly low interest rates. All combined, that made buying a Corvette a no-brainer. Although his was now a decade old, it was as good as the day he had received it in the Michie Stadium parking lot, still shined and shining. To keep it that way, he rarely drove it in DC, using the metro as often as possible and allowing the car to live a quiet life in its cozy garage. But today was a day for it to do its thing, and very shortly, he was driving down the rear alley, taking the sharp right turn onto Pennsylvania Avenue Southeast and heading toward the White House.

Jackson Place was the small street between the White House and the EOB. It was actually more of a parking lot than a "place," but it had tightly controlled access. A permanent parking spot in Jackson Place was a mark of distinction, and it was not a distinction Carter had yet obtained. As he pulled up to the guard shack off Seventeenth Street, he flashed his badge to the uniformed Secret Service agent stationed there, who casually waved Carter through. Pat had, as always, made it happen.

After parking his car in an unassigned spot, he quickly headed to the EOB's midbuilding entrance and briskly bounded up the three flights of stairs before dashing down the hall to his already open office. He was still several feet from it, but he could already smell Pat's coffee. As he entered the door, she was standing there with his cup already filled.

"Take a few minutes, catch your breath, and review your notes from yesterday," Pat instructed. "Dr. Brzezinski is not even here yet. Evidently they had some charity race on the GW Parkway, and it blocked his usual route in from McLean. Margaret will call when he gets here."

"Yesterday's notes?" Carter asked. "So, it's about the topic I raised with him yesterday?"

Pat shrugged. "Either that or he felt your discussion yesterday was so bizarre that he's reserving to himself the pleasure of firing you."

Carter didn't laugh, but Pat did—slightly. "That was a joke, Carter. Go sit down, drink your coffee, and review your notes. My guess is that he has given some more thought to what you discussed yesterday and wants to explore it some more. I've seen this before. That's how he operates."

Carter's brow furrowed a bit. "How do you know what we talked about yesterday?"

"Oh, come on. Give me a little credit. The pope dies. You have an Agency report on it. You spend the day reviewing the history of electing popes—the how and the why. I didn't fall off the turnip truck yesterday, Carter. Nicely organized briefing folder you put together, by the way."

Carter grinned and headed into his office. He pulled the folder from his bottom desk drawer and started to review it, but before he had gotten very far, he heard Pat's phone ring. Shortly afterward, she was standing at his door. "You're on," she said. "Be calm and don't take any crap from him."

Carter quickly gathered his folder, along with some other papers, and headed toward the West Wing. He made the short walk even quicker than he had the day before, with his mind in a whirl the whole way. "What would Brzezinski ask? Had he rethought the discussion from yesterday? Had he spoken with someone about it? If so, whom? Or, was Pat correct: this was his way of telling Carter he was done. Pack your bags, and report to Ft. Polk by COB tomorrow!"

As he hit the top of the stairs, he found Margaret sitting on the corner of her desk. She didn't say a word, just motioned for Carter to go right in. Brzezinski's door was open, and Carter could see him rustling through the stack of reports still piled high in the second chair. The national security advisor was casually dressed; in fact, his shirt seemed to be something that would be in style in Texas, which struck Carter as oddly out of place for a Columbia University professor. Carter knocked on the doorframe. Brzezinski briefly looked up and motioned for him to enter and then pointed again at the empty chair to the left of his desk.

No words had yet been exchanged, so Carter sat down and waited for Brzezinski to finish his search. After a few moments, the old professor found what he was looking for, opened it, and gave it a quick scan as he slipped past Carter to the chair behind his desk. Plopping hard into the seat cushion, he closed the documents and looked directly at his young aide.

"Caldwell, I have been thinking about our discussion yesterday, and I have concluded that you may, indeed, have seen an opportunity that I was about to overlook. Yesterday, my mind was still down at the tactical level, pondering the irritating challenges posed by Israeli settlements on the West Bank and the obstacles they present for substantive discussions about a comprehensive peace addressing both the Palestinian situation as well as the state of belligerency between Egypt and Israel."

Brzezinski continuously amazed Carter. The security advisor always spoke in precise yet complex sentences heavily laden with multisyllabic words, the lingering legacy of many hours giving graduate lectures at a major university. But he had a magical presence, which when combined with his slight European accent, made even ordinary comments about the weather seem interesting.

Brzezinski continued, "Your comments, Caldwell, shifted my thinking back to the strategic level. What we have initiated in the Middle East is a tremendous accomplishment, and President Carter will rightfully receive great credit for it. But after some further reflection, I can see that what you were suggesting could have far greater and longer-lasting implications for the bipolar relationship that has defined global affairs since 1946. And besides, we have another pressing issue that has just arisen."

Carter fidgeted a bit in his chair. "What issue would that be, sir?"

Brzezinski let out an audible sigh and slumped back into his seat. "Well, it seems the Soviets are preparing to invade Poland."

Carter stiffened. "*What*? Why do we think that? I haven't seen anything from the Intel community suggesting a Soviet invasion of anyone. It wasn't in the Poland report we just received."

"No, of course it wasn't. It's too sensitive. This has come from the highest-placed source we have in Moscow—our best mole in the Kremlin. He only contacts us on matters of the greatest urgency, which, of course, means we very rarely hear from him. But he says it's certain. They are beginning to panic about the deteriorating Polish economic condition, the strikes and riots, the growing strength of the Polish labor movement, and the diminishing ability of Gierek to control events. An unreliable Poland will break the Warsaw Pact. If Poland becomes another Czechoslovakia, or worse still, another Hungary, it could be disastrous for them. And Poland has three times the population of Czechoslovakia and four times that of Hungary. Invading it will require many Red Army divisions from the western Soviet Union, and they'll likely have to shift others eastward from Group Soviet Force in East Germany. It will be bloody and brutal, and they know it, which shows how seriously concerned they are."

Carter's military training and education kicked into gear. "An invasion of Poland will require some significant logistical preparation. Have we detected them moving log units forward?"

"Yes, of course. We know they are already positioning the stocks of fuel and ammunition needed to support a large invasion force. As I said, perhaps as many as twenty Red Army divisions, maybe more."

"What about combat units?"

"Many have already been alerted. Others have been told to start planning. A few are already repositioning within the western military district. And we have detected unusual troop movements in East Germany."

"Do we have verification of this? We're not relying on the senior source alone, I assume?"

Brzezinski shook his head. "No, of course not. We have satellite imagery and some very high-level communications intercepts…and you did *not* hear me say that! Bill Odom at NSA would fry me if he knew we were having this discussion."

Brzezinski glanced briefly at a piece of paper on his desk that was bounded in red stripes, indicating it was highly classified, and then took a few seconds to collect his thoughts. "Caldwell, this would be a major setback for us—internationally, diplomatically, domestically, even militarily. And the president doesn't need another major problem at the moment. The SALT negotiations, as you know, are at a delicate spot, and the president badly wants a new agreement. We are about to start working on the details of the Camp David peace agreement with Egypt and Israel. And…and this is my personal view, so don't repeat it to anyone, I expect the Shah of Iran to collapse by the end of the year…early next year at the latest. In the wake of all that, the last thing the president needs is a Soviet invasion of Poland followed by a brutal occupation. Were that to happen, all the initiatives I just mentioned would stagnate, and any chance of slowly peeling away the East European satellites from

Moscow would be lost for another fifty years. Not to mention that the pressure on the president to act would be enormous, especially from the Polish-American community...particularly the one in Chicago. But, of course, there's nothing much he could do, just as Eisenhower was forced to accept there was little he could do in 1956 regarding Hungary, and the same for Johnson in 1968 with Czechoslovakia."

Brzezinski paused for a moment and again looked at the classified report on his desk before returning his gaze to Carter. "So, the question I have been wrestling with, Major Caldwell, is how do we sufficiently raise the stakes for the Soviets so they will conclude that invading Poland will be far too bloody and far too costly? And, I freely admit, I had no ideas. That is until I saw your memo on the pope. It's a long shot, but perhaps an East-European pope, or at least a non-Italian pope, one who is as much interested in international events as church theology, just might cause Moscow to think twice...perhaps even three times, maybe four! Facing very nationalistic Poles would be hard enough, but if you also have to deal with any increased fervor stoked by the Catholic church—and Poland is ninety percent Catholic—now you have a very big problem. So, what I want to do here this morning, for as long as it takes—it is Sunday, as you know..."

"Actually, sir, I hadn't noticed," Carter inserted, believing such a comment might lighten the conversation a bit. It didn't.

"Well, it is Sunday, so let's brainstorm about this—as reluctant as I am to talk about the intricacies of the Catholic church with a badly misguided Presbyterian. But I think there may be a chance here. I'm sure it's one with very low probability, but I think we have to give it a try despite the odds."

"Certainly, Dr. Brzezinski. I'm not sure what I can add, but...well, thank you for sharing your insights on the bigger picture and bringing me into this. I had no idea the stakes were this high. And I'm still processing your prediction about the Shah collapsing...I mean, Jesus! I thought this idea about the next pope was in the 'nice-to-do' category, not something closer to a national imperative. Anyway, sir, here are my initial thoughts and observations." Carter made himself more comfortable in the chair and pulled the notes from his folder. "After reviewing the report from Langley and doing some research, it seems to me that—fortunately—this may be the best time in centuries for the election of a non-Italian pope. And I believe that any non-Italian will be much more likely to delve into broader global issues."

"So I would presume, but why exactly do you think so?" Brzezinski quickly inquired.

"Several reasons, Dr. Brzezinski. First…"

Brzezinski interrupted again. "Caldwell, just call me Zbig…at least for today. OK?"

Carter smirked slightly. This was a good sign. "OK…Zbig. First, the center of gravity of the church has shifted out of Europe to the third world, mainly Latin America and Asia. Yet, nearly half the cardinals come from Europe with the largest single bloc being Italian. Second, despite this, the Italians are very divided along numerous fault lines: the curial verses the pastoral, those who feel the church must embrace modernism versus those who feel it must resist it, theological conservatives verses theological moderates and liberals, those who focus on theology versus those who want to focus on the real demands of daily life, even northern Italians verses southern Italians. So the Italians are a large but highly fractured group. Third, the Latin American cardinals have stepped forward, insisting that their numbers be given greater weight in selecting the church leadership and setting the church agenda."

"How many cardinals are from Latin America?" Brzezinski asked.

"I think seventeen, in any event less than twenty. But consider this: Italy has a population of fifty-five million and twenty-five cardinals; Mexico has a population of nearly seventy million and one cardinal; and Brazil has over twice the population of Italy and a quarter the number of red hats."

"Are any Latin American cardinals serious candidates, Caldwell? I'm not sure one from there would serve our immediate interests."

"I agree, but two might be viable candidates, both of them actually of European heritage. There is Brazilian Cardinal Aloísio Lorscheider, who is from a first-generation German family, and one of the Argentinian cardinals, Eduardo Pironio, whose parents are actually Italian. Conceptually, he would present a way of electing an Italian who is not actually Italian, and he currently serves in the curia as the prefect of religious institutes—or something like that—so he would be well-known to the curia. But, on the other hand, Pironio would carry the baggage of being a curial cardinal, which most of those from outside Rome, whether Italian or not, find unappealing. As for Lorscheider, he is believed to be stridently anticommunist and has taken some vocal and controversial positions on social issues, and—"

Brzezinski was intrigued. "What sort of social issues?"

"Lorscheider has been challenging this misallocation of power within the church—the red hat distribution, let's call it. And he feels that is one of the reasons the church is insufficiently focused on poverty. He has been quite adamant on this, and even some of the European cardinals are taking note. They tend to fight theological battles over issues such as birth control, while the third world cardinals, understandably I suppose, are more interested in poverty, income distribution, and the church's position on things such as political oppression—human rights as we prefer to call them. For the third-world cardinals, Rome's edict about birth control was not something theological but something practical. Cardinal Pironio is the youngest of twenty-two children, so you know he has personal feelings about this. They have seen the impact on their societies and economies of unconstrained population growth."

"So, what are you telling me?" Brzezinski asked. "They might elect one of the Latin Americans? If so, I don't see it."

"No, certainly not," Carter replied. "Lorscheider himself has said the European cardinals, in his words, are far 'too arrogant' to select a Latin American, at least right now. But I think he sees the chance, as apparently many do—including the Italians, for the election of a non-Italian European, something of a first step toward aligning the church's leadership with the reality of its current demographics. So, in my view, that's what we should encourage—the election of a non-Italian European, someone who will be useful to us in using the authority of the church to confront Soviet aspirations. And there are a few European cardinals who have been interested in East-West issues…more interested in those than in doctrinal issues. But when I thought of this, I wasn't considering any invasion."

"OK. Let me extrapolate on your thesis from there," Brzezinski interrupted. "So if we were somehow, to use your word, to *encourage* someone's election, there are obviously two questions to be considered: the who and the how. Let me lay out the who, as that is very much my area of expertise. A non-Italian European would have to be someone from a relatively minor country, as any of the major European powers would make the communists far too uncomfortable. But to be useful, he has to be someone who has spent significant effort and energy focusing on East-West affairs. I only see two European members of the college who fit such criteria…"

"Koenig and Willebrands," Carter inserted, finishing Brzezinski's thought.

"Yes, that's my view, Koenig and Willebrands," Brzezinski replied. "And I think Koenig more than Willebrands. I've met him several times and greatly respect him. I exchanged some thoughts with him when he was working to get Mindsvinty out of Hungary. Mindsvinty was a real hero, a very determined and courageous fellow, but one whom we all felt was a bit too willing to go down with the ship—and it was our ship he was a passenger on! Koenig is calm and persistent; plus, I think he speaks six languages."

"Actually, seven, Zbig. But I agree with you. I think he's the man we should support. The problem is that he's seventy-three years old, a bit long in the tooth."

Brzezinski waved his hand dismissively. "Caldwell, I don't think it matters. As I recall, John XXIII was in his late seventies when they elected him in 1958. I can tell you from personal experience that papal politics, unlike American politics, is a sport for old men. Koenig is in good enough health and quite active. His mind is exceptionally sharp. And he has well-known issues with the curia…has for years. That alone will garner him quite a few votes. As you army fellows like to say 'higher headquarters is your natural enemy.' So, I think he's as good a bet for us as any. But I must tell you, as an American of Polish decent, I like the idea of Cardinal Wyszynski. He would seriously concern the Soviets."

Carter subtly shook his head. "Zbig, I understand your sentiment, but given his history, don't you think the Soviets would see that as a major threat? His election might very well spur the invasion we're trying to avoid. And he's seventy-seven, no young buck by any means."

Brzezinski again gestured disagreement. "East Europeans are a hearty stock, Caldwell. They live a long time and are active well into their twilight years. So, I still feel the age issue isn't disqualifying. How about Cardinal Tomášek from Czechoslovakia? Is he feasible? Taken a look at him?"

"No, not in detail. But I believe he's even older than Wyszynski."

The security advisor nodded in agreement. "Probably true. But he's very much like him, only not as well known, mainly because the Czech community in the United States is much smaller and less active than the Polish community. Tomášek resisted the Soviets and was thrown in jail for several years…he even supported Dubcek in 1968 as the Red Army was marching into Prague. He's a courageous man. And for reasons that still befuddle me, the Czech government allowed him to attend the Vatican Councils in the early sixties, so I would imagine he used the time to become acquainted with the curia and many of the Italian cardinals. I presume he developed positions on the theological issues while in Rome, so he should be conversant enough about them to satisfy the doctrinal purists. Unless I am mistaken, he earned a doctorate in theology from somewhere."

Carter had briefly evaluated Cardinal Tomášek, and all that Brzezinski had said about him was correct. But Carter still felt he was too old, a factor that, despite his boss's opposing view, he believed was certain to be a large demerit after John Paul's sudden death. "Sir, I think you are being too cavalier about age. They'll want someone younger. Koenig may even be too old now. But, I believe he's the best alternative, and the Langley report says he's quite respected by the other cardinals. We think he had more than a few supporters in the last conclave."

Brzezinski smiled. "Scowcroft was right about you, Caldwell. You are thorough and perceptive. And I think you're correct. OK, I agree. We'll focus on Koenig. So, what are your thoughts on the how? How do we actually make this happen? How do we *encourage* people who are seemingly immune to encouragement?"

Carter held up his hands, signaling they were now in a murky area of considerable uncertainty. "Sir, this is where I had hoped you could help. Frankly, I'm not sure. And the Langley report is pretty good at arguing what outcome we should want, but it's totally silent on how we might achieve it."

"I know. I've spoken with Stansfield about it," Brzezinski replied, referring to Admiral Stansfield Turner, director of the CIA. The comment confirmed to Carter that the national security advisor had, in fact, further explored the issue after their meeting the day before. "I'd like to tell you we have a well-placed mole at some senior level in the Vatican. But, surprisingly enough…we don't. We have a couple of what I would call solid peripheral sources in the Vatican and around Rome, but nothing in the upper strata. Can you believe that? We have better sources in the Kremlin than the Vatican!"

Carter shook his head. "Well, Zbig, I had hoped you would tell me that Langley had Villot on the payroll," he replied with a mischievous grin.

"Villot!" Brzezinski exclaimed. "That pompous ass! And he's just that…an ass. And still worse…a French ass!"

"Many seem to share that view, sir. So, did Admiral Turner have any ideas?" Carter asked.

"Yes, Turner does have some ideas," Brzezinski quickly replied. "He's assigning a young agent to us to help with this. So our first step is to find a mole that we can use as our, shall we say, *campaign manager*, for one of those we want to be wearing the white robes after the white smoke!"

Carter should have been amused by the security advisor's clever "white smoke" reference, but he was too surprised by what he had just heard. "Dr. Brzezinski, did you say the Agency is assigning someone to *us*?"

"That's what I said, Caldwell."

"But shouldn't we be assigning someone to them? Maybe not exactly *to* them but to coordinate *with* them? This is Agency stuff. They do operations. We just do coordination and oversight."

"You have a solid grasp of the NSC's conceptual organizational and technical role, Caldwell," Brzezinski said, chuckling as he clapped his hands in front of his face. "There are many around here who don't. But the problem we face is that the Agency doesn't wish to get involved in this operationally and at the moment simply don't have the manpower to do so anyway. Stan has reduced their manning rather substantially to meet budget levels, and with what he has left, he doesn't want to commit operatives to nosing around the College of Cardinals. Plus, if somehow it were to come out that the CIA had tried to influence a papal election, the howl of outrage would be deafening. So, what does one do when you wish to undertake something that is potentially important, probably infeasible, possibly imprudent, and politically toxic?"

Carter leaned back in his chair and scowled at his superior. "I guess what you are about to tell me is that you put someone in charge who provides deniability if things go badly and is basically expendable if someone's head has to be served up on a public platter."

"I think you're painting a rather harsh metaphorical picture there, Caldwell. But I believe you have, nonetheless, summarized it accurately. If this succeeds, you will be an unacknowledged hero. If it goes badly, none of us ever had any idea what you and this CIA person were up to. We thought you were just taking a vacation to Italy after a stressful year."

Carter thought about this unappealing offer for a few moments. "Zbig, what if I just say no? This is not what I do, not what I'm trained to do, am positioned to do, and—most importantly—want to do. Maybe I don't want to be expendable while still a young army major. If I was an army general, maybe, but an army major? I don't think so."

Brzezinski smiled broadly and then leaned forward, placing his elbows in the center of his desk. "Well, Caldwell, you and I both know that such sentiments are not in your makeup. This is your idea…perhaps developed with incomplete information, but it's still yours. You're the one who saw the possibility, took the risk of sharing the whole nutty notion with the president's national security advisor, took the bullet between the eyes yesterday—no, you wouldn't pass the ball to someone else. Guys like you don't think that way, now do they?"

Carter didn't reply to Brzezinski's comments, knowing they were essentially accurate. But after a brief pause, he asked, more exhaling than speaking the words, "So, do you have a number I can use to contact this Agency operative?"

"They'll contact you."

"When? Where?"

"Two quick answers: very shortly and I don't know."

Carter nodded his head. "What should I do now?"

"Well," Brzezinski replied, spinning in his chair, leaning back, and briefly looking up to the ceiling, "it seems to me that what we need is to very quickly develop a senior source, someone who'll be on the inside of this. So, that implies to me that you need to start making the rounds and having discussions with a few carefully selected American cardinals. They'll be on the inside, and certainly there must be one among them who believes the times necessitate that he be simultaneously secular and spiritual, an American as well as a Catholic. Since time is of the essence, I suggest you make an appointment immediately with Cardinal Baum down the street here at St. Matthew's."

"How?" Carter asked. "I wouldn't imagine that one just calls up the local cardinal, gets him on the phone, explains he is a Presbyterian with some casual interest in Catholicism, and asks to stop by for a general discussion about religion over a cup of coffee!"

Brzezinski spun back in his chair and looked directly at Carter, his face wrinkled into a mischievous smirk. "I hereby appoint you a senior American government official reporting to the 'highest levels.' It's an easy appointment because that is, after all, what you are, more or less. Don't add it to your résumé. But I find that this phrase is equivalent to a master key; it can unlock almost any door. Use it often…but not too often. If you get resistance, have them call Margaret, who will verify you work in the White House. She's good at this sort of stuff—ex-CIA herself you know. How many American cardinals did you say there are?"

"Nine," Carter answered, trying to sound as if this assignment was a major inconvenience, while increasingly thrilled that it could create the most exciting October of his life.

"Baum is not a very engaging person. I would say the likelihood he would help is small, but he should at least give you a feel for whatever prospects there might be elsewhere…maybe not. But we have to start somewhere. In any event, I would suggest you focus the effort on the East Coast, as you won't have time to fly to LA or Chicago. Besides, my judgment is you'd be wasting time doing so. Cardinal Cody in Chicago is a most unappealing fellow. Manning in LA is a very good man but probably not a possibility. And back here, Cardinal Cooke in New York is too visible and too well known. I'm sure the media is already camped out on the steps of St. Patrick's Cathedral, seeking insights on who the next Pontiff will be. He'll either be locking himself in his office shortly or fleeing town on the first available flight to Rome. Medeiros in Boston might have potential, but he's a bit introverted."

"How about Philadelphia?" Carter asked, starting to accept this new challenge being offered.

"Philadelphia? They have an archbishop?" Brzezinski rubbed his hand across his chin. "I had forgotten that. Philadelphia has always been just another stop on Amtrak between New York and DC for me. I don't even know who their cardinal is. Do you?"

"I believe his name is Krol," Carter answered. "To be honest, Dr. Brzezinski, I didn't spend much effort researching the American cardinals, so I don't know much about them other than what you occasionally hear from the media. I'll verify it, but I think Krol's the one in Philly."

"I've heard of him, now that you mention the name," Brzezinski added. "Seems odd to me that I wouldn't be more familiar with him. Perhaps, for some reason, he keeps a low profile, but as I said, I've not spent much time in Philadelphia other than occasional lectures at Penn and the Wharton School—both excellent schools, by the way—worthy competitors for Columbia."

"And Harvard?" Carter asked, knowing full well why Brzezinski had omitted it.

"Harvard did not offer me tenure, which shows a significant absence of both judgment and strategic thought," Brzezinski countered, with a sly smile. "But you know, Caldwell, sometimes things just work out. Had Harvard done so, I would have never moved to Columbia and New York; in all probability, I would never have made the connections that I did and would likely not be sitting here today having this fascinating conversation. I always keep that in mind, which is why I think that, although the odds are rather long, this endeavor might work out. And we need it to work out, as we have a lot at stake. This could be a stunningly low-cost way of avoiding a major international crisis. So…give me about an hour and then call Cardinal Baum's office. Let's get moving on this. I'm worried about what's certain to happen if we don't at least give this a shot."

Carter nodded. "Very well, sir. I'll try to get up to St. Matthew's and see him this afternoon after Sunday services." With that, Carter rose from his chair and stepped toward the door of the small office. But before he could step outside, Brzezinski's voice stopped him.

"Carter, one last thing, if I may."

Carter immediately froze in place, surprised that for the first time the security advisor had called him by his first name. "I know I was a bit harsh with you yesterday, rather gruff and dismissive to some degree. I hope you didn't take it personally. Sometimes I just get that way. Some feel I am testing them, and perhaps subconsciously I am. It is just part of my personality. My father was much the same. But I want to assure you that I am pleased you are with us, though I realize that sometimes it can be tough playing on my team."

"Thank you, Zbig," Carter replied through a thin smile. "I'm glad—and quite honored—to be here. Believe me; I can take whatever you dish out. Playing on Bobby Knight's team is tough. In comparison, yours is a piece of cake."

With that, Carter headed down the stairs and back to his office. As his footsteps grew fainter, Brzezinski picked up the phone and buzzed his secretary. "Margaret, call research first thing in the morning. See what they know about some fellow named Bobby Knight."

## ROME, ITALY

Gianluca Giordano was working in a large storage area beneath the Vatican Museum, the magnificent building with an even more magnificent art collection that stood adjacent to the northwest edge of the Apostolic Palace. Within the cramped confines of Vatican City, the lower levels of the museum provided, as might be expected, the only ample storage space. It was filled with a treasure trove of priceless historic art pieces silently awaiting their return to the museum floor. Once back on display, they would be bathed in the sunlight of the large skylights and endlessly photographed by the thousands of tourists and Catholic pilgrims who passed through the museum each year. But managing and admiring art was not Gianluca's function within the city-state. He was the deputy facilities manager, assigned the responsibility of fixing windows, patching leaky pipes, and at the upper end of the spectrum, adjusting the heat and air conditioning in the papal apartments.

Those were the routine items he dealt with under the supervision of his immediate superior, Bruno Brachi, but his immediate task was far from routine. He was in the museum storage spaces with several carpenters inventorying the wooden walls left from the August conclave, the walls that would be needed to make—for the second time in six weeks—the temporary rooms for the cardinals. No one had bothered to label the various walls or store them in any particular order, so reassembling the eighty or so "cells" would be like reassembling a giant jigsaw puzzle.

"God help me," Gianluca muttered to himself, as, along with his colleagues, he tried to make sense of what seemed, in the dim light, to be an endless row of wooden sheets. "How in the world are we to do this again in just a few days and make all of these little rooms the same, as the camerlengo has directed?" he thought, throwing his head back and his hands up. The carpenters with him grinned at one another, but just slightly. His problem was their problem, and they knew it. This was going to be an onerous undertaking, carrying all of these wooden sheets out of the basement up often narrow stairways, laying them out on the museum floor near the Sistine Chapel, figuring out what attached to what, and then nailing the rooms back together.

"Gianluca," one of the carpenters said to his boss, the expression on his face a strange combination of humor and horror, "perhaps we should just throw it all away and start over with fresh lumber. It would probably be easier than trying to figure out what fit with what."

"No way," Gianluca brusquely replied, his hands again gesturing expressively, as Italians did during any normal conversation. "Cardinal Villot has directed us to use the wood we had from August. He is already upset about the costs of another conclave, and he's given us no more money to purchase lumber—or even nails. He's watching us like the nervous French uncle he is."

The men laughed briefly—very briefly. It was gallows humor and, given their location in the lower levels of the Vatican, close to accurate.

"Gianluca!"

The carpenters turned and looked through the low archways that were the foundational support of the museum above them. Through the dim light, they could make out the outline of Bruno Brachi, walking briskly in their direction. "What are you doing? You've been down here for hours! Start moving the walls up to the main level! The museum is closed! What are you waiting for? Get moving!"

Gianluca and the carpenters looked at each other and rolled their eyes. Everyone in the facilities office that he oversaw despised Brachi. He was overbearing, always in a sour mood, and a walking inventory of impractical suggestions, which he rapidly translated into undoable orders and undecipherable instructions. It was a constant topic over the sandwiches in the small facilities lunchroom: who had hired this worthless asshole, and why had no one fired him?

The relationship between Bruno and Gianluca had never been good, and with all the pressures of the past few weeks, it had degenerated further, moving from bad to very bad. The two had nothing in common other than being middle-class Italian men. Whereas Gianluca was tall, slim, and still relatively good-looking for being in his early forties, Bruno was short, round, overweight, balding, and invariably irritating. Many in the facilities office felt that Bruno was simply jealous of Gianluca, saw him as a threat, and therefore was constantly looking for some excuse to have him fired. It seemed odd to the staff that Gianluca took such constant abuse. But he did and with what seemed to be good humor. There was continual discussion among the staff as to why the Vatican higher-ups kept Bruno on the payroll and why Gianluca did not merely move to a position handling the repairs of one of the major luxury hotels in the city. Everyone felt he would be good at that.

Gianluca turned to face Brachi as he approached. "Bruno, we're trying to sort out the pieces to see what fits with what before moving them upstairs and laying them out on the museum floor. We should have marked these in some way or stored them with some sense of order."

"Are you criticizing me again?" Brachi roared. "Are you saying I should have known that the Holy Father would die in his bed, so we should have been prepared to do another room construction? We hadn't done one for fifteen years, so who would have thought we'd need to do another so soon!"

"I wasn't criticizing anyone," Gianluca replied. "Of course you couldn't have foreseen the Holy Father's death. Nor could I. I supervised the disassembly of the rooms. All I am saying is that it would not be such a problem now had we not rushed to clear the museum floor so soon after the conclave ended."

Brachi was unmoved. He hated Giordano, and did not trust him. There was no concrete reason for his feelings—he just didn't like his deputy. He had not hired him. He had wanted to hire a cousin from Naples, someone he knew and trusted. That would make his job easier. But there was nothing he could do about it right now. He had to get the cardinals' living spaces reassembled quickly and do it in a way that cost the Vatican treasury as little as possible. And if during the process he could get Giordano to resign, so much the better. If something went badly wrong, and Cardinal Villot became angry, he'd blame it on Gianluca.

"Bruno," Gianluca calmly replied, "I'll take care of it. Now, would you just let us get on with this job? I may need more men brought in early to assist with moving the lumber as well as reconstructing the rooms. Eighty or more rooms cannot be put together quickly by a handful of men. Certainly you realize that."

"Just do your job, and don't tell me how to do mine!" Brachi shouted. With that, he turned quickly and disappeared into a connecting tunnel, one of the many comprising the Vatican's enormous underground labyrinth.

Gianluca waited until Brachi was out of sight, trying mentally to predict which of the various facilities personnel he would be terrorizing next. He grinned and slightly shook his head. He was used to such confrontations. And he had been trained to deal with such things while remaining cool and calm. "OK. So much for that," he said to the men sorting through the wooden walls with him. "I think we need to just carry the wood upstairs and lay it out on the museum floor. We don't have enough light or floor space here, and we'll have to carry it upstairs anyway, so let's just get started. I'll get help down here for you…from somewhere."

"Just don't send Brachi," one of the men replied with a chuckle.

"I said I'd get you some *help*." Gianluca grinned. "Obviously that would disqualify Mr. Brachi."

The men laughed and then began lifting the awkward wooden walls. Gianluca turned and headed down the tunnel toward the small, curved staircase leading up to the main level of the museum. As he reached the first stair step, he saw a tarp covering something in a space beneath the steps. "I've never noticed this before," he thought as he reached around the railing and lifted the discolored old tarp to take a quick peek beneath it. "Well, I'll be," he whispered softly to himself, staring at his discovery. "I had no idea we stored it here." Gianluca stared for a few more moments, his mind slowly formulating and evaluating an idea. Still in thought, he tossed the free end of the tarp back in place and headed up the stairs. He still had to find some more carpenters.

## Moscow

The phone was ringing on Dimitry's desk. Unlike those much higher in the KGB, his desk only had two phones. The more phones, the less desk space, but the more rank and prestige, the more phones. All things considered, it was an odd symbol of status. "Zhukov," he crisply said, jerking the phone from its cradle.

As he had known, given the line that was ringing, the voice on the other end was that of his boss. "Zhukov, come to my office immediately!" Sergei Kornilov barked. "Quickly!"

"Certainly, Comrade Kornilov," Dimitry replied calmly. He hung up the phone, thought to himself for a moment, grabbed a notepad from his desk, and headed toward the door. As he walked through the small space occupied by Elena, the two of them exchanged nervous glances but no words. Dimitry worried about Elena constantly. She seemed far too apprehensive and fearful to work at Lubyanka. He felt her blood pressure must be a hundred points above normal, both systolic and diastolic. He stepped into the hall and quickly made the rather short walk to Kornilov's office. As he stepped inside, Kornilov was waiting.

"Come in." The greeting was short and blunt, as Kornilov pointed for Dimitry to follow him through the door. The older KGB veteran went straight to the chair behind his desk, while Dimitry gingerly seated himself in one of the chairs facing him. Kornilov fetched a pack of cigarettes from his center drawer, pulled one from the wrapping, and lit it. After taking a long drag, he leaned back in his chair and exhaled a mouthful of the smelly tobacco, a product the Soviets had never mastered. "Care for one?" he asked Dimitry, holding the pack out to him.

"No, thank you," Dimitry replied. "I don't smoke."

Kornilov glared at him for a moment, looking as if he were calculating some biting reply, but he said nothing, electing instead to get to the point of the meeting. "Zhukov, we are sending you to Rome."

"Rome?" Dimitry replied with obvious surprise. "When?"

"Immediately. Tonight if we can get the proper papers put together."

"Why?" Dimitry was baffled at this decision. "What do you want me to do in Rome?"

"Comrade Andropov wants you to take charge of this issue regarding the pope."

Dimitry leaned forward in his chair. "You mean take charge of the effort we discussed to elect an Italian?"

"Unless you are aware of some other effort regarding the pope, yes… that would be the one."

Dimitry fidgeted in his chair. "But, Comrade Kornilov, that is work for operatives…experienced field operatives. I'm an analyst. I evaluate things for operatives to do; I don't do them myself. I did some work with the Rome operations office when I was there studying, and it was useful to get some familiarity with what they do, but I had the clear sense they were just tolerating me. Most of it was liaison work with the Italian Communist Party. I don't see—"

"Enough!" Kornilov snapped, cutting off Dimitry's protest. "The decision has been made. Andropov made it himself. You're going to Rome, and you're going right away. So, go home and get what personal items you will need and be prepared to leave tonight. A car will come get you at your apartment."

Dimitry half nodded. "But why?"

"Because Andropov does not trust our Rome operatives. He believes they have been there too long and have gone native. They are more Italian than Russian, more coffeehouse patrons than intelligence operatives. They have gone soft, grown lazy. They don't remember how to do tough things, make the hard calls, take strong action if it must be taken."

"And he feels I do?" Dimitry countered.

"You, young man, are a Zhukov. Making hard decisions and taking tough actions are in your biology. Your grandfather destroyed whole cities during his relentless march into Germany in 1945. He was tough. He was hard. He did what had to be done. These clowns in the Rome office no longer possess such qualities, if they ever did."

"Well then, why not just replace them with other operatives?"

"Come on, Zhukov, you know better than that. Operatives need to be in position. They need to understand the ways of the places where they operate. They need to have contacts and confidants. You don't develop that in a couple of days. That takes years. We will have to take advantage of the positions they occupy, but we also have to give them firm direction. This thing could get messy. People may have to be eliminated. Neither Andropov nor I feel they are up to the challenge. So, you will go to Rome and take charge. Kick some ass if you have to. Messages have already been sent to them with these instructions."

"And I am sure they are thrilled at the prospect of a young analyst from Moscow flying in to Rome on short notice and taking over their operations."

"Well, I'm sure they're quite pissed. I'm also sure they lack the balls to say so. And I'm equally sure you'll find a way to make them happy to have your—shall we say—*assistance*."

Dimitry squirmed a bit in his chair. "But I don't…"

Again Kornilov cut him off, this time with such a strong gesture that ashes from his cigarette flew across his desk. "Enough, Zhukov! You are going. Go home and get your things. You are wasting time we don't have. When you get there, send me an assessment. If you need anything further, tell me what it is. Our people in Washington are checking their sources to see if the Americans are up to anything regarding this.

Personally, I think they are too distracted on other matters, but I'll let you know what they report. If they are doing something to engineer an outcome favorable to them, of course, they must be stopped."

"So we don't know if they are?" Dimitry asked.

"There are no indications that they are…yet. And the Carter administration has been totally focused on Israel and Egypt…God, we should have taken out that imbecile Sadat when we had the chance. I don't know what they think they might do, but it would be foolish to think they won't do something. Brzezinski hates us; we know that. And being Polish himself, he blames us for many things—the Soviet Union in general and the KGB in specific—things such as the Katyn Forest episode. So, we have to be alert. Now go!"

Dimitry rose from the chair and headed toward the door. As he was leaving, Kornilov called to him. "Zhukov, this is a great chance for you. Comrade Andropov has been impressed with you. Don't fuck this up."

Dimitry nodded his head and stepped outside, closing the door behind him. Within five minutes, he had grabbed what he felt he would need from his office, told Elena he would be gone for a few days, and was running toward his apartment through the dimly lit streets around Lubyanka Square.

CHAPTER 6

# Monday, October 2, 1978
# Washington, DC

• • •

IT WAS A BRIGHT, SUNNY day in Washington. The temperatures were in the mid-seventies, the annual summer agony of oppressive heat and humidity was long past, so Carter had decided to walk the eight blocks from the White House to St. Matthew's Cathedral. The stroll down Connecticut Avenue would be pleasant enough and give him time to think about how exactly he would handle his meeting with Cardinal William Wakefield Baum, the archbishop of the Archdiocese of Washington.

Clearly, Dr. Brzezinski had followed through with the discussion from the previous morning, for when Carter had arrived at his office, Pat had placed a note on his desk saying simply, "Meeting with Cardinal Baum, St. Matthew's, 10:00 a.m." Carter had done some research on Baum Sunday afternoon and had learned the basic information on the man, but he was unable to get anything detailed and therefore had little idea what to expect. He didn't know if he would be welcomed by the cardinal or shown the quickest way to the front door after he explained the purpose of his visit.

Baum was fifty-two years old and had only been a prince of the church for two years. He was born in Texas but had spent most of his adult life in Missouri where he had served for five years as the archbishop of Springfield-Cape Girardeau. During that period, he had been an American delegate to the World Synod of Bishops and served on several committees taking advantage of the doctorate in theology he had earned during studies in Rome. With this background, Baum was familiar to the cardinals of the curia, well known to his fellow American cardinals, and recognized by others from the third world. But the August conclave had been his first, and how he had perceived it and the role he had played in it were anybody's guess. So when it came to approaching this meeting, Carter was basically flying blind.

St. Matthew's presented a rather austere brick facade, combining Romanesque and Byzantine architectural qualities with no particular enhancement to either. As he turned the corner onto Rhode Island Avenue and approached it, Carter was reminded of that singular moment in its history that had made St. Matthew's famous: the sight of a two-year-old John F. Kennedy Jr. standing on the top step outside the main entrance door, saluting his father's coffin following the funeral Mass held inside. It was an image burned forever into the American consciousness, and whenever Carter passed the old church, it appeared in his mind, as it did now. But rather than the president's young son standing on the top step in front of the cathedral, today there was a young priest, who spotted Carter coming down the sidewalk and headed in his direction with his arm extended.

"Mr. Caldwell, I am Father James Hanlon, Cardinal Baum's personal secretary. Welcome to St. Matthew's. If you'll follow me, I'll escort you to Cardinal Baum."

"Thank you, Father. Nice to meet you," Carter replied, shaking the young priest's hand.

Hanlon turned and headed to a town house two doors to the right of the cathedral that served as the rectory. Upon reaching it, the two walked up the steps. As they approached the door, it opened as if commanded by some mysterious force, but that force was actually Cardinal Baum, who stood smiling in the doorway.

"Dr. Caldwell, I presume," the Washington Archbishop said, welcoming Carter and shaking his hand. "Please come in."

After exchanging brief pleasantries, Baum led Carter to an austere sitting room and motioned for him to take a seat next to a small table holding a porcelain teapot and two cups. Without asking if Carter cared for anything, the cardinal poured a cup of tea for each of them, handed Carter his, arranged himself into a comfortable position in his chair, took a sip, and then turned his eyes to his government guest. "So, Dr. Caldwell, how may I help you?"

Carter smiled at Baum. "Your Eminence, actually it's Mr. Caldwell. I don't have a doctorate. And technically, I guess, it's Major Caldwell. I'm an active-duty army officer on assignment to the National Security Council."

"Really," Baum replied, taking another sip of his tea. "Very well, how about if I just use Mr. Caldwell in that case?"

"That would be fine, sir…I mean, Your Eminence."

Baum smiled. "You're not Catholic, are you, Mr. Caldwell?"

"No, I'm Presbyterian, Cardinal Baum," Carter replied, firmly but respectfully.

"Isn't your first name 'Carter'?" Baum asked.

"Yes, it is, Your Eminence."

"Very well," Baum replied. "Let's keep it simple between the two of us here. I'll call you 'Carter,' and you call me 'William.' Would that be more comfortable for you?"

"Yes…it would," Carter answered, relieved at the offer of informality and suddenly hopeful that this session might go more easily than he had expected. He took a breath and then got down to business. "William, as a member of the College of Cardinals, and a cardinal elector, I presume you will be departing for Rome shortly to participate in the conclave to elect a new pontiff."

Baum took another sip of his tea and nodded his head. "Yes, I will, Mr. Caldwell." He sighed. "I'll leave tomorrow, as the Holy Father's funeral Mass will be on Thursday and I plan to be in attendance. Then there will be nine days of official mourning before we gather in the Sistine Chapel, on October 14, I believe, to begin the process of electing the new pontiff."

Baum paused for a moment and looked away before returning to the topic at hand. "This has been such a great disappointment, such a terrible tragedy. Pope John Paul was a wonderful man, a great teacher, a great example, a man of great humility, and blessed with an electric smile. People were drawn to him…I know I was. I had only met him once prior to the August conclave, and I must admit I did not view him as a *papabili*. Are you familiar with that term?"

"Yes, I am," Carter answered. "Possible pope…in Italian."

"Well, I see for a Presbyterian, you know more than one might expect about the Catholic church." Baum grinned while settling back a bit deeper into his chair, an expression of introspection slowly returning to his face. "As I said, I did not know him well, but it was clear, as we got to know him during our sessions in August, that he was a most special man."

Baum paused once again and fell quiet for a few moments.

Carter thought this might be the opening he had hoped would arise. "Your Eminence, do you see another among you having his same qualities?"

Baum squinted his eyes and wrinkled his nose. "Well, of course there will be someone from among us. That is how the Holy Spirit moves us to make the choice. During the course of our time together, he will come into our hearts and reveal to us the one best prepared to be the next heir to Saint Peter."

It was slowly dawning on Carter that this discussion with Baum might be challenging. Baum was a relatively young cardinal, and unlike Siri, he had not attended many such gatherings and evidently still viewed them as more a spiritual than political event. But Carter was with Baum for a purpose, so he decided he had to press ahead. "Your Eminence, what is—in your view—the possibility that the next Holy Father might not be Italian?"

Baum's eyes quickly shifted upward to Carter, his gaze narrowing and focusing on his young guest. "It is possible that he might not be an Italian," he slowly answered. "But that is not for me to say. The Holy Spirit guides us to such decisions."

Carter pressed ahead, deciding it was time for a full-frontal assault, a roll of the dice. "Your Eminence…William, there are many great issues that one must face in the world, that in my life I have to address every day. Many of them are theological and spiritual, but many others are practical, political, and immediate—issues less concerned with the conditions of the next life, than those of this life. And among the most pressing is the balance of power between the two superpowers, a balance that President Kennedy once referred to as the 'balance of terror.' For over five hundred years, there have been Italian popes, chosen because the immediate issues confronting the church in Rome very much involved its relationships with the Italian states and the other European powers. But those times are long gone and those conditions very much changed. Wouldn't the world be a better place if the Holy Father was someone who had a global view, who saw the great issue of our time as the confrontation with communism, who was willing to use the enormous influence and prestige of the church to help in advancing Christian and therefore Western ideas?"

Baum stared straight ahead, seemingly focused past his guest and on the wall across the room, and Carter could see great discomfort in his eyes. A long silence came between them, Baum trying to process what Carter had just said and Carter trying to predict what the cardinal would say when he replied. Baum looked left, then right, then back to Carter. "What are you trying to tell me, young man? Or are you trying to ask something of me? Are you trying to suggest that the conclave should select a new pope who, in some way, is the preferred choice of the American government as opposed to the preferred choice of the Holy Spirit? No secular government has ever determined who would be pope."

Carter took a deep breath. "William, you certainly know that isn't quite correct. As late as 1903, the Austro-Hungarian Empire sent a message to the conclave opposing the election of Cardinal Rampolla, who was by many reports, close to being elected. So, the conclave turned to Cardinal Sarto of Venice, who was elected Pius X…and who, as you know, is now a saint. So, such considerations have, at times, managed to find their way inside the Sistine Chapel."

"I am not familiar with this particular story," Baum countered. "Maybe it happened; maybe it didn't. Maybe the Holy Spirit chose to express itself in such a manner. Who can say? But even if your tale had any substance, that was seventy-five years ago. It could never happen today. And besides, your example is one of opposing a potential pope, not proposing one."

Carter retreated slightly, shifting back to a more formal footing. "Your Eminence, I am merely asking your view as to whether there might be great merit if the next pontiff came from somewhere other than Italy. Italian cardinals are over 20 percent of the college, yet Italians comprise less than 3 percent of the church. I am merely suggesting that the time might have come to place greater weight on the presence of the other 97 percent, and perhaps the time has come to place more emphasis on looming issues that pose serious threats to mankind."

"I see," the Washington archbishop replied. "You have decided there is someone among the cardinals that the American government wants selected as pope, and you are here to ask me to help in some way. Is that it?"

"Your Eminence, I am merely suggesting that in the various *prattiche* you will be a party to—"

"The *prattiche*? For a Presbyterian, you *are* exceptionally well versed in the history and the ways—and even the words—of the Catholic church." Baum paused for another sip of his tea. "So what you want is that you give me a name, or perhaps a couple of names, and in the preconclave *prattiche* with other cardinals, I become something of an advocate for someone—something of a campaign manager. Is that it?"

Carter decided to be frank. "Your Eminence, yes. I guess I must say…yes, something like that. You are the archbishop of Washington, the capital of the free world. You have clout and visibility and, I would presume, influence. There are cardinals we feel should be supported, and we feel you would be useful in advocating them."

"Who are they?" Baum asked, his face expressionless, his tone suddenly icy.

"They are…" Carter began, but before he could utter a name, Baum raised his hand, cutting him short.

"No. Just stop right there. This is not appropriate. This is not how we select the Holy Father. No…this is wrong. And if I were the archbishop of Moscow, I would be saying the same. I won't be involved in any such thing. I won't." With that, Baum placed his teacup back on its saucer and stood up. "It has been a pleasure meeting you, Mr. Caldwell, and may God bless you, my son. Father Hanlon will show you out."

Carter stood and extended his hand to Baum, who shook it firmly, a smile on his face, suggesting there were no hard feelings. But Carter could tell there were. Without saying anything further, he stepped into the small hallway of the rectory where Hanlon was waiting. The priest motioned for Carter to follow him, but rather than exit as they had entered, they passed through another door, down a passage, and emerged near the altar of the cathedral.

"Thank you for coming to see us," Hanlon said, pointing to the open doors at the main entrance of the nearly empty church.

Carter took the hint.

"Thank you for seeing me," he softly said as he turned and started walking down the cathedral's main aisle leading to the front door. About halfway to the massive doors, he stopped and looked back toward the altar area. Hanlon was gone.

Carter was pondering what his next step might be when he heard a soft voice coming from a pew to his left. "He blew you off, didn't he?"

Carter looked over to the source of the comment. Sitting along the aisle in one of the wooden pews was an incredibly beautiful young woman, wearing a well-tailored business ensemble, complete with a pleated skirt and a form-fitted top cut to allow just the right amount of a lace collar to peek out from her white blouse. She looked like she might have just finished a photo shoot for the cover of *Cosmopolitan*. Her shoulder-length blond hair framed a perfectly formed face, and her hazel eyes seemed to be on loan from Elizabeth Taylor.

Carter stared for a moment before realizing that he was acting like a stunned mullet. He shook his head slightly and did all he could to reenergize his vocal cords. "Excuse me. Who are you?" he asked, struggling to string together a coherent sentence.

The young woman did not answer. She slid a couple of feet further into the pew and pointed for Carter to take the seat she had warmed for him. He paused for a moment, glanced around, and then cautiously slipped into the pew beside her.

"Have we met?" he asked, still working on short sentences.

"Not really, Carter," the cute blonde replied. "Perhaps figuratively, but not personally—at least so far as I can recall."

Carter was thoroughly intrigued by this evasiveness. "OK, you seem to know who I am, and you have my first name memorized. Now would you mind telling me yours…along with your last name?"

The young woman rewarded his question with a most beautiful smile. "Yes, of course. My name is Katherine O'Connor. That's Katherine with a 'K.'"

Carter's mind shifted into rapid-recall mode. He was quite good at recalling names, dates, events, historical facts, the types of things he had just displayed to Cardinal Baum. "I don't know any Katherine O'Connor," he thought, his mind still sifting through his mental Rolodex. "Katherine O'Connor. Katherine O'Connor. K. O'Connor. Whoa! K. O'Connor! The Agency blame line!"

Carter tried to show no hint of an expression, but a slight smile emerged that he couldn't fully suppress. He looked around the great church. There were only a few other people in the cathedral's pews, and none were nearby. "Ah, so might I assume you are the K. O'Connor who authored Langley's analysis about the death of the pope and its possible implications?"

Katherine also looked around the great cathedral and then turned back to Carter and nodded. Neither spoke for a moment, but after a few seconds, she broke the silence. "I could have told you Baum would be of no help in this," she said, looking to the front of the church. "He's a young cardinal, and he's very much into the theological issues of the church. I think he sincerely believes that the Holy Spirit descends into the Sistine Chapel and marks the ballots."

"And you know that how?" Carter asked.

"Because I have worked up psychological profiles on all of the cardinal electors, at least to the extent one can do such a thing. It's not easy, as you might imagine. I think there is more public information available on the members of the Soviet Politburo and certainly more private information."

"Is this something the Agency does routinely?"

"Well, not routinely. But as it became clear that Paul VI was in declining health, someone thought it might be useful to have some insights on who the likely successor might be and who would be selecting him."

"And who did you think it would be?"

"Why, Benelli, of course. I think we all thought it would be Benelli. We knew he would play a big role in the conclave. We just thought it would be for himself rather than bad-mouthing Siri and pushing Luciani."

"So, who are you predicting this time?"

Katherine smiled and turned her head away briefly before answering. "Well, logic tells me Benelli, but I don't know if he can put together a large enough coalition given those in the curia who hate him. And after the last experience, I think we can count on Siri strongly opposing him. So, that leaves the field open to someone else, maybe someone very different. So, isn't that why you and I are here having this discussion?"

Carter thought for a moment about what she had just said. He was reassured that her detailed study of the coming conclave seemed to match his own more casual assessment. But he was still bothered that the report Katherine had sent to the White house did not have any strategy or action plan. But that was a professional concern; his immediate interest was to gain more personal traction.

"Do you prefer Katherine or something else? Kathy, perhaps?" he asked, deciding this was going to be very useful information.

"Either," she answered. "But most of my close friends and colleagues just call me Kath. You're not a close friend, but I understand from Admiral Turner that we're going to be colleagues for a couple of weeks. So, I guess I'll give you honorary status."

Carter nodded, believing her comment provided the go-ahead for the next step. "OK…Kath. So, let's get down to business. Is it really true we have no one inside the college that we can work with on this? We don't have a campaign manager, so to speak?"

"That's true; we don't," Kath replied. "But that is what you and I are supposed to accomplish—find one. Isn't that your understanding? If not, why are we sitting here on this hard pew?"

"Well, that's our job as far as I know. That's what I've been told to do, or more accurately, attempt to do, by Brzezinski. I assume you have similar instructions from Admiral Turner."

Kath nodded her head in agreement. "Basically, I've been told to give you whatever help you need, serve as liaison between you and the Agency and the Agency assets on the ground, and do what I can to prevent you from failing."

"I note that you chose the wording of 'prevent you from failing' as opposed to 'help you succeed.'"

"An inconsequential choice of words, Carter—I am calling you Carter, correct? As opposed to Major Caldwell."

"Carter works for me, if Kath works for you."

Katherine smiled. "Well, Carter, are you ready to go?"

Carter gave her a quizzical look. "I guess so, but…where exactly are we going?"

Katherine reached into her large, stylish handbag and pulled out two Amtrak train tickets. "We're going to Philadelphia, on the 12:30 train. We have a 3:00 p.m. appointment with Cardinal John Krol, the archbishop of Philadelphia. I think you'll want to be part of it. He's the fellow you should have talked to in the first place. I'm sure you'll find him much more receptive than Baum."

Carter looked at the tickets. This gal clearly did not fool around. "Is that enough time to get there?"

"Trip time is an hour and thirty-eight minutes. That gets us there just after 2:00 p.m., which should be plenty of time to make a 3:00 p.m. meeting."

"Have you already spoken with him?" Carter asked. "Does he know why we're coming?"

"No. Of course he doesn't know why we are coming," Kath replied through a slight smile. "At least so far as I am aware. Admiral Turner called him and arranged it, following my suggestion."

"Why do you think he'll be receptive?" Carter asked.

Katherine grinned slightly. "You have done a fabulous job of acquainting yourself with the details of the conclaves, Carter. And you have done a pretty good job of learning about the key participants, but somehow through it all, you missed an obviously great possibility."

"In Krol?" Carter queried. "Why are you so high on him?"

"Two big reasons," Kath replied. "First, as I understand it, everyone feels the cardinals we should advocate are Koenig and Wyszynski, right?"

"Right," Carter answered in agreement.

"So, therefore, second…Krol is close to Koenig and shares many of his views—they have known each other for years, and—perhaps most importantly—Krol is Polish."

"Polish!" Carter exclaimed. "What do you mean he's Polish?"

"Second-generation Polish," Kath replied. "His parents were Polish immigrants. Came from the Tatra Mountain region. He speaks something like ten languages and is theologically quite conservative, which makes many who would be supporting Benelli uneasy. But he is also quite a practical man and has taken progressive positions on social and humanitarian issues, largely because he realizes they are implicit criticisms of communism in most cases. He has advocated nuclear disarmament, as an objective, but has otherwise been supportive of the American nuclear posture. As a result, I see him as being able to work with both the Italian conservative and moderates—with Koenig, with Wyszynski, and with many of the third-world cardinals with whom he seems to have a good rapport."

Carter frowned. "Well, I wouldn't say he has been supportive of our nuclear posture if he has been supporting nuclear disarmament. How do you feel that means he supports our position?"

Katherine was ready with a quick rebuttal. "I think he does eventually want nuclear disarmament. But he does not advocate unilateral disarmament. He is realistic and feels any moves toward nuclear disarmament should be 'mutual, negotiated, proportional, and reciprocal'—I think those are the words he frequently uses when addressing the topic. But to me, that sounds a lot like our position on SALT. And if the *Post* this morning is accurate, those talks are now being delayed until the spring, so it doesn't sound to me like worrying about positions on the SALT negotiations are an immediate priority. I presume that means we have time to work on selecting the next pope. Right?"

Carter paused for a moment to digest what he had just heard and then looked down at his watch. "Well, if we're on the 12:30 out of Union Station, I guess we had best grab a cab and head down there. Do you have all you need?"

"Yes," Kath said, pointing toward her large handbag. "How about you?"

"I'm good, presuming you have a round-trip ticket and we'll be coming back late this evening. And it looks like it could be pretty late."

"I do have round-trip tickets, and the last train leaves at eight. The cardinal's office is not far from the Philadelphia train station, so it should work, unless our chat with him goes late into the evening. Then, I guess we'll just see."

Carter nodded. "OK with me. Let's go." He stood up from the pew and stepped into the aisle to allow Kath to step out and walk out with him. She gently slipped from the pew, quickly knelt by it, made the sign of the cross, rose to her full height, and headed toward the cathedral entrance onto Rhode Island Avenue.

Carter paused for a moment to watch her walk away and then quickly engaged his own gears and caught up with her. "My goodness," he quietly commented. "I wasn't aware how tall you were while we were sitting in the pew."

Kath smiled. "A bit under six feet," she replied. "But you're not exactly one of the seven dwarfs. How tall are you—six four?"

"Six four and a half," Carter answered. "And don't dismiss the half. It's a big deal to me. Makes me taller than my dad."

"I'll try and remember that," Kath answered as they approached the large doors.

"And you're Catholic?" Carter continued, increasingly convinced this was a young lady worth knowing better.

"Yes, I'm Catholic. Makes it a bit more natural to do analysis on the worldwide church if you're actually a part of it, wouldn't you agree?"

"Well, yes. I suppose I would."

"Aren't you Catholic, Carter?"

"Uh…no. Presbyterian…more or less."

By then they were at the curb and Kath was hailing a cab. One quickly pulled up, and the two of them piled into the backseat, which quickly became a tangle of long legs. After they had arranged themselves so that both fit with some degree of comfort, the cab pulled away and headed toward Union Station.

## Florence

Cardinal Benelli was alone in his simple bedroom. He had his three travel bags packed. All were quite full. One held the personal items that he would use: toiletries, sleeping pajamas, a book on the evolution of religious thought in the twentieth century, and two large folders of notes regarding the conclave. The other two bags were stuffed with the well-tailored outfits that would be required by a prince of the church for participating in all of the meetings and ceremonies associated with the pope's funeral, the conclave, and the official—and unofficial—meetings that would occur in between.

He would be leaving in the morning, taking a private limousine that was being provided by Angelo Sardi, a much-appreciated luxury that would allow him time to review his notes, and collect his thoughts. And he had some considerable collecting to do given the complexity of the task that he had taken upon himself.

Benelli rose from his small desk and looked around his bedroom. "I had best get to sleep early," he thought. "This may be the last good night's sleep I get for a while, if ever again. And while in Rome, who knows what sort of rooms Villot may have built for us this time. Hopefully he won't leave instructions to give me the most uncomfortable mattress available. At least the summer heat has passed."

Moving slowly, like a man carrying a great weight, which he felt he was, Benelli walked out of his bedroom and slipped into the small private chapel adjacent to his sleeping quarters. It held a compact altar, illuminated for the moment by a single candle, whose flame flickered across a small framed picture of the late Pope John Paul. Benelli shuffled in and knelt before the altar. The face of John Paul seemed to be fixed on him, the dead pontiff's eyes glimmering with something close to the glow that was always present whenever anyone was in his presence.

"I will do all I can, Albino, to ensure that your successor is worthy of your great legacy and sacrifice," Benelli whispered. "I will do all I can, but you were a comet in the evening sky, one that appeared, illuminated, fascinated, and then vanished. I am unsure there is another like you. But, forgive me, I know some who covet your seat are not worthy of it… not worthy in any way. Not worthy by temperament, by vision, by piety, lacking in humility."

Benelli paused for a moment, rested his forehead on his clasped hands, and thought deeply. "We must find another Luciani, but is there another such precious presence among us? Is there? And what if there isn't? Where would we look then?" He exhaled a deep sigh, crossed himself, and rose to his feet, slowly turning and then heading back toward his bed. It would be a most tiresome two weeks, maybe more—yes, most tiresome. He needed to get some sleep and prepare for it. And he knew his own mattress was quite comfortable.

## Genoa

Cardinal Siri's bags were also packed, and Monsignor Grone had checked them thoroughly to ensure all that his superior would need was tucked inside. That included the small flask of cognac that Siri had used in the last conclave. Siri knew in great detail what he wanted to carry to Rome. When it came to conclaves, he was, at this point, a well-practiced authority.

Siri was seated at his small writing desk, wearing an old-fashioned nightshirt, the simple sleeping attire he had always preferred. He was reviewing two items, switching back and forth between them as the random thoughts generated by each congealed in his mind. The first was the list of cardinals that Grone had prepared—sorted in the order and precedence he had directed. To be elected pope, he would need the support of seventy-five cardinals, and it was a challenging mental exercise to determine who the seventy-five might be. He felt he could count on perhaps eighteen of the Italians, including nearly all in the curia and many of those who led the major archdioceses around his native country. He had lost the support of some in the curia and many from the more pastoral ranks back in August, but he felt he was in a stronger position with the latter group now. He had called many, both the Italians and others he felt were, like him, theologically conservative, not to ask for their support—as that would be far too forward—but to simply pray with them over the death of John Paul, discuss major issues before the church, and subconsciously remind them that he had now been a cardinal for a quarter century, certainly a lengthy enough tenure to have prepared him for greater responsibility and endowed him with uncommon insight.

"Your Eminence."

Siri turned in his chair to see the young face of Monsignor Grone peeking in from the doorway. "Is there anything further you might need, Your Eminence?"

"Have you called Sarac?" the old cardinal asked.

"Yes, I did. And as you had predicted, he was most amenable to granting your request on the location of your temporary room. I think it will meet all of your requests."

"Did you tell him I want a comfortable bed this time?" Siri asked, a broad smile extending across his face.

"No, Your Eminence. I did not raise any issue about the bed. Do you want me to call again?"

Siri laughed and looked away toward his small table. "No, it is best not to push such things too far. And we have pushed a bit far already."

The cardinal grabbed a folder and thumbed through it slowly. The interview he was to have in the morning with Gianni Licheri was on his mind. He was uncertain how far he should go in raising his concerns about the Vatican Council reforms. He certainly could not condemn them, as that would be seen as a direct challenge to the wisdom of both Popes John XXIII and Paul VI, but he must make it clear that he felt they had gone too far. He knew he was not alone in his concerns. He chuckled to himself at recalling his brief exchange with British Cardinal Basil Hume at the last conclave when they had seen a sign held by an old man in St. Peter's Square, imploring the college to elect a "Catholic Pope." Basil Hume had chuckled and commented to Siri, "So, does someone feel we are here to elect a Protestant?"

"Grone, what are your thoughts about the interview with Licheri," Siri asked. "How specific should I be about my reservations on the Vatican Council reforms?"

"I would not be specific at all," the young monsignor answered. "I would focus on this strange idea some are advancing that the leadership of the church should be more decentralized among the cardinals or even down lower to the bishops, rather than being the strict domain of the supreme pontiff. This idea they call 'collegiality.' I am not sure what that even means. But if the next pontiff..." Grone paused and glanced over at his superior, "whoever he may be, plans to be a powerful leader intent on rolling back some of the more contentious reforms, then this 'collegiality' idea is a relatively threatening concept that should be attacked."

Siri pressed his lips together, making his thin mouth disappear into little more than a fine line. "That is a very good idea, Grone. Focusing on that issue is on safe theological ground, and if the next pontiff—whoever he may be—signals such a position, nearly all other issues would be subsumed into it. That's brilliant!"

"Thank you, Your Eminence," Grone replied, pleased with how warmly Siri had embraced his proposal. "And besides, if the interview does not come out until after the conclave is concluded, all that anyone can say is that it shows a pontiff who has a strong grip on his papal ferula."

Siri was always impressed with his young aide. He had a quick intellect and a sharp mind for the political currents that were always swirling around the church's complex internal relations. "Grone, Licheri and his paper understand this is not to be published until after the conclave is over, correct? You have made that quite clear, I trust?"

"Yes, Your Eminence. Quite clear."

Siri smiled. All seemed in order. He had a well-positioned room reserved, courtesy of Cardinal Villot. He would go to Rome for the pope's funeral, return to Genoa, and then return again to the Vatican prior to the conclave—the Montini strategy. He had made nearly forty phone calls. He was ready. It seemed that the fourth time would be the charm in this case.

## The Vatican

Sister Elizabeth Cummings was taking a quick look around what was to be her primary place of duty for the next two weeks—the Vatican kitchen. It was normally used for two purposes: preparing food for the Swiss Guards, the curial cardinals, and their immediate staffs. But for the next two weeks, it would have to provide food service to nearly eighty additional cardinals and, as Cardinal Villot had already come down to remind her, they were unhappy with the food from the last conclave. He was quite emphatic that he wanted no complaints this time. Sister Elizabeth had listened politely and reverently to the camerlengo, but as her own mother used to tell her, "Well, my dear, people in hell want ice water."

She understood Villot's concern and his expectations, but he had not given her a single lira to make it happen. And expecting something for nothing was a sure way to fire up her Irish blood. She was a redhead, and her personality displayed all of the traits of temperament that went with that condition. She had been given a staff of about twenty additional nuns to help her; however, only a couple had arrived and Villot was vague about when the others might appear. It had best be soon. The Holy Father's funeral was in three days, and the other members of the College of Cardinals would soon descend upon her, asking for everything from the minestrone soup favored by Siri, to the wurst preferred by Koenig, to the tinga de pollo preference of the Latin Americans. And where was she to get all this on such short notice?

She was at a small table furiously going over a large shopping list, trying to reconcile it with a meager budget and expansive palates, when the door to the kitchen opened and in walked one of Sister Elizabeth's least-favorite people, the facilities director himself, Bruno Brachi.

Brachi walked up to the feisty nun and asked exactly the wrong question in precisely the wrong way. "Sister Elizabeth, do you have everything set for the meals? Is there anything you need?" As soon as the words had left his mouth, Brachi realized that he couldn't have created more heat had he simply walked over and set Sister's Elizabeth's habit on fire.

"You can't be serious, Mr. Brachi! Tell me you are not serious! Only one person has ever succeeded in feeding the multitudes from a small basket of fish and bread, and I certainly am not him! And I'm quite certain that you don't have that divine gift either you pompous ass! How dare you walk into my kitchen and ask me if all is in order when you know…we both know…and we both know you know…that it's not! And we both know that you have done absolutely nothing to help, to get things in order, to find others to help, and to get some assistance from beyond the Vatican walls!"

A large carving knife was lying on a preparation table, and Sister Elizabeth reached over for it. Taking it by its black handle, she held it up, its sharp blade reflecting the fluorescent lights above the kitchen area, pointing it at Brachi. "I have taken many vows in my life, Mr. Brachi, but none of them were to tolerate the likes of you. Now get out of my kitchen and don't come back unless you bring some food, some staff, or some money. And if you come back without anything, you'll see how the Almighty's terrible swift sword is wielded by outraged nuns! Do we understand each other?"

Brachi held his hands up and backed toward the door. "Yes, Sister. I'll see what I can do. I truly will."

With that, the facilities chief fled the room, dust flowing behind him in the slight vortex created by his escape. Sister Elizabeth stuck the knife into a wooden carving table, crossed her hands, and then returned to her desk. "Forgive me, Father," she quietly said, turning her eyes to the ceiling. "It's the Irish, you know."

## ZADAR, YUGOSLAVIA

The evening mist was rolling in from the Adriatic, a common occurrence all along the central Yugoslav coast at this time of year. Standing in the small, treed garden on the northwest side of the Cathedral of St. Anastasia in the seaport city of Zadar, Cardinal Jedar Katic, his large hands clasped tightly behind him, was deep in thought. His gaze was fixed on some unfocused spot across a peaceful public square leading to the seawall that surrounded the old city, one that sat postcard-like on a small peninsula. The mist rolled toward him in a steady, inexorable way, slowly shrouding his view of the large, rocky barrier island that was about a mile away on the far side of the sea-lane approach. Katic was very uneasy and—as always—unhappy.

Zadar was a compact port town in the Yugoslavian province of Croatia. Unlike the other sections of the artificially created and tenuous Yugoslav state that had emerged after World War I, Croatia remained the closest to Western Europe in culture and outlook. The other portions of Yugoslavia had ties to the East, but Croatia's were to the West. Although the Croatian language had roots in the South-Slavic tongue and was commonly called Serbo-Croatian by many, the Croats themselves worked hard to keep it from outside corruption, even by the Serbs. Whereas the Serbs of Yugoslavia wrote with Cyrillic characters, the

Croats used the Latin alphabet. Latin had even been the official language in much of Croatia until the nineteenth century. It was natural, therefore, that the Catholic church had maintained a firm foothold in Croatia throughout its turbulent past and into the communist present. Statistics were difficult to determine in any communist country, but it was widely known that over 80 percent of Croats were Catholic, an uncomfortable reality for the central government in Belgrade, led by Marshall Josef Broz, known throughout the world as "Tito."

Tito and the church had been at odds since he came to power in the latter days of World War II. Although the two had made common cause against the Nazis during the war, their fundamentally different philosophies of life emerged in full bloom when it ended. And the most vocal leader of the church's opposition to Tito's regime was Bishop Aloysius Stepinac, the archbishop of Zagreb, Croatia's capital city. Eventually in 1946, Stepinac was put on trial by the government, one of those stage-managed travesties known in the West as a "show trial," was predictably found guilty of treason along with numerous other vaguely worded crimes against the state, and was sentenced to sixteen years in prison. The Vatican sternly responded to the conviction by excommunicating all of those on the jury who were Catholic.

Stepinac was held behind bars for five years, but following a visit by a senior American congressional delegation, Tito agreed to release him in exchange for American foreign aid. Stepinac refused an offer to leave the country and was kept near Zagreb under house arrest. In late 1952, the Vatican upped the ante by elevating Stepinac to cardinal, prompting Belgrade to immediately break diplomatic relations with the Holy See.

Like Cardinal Stepinac, the city of Zadar had lived its own difficult history. Although a prosperous trading town with a natural harbor, it had always been a secondary economic force behind Dubrovnik to the south, and the much more powerful and prominent Venice to the north. And being a secondary economic force meant it was a secondary military force. On countless occasions, Zadar had been attacked, captured, and ransacked by the Venetians. All of this had happened centuries before, but in the Balkans, people had very long memories, and the bigger the grudge, the longer—and clearer—the memory. Things that had happened seven hundred years earlier were frequently recounted at sidewalk cafés as if they had just been reported on the evening news.

Cardinal Katic had lived the contemporary stress between Belgrade and the Vatican, and being a native of Zadar, he had been schooled on its past since he was old enough to follow his grandfather's stories of the town's tortured history. He wanted to be helpful and tend to the downtrodden, an essential motivation for anyone entering the clergy, but he had mainly gone into the priesthood to get a good education. And much of that education was learned at the feet of a young priest named Aloysius Stepinac.

Stepinac admired his young protégé's quick mind, and Katic admired his mentor's courage and strong convictions. A few years after his ordination, Stepinac had Katic posted to Belgrade to attend to the spiritual needs of the small Catholic community there, one that was largely isolated in an Eastern Orthodox stronghold. In Belgrade, Katic found himself more and more attracted to the other strong Yugoslav personality with courage and convictions, Marshall Tito.

Tito, on occasion, would come by Katic's church to try to explore ways in which the church and his government might better coexist. Looking for coexistence was a constant effort for Tito, who spent enormous time and energy trying to maintain peace among the numerous ethnic adversaries who were now locked together within the Yugoslav state. The old marshal liked the young priest, and the young priest liked the loud laugh of the old marshal as well as his clear commitment to building a prosperous and peaceful country, one where the Communist Party would be a guide but not an ominous, forbidding presence, and one with a degree of independence from Moscow. Over time, Yugoslavia became relatively open, and slowly German tourists and vacationers began to find their way down the gorgeous Dalmatian coast, leaving behind their highly cherished German marks. Tito's efforts seemed to have paid off handsomely when in the Spring of 1978, the International

Olympic Committee announced the award of the 1984 Winter Games to Sarajevo.

When Cardinal Stepinac died in 1960, still at odds with the Tito government, Bishop Katic suddenly became a human bridge between two adversaries: Pope Paul and Marshal Tito. When the archbishop position opened, Katic became an easy and satisfactory choice for both parties, with each thinking Katic would be a strong advocate of his position to the other. Katic accepted the role and the eventual promotion to cardinal but only on the condition that he fill this function from Zadar rather than Zagreb. Tito quickly agreed; the Vatican grudgingly followed. Tito liked the move, feeling it showed Katic was not Stepinac, while the Vatican disliked it for exactly the same reason. Nonetheless, Cardinal Katic, a child of the Dalmatian Coast and Zadar, a committed enemy of Italy and Germany, and a sympathetic advocate of Tito's brand of communism, assumed his new office.

That was ten years ago, and much had happened since. Katic had been to Rome many times, most of his trips related to his strong differences of opinions with the curia. Katic was clearly not a Vatican favorite. The mother church liked neither his closeness to Tito nor his continuing refusal to relocate the cathedral in Zagreb. In the August conclave, Katic had been among those who fell in behind Cardinal Luciani, but he had done so with little enthusiasm. Like so many cardinals from around the world, Katic had no warm feelings for the curia, fewer for Italians in general, and fewer still for Italians who were also Venetians—and Luciani was both. Like so many from Croatia, Katic harbored the historical resentments and old hurts. It was just the Balkan way.

As the Adriatic mist began to descend on the garden at St. Anastasia's and slowly wrap around the cardinal's feet, all of this old history sat heavily on Katic's head, like the weight of a lead mitre. He watched the waterfront slowly disappearing in the soft natural shroud. "What a strange turn of events," Katic thought, slowly turning his eyes toward the darkening sky. "Another conclave, and another pope. And probably another Italian. I am so tired of Italians—Italian merchants, Italian sailors, Italian fishermen, Italian tourists, and most of all Italian popes! But there will be another. That is the way of the church. That is what they want—or what they think they want."

"Bitte."

Katic glanced down at the foot of the three steps leading from the garden to the street that circled the square. He could see a man, a woman, and a child standing there in the mist. The man was holding a camera and wearing the leather hiking shorts common in Bavaria. They were clearly German, and German was one of the languages that Katic had mastered. "Guten Abend," Katic responded, covering his face with a smile suggesting a kindness he did not feel. Croatia and all the Yugoslav states had suffered horribly in World War II at the hands of the Germans and had united in the common effort to drive them out. It had been a brutal struggle, but the Yugoslavs had succeeded. And now, a mere three decades later, the Germans were back, this time with families and cameras—and money. It was a much different type of invasion, quite benign, economically even essential, but Katic still did not like it.

"Darf man fotografieren?" the German asked, holding up his camera.

"Ja," Katic responded, trying not to engage the German any more than necessary, nor reveal that he was quite conversational in his language.

The German fumbled with the settings on his camera, trying to get the right light and photo angle, wanting to get a picture of both the church and the clergyman standing outside it, not realizing his human subject was a Catholic cardinal.

"Was fur ein Gebaude ist das?" (What building is this?)

Cardinal Katic glanced over his shoulder and then back to the German as he raised his camera. "St. Anastasia," he replied, correctly assessing that would satisfy the question.

"Vielen Dank," the German answered, as the shutter clicked and the flash illuminated the garden. "Und wiedersehen."

"Ja. Wiedersehen," Katic answered as the German family disappeared into the mist. The cardinal of Zadar watched as the figures slowly vanished and then turned to go back inside his church. He needed to start packing. He was not leaving for a couple more days and did not plan to be in Rome for John Paul's funeral, which he would skip, offering the usual excuses about the slow, tedious process of getting travel authorizations from Belgrade. But he needed to get ready anyway. Packing was such a chore for a traveling cardinal.

And he needed to carefully reread the two messages he had received earlier in the day, especially the coded one. That was the one that tormented him, bothered him, made him question who he was and what he was doing. But those emotions were part of his life. He had learned to deal with them and to compartmentalize them in that secluded, isolated part of his brain. It created a conflict with his faith, which fought to stay the most important element of his life, and such conflict created tension and stress. Physically, he felt it. He wondered if John Paul had ever felt something similar. It would have been useful to ask him. But that was not a possibility. After all, he had been a Venetian, and now he was dead.

CHAPTER 7

# Monday, October 2, 1978
# Philadelphia, Pennsylvania

● ● ●

Carter's watch showed 2:35 p.m. when the cab he and Kath had taken from Philadelphia's Thirtieth Street Station pulled up in front of a town house on Spring Street, about three blocks across Logan Circle from the Basilica of Saints Peter and Paul. The street was tree-lined, quiet, and pleasant, not fully consistent with Carter's preformed image of downtown Philly. The trip up from DC had gone easily and, contrary to Amtrak's reputation, had departed and arrived on time.

Carter pulled some cash from his wallet and paid the cabby, as Kath stepped out onto the street, stretched her arms, and took a deep breath.

"Keep the change," Carter casually told the cabby and then momentarily considered whether any of this trip would be expensable when reviewed by the stern-faced accountants in the NSC travel section.

"Thanks, fella," the cabby shouted with a sort of half wave before speedily pulling away from the curb. Carter began to wonder how big a tip he had actually left as he walked over toward Kath, who was looking at the number above the transom of the house's front door, verifying they were at the right place.

The two of them had enjoyed a wide-ranging discussion on the way up, and among the things they had determined about each other was that his sense of direction and spatial relationship was far superior to hers, a discovery confirmed when she had misdirected the cabdriver taking them from St. Matthew's to Union Station, and then wanted to exit the train in Wilmington, one city short of Philadelphia. Carter's skills had served them well in both cases, drawing heavily on experiences ingrained in many map-reading classes and while stumbling through the woods on night navigation exercises outside Ft. Benning, Georgia. Compared to that, getting to the right address in Philadelphia was a snap.

"Looks like this is the place," Carter said, admiring the elegance of the town house—which was far superior to his in DC, as Kath continued to evaluate the street itself. "We're early. Think we should just go up and ring the doorbell or walk around for a few minutes?"

"I think we just go ring the doorbell," Kath replied, continuing to eye the surroundings.

Carter may have been trained in navigation, but she was trained in surveillance.

"Interesting that he wanted us to meet him here rather than at the cathedral. That's encouraging, I think."

Carter nodded his head in agreement, although he was unsure why he actually was in agreement, or why this location might somehow be encouraging.

"OK. Let's go ring the bell," Carter said, pointing to the stone stairs. They walked up to the top step, but before Carter could touch the button subtly embedded in the doorsill, the decorative door opened, its beveled-glass sections reflecting the light from the ornate chandelier hanging in the hall. Standing before them was a tall, erect gentleman wearing a black suit topped with a white clerical collar, his face covered with an engaging grin.

"Good afternoon," he said, extending his hand to Kath, evidently taking notice of her more quickly than he did Carter. "I'm John Krol. It's a real pleasure to meet you, young lady."

Kath's eyes widened as she looked at the cardinal, whose picture she had seen but whom she had never met. "Thank you, Your Eminence," she shyly answered. "Believe me, the pleasure is all ours. We very much appreciate your seeing us on such short notice. My name is Katherine O'Connor, and this is my colleague, Carter Caldwell."

Krol turned his warm, shinning eyes towards Carter and grabbed his hand in a firm, athletic grip. "Good to meet you as well, Mr. Caldwell." Krol took a step back and gazed for a long moment at the two professionally dressed visitors at his door and then held his arms wide. "Goodness. Where are my manners? Please. Come inside."

Carter and Kath stepped into the town house, pausing briefly in the entrance hall to admire its patterned marble floor and the elegant staircase leading to the upper levels.

"Is this the rectory?" Kath asked, surprised at meeting Krol in such a lovely setting.

"Oh, certainly not," Krol answered with a chuckle. "This was given to the diocese by one of our wonderful—and wealthy—members. I use it for receptions on occasion or off-site meetings to discuss various issues involving the cathedral. And it's useful for quietly meeting people, such as mysterious visitors from the nation's capital." Krol playfully looked around the entrance hall and then whispered, "Don't tell anybody."

All three of them laughed lightly as Krol directed his guests toward the sitting room to their right. The entire house was very wonderfully furnished, and Krol motioned Carter and Kath toward a very plush sofa in front of an ornate fireplace while he slipped into one of the two large wingback chairs flanking it. A slightly steaming pot and three cups were on the coffee table in front of the sofa. "Please, just help yourself," Krol gently instructed, pointing at the items on the table.

Kath glanced at Carter, who nodded. She poured a cup of coffee for each of them, handed one to Krol and the other one to Carter. He preferred his with cream and sugar, but he smiled appreciatively, took the cup, and wisely said nothing.

Krol made himself comfortable in his seat and flashed a slight, sly grin toward Carter and Kath. "So, as I understand it, the two of you somehow want me to fix the election of the next pope, correct?"

Carter and Kath exchanged uneasy glances.

"Why do you say that?" Carter asked.

"Because Cardinal Baum called me, Mr. Caldwell," Krol responded, the slight grin still on his face.

Carter and Kath exchanged another uneasy glance.

"And what did he tell you?" Carter continued, as calmly and innocently as possible.

Krol leaned forward in his chair, his expression suddenly more serious. "Mr. Caldwell, you know very well what he told me. He was rather unhappy, I'd say even a bit irate. He seemed more than a little disturbed that you would even suggest a sort of advocacy campaign to elect someone to the Throne of St. Peter. Did you actually ask him to be a 'campaign manager'?"

"Your Eminence, those were his words, not mine," Carter responded, feeling his coffee cup slightly rattling on its saucer. "I certainly suggested no such thing. Nor did I use that description."

"I'm sure," the cardinal quickly answered. "Cardinal Baum is a good man…a very good man. I like him very much. But I believe he occasionally sees things in very simple, conceptual, sometimes even innocent terms. His views on the process of papal elections certainly reflect that, as did my discussion with him."

Kath jumped in. "Certainly, he didn't tell you that Mr. Caldwell and I were on our way here, did he?"

"No, of course not," Krol responded with a wave of his hand. "He was just venting about Mr. Caldwell's visit. We talk frequently. He didn't indicate at all that he felt anyone was headed here. But after the call I received from Stan Turner yesterday, I knew that someone was coming to see me for some unknown reason, and William's call very strongly suggested what it was. I'm a theologian, not a mathematician, but even I can add this up." The cardinal leaned forward in his chair, moving his face closer to Carter and Kath, lowering his voice to a near whisper. "So, I'll make this easy for you."

Carter braced for his second cardinal-level lecture of the day about the purity of the papal selection process, certain that he had enjoyed all of the coffee he was likely to have.

Krol rested his elbows on his knees and looked directly at Carter. "Mr. Caldwell, you want a campaign manager for the conclave? Well, young man...I'm your guy!"

Carter was stunned and for a moment could not speak. He flashed a perplexed look toward Kath before turning his eyes back to Krol. "Did you tell Cardinal Baum that?"

Krol leaned back into his chair and chuckled. "Please. Of course not! When we spoke, I told him I was as shocked as he was at any such suggestion. You know, even princes of the church can be a bit evasive with each other from time to time, especially on occasions such as this." The cardinal's light mood quickly dissipated. He shifted his large frame in his chair and let out a long sigh. "This has been a very trying experience for all of us, as I'm sure you know. The selection of the Holy Father last August went smoothly, as I believe was obvious by the quickness with which we all gathered around Cardinal Luciani, may God bless him. I thought he had all the qualities we needed for the supreme church leadership, given the challenges of the moment. But it was God's will—his quick death, so the question before us now is...what next?"

Carter and Kath sat quietly as Krol slipped into a moment of introspection. Both of them had mentally concluded it was best to let him simply think aloud while they listened. The cardinal reached for his coffee cup, took a sip, and then gently placed the cup and saucer back on the coffee table. "Did you hear what Cardinal Carberry of St. Louis said the other day?"

Carter and Kath shook their heads.

"He said in the last conclave that he had seen an invisible light shining on Cardinal Luciani, suggesting to him that Luciani was the choice of the Holy Spirit. Well...if he saw such a signal, who am I to question it? I myself certainly saw no such light, but the Holy Spirit comes to and speaks to each of us in different ways. For me, that happens most commonly during prayer when my thoughts begin to sort through the complicated problems of the day, be they large issues or the smaller concerns of one single individual I may have met during the course of my day. It would be nice if the Spirit had a TV channel that we could merely tune in to at night and be given thoughts and guidance for tomorrow, along with clear answers to confusing questions. But I'm sure we all agree it's not so simple."

Krol paused to further gather his thoughts, obviously weighing his words with care as Carter and Kath continued sitting silently on the couch. After glancing around the room for a few moments, his expression softened as he turned his eyes toward his guests. "Given what we are discussing, would the two of you be comfortable being a bit more informal."

"In what way, sir?" Carter asked.

"In how we address each other," Krol instantly replied. "How about if I call you Carter and Katherine, and you just call me John. I get a bit fatigued hearing 'Your Eminence' all day long. And I think we would be better served with a comfortable relationship, given what we are discussing."

Carter looked to Kath. She was the Catholic. If she could dispense with formalities, he was sure he could also, despite his years of military indoctrination to the contrary. "Fine with me…John," Kath slowly answered. "Carter?"

"Sure. That would work with me," Carter replied.

"Good," Krol continued. "Let's try that. I think it will make things more comfortable for us, and make the conversation easier." Having that issue settled, he resumed the discussion in a more reflective tone. "God uses each of us in different ways, you know. And he also communicates with us in different ways. It is up to us to decide how to act, how we should do our part to carry out his will. I suppose on occasion he might provide an 'invisible light,' and I suppose on occasion he might place in your presence an attractive young couple from Washington, DC, who have had their own experiences with trying to determine divine will. Have either of you ever read President Kennedy's inaugural address?"

"Many times," Carter quickly answered.

"Really! Do you recall how it concludes? I mean, at the very end."

"Yes, I do. He concluded it by saying that, 'Here on earth, God's work must truly be our own.'"

Krol smiled. "Very good, young man. Very good…I'm impressed. Are you Catholic, by the way?"

"No, uh…John. Presbyterian…more or less."

Krol shifted his eyes to Kath. "And you?"

"Yes, Your Eminence, I'm Catholic."

"Well, I suppose one out of two isn't bad. And it's 'John,' right?" Krol chuckled to himself as Kath nervously adjusted herself on the couch, aware that a good Catholic girl would find it hard to be so informal and familiar with a prince of the church. The cardinal paused for a few more moments as he shifted his thoughts onto a more serious track. "I want you both to understand something quite clearly. What I do, I do because I think it is best for the church and all of those who are Catholic. But I also know there are moments in history where other considerations have to be given great weight. I presume the two of you are well aware that I have been quite concerned—and outspoken—about this whole idea of nuclear war and nuclear deterrence. There are differing views, of course. For example, Cardinal Cooke and I are not in complete agreement on this. But this is, in my view, a daunting challenge, a huge danger, a Sword of Damocles hanging over the head of mankind. And I am comfortable in my conclusion that we must bring all the pressure we can to remove this terrible threat, or at least lessen it. In this country, we have many ways to express such views and generate such pressures. I can preach about it, talk about it, write newspaper articles about it; being who I am, I can even from time to time firmly express my views with senior government officials—such as my friend Admiral Turner. But in the Soviet Bloc, there are no such mechanisms for shaping government opinion or policy. Doing so requires carefully calibrated pressure. Too much pressure, as we have seen in the past in Hungary and Czechoslovakia, and the results are disastrous. Too little pressure, and nothing happens. In my view, the space between too much and too little is where the church can operate…or where it *should* operate."

"And how, in your view, will the church do that?" Carter asked, trying to interrupt as courteously as possible.

"A very good question, my Presbyterian friend," Krol replied, rubbing his hand on his chin. "In my view, and I suspect in yours—which is, no doubt, why you are here to begin with—right now that means a non-Italian pope, someone who has an interest in and a sensitivity for such issues. But given that the real pressure points for Moscow have always been in Eastern Europe, he must be a European. I know many of my third-world colleagues, particularly the Latin Americans, want the selection to be one of them. But I think that is premature. One must first step outside of Italy, then at some point in the future, outside of Europe. Do you agree?"

"We do," Kath quickly responded. "Carter and I have both looked at this, and we agree with what you have so precisely laid out. So, the big question is: who do you see in that role?"

"Ah," the cardinal replied, pointing his finger at Kath, "the big question. Given my position as a cardinal elector, I am reluctant to answer that. So, let me turn it around. Who do you see in that role?"

Carter now jumped in, feeling this was a question best answered by the Presbyterian in the discussion. "Your Eminence…John, we have looked at this from the perspectives you have described, the broader needs of the moment, the opportunity before us, and we feel the best outcome would be with either Cardinal Koenig or Cardinal Wyszynski."

Krol leaned back in his chair and cocked his head slightly. "Very good men, both of them. I know them both well, and I am sure—like most others, greatly respect them. However, both are, shall we say, a bit up in years. And I think that will be a bigger issue this time given the unexpected death of the Holy Father. But both are European and I like that you have given serious thought to a Pole. I'm sure you are both well aware that I am myself first-generation Polish. I was born in Cleveland, but my parents emigrated from Poland."

Kath chuckled at the comment. "Well, Your Eminence, one of us was aware of that. Somehow that little tidbit escaped the other. But I won't say which one of us was sloppy in the homework."

Carter rolled his eyes and looked away.

"Well…and it's John, right?" Krol replied. "I am no authority on body language, but I'll bet I know who is who in this regard. But do we agree that Poland is the crown jewel here? That it has all of the conditions to greatly complicate life for the Soviets? The trick will be to pressure them in a way that goes far, without going too far?"

"I would say we certainly agree with that," Carter answered.

"Then let me suggest another Pole who I believe would very ably occupy the throne of Saint Peter—Cardinal Wojtyla of Kraków."

Carter and Kath quickly glanced at one another. "But he's young for a cardinal and not that well known," Kath countered, anxious to hear Krol's reply.

Krol laughed again. "Oh, he's certainly young compared to many who have been named before—about fifty-eight, I believe. He and I were both elevated to cardinal at the same consistory in 1967, so I have known him for quite a while, and I assure you he has an appealing personality, a forceful presence, a grasp of contemporary theological issues, and a keen intellect—very keen. He is very respectful of Wyszynski and has stayed very much in the prelate's shadow, as you imply. And he is very fit, quite the athlete, an accomplished skier. In fact, to combine the two comments I just made, he once commented that forty percent of Polish cardinals ski. And when asked by someone how the number could be forty percent, as there were only two Polish cardinals, he answered, 'Of course. But Wyszynski counts for more than half.' Is that quick or what?"

"But how do other cardinals feel about him?" Kath asked, impressed at this anecdotal evidence that Wojtyla indeed had a quick mind.

Krol narrowed his eyes slightly and pressed his lips together. "My take on it is that he has a greater following than you might expect. He is surprisingly well known to the third-world cardinals. I believe he and Lorscheider of Brazil are close and correspond regularly. He is also well known to some of the African cardinals, such as Cardinal Rugambwa of Tanzania. I think Karol speaks six languages, maybe seven—linguistic skill is surprisingly common among us East Europeans. I speak ten languages myself—something that always amazes Americans, but as I say, in Europe, that only gets you a concierge job at a first-rate Parisian hotel."

All three shared another brief laugh, recognizing that Krol's comment was close to the truth.

"Can he stand up to the Soviets?" Carter asked, still unconvinced that Wojtyla had the appeal to trump Koenig or Wyszynski. "And did he have anyone supporting him in August?"

"On your last question," Krol answered, his voice suddenly firmer, "I won't say. The proceedings of the conclave are secret. To twist a well-used line, what happens in the Sistine Chapel stays in the Sistine Chapel."

It was a lightly made but simultaneously serious comment, so Carter smiled rather than laughed. "I apologize, Your Eminence…uh, John. But that was a very effective comeback." He hoped Krol would take no offense.

Krol grinned. "Well, thank you…I suppose. As for standing up to the Soviets, he has certainly done so on occasion but has been much more subtle and quiet than Wyszynski. I fear the Soviets would see the election of Wyszynski as a direct affront, and they might make it difficult for the church in Poland and therefore for all Poles…given the large percentage who are Catholic. I don't think anyone wants to experience another Prague Spring."

Carter and Kath weighed the cardinal's comments, Carter a bit more soberly than Kath. This was certainly an unexpected turn. They had expected it would take some careful debate to convince Krol to play any role at all; instead, they now found themselves speaking to a man not only volunteering to be their campaign manager but actually presenting his own candidate.

Kath was encouraged but also concerned. She hesitated a bit, picking her words carefully. "John, I wouldn't be so presumptuous as to suggest who the conclave should chose, but I think we need—the church needs—not only a non-Italian but also a man of great substance. Despite their ages, which I agree may be an issue, we think that argues for Koenig or Wyszynski."

Krol did not reply immediately, and his silence made Kath uneasy. "Yes, substance," he finally responded in a low voice. "We will definitely need someone of substance, young lady." His voice was now a bit cold, and he looked away without adding any further comment.

"Well," Carter finally added, breaking what was becoming an uncomfortably long silence, "we have some thoughts and ideas, but we don't actually have a specific candidate, John. It's not like there have been a series of polls and primaries. None of these people have been in Iowa or New Hampshire. We just have an opinion, and we all know what opinions are worth. After all is said and done, we'll have to accept the decision of an electoral process over which we have little influence. And our only real influence will be in hopefully shaping the actions and sensings of people such as you. I couldn't agree with you more: the center of gravity of the Soviet sphere is Poland. And Poland is a growing problem for them. It has economic problems—as all the Soviet satellites do—and it has social unrest bubbling just below the surface; we're sure of that. An Eastern-European pope would give them a reason to look west—even if just a little—and presumably provide them a strong advocate."

Krol slowly nodded. "So, we're agreed on that. If you go in, go in all the way. You don't want a toehold in Eastern Europe, you want a beachhead, and in that regard, we need Poland to be Normandy, not Dieppe."

Carter smiled at this comment, referencing as it did the success of the Allies' major invasion of World War II, which had followed the failure of a smaller-scale raid on the French coastal town of Dieppe. "Well, Your Eminence, a good military analogy. It works for me."

"Just came to me," the cardinal grinned, rejoining the discussion with some enthusiasm and animation before turning to practical matters. "Now, I leave for Rome tonight to be there for John Paul's funeral on Wednesday and have a few meetings beforehand. I understand that the president's mother, Lilian, will represent the United States. That's surprising to me. I've never met her but hear she is quite the personality.

Nonetheless, the real issue for me is…what now for the church? I think it's obvious what my role is: trying to build support for one of those we've discussed. I'll advocate for Koenig or Wyszynski and see if there is any traction there. Maybe Willebrands could be a fallback. Perhaps even Lorscheider if things move that far—which I doubt. But what's your role? How will you help me? Or perhaps should I ask, can you help me?"

Carter looked at Kath. This was her world that Krol was gently referring to, and he knew he would have to follow her lead in discussing it.

"Your Eminence," she began, "we have some people on the ground… within my organization, we simply call them 'assets.' One of them will contact you; I don't know which one exactly, so descriptions will not be useful. We will decide that on the ground once we have communicated your role to them. But you will be asked by someone, 'Is it true Benjamin Franklin was actually born in Boston?'"

"What a silly question," Krol interrupted. "Everyone knows he was born in Philadelphia."

"Sorry to tell you this, Eminence, but no…he was actually born in Boston. He ran away to Philadelphia when he was a teenager. But you have validated why we are using that question—very few would know the correct answer, and given your office, it's something you might be asked by a curious person. Even a curious Roman."

"Goodness," Krol replied through a wide grin. "How bloody embarrassing. OK, Boston. So what then?"

"That will largely be up to you, Your Eminence. You will be passed information on what our assets believe is going on, and you can pass information to them on what you feel is happening and where you would like help or for us to take action."

"What sort of help or action? I presume they won't threaten people," Krol said with a slight chuckle.

"No, nothing like that; it's not our style, shall we say. But they can arrange for certain things to happen, information to appear, maybe even rumors to circulate. You'll have to trust us on this. We won't do anything damaging to anyone, but we may do things that are discouraging, so to speak. Anything we do will have a factual basis that can, we hope, help you make your case. And, from another perspective, we can maybe, shall I say, *encourage* the stalemate between the two Italian blocs that seem to have formed: one side against Siri, the other against Benelli; evidently no one is really passionately for either one."

"They are both quite honorable men, and great servants of God, each in his own way. I will not be party to any effort to discredit either," Krol interjected. "I mean, who knows? One might yet be selected. Of the two, I would prefer Benelli, but Siri has been a serious possibility for over twenty years, and for good reason."

"True, but we need someone else," Kath countered. "So we will have to take advantage of any possibilities presenting themselves that allow the cardinals to look for that invisible light. That's the only way to play this."

"Agreed," Krol replied, nodding his head after a brief moment of reflection. "But do you feel the Soviets will be in the background working for another outcome? Certainly they have decided they don't want an Eastern-European pope, even one who has worked rather well with them, such as Koenig?"

"We have reason to believe they've reached that conclusion. We have that on good authority. We don't know what they might do, or how they might do it, but I must advise you to be watchful and careful. We must assume they have their own assets on the scene, and I need not tell you that they play by different rules—much different. So, please be careful. I am sure they have already figured out that you might be advocating an East European, probably Wyszynski, so you'll have to be on guard."

Krol's eyes narrowed as he considered what Kath had just said. "Very well, young lady. I'll do what I can do, within the confines of, well… within the confines of what I can do. How will we communicate once the conclave starts? Pope Paul established procedures that are very tight, very secretive, very much on-guard against intrusions and intruders."

"I'm not sure yet, Your Eminence," Kath answered. "This is all being pulled together on the fly, almost literally. We will need some way to communicate after the doors to the Sistine Chapel are closed and the first vote is taken."

"The first scrutiny, you mean."

"Excuse me," Kath answered, her face reflecting surprise.

"A vote during a conclave is called a *scrutiny*," Krol crisply responded, his expression revealing a slight satisfaction that his guests were unfamiliar with the term. "So, we will need to communicate in some useful but brief way after the first scrutiny when the initial sentiment becomes clear. So how do we do that? The chapel will be closed, guarded, and swept for listening devices."

"I understand," Kath said in acknowledgment. "We're working on that. I don't have any details of what is being done, or even the basic concept, but I do know we are working on some way to communicate with you. We have very talented and creative people."

"You mean such as 'Q'?" Krol interrupted.

Kath looked over at Carter, who shrugged his shoulders in silence. "I'm not following what you mean," she said to the cardinal.

"Q," the cardinal replied, with an expression of false exasperation. "The technical fellow in the James Bond movies who is always developing those really cool special devices for 007! The role played by Desmond Llewelyn. What a wonderful character actor."

"You watch James Bond films?" Kath asked, surprised.

"Well, one has to stay attuned to modern culture," Krol replied with a grin.

"OK, we have some people like Q. And they'll come up with a concept for communications. As I said, we'll discuss it with you when we are in Rome. We'll arrange to meet with you before the conclave and we'll give you instructions on what to do and how to do it. I know that sounds rather vague, which it is, but that's all I can tell you right now."

The cardinal thought for a few moments, rubbing his large hands together in front of his chest. "Very well," he said at last. "I'll wait to hear from you in Rome. And I'll trust you know what you're doing on this. For now, I have to get to another appointment across Logan Circle."

With that, Krol stood, signaling that the meeting was over, strolled out to the entrance hall, and turned toward the front door. "Thanks for coming by to see me. As I said, I'll do what I can—either with you or just alone." He paused for a moment and gazed at Carter as he and Kath stepped through the door. "Do you know what 'Krol' means in Polish, young man?"

Carter turned and slowly shook his head. "No, Your Eminence, I don't actually."

"It means 'king,'" Krol answered with a smile. "So, I guess in this instance, perhaps, I can help in some way to be a 'Krol-maker.'"

Without any further words, Kath and Carter stepped through the door, and the cardinal closed it behind them. Krol turned and slowly made the short walk across the entrance hall to the small closet holding his overcoat. He thought about the discussion. Was this the right thing for him to be doing? Should he have feelings like Cardinal Baum's? Should he be like Cardinal Carberry and wait for a sign from God? As he opened the closet door and reached for his coat, he thought about the questions he was posing to himself, especially the one about a sign from God. After pulling the garment from the closet, he slowly slipped his muscular arms into it and drew the lapels down over his broad shoulders. "Maybe," he said quietly to himself, "I just had a sign from God."

## **WILLIAMSBURG, VIRGINIA**

As Kath and Carter headed back toward the Philadelphia train station, a well-groomed, middle-aged gentleman slowly drove his aged Ford Fairlane north along Route 143 past Williamsburg, Virginia. The official name of the road was the Merrimac Trail, but the locals tended to prefer its state road number. The area around Williamsburg was historic and beautiful. But being historic, it was also old, the site of the first permanent European colony attempted on the North American continent, the ill-fated Jamestown, whose story was a tangled mixture of the heroic, the mysterious, the tragic, and the controversial. None of that was of much interest at the moment to the nondescript man driving his equally nondescript car. He had been summoned. He was on a mission.

Moving past the intersection of Routes 143 and 132, the gray-haired gentleman proceeded straight ahead, crossed over the bridge spanning Interstate 64, passed the Exit 238 sign to Richmond, and immediately slowed as he approached a rather simple, wood-framed building that sat across the road, anchored to chain-link fences on both sides, which disappeared into the thick woods covering the area. There were no markings on the building, only an usually large red stop sign attached to a gate and a couple of simple metal signs clamped to the fences saying, "US Government Property. Access Restricted."

As the old Ford approached the gate, a guard, dressed in a dark-blue police-type uniform, stepped from the small guard shack and signaled for the car to stop. The distinguished-looking driver behind the wheel knew the drill. He slowed and rolled to a stop just in front of the gate, grabbed the squeaky hand crank, and rolled the driver's-side window down, simultaneously reaching for a badge hidden in a brown folder lying on the passenger side of the frayed front seat.

It was a common drill for the guard as well. He knew the old Ford's driver and had waved him through the gate on many occasions. This would just be another. Both the guard and the driver were aware that this was the entrance to Camp Peary, commonly referred to as "the Farm" by those in the CIA. It was a training facility used to instruct field agents and operatives on all kinds of techniques, ranging from escape and evasion, to trailing someone without being seen, to both withstanding and administering interrogations. It had once been a navy facility, but it had been closed to the public ever since the Agency took it over in 1951. The guard knew it was a CIA facility, the man behind the wheel knew it was a CIA facility, but the American public officially did not—and unofficially didn't really care.

As the guard stepped to the car, the driver held up his ID cards for inspection. "Good afternoon. How are you today?" the guard asked. No names were used, no other outward signs of recognition revealed. The guard pretended not to know the man's name, and the man pretended not to know this was the entrance to a CIA facility, and both of them pretended not to know that the other knew all of that. "I see you have a meeting today. Can you tell me where it is on the compound?" the guard continued, completing the usual gate ritual.

"Certainly, Building 121," the driver replied, dangling his ID badge and extending it through the window. The guard glanced at it quickly, stepped back from the car, and motioned the old Ford through with a smile and a quick wave of the hand. The chain-link gate retracted to the right, and the creaky old car drove into this place of many secrets.

It was a rather short drive through the compound's thick forests to Building 121, a nondescript one-story building that looked as if it had been built by a firm specializing in the small rural golf clubhouses that were common in Virginia's Tidewater area. It appeared completely ordinary, as did all of the buildings inside the fences of Camp Peary, but of course none were. All were positioned in a way that screened them from overhead surveillance satellites, what the United States and the Soviet Union called "national technical means" in their preferred Cold War jargon, and all had interior shielding preventing the emission of any sort of telltale electronic signature from the numerous computers inside. And most, like Building 121, were somewhat like icebergs—most if it was beneath the surface and unseen.

After navigating his way to Building 121's familiar parking area, the man parked the Fairlane in a slot marked for visitors. He had to jerk on the latch of the Ford's old glove compartment a couple of times before it reluctantly popped open, allowing him to withdraw a somewhat yellowed parking permit. He tossed it onto the windshield, grabbed his envelope, stepped from the car, and circled back to the trunk. Opening it, he glanced at the mess scattered around the trunk's spare tire, a random collection of junk, including old clothes that had never quite made it to Goodwill, some unopened oil cans—as the old vehicle was always burning oil and its owner never seemed to want to take it to a repair shop, and an eighteen-inch cube of a cardboard box that he reached in to retrieve. He laid the folder on top of the box, balanced both on his knee, closed the trunk, and headed toward the front door of Building 121.

Reaching the building's entrance, he struggled a bit to balance his load but finally succeeded in pushing the small doorbell after two failed jabs with his right index finger. He waited. He always had to. After a few seconds, the door was pushed open by a young woman who served as the receptionist—the man was sure she had other duties, but this was the only role he had ever actually seen her perform. "Thank you," he said as he pushed on by. The young woman smiled and said nothing. Camp Peary was just not the sort of place where people engaged in conversation. She motioned for him to head back down the hallway that extended before them, and the man did so with only a slight nod of the head. About twenty feet ahead was an elevator, and upon reaching it, he pushed the only button.

The doors slid open quickly and quietly. He stepped inside and again struggled to balance the box with his free hand while trying to push the button for the third floor. That would be the third floor down. It was a conventional elevator with a conventional button pad, but for this building, one pushed buttons going up to go down—to the lower levels. He hit the "3" on the third try; the doors closed, and he felt the slight jolt and heard the hum as the elevator started its descent. It was a quick trip. The doors opened, and the old man looked out upon the familiar large room he had seen many times before.

The third lower level of Building 121 was a very large lab that had open space about the size of a football field. Bright neon lights hung overhead, and technicians strolled leisurely around in white lab coats, focusing on their immediate projects. The large space was bright, quiet, sterile, and almost antiseptic. The room was laid out with three long aisles, each delineated by rows of worktables that had all sorts of contraptions in various stages of assembly and disassembly scattered across them. The man had no idea what the vast majority of these little projects were or what purpose they could possibly serve, but he knew not to ask. Everything there was strictly "NTK," acronynese for "need to know."

The man walked to his right a few steps and headed down the long aisle closest to the wall. No one seemed to pay much attention to him. They knew him and had seen him on other occasions coming and going—when needed. A few smiled and nodded, one waved, but as always, words remained rare. The visitor walked slowly down the aisle with his box awkwardly tucked under his left arm until he saw the man he was looking for, the young one with the red hair, quickly flipping through a set of blueprints. The older man knew the younger one well. He had taught him in class a few years ago and knew him as Larry Thomas. Given their relationship now, he had concluded that was not actually his name, but the two of them used it anyway. Seeing his former teacher approaching, the younger man looked up at him, smiling.

"Professor Ames, thank you for coming by. How have you been?"

"Fine, Larry. And you?"

"Very well. Always busy…which is good. And always working on interesting little projects, which is even better. There's never a dull day or even a dull moment down here."

"Great to hear," the professor responded, certain that this was as much small chatter as they would likely exchange. "I have what you asked for…I think. I have to admit I haven't had time to test it thoroughly, given the short notice and quick response needed, but I'm pretty confident it'll meet your needs." The professor scooted the box onto Larry's worktable and pulled open the top flaps. He reached inside and pulled out a small compact structure covered with a rough, dark-gray coating and having a small hole in one corner. Larry pushed it to the center of the table and reached across to the other side, grabbing a tape measure.

"Let's see," the younger man said as he hooked the tooth of the tape measure to a corner and pulled the tape to the other side. He checked the width and wrote down the dimensions on a small pad of paper lying nearby. He then measured the length of the structure, followed by its depth, again taking note of the measurements in metric rather than English units. "Seems to be about right, twenty-seven centimeters by nineteen by eleven. How does it come apart?"

The old professor reached over to the boxlike structure, dug his fingernails into a corner, and gave a tug. The top of the gray box lifted apart, exposing an interior that was also covered with the same gray coating. "Pretty simple, as you see. This is really not that complex. And as you note, there is some shaping along the cut line between the top and bottom providing a small lip, which will provide a sufficient seal to maintain thermal integrity."

"What is the thermal integrity?"

Professor Ames let out a slight sigh. "Well, as I said, with the short time to construct it, I haven't had the chance to test it as thoroughly as I'd like, but the material I used and the gray coating you see here on both the inside and outside come from a new composite compound we've been working on, the latest in ceramic engineering. No one else has it."

"So what heat differential should we expect?"

"Much more than you need. My earlier work with the material in my lab has shown that, when coated—as I have with this one, the differential between the inside and the outside can be as high as four hundred degrees?"

"Celsius?"

"No, Fahrenheit. I assumed you meant Fahrenheit when we discussed this."

"Well, it's irrelevant. Four hundred Fahrenheit is more than enough. I don't think we really need more than 150 degrees, so this should more than meet that. And you have the measurements down just as we asked. Are these the tubes we discussed?" Larry reached into the box and withdrew several bundles of tubes that were tied together.

"Yes, that's them," the professor replied, grabbing one of the bundles himself. "They just slip together—snugly—and provide the same sort of thermal differential. When you put them together, you have about twenty-five meters of tubing, but the material and coating make it a bit heavy so unless you brace it somehow, it won't stand up on its own. Of course, if you want to lay the tubing down, that won't matter."

"This is fine," Larry quickly answered. "We'll have the bracing needed. And we've made some more tubing that fits into the top well beyond the point where we are concerned about the thermal protection. But you're sure about the four hundred degrees?"

"Well, as I said…I'm not sure without testing it, as I would have liked, but I'm pretty certain we're talking about a variance of no more than twenty-five degrees, which should be well within tolerance of what you said you needed."

Larry smiled. He was satisfied. Professor Ames was one of the most accomplished ceramic engineers in the country. He had spent many years at Alfred College in western New York, where he was a legend among many of the ceramic engineers from DuPont and Corning. At Larry's request, the Agency had arranged to have the College of William and Mary offer him tenure and move him to Williamsburg, with a significant salary increase, most of which was provided by the CIA comptroller in Langley. It was best to have him close to Building 121 and Camp Peary, specifically for jobs such as this one and a wide variety of others. Ames didn't really look the part, but he was quite the traditional mad scientist.

Larry glanced at Ames again, giving him the smile of a satisfied customer. "Thank you, Professor. I think this will work perfectly well given the specs. What is this material being designed for anyway? I'm sure you had it available on such short notice because you are thinking of some commercial use."

"I am," Ames answered, looking around the room to see if anyone was listening to the discussion, momentarily forgetting where he actually was. "I think this material has enormous potential for coating buildings—walls and structural members. With the right density of application, I believe you can have up to perhaps 750 degrees of thermal differentiation, meaning that if a building were on fire and if the emergency stairwells had this as a coating, if the fire was burning at 500 degrees, people running down the stairs inside the stairwell wouldn't feel a thing. Moreover, if the structural members were coated with it, they should be able to maintain their tensile integrity long enough, under even the worst of circumstances, for the fire department to arrive. That would prevent building collapse—it's very exciting. Plus, it should do the same on ships, which means a navy destroyer, if hit by a missile, could maintain enough structural integrity to allow the crew to escape. There have been materials in the past that do that, but they were too heavy when applied and too expensive to be economical. This material is both light and inexpensive."

"Wow," Larry replied, truly impressed. "Well, I think it will meet our needs. Thanks for your quick response, as always."

Professor Ames recognized that this was his cue to leave. He had been asked to provide a product; he had, it was appreciated, so this little tasker was finished. Although he was dying to know what this particular, simple product was to be used for, he also knew asking would neither be appreciated nor rewarded with a reply. He gave Larry a semi-military salute and turned to depart. Larry smiled and returned the semi-salute, his salute looking more like that of Boy Scout than a soldier, which made sense, as he had once been a Boy Scout but never a soldier. He watched as Professor Ames walked back toward the elevator, pushed the button, and stepped inside as the doors opened. They closed, and he was gone as quietly as he had arrived.

"Chris!" Larry called to a young woman with flowing auburn hair who was at a worktable three down from his. She nodded, waved a finger that she would be there momentarily, picked up a plastic basket from beneath her table, and carried it over to Larry's table. "Let's be sure it fits," Larry instructed, motioning for Chris to lift a metallic box from the basket.

Chris grabbed the gray metal box with clusters of small instrumentation nodes visible on three of its four sides, lifted it from the plastic basket, and held it above the open box Professor Ames had constructed. She gently slipped it down inside. It fit perfectly.

"Looks good to me," Chris said, smiling at Larry, on whom she had developed a serious crush since coming to work in Building 121 two years before.

Larry leaned in close to give their project a closer inspection. "Well, all things considered, the thermal box was the easy part. The big question is will your device work? It's a lot more complicated"

"It'll work, Larry," Chris replied, trying to look as admiring as possible. "I guarantee that. The bigger question is can we teach anyone how to use it when it does?"

## The Amtrak Train to Washington

The sun was disappearing behind the trees intermittently bordering the western edge of the Amtrak tracks heading to Washington. Carter reached up and pulled down the window shade by the seats he and Kath had occupied. The combination of the sunlight from an autumn sun, a moving train, telephone and power poles, and the increasingly barren trees of the early fall made the lighting inside their passenger car resemble that of a strobe light or a rotating mirror-ball at a disco. In those settings, flashing lights could be entertaining, but in the passenger car of a train, they were highly annoying.

There was no one seated around them in any direction, and the car itself was half empty, perhaps an indication of the declining popularity of Amtrak. Regardless, this gave Carter and Kath some needed privacy, and they had spent the past hour reviewing their meeting with Cardinal Krol. They had been surprised and satisfied with the outcome; it had exceeded their expectations in about every possible way. The question now was: how did they operationalize it? Carter wanted details, any kind of details, but Kath simply didn't have them…not yet.

"Look, Carter," she said, turning to her inquisitive companion, "the operational part of this is still sketchy. Our people in operations are working on it. This is truly going to be an effort constructed on the fly—with many variables and many players, many of them having bit parts, some of them assets that we've never used…at least so far as I know. But this is what we do. This is how we do it. We're not like the army, you know."

Carter clasped his hands together in front of his face and slowly lowered his chin onto them before cutting his eyes to Kath and giving her a skeptical look. The utter vagueness of it all made him very uneasy. "Look, Katherine, at heart, I'm still an army guy. For better or worse… I'll probably always be an army guy. Our operations are conducted by trained units stocked with disciplined soldiers, each of whom plays on the same team, knows his assigned role, and has a specialty learned in a structured, controlled manner. We have what we call the five-paragraph operations order that covers everything from soup to nuts. Everybody reads it and understands it. It's the sheet music we're all on. What you're telling me is that the Agency, by contrast, is a gathering of cats and dogs coming from many places, some well-known and trusted, others having murky backgrounds, and with loyalties that might not be fully known. There is no operations order for everyone to read, much less one that has a structured format. So, this is a very different beast for me, and if I'm going to be a part of it and held accountable for it by some very senior people…I want to know what we're doing, how we're doing it, and who's doing it. That's all I'm asking."

In truth, Kath was more sympathetic to Carter's concerns than she was revealing, but at this point in her career, she was now a "company girl," and since it was her agency doing the work and pulling this effort together, she was determined to put a positive spin on it. And she was convinced the chances of success were good; she had seen it work before, although usually from the safe distance of the headquarters complex at Langley. She glanced back up at the shade next to the seat. "Could you pull that down a little further, Carter. I still feel a bit like I'm living beneath an airport beacon."

Carter reached across her and pulled the shade lower, an effort that gave him a chance to enjoy her beautiful eyes as the sun reflected in them. "How's that?"

"That's great," she replied, leaning back in her seat and adjusting her body into it, trying to relax a bit after what had become a very long day. "How about we change the topic for now, Carter. I've told you about all I know about what we're doing. I understand your concerns, and I'll know more tomorrow once I get briefed by the director of operations. But for now, I've told you about all I can. Or would you prefer I simply make stuff up so you can relax a bit?"

Carter stared at his CIA companion for a moment. He had decided that staring at her was a good investment of time, but he had also learned not to let it linger too long. "You said change the topic. Change it to what?"

"Well, Major," Kath answered with a sly smile, "since we are going to be working together on this thing for a couple of weeks, I thought it might be useful to learn a little bit about each other. So what can you tell me about yourself?"

Carter smirked as his reply was going to be an obvious one. "Are you suggesting to me that the CIA doesn't have a file on me and that you did *not* read any of it before ambushing me in St. Matthew's?"

"Goodness," Kath answered, laughing lightly. "Of course we have a file. And of course I read it. But I guess out of deference to the White House and the NSC staff, it was quite sterile. Pretty complete on data, but fully devoid of details. So, how about giving me some details? I know the basics about you, but that's about all."

"What basics?"

"Well, I know you were born in Lexington, Kentucky, in 1946. Your father was a professor of history at the University of Kentucky. You graduated from West Point in 1968 and went to get a graduate degree almost immediately thereafter—which I found odd. And I found it even odder that there was no mention of where you went to earn it. So, we have about an hour before we get to Union Station; how about filling in the blanks for me."

Carter leaned back in his seat so that their faces were level with one another and smiled. "OK. Fair enough…I guess. But if I fill in some blanks for you, I expect you'll do the same for me…with equal detail. We don't keep personnel files at the NSC, and all I really know about you is that you wrote the first report that came over to the White House about the pope's unexpected death. So, I'll expect at least as much as I give… and, I'll expect it to be accurate. None of the usual Agency false names, fake IDs, cover stories, phony résumés, and all that other sort of stuff you people are famous for. Deal?"

Kath grinned and nodded her head. "Sure. It's a deal. But you go first."

"OK," Carter began, squirming himself a bit deeper into his own seat. He genuinely disliked talking about himself. "As you said, I was born in Lexington and my father was a professor of Middle-Eastern history at UK. We lived very near the center of town in a nice old duplex just down the street from Henry Clay's home, Ashland—which is a great old house, by the way. My mother taught music at Henry Clay High School, which was only a mile or so from our home, and that's where I went to high school."

"What was your major interest in high school?"

"Basketball. I lettered all three of my varsity years. And we went to the state basketball championship when I was a senior. We didn't win it, lost in the quarterfinals to Breathitt County, a school way out in Eastern Kentucky, the poor coal area of the state. But just making it was huge. You have no idea how big the state high school basketball tournament is in Kentucky! I mean—*big*!"

Kath's face lit up at the mention of basketball. "I love basketball and follow it closely. You must have been happy when the Wildcats won the championship last April. It had been a long wait."

"I was thrilled. It had been twenty years since Adolph Rupp last won it for UK. But Duke really made it a great game—94–88! They made the Cats hustle until the final buzzer. I was glad when it was over. As, I'm sure, Coach Hall was."

Kath turned slightly in her chair, angling herself a bit more toward Carter. "So, if you were growing up in Lexington and playing on a pretty good high school team, why didn't you go to Kentucky and play for Coach Rupp?"

"That's pretty simple," Carter replied with a chuckle and toss of his head. "I wasn't good enough. My coach at Henry Clay used to say I was fast…but not quick. And I was physically in an awkward spot: too tall to be a guard but too small and skinny to be what they now call a 'power forward.' But I did have a good, reliable jump shot from about twenty-five feet, better on the left side of the hoop than the right. And I was disciplined enough to follow the shot so I got a lot of put-backs and trash baskets. And if you fouled me, I was over ninety percent from the line. Coaches love that. Free throws equal free points. But, bottom line, I only got one offer—from Army."

"Army. Really? Was there some military connection in your family?"

"Absolutely none. But I had some good games in the state tourney, and that attracted the attention of the Army assistant coach handling recruiting for the Midwest area. He felt I'd fit into the style of play being developed at Army…a style that was the only way he saw where they could be competitive: aggressive defense and high-percentage shots. He believed I was fast enough for his defensive scheme, as big as anyone they were likely to bring in given the academy's height restrictions, and he liked my high-percentage jump shot. He convinced my parents and then me, so I went to West Point."

"Did it work out, the basketball, I mean?"

"Pretty well. We were 20–5 my senior year, led the nation in defense, and got invited to the NIT. We lost in the first round to Notre Dame sixty-two to fifty-eight but held them well below their scoring average… and I made a couple of key baskets that kept us in it down the stretch."

"Goodness! Really! Army was 20-5! In all honesty, I never paid much attention to the East Coast schools. But I was a huge fan of Wooden and the UCLA Bruins back then. Is the Army coach who recruited you still there?"

Carter grinned widely. "No, he moved on. If you can be successful at Army people start knocking on your door. He went back to the Midwest. He's head coach at Indiana now."

Kath's head snapped strongly in Carter's direction, and her mouth dropped open. "Oh, my God!" she exclaimed. "You played for Bobby Knight! He was the Army coach back then! I completely forgot. Was he as crazy then as he is now?"

Carter laughed. "Oh, he's pretty tame now! Back then, he was something like twenty-five years old and determined to make a name for himself. Those little temper outbursts you see today are tame compared to what we went through. If you missed an open twenty-footer, you had better plan on going back to the other team's bench during the next time-out."

"Who coaches Army now?" Kath asked, smiling and chuckling at Carter's comment about a missed shot.

"A fellow I played with named Mike Krzyzewski, class of sixty-nine. He was a pretty good point guard and captained the team the year after I graduated. He assisted Knight at Indiana a few years back, left the army, and then went back to the academy where he's had some good success... like Coach Knight. I'm sure one of the big schools will discover him one of these days...like they did Knight." Carter paused for a few moments. "You seem to have a great interest in basketball, Kath. Did you have brothers who played?"

"No brothers," Kath answered. "I played women's basketball at Stanford. As I said, I'm a West Coast girl...from LA."

Carter sat up a bit straighter in his seat. "Really! You played basketball at Stanford! Well, I wish I had known that when I was getting my graduate degree across the bay at Cal."

Now it was Kath's turn to straighten up further in her seat. "You got your graduate degree at Cal? Seriously? Cal! A guy from West Point at Cal Berkeley! How and why did you wind up there?"

Carter laughed, understanding both the surprise and the irony. "Well, Katherine, I always wanted to experience the West Coast. I had, of course, heard a lot about it—even in Lexington. *Especially* in Lexington as Wooden and UCLA became such a rival basketball powerhouse. But I had never been there. I graduated high enough in my academy class that I had the option to go to grad school right away. It seemed too good a deal to pass up, especially since the alternative was an immediate tour in Vietnam. It looked like a sanity test to me. So I opted for grad school, applied to Cal, and then went to Ft. Benning for Airborne and Ranger schools, followed by the infantry officers' course. While at the course, I got my acceptance, so after the first of the year in sixty-nine, I found myself at Berkeley studying international relations, and avoiding the various—and numerous—antiwar demonstrations. And don't try to tell me the Agency knew nothing about any of that."

Kath mischievously hunched her shoulders. "Well, I don't know if the Agency knows anything about it, but I certainly didn't. Really...I decided not to read your complete file, as it seemed to me that'd be a bit intrusive given we were going to work together on this assignment. I figured we'd have some time together, such as this, and it seemed it would be easier if we got to know each other personally rather than by reading files. Don't you agree?"

Carter nodded his head.

"But I'm curious," Kath continued. "How did you avoid getting involved in the daily confrontations about the war? Back then, especially after the Tet Offensive in early sixty-eight, Berkeley was in a constant state of antiwar turmoil. Or, by that point, were you against the war as well?"

"Well, while I was at Berkeley, my views began to change, as it became apparent that we simply didn't have the national will or the time needed to win. As for avoiding confrontations, that part was easy. I grew my hair longer, grew a beard, and wore jeans and sandals to class."

"The army let you do that?"

"Not only let me do it, they encouraged those of us studying at civilian universities to do it. It was a form of academic camouflage. I don't think more than a handful of those I attended class with ever had any idea who I was or who was paying my tuition. And as I said, after four years with Bobby Knight, riots and tear gas where far from intimidating." Carter paused for a moment, deciding it was time to switch the topic to Katherine. "Anyway, enough about me. So, how about you, Katherine?"

"Well," Katherine began, slowly drawing out the *well*.

Carter shook his head and jumped back in. "OK, don't try the old 'there's really not much to tell' ruse. Anyone from LA, who played women's b-ball at Stanford, and now works at Langley for the nation's spy agency will inevitably have an interesting story to tell."

Katherine raised her hand to cover the smile slowly sweeping over her face. "Well, Carter," she began again, "actually, as much as I hate to say it and as unlikely as you are to believe it, I think you have it pretty well summarized. With one exception."

"And what would be the exception?"

"The exception is that I was somewhat bred for this work. Both my parents were with the CIA. We lived in LA because they were both Asia operatives. Dad was more on the operational side; Mom was like me, an analyst. She did a lot of work on Indochina, and I can tell you, were she seated here with us, I bet she would agree with you a hundred percent about Vietnam. She felt, still does, it was a slow-motion train wreck—although maybe I shouldn't use that analogy while we're on a train. Dad had many interesting assignments, I'm sure…Even now, he only ever talks about a few of them. I know in World War II he had a role to play with the OSS in getting the Doolittle raiders out of China after their famous thirty seconds over Tokyo."

"Really! Wow!" Carter exclaimed, louder than he meant to, causing him to glance quickly around the car to see if anyone had noticed them. No one had. "I think the Doolittle raid was probably the most consciously courageous act by any group of men in the army's history," Carter added with a smile.

"I thought they were air force," Kath responded. "Wasn't Doolittle an air force general?"

"Later in life. But in 1942, there was no air force, so he and his seventy-nine men were army air corps."

"OK, they were army," Kath conceded. "But Dad had some role in setting up their escape from China. And he did many other things in Asia after the war, although I couldn't tell you much about any of them. Right after the war, he met Mom at UCLA where she was a student, they got married, and I came along in late 1950. He had been in China just before the communist takeover in 1949, again, doing something—I'm not exactly sure what. Certainly with the Nationalists, whatever it was. I know he met General Marshall several times. But, given the turmoil in Asia, especially after the Korean War broke out, we stayed in LA except for a brief two-year tour in Saigon in the late 1950s. I went to a Catholic school there where I met many of the children of the South Vietnamese Catholic community—I often wonder what happened to many of them. We came back to LA after that tour and never left. Dad worked from home, so to speak, and Mom did some teaching at UCLA, so it was a natural for me to study international relations…like you. Although, like most young women, I wanted to get out of the house so I applied to Stanford."

"So, is that how you got into the CIA?" Carter was unaware that the CIA had such family traditions and connections. They were quite common and clearly natural between West Point and the army, where many of his classmates had been "army brats," but he had never considered that similar lineages might be reflected in other government agencies.

"Basically, yes," Kath answered softly. "The Agency has recruiters, and one of them approached me. Dad probably set it up, but he'll never admit it. Anyway, I knew it could be fascinating work. Demanding work, of course, and sometimes dangerous, but always fascinating."

"And the basketball? How did you get into basketball?"

"Come on, Carter! We lived just off campus in Westwood. The Wizard of Westwood was in full flower back then. It was so exciting. Dad and I went to the UCLA varsity–freshman game the year Alcindor was a freshman. The frosh won by about twenty points! Imagine, the UCLA varsity were the top-ranked team in the country, and they were the second best team on campus. We were all basketball nuts! Sound familiar? Maybe a little like Lexington? Women's basketball was a true backwater then, but my high school had a team, so I played, and Stanford had a team. So, I went there, played ball, and—like you—lettered all three varsity years."

"Are your parents still living in LA?"

"They are. Been in the same house for about twenty years."

"And you've been with the Agency how long?"

"A bit over six years…nearly all of it at Langley after finishing the course at the farm. But back to you. What did you do after Cal?"

Carter grimaced slightly. "Well, about the time I finished the master's, I went for my annual physical and they discovered I had developed a form of adult asthma. It was severe enough there was a treatment but no fix, so I couldn't continue as an infantry officer and certainly couldn't go to Vietnam."

"That bother you?"

"Not really. But it did cause a little friction with some of my academy classmates. I think a few, especially those who had pulled a tour over there, were a bit suspicious about a fellow who had spent two years at Cal and was then excused from the war. But I worked it out with most of them—at least I think I did. So, the army had me stay on at Cal another year while they decided what to do with me. I applied to be reclassified—as the army calls it—from infantry to intelligence. It was surprising how long it took to make that happen, but while the personnel bureaucracy worked, I got most of the course work done on a PhD."

"Have you finished it? Are you also Doctor Carter?"

"Nope. Haven't even started the dissertation. Haven't even decided what to do it on, but I'm sure it will involve nuclear issues and SALT."

"The Strategic Arms Limitation Treaty? That SALT?"

"That's the one," Carter answered, enjoying the chance to talk with someone who had the security clearances that allowed him to discuss his work and his doctoral topic. "So, in seventy-one, I was assigned to West Point as an instructor in the Department of Social Sciences, which was a very fun tour."

Kath's eyebrows arched a bit, at least the left one did. Carter had noticed that although her eyes were like Elizabeth Taylor's, her eyebrows were those of Vivian Leigh, and it was a wonderful combination. "Is that the 'Sosh' Department?" Kath asked. "That's a pretty famous incubator of army leaders. Goodness, we have several key people in the Agency from the Sosh Department."

"Yeah, that's it," Carter replied with a smile, once again pleased with Kath's scope of awareness. "I stayed, became a member of the permanent faculty, helped Coach K a bit with the basketball team, enjoyed it thoroughly, then I got a call one day from General Scowcroft who asked me to come to Washington for a 'discussion.' He was a Sosh alum and felt it would be useful to have some continuity regarding SALT between the

Ford and Carter administrations, said he had recommended me to Dr. Brzezinski. So, here I am." Carter paused for a moment before changing the subject. "You know, Kath, despite my best efforts, it still seems like you learned more about me than I did about you."

Kath looked away, again arching the left eyebrow. "We're approaching Union Station, so more about me will have to wait," she replied. "Anyway, all things considered, it seems there is more to be told about you. We've certainly traveled different roads, but we're evidently on the same one now."

"And, for the moment at least," Carter said, grinning at what he felt was certain to be a clever comment, "all roads lead to Rome."

Kath smiled and nodded her head. "Yeah, I guess they do," she replied, as the train squeaked to a stop inside the station. "And tomorrow that's exactly where we're going."

CHAPTER 8

## Tuesday, October 3, 1978
## Fiumicino Airport—Rome

● ● ●

It was slightly past 8:00 a.m. when Pan American Airways Flight Number 44 touched down in Rome. It was a direct flight from Philadelphia, and Cardinal John Krol had managed to sleep most of the way. He was traveling alone, as he saw no need to bring a young priest as an aide, and he knew the Vatican would assign to him one of the young American seminarians studying in Rome for the priesthood. In August, he had brought along his own secretary, as much for educational as administrative purposes. But since his young priest had already seen one conclave, Krol did not feel observing another a mere six weeks later was worth the expense.

The plane quickly taxied to the terminal. Being an early arriving flight, there wasn't much air traffic and nearly all the parking spaces on the tarmac were empty. For Krol, the plane had hardly slowed down before it came to an abrupt stop in front of Fiumicino's modern terminal building, one he had frequented many times when making this familiar trip.

Because it would be a grueling couple of weeks, he had considered booking a first-class ticket but decided to economize and book coach. He got a small perk, however, as when he checked in, Pan Am had upgraded him at no charge, a courtesy he greatly appreciated, knowing he would need the sleep. Seated at the front of the plane, he saw the door open, and the first person who stepped through was obviously his young seminarian host. They immediately made eye contact, and Krol offered a smiling nod of recognition. "Cardinal Krol, my name is Albert Pierce, and I'll be your assistant and guide while you're here in Rome. There is a car at the bottom of the ramp. If you'll come with me, Eminence, we'll get you to the Vatican. I'm sure you must be quite tired."

"Thank you, Albert. I appreciate your coming to get me. What about my bags?"

"They are being taken care of, Your Eminence. We're going to the Vatican first so you can be welcomed by Cardinal Villot, who will discuss details of the Holy Father's funeral Mass tomorrow; then we'll get you to your room at the American Catholic Conference. I understand you're staying there until the conclave begins, correct?"

Krol nodded, pleased that he would sleep well for at least a week before he had to endure Villot's cots. He stood up to retrieve his small flight bag from overhead, but the eager young seminarian beat him to it. Meanwhile the other passengers in first class remained seated, offering silent respect to the cardinal, aware of the reason he was on the plane with them. Krol turned and looked at them before stepping toward the door, raised his hand in a sign of blessing, and then crossed himself. The majority of those who saw him also made the sign of the cross and then broke into polite applause, another gesture of respect for the unique responsibility they knew their fellow traveler bore.

Krol and Pierce bounded down the mobile steps, jumped into the backseat of the car, and headed off to Rome. It was about an hour's drive down a broad *Autostrada*, a highway similar to an American interstate, but as was the European style, one that abruptly ended on the city's edge, dumping all vehicles straight into Rome's congested and contorted streets, which were already alive with morning traffic. Pierce offered only the barest of details to the cardinal, and it was obvious to Krol that he had been instructed to let Villot do the talking when they arrived at his Vatican office. So, for most of the trip, they simply sat in silence, Krol staring out the window deep in thought, and Pierce wondering what those thoughts were.

Their driver obviously knew how to deal with the infamous Roman traffic, as they arrived at the Vatican much faster than Krol had expected, were waved through one of the wall openings by a Swiss

Guard, navigated through a couple of narrow internal streets, and came to a stop at the entrance to the Apostolic Palace outside Villot's offices. As they pulled up, another car was waiting, having itself just arrived. Krol looked through the windshield, saw its door open, and recognized the familiar face of an old friend stepping out of the rear seat. It was time to get on with business. Krol quickly exited from the rear seat of his car and stepped forward, holding up his hand in greeting.

"Cardinal Koenig…Franz! How are you? How good to see you…despite the circumstances."

Koenig turned toward the voice from behind him, his round face breaking into a soft smile. He walked over to Krol, and they embraced. "German or English?" Koenig asked in English.

"I guess English, since you asked in my mother tongue," Krol replied with a laugh. "And your Austrian English is superior to my Polish German."

Koenig tossed his head back in slight amusement. "I doubt that, John, but I appreciate the compliment." The two cardinals stepped through the doorway as the Swiss Guards on duty snapped to attention. "Well, here we are again, John. Another period of *Sede Vacante*, and another conclave. So soon. So tragic. I had not expected to ever do another. And I fear this time, it'll be more difficult than the last. Luciani's smile and demeanor were highly attractive in August. And what an instant global phenomenon he became! I don't see anyone with similar appeal…at the moment. But I hear that Siri and Benelli are already quietly making their cases."

"Who's told you that? I haven't heard from them…or anyone else."

"Of course you haven't, John. You're not old, and you're not European. So, Villot hasn't personally called you?"

"No."

"Me neither. But he included a handwritten note in my official notification asking that I play a role in trying to unite the 'necessary' forces, whatever that means. He said I have 'uncommon diplomatic and political skills,' as he put it."

"Well, Your Eminence, you do," Krol respectfully replied, turning his head and angling it toward Koenig's to ensure the Austrian could see how genuine and serious the comment was intended to be. "In those arenas, there is no one among those of us sharing this heavy responsibility who is as skilled." Krol fell silent briefly as they rounded a corner and started up the staircase toward Villot's office. "You know, Franz, you had some support in the last conclave. Perhaps you should be given some serious consideration yourself."

Koenig smiled, continuing to take the stairs with a slow, measured pace. "Forget about it, John. I am humbled by your suggestion and the deep friendship that lies behind it, but I'm not what is needed and not whom we seek."

"Why not, Your Eminence?" Krol replied, feeling that if he switched to the titular, it might somehow change Koenig's view.

"Many reasons, John…many reasons. First, I am not well liked in the curia. I have been as strongly opposed to abortion as anyone and quite vocal about it. Fought with the Austrian government over it. But I am also of the view that *Humanae Vitae* was a terrible mistake, even though I have been less vocal on that topic and always very subtle in public. It has placed a great burden on many good Catholic couples, forcing them to choose between being responsible parents or being observant to the teachings of the church. They shouldn't have to make such a choice, but many have made it…and quietly broken with the church. The church mustn't place itself in such a position. I believe Luciani had the same view." Koenig paused briefly to catch his breath on the stairs before continuing. "But more important, John, I am seventy-three years old. That is too old. After the death of the Holy Father, we clearly want someone younger. I have never liked the idea of 'interim' or 'transitional' leadership, and anyone of my age is certain to be seen in that light. Besides, to put it quite frankly, I don't believe I have the energy required. But, perhaps most importantly, I am not Italian, so there is considerable history stacked like bricks in the road for anyone who was not born in this beautiful—if undisciplined—country."

The cardinals shared a slight chuckle at the last comment. It was, of course, difficult for either of them to see modern Italy in any other way.

By then, they had arrived at the doors to Villot's office suite. Surprisingly, there were no guards stationed there, so Krol simply grabbed the door latch and stepped inside with Krol right behind him. As they did so, they found themselves face to face with both Cardinal Villot and Monsignor Sarac, who were discussing items detailed on a small notepad that Sarac held in his hand. As soon as Villot looked up, he immediately halted the dialogue with Sarac, turning his attention to the two cardinals. "Franz! John! How good to see you both," the camerlengo effused, as he walked across the office toward his guests, his hand outstretched toward Koenig. "Thank you for coming by to see me. I am sure you both must be tired after your journeys, especially you, John. Please come into my office so we can chat. I apologize that I only have a few minutes. So many details are still unresolved. And we are still severely shaken by these tragic events, as I am sure you recognize. Can I get you both some tea?"

Koenig and Krol followed Villot into his office, both nodding at the offer of tea. Villot motioned toward Sarac, who called down to the kitchen. Villot closed the door and moved to the large chair behind his desk while directing the visiting cardinals to the chairs facing it. Koenig slowly lowered himself into his seat, while the younger and more athletic Krol quickly occupied his. "I understand you have already spoken with Benelli and Siri," Koenig began, getting right to the point.

"I have," Villot replied.

"But you just sent me an official letter with a note. So why did the two of them get personal phone calls?"

"They are Italian and in the same time zone as Rome," Villot answered, uneasy at the direction Koenig was taking whatever it was.

"So am I," Koenig quickly countered. "In the same time zone, I mean. I think you realize I am not Italian. My accent always gives me away."

Villot relaxed, as did Krol. Koenig smiled and then continued, "But I am curious…as are others, why you contacted Benelli and Siri so quickly and so directly. You are not picking favorites, are you, Jean?"

Villot shook his head and scowled. He did not like being accused of favoritism, even by such a respected senior cardinal. "Of course not, Franz.

I don't know why you would say that. I'm just one vote, and like you, I am also not Italian—although I'm told my accent is hardly noticeable."

Koenig smiled and nodded. "That is true," he softly answered. "But perhaps that is because you have been here in Italy for a rather long time. Agree? Well, never mind. I apologize. Perhaps I am just getting old and a bit touchy."

Krol sat silently, observing this exchange. It was obvious to him what Koenig was doing. The wily old cardinal was lightly but firmly signaling that he was not interested in being considered for the papacy and simultaneously putting Villot on notice that the election should not be conducted in any way that played favorites or stacked the deck—especially in favor of an Italian. Krol admired the approach. Koenig's reputation for being a skilled diplomat and a worthy debating adversary was on full display. Krol had always admired Koenig, but never more than now. He was content to simply listen and learn while he contemplated the strategy for his own agenda.

"Your Eminences." The voice of Monsignor Sarac came from the door that he had quietly opened. "The tea is here." Sarac pushed the door open wide, revealing a nun carrying a tray with three cups and a pot of tea.

Villot came to his feet behind his desk. "Thank you, Petar." He motioned to the nun. "Please, come in, Sister." The nun walked into the room, carefully balancing the heavy tray. "Your Eminences, allow me to introduce Sister Elizabeth Cummings. She will be quite important for us all during the coming two weeks. Sister Cummings will be running the kitchen and preparing your food, which she assures me you will all find delicious."

Koenig remained in his chair, but Krol came to his feet. "Sister Cummings, it is a privilege to meet you, and allow me thank you in advance for taking on such a fundamentally impossible task."

Cummings nodded to the tall American cardinal. "It's an honor, Your Eminence. My task is insignificant in comparison to yours. I have heard many great things about you from family I have in Philadelphia."

Krol grinned broadly. "How wonderful, Sister. Let me have their names before I depart Rome, and I'll be sure and tell them we met. And the important role you had in the conclave!"

Sister Cummings smiled at Krol, poured the tea, placed the pot on the corner of Villot's desk, and quickly departed. She had just accomplished her major mission for the day.

## GENOA, ITALY

Monsignor Mario Grone gently cracked open and lightly tapped on the large, oaken door to his superior's office in the Cattedrale di San Lorenzo. He heard a firm reply from inside.

"Yes. Who is it?"

Grone cracked the door open and stepped inside, looking across the space covered by a worn oriental carpet that stretched to the desk where Cardinal Siri was bent over, reading one of the morning Genoese newspapers, his glasses perched on the end of his nose. Siri lowered the paper and looked up, his eyes asking his secretary why he had knocked. Grone cleared his throat. "Your Eminence, Gianni Licheri from *Gazzetta del Popolo* is here for the interview."

Siri leaned back in his large chair. "Very well, Mario. Have you briefed him on the ground rules that I requested for the interview? Does he have any issues with them? If he does, then no interview."

Grone nodded. "Yes, Eminence, I have gone over them with him once again. In fact, that has taken the better part of a half hour, which is why we are a bit behind schedule. And, yes, predictably, he is unhappy with your restrictions but says he will accept them."

"Very well," Siri replied, a smile of satisfaction on his face. "Bring him in and let's get on with it." Siri could see that Grone still had concerns. After their years together, they each read the other's mind and moods well. "Mario, do you have something you want to say?"

"Yes, I do, Eminence. Far be it from me to question your motives or your wisdom…That is not my intent. But are you sure this is a good idea? I mean, giving this interview at this moment? Are you sure about what you want to say? And are you fully confident that Licheri will follow our instructions on this? He is, after all, a reporter, and they are not known for always playing by the rules. They don't even follow their own rules, much less those of others. I'm most uncomfortable with this."

Siri lowered his gaze to the floor and reflected for a moment. Grone's reservations were not to be lightly dismissed. He raised good points. But the old Cardinal had set his mind on how he wanted to approach the days ahead, and besides, it was too late to change direction now. He had good reasons for wanting to have the interview with *Gazzetta del Popolo* and understood the risks, but he thought the benefits might be great and certainly worth the effort if he was right. He would be the senior cardinal elector in the conclave, and he was obviously a *papabili*. He knew what he wanted to do, and he was going to do it. He looked up at the young monsignor. "Mario, I appreciate your concerns. And I appreciate even more your willingness to share them with me. You show great courage and character, which is why you have the burdens of your position. But I have decided on my path, so please bring Mr. Licheri in."

Grone paused for a minute, debating whether he should offer additional reservations but decided it would be pointless. The old cardinal's mind was made up. And once it was, experience told Grone that nothing could change it. He turned and walked back through the office door and headed down the hall to the small reception area in front of his own desk. Licheri was sitting in the rickety chair where Grone had left him. He came to his feet as he saw Grone approach.

"Are we ready, Monsignor Grone?"

"Yes, all ready," Grone answered in a soft voice. "Please follow me."

The two of them walked back down the hallway, and Grone motioned for the reporter to step through the open door and into the Siri's office. The cardinal was standing in front of his desk, and Licheri quickly crossed the floor to kiss the ring on Siri's extended hand. The two of them then moved to the couch to the right of the desk, Licheri seating himself on one end after Siri had plopped into the other. Grone went to his usual chair to the right of the cardinal's desk and rotated it so he had an easy view of the couch.

"Thank you for coming by this early," Siri said, opening the conversation casually. "I assume Monsignor Grone has suggested a set of topics that you might want to discuss with me."

"Yes, he has, Your Eminence." Licheri reached into his small attaché case and removed his reporter's spiral notepad. "When are you leaving for Rome?" he asked, flipping to a blank page.

"Later this afternoon. Which is why I wanted to see you now before we depart. We will be very busy this afternoon, as you might imagine."

"Well, may I wish you a safe trip and God's guidance in the important deliberations to follow."

"Thank you, my son. So, shall we begin discussing the important matters facing the church?"

"Yes, certainly, Your Eminence. But I would like to start with a general question…well, actually a very specific question about the coming conclave. There is some discussion going around that perhaps the new pontiff might not be Italian. Do you see that as a possibility?"

Grone was horrified. This was not among the questions and topics he had discussed with Licheri. He was suddenly concerned that his enormous unease about this interview was well founded. He felt a slight chill as he saw Siri glance toward him with an expression of unhappiness. Perhaps the cardinal would just end the interview; perhaps now he was also concerned. But, no…Siri turned his gaze back to Licheri.

"All things are possible, my son. But some are not all that probable. And I would not see that outcome as probable. But I feel our time this morning would be better spent on important theological issues facing the church. Would you not prefer to discuss those?"

Licheri paused for a moment. Siri's reply and tone of voice made it clear to him that he had best stay within the bounds that Grone had described. "Of course, Your Eminence. There are some who say that the reforms of the Vatican Councils have had unfortunate, if unforeseen, outcomes. Do you think that the next pope might review how these reforms have impacted the church overall? Might it be time for another council to review the earlier councils and evaluate the impact of the reforms directed by Popes John XXIII and Paul VI?"

Siri looked over to Grone and smiled. This was the turf he wanted to leave footprints on. This was why he had wanted to have this interview. He turned his face back toward the reporter and began a lengthy, detailed reply, one that he had thoroughly practiced. As Siri spoke, Grone felt better, but not much.

## ANDREWS AIR FORCE BASE, MARYLAND

It was late afternoon at Andrews Air Force Base just south of Washington, DC, on the Maryland side of the Potomac River. A large C-137, the air force's version of the venerable Boeing 707, was parked on the tarmac outside the passenger terminal operated by the Eighty-Ninth Airlift Wing, the Special Air Missions organization charged with carrying the president and other senior government officials to meetings around the world. This particular C-137 was similar to the one used by the president as Air Force One. But aircraft on Special Air Missions only had the Air Force One call sign if the president was on board, and President Carter was not making this evening's trip to Rome. But, perhaps, the aircraft should have been given some notable call sign anyway, as his mother, Lillian Carter, was, heading the US delegation for the funeral of Pope John Paul.

The passenger terminal at Andrews was similar to those one would find at any small Midwestern airport, but there were no long jetways used to board the planes. At Andrews, it was done the old-fashioned way: you walked out on the tarmac, went to the designated plane, and walked up a mobile staircase that had been rolled to the fuselage door.

The crowd gathered in the Andrews VIP lounge heading to the funeral of Pope John Paul was rather large, but not as large as the same gathering six weeks earlier. Among those gathered this evening, in addition to the president's mother, were Senator Thomas Eagleton of Missouri, the Democrats' original vice presidential nominee in 1972;

Governor Ella Grasso of Connecticut; and Mayor Edward Koch of New York City. And, of course, each came with an assortment of aides and assistants, all scurrying around when not competing for one of the four telephones in the small open booths hung on a far wall.

Off by themselves in a far corner of the room stood Carter Caldwell and Katherine O'Connor, trying to look as inconspicuous as possible, which was a relatively easy task given the crowd they were with. Nobody paid them much attention, assuming they were merely junior aides to someone else—that is, everyone but the person Carter and Kath were standing with. His name was Bruce Harrison, and he was listed on the official manifest as an aide to Senator Eagleton, but in actuality, he was the deputy director for operations at CIA headquarters in Langley.

"Ladies and Gentlemen, may I have your attention, please?"

The room fell quiet, and all eyes turned toward the doorway where a young air force captain, dressed in his service blue uniform, had appeared. "Ladies and Gentlemen, if you'll kindly follow me, we'll move to the aircraft and prepare for departure." As the officer turned and headed out the terminal door, the conversations that had gone quiet immediately returned to their previous murmur level as people reached around to gather coats and carry-on bags and then, falling into line behind Miss Lillian, began filing through the door and out into the chilly autumn air.

Carter and Kath were near the rear of the entourage with Harrison. Bruce leaned over to them and offered a low-voiced observation. "Only in Washington can you expect that everyone will line up according to protocol and rank whether there are instructions to do so or not." The three of them shared a quiet laugh. It was so true. And the three of them knew their spot: at the end of the line. They smilingly took the place protocol suggested and headed directly out onto the tarmac and toward the mobile stairs.

Within ten minutes, everyone was on board and seated, the engines had spun to life, and the aircraft had taxied, accelerated down the runway, and lifted off, departing to the north and banking slowly to the right, heading to Rome. Kath, Carter, and Bruce settled into their own small corner in the rear of the aircraft's cabin, occupying three seats together near the galley. Bruce waited until the aircraft had crossed Maryland's Eastern Shore and was out over the Atlantic before reaching under his seat, pulling out a bulky worn briefcase, and lifting a thick manila folder from it. He looked at the young people seated with him, "OK, let's go over what we have and where we are on this…and before either one of you offers any judgments, remember, this is being done with minimal assets, minimal planning, and—in my view—minimal chance of a favorable outcome. But, given all of that, we're doing the best we can and this is what we've come up with. OK?"

Carter and Kath nodded. He was eager to see what Langley had concocted, and she was eager to see how he would react to it. Harrison lowered the seat tray, pulled out a pile of dog-eared notes, and continued, "First, no surprise to you, I'm sure, but we don't have extensive penetration of the Vatican. Crap! We've got more moles inside the Kremlin than the Vatican. Of course, we've tried hard to get inside the Kremlin and never seen any reason to bother with the Vatican. But we're not at ground zero either. And the two of you have made this thing…well, at least a little interesting. It's not a hopeless wild goose chase since you've recruited Cardinal Krol, in some way or another. We'll just have to see what he can do and what he's willing to do. But he's by far the senior mole, OK? All the others are low-level functionaries; they can pass messages and be observers, but I think there is only one we could expect to be operational."

"What does that mean?" Carter interrupted. "Being operational?"

"It means do something," Harrison answered rather coldly, almost dismissively.

"Like what?"

"Like blow something up, take somebody out, or set someone up so that someone else would take them out. That clear enough for you?"

Carter was liking Harrison less and less. But he also realized popularity was never the objective of anyone who worked operations at Langley. "Clear enough, Bruce. Sorry for the interruption. Go on."

"OK…moving right along—our assets inside the Vatican are low-level but well placed enough that they won't be suspected…hopefully! But we'll have to be careful not to expose them. We'll want them there after the conclave is over to give us some insights on whoever gets the nod and puts on the white robes. Now, we have some information from Moscow that Andropov and the KGB are apparently quite seriously worried about this thing, and have made some plans of their own. We don't really know what their plans are, but we are pretty sure they're the opposite of ours: we want a non-Italian pope, and they don't. What will they do? Who knows? How important is it to them? Who knows? But we do know they've sent a relatively senior operative from Lubyanka to direct whatever they're doing. I mention this just so everyone knows that we'll need to be on our toes. They play rough."

Harrison paused for a minute and sorted through his papers before pulling a smaller folder from inside his large manila file. "We have one technical device we'll be installing, which should give us some idea of how the voting is going when it starts. I think it's pretty damn clever—if we can make it work and have the right guy who takes the time to learn how to use it.

"Which brings me to the next item. We have a fellow who's a journalist covering the Vatican, been there for a few years now, who has excellent access to the Vatican Press Office…which seems a bit fucked up right now—excuse me, Kath, sorry—and he's comfortable with all the prestige media in Italy. We think we can get some, shall we say, unfavorable press coverage on any of the Italians who starts to show strength in the conclave. I liked Katherine's report. I don't think either Benelli or Siri have enough solid backing to win this thing, but we'll have to move quickly should one of them get close. Same thing with the other Italians who are believed to be contenders. What are their names? Yeah…Poletti and Colombo. We'll have to derail their trains as well if we sense they are picking up speed, and we'll likely only know that from Krol. So, we need to get him wired in so he can help us and at the same time make sure we cover his back. I have to believe the KGB has a mole who'll also be inside the Sistine Chapel, and I assume if they get desperate and concerned enough, they could arrange a convenient heart attack for someone. Hell, some are saying that's what happened to John Paul when he checked out early. I doubt it, but you never know with these guys."

"Gentlemen, ma'am." The three of them looked up at the young air force flight steward who had appeared from the galley. "We'll be serving dinner in a few minutes. We have a wonderful selection this evening from which you can choose: a filet mignon, an Alaskan halibut, and—since we're headed to Rome—a very good manicotti. All are good, but I'd really recommend the manicotti."

The meals were quickly ordered, with Carter being the only one willing to take the highly recommended manicotti. They ate quickly and quietly, and each finished with a cup of coffee, figuring they would have to delay sleeping for a while longer. After their trays were cleared, they returned to working on the details of the operation—such as they were.

"So this is it?" Carter asked, pointing to the rather thin stack of folders that were piled on Kath's lap between them. "I can't believe this is all we know and all we have to work with."

"Drop it, Caldwell," Harrison snapped back. "This whacko thing was your idea. Had we known the pope was going to die in his bed after a month on the job, we would have—perhaps—taken some steps to prepare. But, we didn't know, and we didn't prepare, and had we known we probably wouldn't have prepared anyway. The Vatican is the smallest 'country' on the planet, if you can even call it that, and we haven't had much interest in it. The pope has become a bit player on the world stage, at least in my view, and I doubt you'll find anyone in the Agency who really gives a shit about who he is—unless they are Catholics who go to church regularly, which I guess might include Miss O'Connor here, but certainly not many of the rest of us. So, get off my back, Caldwell. We'll do what we can, but don't expect any sort of a miracle. Personally, I don't expect the heavens to open up and announce to the cardinals they need to pick one of our guys! And truth be known, I don't think there's anyone of them we could call 'one of our guys' anyway!"

Carter glared back at Harrison. "So, you're just in this for what? A free trip to Rome for a few days?"

"I didn't say that, Caldwell. I said we'll see what we can do. We'll try. That's it. I'm doing what I've been ordered to do. But let's set expectations, OK? I don't expect we'll succeed, and you shouldn't either. Maybe I'm wrong. Maybe this will work. And if it does, we're all heroes. If it doesn't…well, no one thought it would work anyway. I said we'd try. That's all any of us can do."

Carter could see they were done with the discussion. He still had many questions, but he could tell Bruce had few answers. They'd just have to see where things went. Basically, it all hinged on Krol, and none of them knew what that really meant.

It was getting late, and they were out over the Atlantic. Army training dictated that "when you can eat, eat, and when you can sleep, sleep." He'd already eaten, so now it was time to execute the second part of that timeless guidance. Carter got up and moved to the aisle seat in the empty row directly across from them, allowing Bruce and Kath to stretch out a bit. Nonetheless, he felt it was something of a sacrifice, as he was beginning to enjoy being close to her, but they all had to get some rest. There was no doubt they would need it. He reached into the overhead space to grab a pillow and then pushed his long body into the reasonably comfortable seat, reclining it back as far as it would go and adjusting the pillow around his head, winding up with his eyes looking across the aisle at Kath. He was surprised but enormously pleased to see that she was looking back at him. They smiled and then dozed off.

## WEDNESDAY, OCTOBER 4, 1978
## OUTSIDE MOSCOW

It was very early in the morning, and Dimitry Zhukov had been waiting at a small military airfield outside of Moscow for over an hour. He was told to be here by 4:00 a.m. where a Soviet Air Force jet would be waiting to take him to Rome. The jet was painted in the colors of Aeroflot, the Soviet national airline, but the crew was military on this otherwise routine flight. It made this Rome run once a week and then continued on to other Western European capitals, carrying diplomats, sometimes their families, and the latest mail and other dispatches that were the life's blood of diplomacy—and, of course, espionage.

But when he arrived, Dimitry was informed the flight was being delayed for an hour, as there was an item being rushed to him from Lubyanka. That was over an hour ago, and Dimitry could see that his fellow passengers, some of whom he recognized as senior members of the Soviet foreign service, were increasingly unhappy, whispering among themselves about why they were being held up—because of something involving this unknown young official.

Dimitry took refuge in a hard plastic chair in an empty corner and tried to act nonchalant. There was no place to hide in the Spartan waiting area, which had the usual absence of style and overall crudeness common in all public buildings in Moscow, with the exceptions of the Kremlin, the Moscow subway, and—of course—Lubyanka. It was difficult to pass the time by simply reading a book, as the light fixtures were haphazardly placed around the room, many hung crookedly on the wall, with few having a full set of functioning light bulbs. The room itself was two-toned: half painted off white, the other half a dark beige, with the boundary between the two going right down the middle of one wall. The colors did not blend and like most such efforts in Moscow reflected what was available rather than what was preferable. The double doors at the far end of the room opening to the tarmac didn't close fully, and the floor beneath them was covered with muddy bootprints, partially absorbed by a jagged-edged piece of cardboard that had been tossed there, probably the remains of a discarded shipping box.

Glancing yet again at the front doors, Dimitry saw headlights shining on the glass as a black car pulled to a stop in front of the terminal. Its doors quickly opened, followed by the trunk, and soon a man in a long winter coat was headed into the lounge, carrying a briefcase. The whispering mostly stopped, except for that between a couple of the senior diplomats, who recognized the fellow carrying the briefcase as Sergei

Kornilov and who knew he was a senior official in the KGB. Kornilov paid none of them any attention. He knew they would be unhappy about this forced delay, and naturally he could care less, knowing that nothing would be said directly to him. He spied Zhukov seated off by himself and headed straight to him. Dimitry quickly came to his feet to greet his boss.

"Please sit down," Kornilov growled. "This will just take a minute. I have here a special briefcase I want you to carry to the embassy in Rome. There are some special contents inside, but none are of importance to you, so do not—under any circumstances—open it. *Ponimayete?* Understand?"

Zhukov nodded and grabbed the briefcase. It was brown, and seemed to be made of fine leather, but his eye quickly wandered to two small insignias embossed on the top. And the case seemed unusually heavy. His eyes looked up to Kornilov, who reached out and patted his young colleague on the shoulder. "As I said, Dimitry. Just deliver this to Viktor, our chief at the embassy, nothing else need be done."

Zhukov nodded again. "Understood, Sergei. I'll take it to Viktor. I know him."

"*Da!* We all know him. No great honor in that." With that, Kornilov stood up and briskly walked to the entrance where he had just arrived, jumped into his black limousine, and disappeared into the foggy night, leaving Dimitry with a roomful of unamused people, most of them staring daggers at him.

"Comrades, please walk out to our aircraft and we can depart." Dimitry looked over to the door where the aircraft's first officer had appeared and announced it was time to go. He appreciated the timing, as it shifted the angry eyes off him and onto the search for handbags and carry-on luggage. Still, no one dared to ask what was important enough about all this to keep them waiting for over an hour on a chilly October night.

Dimitry grabbed his own small bag and the just-delivered briefcase, and headed toward the door. He paused and looked back into the room. Everyone had coats on and personal effects in hand, but no one had moved toward the door. Dimitry was momentarily puzzled and looked around the room from person to person. It slowly dawned on him that they were all waiting for him to board first, even the senior diplomats. He turned and headed toward the door. A slight smile came to his face. It was his first realization that within the Soviet power structure, he had arrived. He was KGB. The others did not like that, but they understood what it meant. And suddenly, so did he.

## Near Altenberg, East Germany

Sergeant Pasha Petrov was underneath tank C-12, in the mud, with a socket wrench, trying to remove the bolts from a plate covering the engine oil drain. The T-72 was a crude contraption with a poorly designed and loosely engineered engine that burned a liter of oil for every ten liters of diesel fuel. This made refueling a challenge, as you had to add both fuel and oil. The road march yesterday had gone so long that the oil truck had never caught up to them, leaving C-12, along with the other still-operable tank in his platoon, belching blacker smoke than ever. His oil had fried, and he had to drain what was left out and replace it before they could continue.

"Sergeant Petrov!"

Pasha rolled his eyes upon hearing the always unwelcome voice of Captain Belikov. Looking from under the tank, he could see the officer's boots. He crawled through the mud to the rear of the tank and came to his feet, mud dripping from all over. "Yes, Comrade Captain."

Belikov glared at him. "Petrov, I am very displeased. You've already lost one tank in the river and perhaps another for not sufficiently refilling the oil reservoir. If C-12 is not repairable, you'll have a one-tank platoon. That is unacceptable."

Pasha was tempted to slug the officer, but he knew that would land him in jail—and his family in the street. He withstood the urge and chose his words carefully. "Captain, the lateral control on C-11 broke because—"

"Because you didn't check to see it was tight!" Belikov interrupted.

"No, because the connecting bolt sheared off," Pasha countered. "And as for my tank, I didn't add oil because the oil truck broke down and never made it to the refuel point."

"It was there when I went through!" Belikov snarled.

"Because you went through after I got there!" Pasha snapped, trying to control his temper. "When my platoon arrived, there was no oil truck."

Belikov's steely eyes fixed on Pasha for a few seconds. "I'll get oil for you," he said after a pause. "We'll need all our vehicles for our mission, so don't lose any more, *ponimayete*?"

"Understood, Captain." The two men continued their silent staredown, until Pasha ended it. "And when will you tell us what our mission is, Comrade Captain? The men are cold, tired, hungry…and don't understand why we are heading east."

"Why do you think we are heading east, Petrov?"

"Sir, please. We may not be officers, and we may not have maps, but we know where the sun rises in the morning. And some of the men have been to Altenberg. They know it's east of Weimar. It's been four days. When are you going to tell us why we're out here?"

"When you need to know," Belikov snapped and then slowly turned and walked away.

Pasha shook his head as he watched Belikov leave and then got back into the mud and crawled under C-12.

CHAPTER 9

# Wednesday, October 4, 1978
# Fiumicino Airport—Rome

● ● ●

U.S. AIR FORCE SPECIAL MISSION aircraft do not follow the procedures of the airlines. When landing, there are no general instructions to return seats and trays to the upright and stored positions. For one thing, given the long duration of trips such as the one between Washington and Rome, many people are asleep and it is best to let them rest as long as possible. For another, given the egos involved, the likelihood of getting the chairman of the House Appropriations Committee to pay any attention to an air force flight attendant was close to zero. So, why bother? Getting everyone into his or her seat was about all that could be reasonably expected. It was herding cats at its best.

Carter and Kath were awakened simultaneously when the wheels of the big plane hit the runway. The landing was a bit harder than normal, as a pesky crosswind had challenged the pilot, but it was still better than anything one would likely see on a commercial airliner. The pilots and copilots of the Eighty-Ninth Wing were among the very best in the world. They had to be.

"Good morning, Carter." Carter sat up in his seat and rubbed his eyes. He looked to his right to see Kath's smiling face, and he was surprised to see how perfect she looked after a long night sleeping in an airliner seat. Certainly she couldn't look that great right away. He decided she must have gone to the lavatory earlier and freshened up.

"Morning, Katherine. Sleep OK? Man, I went out like a light."

"Yeah, me too. I was talking with one of our liaison guys a while ago, and he said transportation will meet us at the bottom of the stairs. We're to get into the green Fiat van having an 'Embassy 9' placard in the windshield. It'll take our bags and us to the hotel to check in and freshen up. Then we're going to the embassy with Bruce to meet with the CIA station chief and some of the embassy staff—old Rome hands. They should have some more info for us."

Carter nodded. Suspicion confirmed. She had been up, wandering around, coordinating, and no doubt spending time in the lavatory. She was already "freshened up." And as she looked fabulous, it was time she had spent well. The plane came to a halt, and Carter looked out on the tarmac. A veritable convoy of vehicles was gathering around the plane, and he could see air force personnel setting up a guard perimeter. It was a clear morning, but he could tell from the dress of the ground crew that it was chilly. He wished he had brought a heavier coat, and as he looked toward the front of the plane, he could see that many others were pulling theirs on as they gathered their bags and other belongings, mainly briefcases. Well forward in the cabin he caught a glimpse of Miss Lillian, despite her advanced age already moving with the energy for which she was famous.

Everyone was getting set. They were on the clock. The official delegation had to get off the plane, be loaded into their transportation, taken to their hotels, and then to St. Peter's for the funeral Mass. Rome was nearly an hour's drive away, and between the airport, the hotels, and the Vatican lurked the ever-exciting Rome traffic. Carter hoped all would go well, as he could see through the plane's windows that *Carabinieri* vehicles of the Italian national police had joined the various vans and cars gathered around the plane. They were clearly getting an escort, which should speed things up considerably.

As he waited for the aisle to clear so that Kath, Bruce, and he could start making their way to the front of the plane, Carter's eyes glimpsed another airliner pulling in next to the C-137. He recognized it as a Soviet-built Ilyushin-62, and his two years of Russian at West Point allowed him to read the Cyrillic lettering running along the fuselage, *Aeroflot*. The question quickly entered and departed his mind as to whether the Soviets would have anyone at the funeral. As he moved to the front of the plane, he looked out the windows again and saw that a large gray bus had pulled alongside the ramp pushed up to the Ilyushin's door, and people were quickly deplaning. Carter stepped through the C-137's door and paused briefly on the top step of the stairs. He looked around at the scene below him, hoping his bags would indeed make it to the hotel, but natural interest drew his eyes back to the Ilyushin, where he noticed one of the Russians standing at the bottom of the steps, a dark briefcase in his right hand, and staring at the American plane, seemingly right at him. Their eyes met momentarily, and then the Russian jumped onto his bus, which sped away.

Carter did not think much of it. "I guess they're as curious about us as we are about them," he mused. He scurried down the stairs and headed toward the van with the "Embassy 9" placard in the windshield. Kath and Jack were right behind him.

## St. Peter's Square

Avery Dugan had spent most of the morning walking around St. Peter's square, taking in the scene created for the pope's funeral that afternoon, talking with those who had made their way to the Vatican, taking copious notes, and grabbing an occasional cappuccino at the little café on the square's western edge. He had worked for the *Christian Science Monitor* for over a decade, half of it here in Rome, an attractive assignment for someone fluent in Italian. His maternal grandmother was Italian, and he grew up speaking her native tongue at home.

Avery had always wanted to be a reporter and had been the editor of the school newspaper at Georgetown his senior year. He loved politics, and had thoroughly enjoyed learning his craft covering campus politics at Georgetown, especially the always exciting machinations of his class's president, a charismatic character from Arkansas named Bill Clinton. It was natural that he remained in DC after graduation, and he was thrilled to be offered a position with the *CSM*. If you liked politics, Washington was the big leagues, and if you were fascinated by personalities, Washington was overflowing with them. Avery had filed one of his first stories when the seventy-six-year-old chairman of the House Ways and Means Committee, Wilbur Mills, had been plucked from the Tidal Basin late one evening after falling in with his strip-club girlfriend.

Avery might have stayed in DC permanently, but he had good reasons for leaving. Sometimes it was best to just get away, to recognize that it might be best to simply go somewhere else and start over. He had a good reason to leave, and Rome was a great place for restoring a damaged spirit.

"Avery! Over here!" Dugan turned to see Rick Smith, his counterpart from the *New York Times*. Rick was trotting over to where Avery was leaning on one of the wooden barricades that had been placed at the edge of the square, doing the best he could to step through those slowly joining the swelling crowd. Avery took a sip from his latest cappuccino as he watched Rick pick his way toward him.

"Heck of a day, Avery," Smith said as he reached the barricade.

"Yeah, isn't it? I thought you had gone back to New York."

"I had, but when this came up they sent me right back. And I had great seats for the Jets game this week. I hear there're still questions about the circumstances of the pope's death. Heard anything?"

Avery slowly shook his head and pursed his lips. "Not really. I think it's just a bunch of talk by those who adore a conspiracy. These days, everybody wants to be Woodward and Bernstein. I think the big problem is that Villot has handled this whole thing like the imbecile he is."

"Is there anything you see as an interest story about the funeral?"

"Nah. The story is the funeral. Lillian Carter will represent the United States. Ed Koch will be here—so I'm sure he'll want to talk with you. No way he misses a chance to be quoted in the *Times*, now is there? Other than that, nothing much I see that's particularly newsworthy."

Rick had known Avery a long time. They had worked several stories together and had collaborated considerably when former Italian Prime Minister Aldo Moro was kidnapped and murdered six months earlier.

They had been nominated for a Pulitzer on that one, much to the delight of their respective editors. Rick had never known Avery to be devoid of angles to a story. He was hiding something.

"OK. So, it's just another papal funeral. They happen all the time, don't they? Hell, I've been to two in six weeks myself. So, let's talk about the conclave. What have you heard about who's next?"

"Haven't heard a thing."

"Oh whale crap! Come on, Avery. What gives? You aren't the sort of guy who sits in the middle of Rome with something like this going on and writes it off as just another boring day at the Vatican. What's eating you?"

Avery stared at the *Times* reporter. "Nothing. Nothing's eating me. Why would you think something's eating me?" Avery spotted a group of nuns walking toward the opening into the square. "Look, Rick. I need to go get more color on this. I'm going to go interview those nuns, see what they think about it. I'll catch you later." With that, Avery slapped Rick on the shoulder and walked away.

Smith shook his head as he watched him go. "Bullshit," he mumbled to himself, "something's eating him."

## SOVIET EMBASSY, VIA GAETA, ROME

Dimitry's Fiat sedan, flying small Soviet flags on the front fenders, pulled up in front of the Soviet embassy on Via Gaeta, the narrow street in central Rome where the building entrance hid behind a high fence topped with a stylish metal grate. As the Fiat approached the main entrance, the large gates were swung open by two Soviet security guards, who held them open just long enough to allow the car to enter the short driveway and then quickly closed them behind it. The car rolled to a stop, and the guard by the door stepped forward to jerk the rear passenger door open. Dimitry quickly stepped out and bounded up the steps, the large briefcase firmly clasped in his right hand.

He had spent considerable time here in the past and was familiar with the embassy layout. He entered the atrium on the main level and immediately climbed the stairs to the second floor, turned right, and headed down the hall to the last door on the left. Little had changed. Little ever did involving a Soviet bureaucracy, even one tucked away in a historic city well beyond the direct supervision of the Kremlin… and Lubyanka. Dimitry reached his destination, opened the door, and stepped inside. The room was relatively small, dominated by a single large desk on the right facing a smaller one on the left. A grim-faced official in an ill-fitted suit sat behind each, but Dimitry knew only one of them. He stepped across the room toward the large desk as the man behind it stood and extended his hand.

"Dimitry, how good to see you. Have you met Vladimir?"

Dimitry took the hand of Viktor Myshkin, the KGB chief in Rome and the coordinator of all KGB activities in the Mediterranean. "Good to see you, Viktor," he said, turning his head toward Vladimir, the man he had never met. "And good to meet you, Vladimir." He did not know Vladimir's last name. Myshkin had not revealed it, so Dimitry knew better than to ask. He stepped over to shake hands with this large, unknown presence, knowing that *Vladimir* was probably not really his name. But that was the KGB way when it came to names: don't reveal more than you have to, and don't ever reveal real names unless necessary.

Vladimir's hand was cold. He grunted in recognition rather than speaking, and Dimitry sensed he had just met a very frosted fish. "Give me the briefcase," the human iceberg directed upon ending the handshake.

Dimitry looked over toward Myshkin, who nodded, so Dimitry somewhat reluctantly handed the briefcase over.

"*Spasiba*," Vladimir half murmured and with briefcase in hand quickly left the room.

"You're welcome," Dimitry replied as the door closed, leaving him alone with Myshkin. "What's in that briefcase anyway?" he asked. "It's rather heavy."

"Did Comrade Kornilov tell you?" Myshkin answered, pulling a cigarette from the pack on his desk.

"No, he didn't."

"Then I guess you don't need to know, do you?"

Dimitry suppressed the anger he was beginning to feel. "Look, Viktor; we've worked together before. But now, I've been sent here to run this operation—"

"Did someone tell you to run it?" Myshkin interrupted.

Zhukov decided to be evasive, for the moment at least. "No, but if I'm not running it, why am I here?"

"You are here to tell us what we need to do, and we will decide how to do it. You are an analyst; we are operators. We operate. You don't. Just tell me what support you need, and I'll provide it. Other than that, stay out of the way. You do what you do, and we'll do what we do."

Dimitry paused for a moment. He did not like the tone of this discussion and had not expected it. He would check in with Kornilov on this, but for the time being, he did have something he wanted done. "Did you have someone at the airport observing the American delegation plane that arrived?"

Myshkin lit his cigarette and with one puff filled the room with an acrid aroma. "We did. We always do. He took pictures of the Americans as they came off. Why?"

"There was a fellow who got off very close to the end. I would like to see the picture you took of him. I think I recognized who he is, but I'm not quite sure."

Myshkin took another drag on the cigarette and slowly exhaled another large volume of gray smoke. "All right. We should have the pictures developed by midafternoon. I'll get you a copy. Now, I'd suggest you go wash up and rest a bit. Your room is in the attic dormitory area. You'll find all your baggage there."

"*Korosho*, Viktor. *Spasiba*. Thank you. I'll check back with you in an hour or so."

Myshin nodded, and Dimitry opened the door and stepped into the hall. Instead of heading to the attic, however, he headed to the communications center. This was not the reception he had anticipated. He needed to call Lubyanka.

## The Vatican

Cardinal Villot and Monsignor Sarac were making the rounds. They had been around the square and checked to see that all of the preparations for the pope's funeral were set, that seats were in place, that security was established, that the media was positioned, and that the attending cardinals were getting ready and had been briefed on the specifics of the funeral Mass. Villot was walking quickly, as quickly as he could, but not so fast that Sarac had any trouble keeping up with him.

"Are all of the cardinal electors here?" Villot asked. "I haven't had time to greet them all, but I assume they have all arrived. How many will we have?"

Sarac flipped to a section of his small notebook he had marked with a paper clip. "Ironically, Your Eminence, we'll have the same number as we did in August—111."

"How can that be?" Villot asked. "In August, one of the attendees was Cardinal Luciani, who we both know is now dead and ready to be carried to his rest. So how do we have the same number? His Holiness had no time to appoint another cardinal."

The always efficient Sarac was ready with the answer. "Eminence, remember that in August, Cardinal Wright from the curia was too ill to participate, but he has recovered sufficiently for this conclave. So the number will be the same."

Villot nodded. "Ah, yes…I forgot Cardinal Wright. Are all of the others here?"

"No, Your Eminence. Several have not arrived and won't be present for the funeral Mass. Cardinal Katic from Yugoslavia has not arrived. He sent word that he has experienced some travel approval complications with Belgrade. He won't arrive until tomorrow. And Cardinal Lorscheider is not here either." Sarac glanced around before lowering his voice to a whisper. "I understand he may have some health issues and may not be able to make the conclave either."

"I hope that's not true," Villot whispered in reply. "Lorscheider has a great role to play here. He's well liked and quite influential. Keep me informed about his circumstances. As for Katic, as always, he's trying to annoy me," Villot snarled. "He gets along well enough with Tito. He could get here if he wanted. But he's not interested. He dislikes Italians, he dislikes me, and he disliked the Holy Father. That was clear in the last conclave."

"How do you know that?" Sarac asked, immediately aware he was intruding into forbidden territory.

Villot gave him a look, showing he was unhappy with the question, but said nothing about it and changed the subject. "Let's go look at the rooms. Did we make the arrangements Cardinal Siri requested?"

"We did, Eminence. I verified that with Monsignor Grone. He will be…well, he will be as pleased as he ever gets."

Villot nodded as they entered the bottom level of the Apostolic Palace and headed up the stairs to the first level. At the second landing, Villot stopped. "Before we go to look at the rooms, let's check out the kitchen. The food still worries me. They'll politely complain about the rooms, but they can get very ornery about the food." The camerlengo turned to his left and pushed open a door that was so blended into the wall that anyone unfamiliar with it wouldn't know it was even there, one of the palace's many hidden stairways. The two robed inspectors walked down a flight of stairs into the grotto-like basement and then down another hall to the kitchen that Sister Cummings, aided by five other nuns who had finally arrived to assist her, now had working at a high tempo.

"Sisters!" Cummings quietly but firmly called to the other nuns as she caught sight of Villot and Sarac heading their way. The group of them stopped what they were doing, faced Villot, and nodded as he approached. "Your Eminence," Sister Cummings said, greeting the old cardinal, "we're pleased to see you, and we assure you that all is under control…or as under control as it can be."

Villot raised his head and looked at the head nun through the bottom of his glasses. He then looked from one side of the large kitchen to the other, attempting as best he could to give the operation a critical inspection, even though he had never cracked an egg in his life. His eyes slowly scanned the room and then returned to Sister Cummings. "It all seems to be going well, Sister. Let me know if you need anything. I realize you can't please such a diverse group of men, but I am confident you will do the best you can. And I will be most displeased if I begin to hear a loud chorus of complaints, understand?"

"Yes, Your Eminence," Cummings replied, struggling to keep her Irish temper under control. "We will do all we can to meet your expectations." She and Villot took the measure of each other for a few moments, while the others looked on uncomfortably, until Villot smiled slightly, turned, and, followed by Sarac, headed back toward the stairs.

Arriving at the main level of the Vatican Museum, they emerged from the stairwell into a scene of furious activity. Looking at it, Villot was horrified. The cardinals' living quarters were nowhere near finished. Sarac heard two voices yelling at each other in loud, excited tones about ten feet away. He quickly stepped over toward the two men to tell them to calm down in the presence of the camerlengo, and as he approached, he recognized that the two were Bruno Brachi and his deputy Gianluca Giordano, who were clearly having another of their frequent altercations.

"Damn you, Gianluca!" Brachi was shouting. "I told you all of the rooms had to be the same! Look at these two! This one is square, and that one is rectangular! Take it down and make them both the same—rectangles or squares! I don't care which so long as they are the same!"

"Fuck you, Bruno!" Giordano shouted back. "You want them the same? Then rip a wall out of the museum and we'll have space to make them the same. They weren't all the same last time, and no one said anything!"

"No one said anything to *you*, asshole! They said plenty to *me*! Now make them the same!"

"*I can't, Bruno*! We can't work miracles here! Dimensions are dimensions, and they dictate what we can do!"

"Gentlemen!" Brachi and Giordano turned to see a very stern-faced Monsignor Sarac staring at them and pointing as subtly as he could toward Villot, who was standing a few feet away, having decided to let his secretary calm the waters before stepping into this fracas. The two facilities leaders fell silent as the cardinal slowly sauntered over toward them.

"Do we have a problem here?" Villot asked, as Brachi and Giordano lowered their heads slightly.

"No, Your Eminence. No problem," Brachi replied, turning his head toward Giordano.

The deputy glared at his boss momentarily and then grudgingly echoed his comments. "No, Eminence. No problem at all. Just a healthy discussion on how best to configure the rooms."

Villot turned away and motioned for Brachi to follow him, leaving Sarac standing with Giordano. While the two of them observed the whispered conversation between Villot and Brachi, one of the workers came up to Giordano.

"Gianluca, I think these four rooms are ready. If it's all right with you, I'll go get the cots and other furnishings and finish setting them up."

Gianluca turned his attention away from Sarac and the conversation underway between Villot and Brachi. "That's fine, Matteo. Go ahead. I think we'll make no further changes to the shape of the rooms..." He paused briefly to look at Sarac before continuing, "Despite what some feel is possible."

"Thank you, Gianluca. I'll take care of it." With that, the worker scurried off.

"Who's he?" Sarac inquired, watching the worker disappear around one of the wooden rooms. "You seem to know him well, but I don't recall having seen him before."

"We just hired him," Giordano replied. "He's a cousin of mine. Matteo Ferrari. He's a very capable fellow. He'll be a great help—especially with this."

Sarac did not reply. He didn't quite know why, but for some reason, he did not like hearing this. He always signed off on new hires in the facilities division, and he was certain this one had not reached his desk.

Maybe in all the confusion after the pope's death, he had just not paid any attention to it or just didn't remember. Maybe. Possibly. Not likely. But there was something about Matteo he didn't like. He wasn't sure what, but something about him just didn't seem right. Nonetheless, he decided to let it go. He didn't have time to dwell on it right now. The funeral was only a few hours away at this point. He lifted his notebook and flipped it open to a blank page, pulled a pen from inside his black jacket, and wrote down, "Matteo Ferrari."

## HOTEL DE RUSSIE

As Cardinal Villot and Bruno Brachi were discussing the austere accommodations at the Vatican, several of the cars carrying the Americans from Fiumicino pulled up at the De Russie Hotel, including the three people in the last van designated "Embassy 9." The De Russie was located on Via Babuino between the Piazza del Popolo and the famous "Spanish Steps," and was one of Rome's more famous and elegant hotels. As their van came to a stop, Carter pulled open the sliding door and jumped out onto the street. Bruce and Kath quickly joined him.

"My goodness!" Kath exclaimed. "We're staying at the De Russie?"

Carter looked around. He had never heard of the De Russie but was suddenly focused on the irony of staying at a hotel that in Italian meant "The Russian." Nor was he relating to Kath's excitement as the entrance to the hotel looked quite unspectacular. However, all that changed as he stepped inside, followed closely by a wide-eyed Katherine O'Connor. The two of them walked straight through the entrance and out into an inner court that served as a bar and lunch area. Beyond this courtyard were fabulously elegant marble steps leading up into a lush, green hanging garden that was terraced into the hill behind. The hanging garden had at least two levels, and Carter could see that it had numerous tables shielded from the sun with large, festive umbrellas, all of it the setting for the hotel's restaurant.

Carter and Kath looked at each other, turned, and headed back toward the lobby. The embassy guide who had ridden in their car met them inside the lobby, having unloaded their luggage—three pieces for Kath, one for Carter. "Excuse me?" Kath asked. "Isn't this like the most expensive, famous hotel in Rome?"

"Maybe," came the short reply.

They had already discovered that their young embassy guide was not very talkative.

"So, why did the embassy put us up here?" Kath continued. "I don't think our *per diem* comes close to covering this place, especially if we're going to be here a couple of weeks. You do know we'll be here a couple of weeks, right?"

"Yes, we know," came the short reply and then a pause. "You're here because this was the only place in Rome we could get on such short notice. And we have an arrangement with the management, so your bill will match your *per diem* allowance; trust me." The guide then went silent again.

Bruce was at the front desk checking in, while Carter and Kath hung back and waited. They were the junior people in the whole delegation, and they decided to wait until Mayor Koch was finished with the desk clerk on the left.

The mayor suddenly grabbed his key and stepped away from the clerk, passing by Kath and Carter, looking at them with his famous twinkle-eyed expression. "How ya doin'?" he asked, as only the mayor of New York could.

"Fine, sir," Carter replied. As the mayor and his room valet headed toward the elevator, Carter motioned for Kath to step ahead of him to the desk. She did while reaching into her purse to pull out her passport.

"Good morning, ma'am," the smiling clerk said to Kath, her English only slightly accented.

"Good morning," Kath replied, handing the passport across the counter. "I'm Katherine O'Connor, part of the delegation, but I'll be staying here a couple of weeks longer than the rest of the group."

The clerk smiled as she grabbed the passport. "Yes, ma'am. We have you on an open reservation until October 21. If you need to extend, that shouldn't be a problem. And the American embassy is picking up your entire bill other than any room incidentals."

Kath smiled. This was sure to be a demanding couple of weeks, but at least the time she could spend at the hotel would be enjoyable and restful. She momentarily daydreamed about perhaps a spa visit and maybe a couple of great meals under the stars in the garden.

"Ma'am." The clerk's voice brought her back to the reality of the moment. "Ma'am, would you ask your husband if I could have his passport as well."

"My what?" Kath answered, looking around to see if anyone had heard her excited comment. Seemingly no one had. "I don't have a husband," she whispered. "Why do you think I have a husband?"

The clerk's face reflected puzzlement. "Ma'am, it says here that you will be sharing a room with your husband, a Mr. Carter Caldwell. We have put the two of you in a wonderful room overlooking the gardens, with a queen-sized bed. It's very nice."

Kath spun around and motioned excitedly to Carter and the embassy guide. Both stepped up to the reception desk.

"What's up?" Carter asked, holding his passport in his hand.

"They think we're married!" Kath firmly but quietly breathed through her clenched teeth.

"What? Married!" Carter answered as he and Kath turned their gazes to the now nervous embassy guide.

"We were told you were a couple," the guide quietly protested. "I assumed that meant a married couple. You're not married?"

"*No!*" Kath replied.

A seemingly long silence followed.

"No big deal," Carter softly said, trying to calm the moment. "I'll just have them put me in another room."

"But, sir," the clerk interjected, overhearing the whispered discussion occurring in front of her, "we don't have any other rooms. Rome is filled for the pope's funeral Mass. Every hotel in the city is filled… believe me."

"That's right," the embassy guide defensively chipped in. "The city is filled. I hate to admit it, but one of the reasons we booked you here was because it was about the last place with any rooms available. Most people don't want to pay these sorts of prices. Look, we were told you were a couple working something together with the delegation. I took that to mean you were a married couple and thought this would be a great—you know—little break for you."

Carter and Kath looked at each other with mouths open.

"Excuse me. Could you two please finish so the rest of us can check in?"

Carter turned to see that another van carrying many of the congressional aides had arrived, and one was now standing behind him, anxious to check in and clean up. Congressional aides were always pushy and famously self-important; that much was clear to Carter and certainly no state secret.

"OK," Carter said to the desk clerk after surveying the situation and determining that the immediate options were limited. "Look, put our luggage in the room you have for us, and we'll sort this out later today. We really have some things we need to attend to rather shortly. Is that all right with you, Kath?"

"No, it's not!"

"Kath, we don't have a choice at the moment. We have to get to the embassy, and we have people piling up behind us who need to get checked in. They're on a schedule too. We'll sort it out later."

"*No*, we won't."

"Yes, Kath, *we will*." Carter turned to the clerk. "Check us in, and I'll see you later today. Meanwhile, see if you can work out something else."

The clerk slyly smiled. She had seen many things in her time working the front desk at the De Russie. She knew there was occasional confusion and sometimes crossed signals, and she had observed many people stand in front of her, reacting to unexpected things. She had learned to read people pretty well. Anyone who worked at a hotel like the De Russie had to develop that skill. And there was one thing she knew for certain about this situation: Miss O'Connor was genuinely quite upset by it, but Mr. Caldwell…well, not nearly as much.

## St. Peter's Basilica

It was midafternoon and time for John Paul's funeral Mass. The cardinals of the church who had arrived in time for the Mass were gathering inside the great basilica. Some were greeting others as the old friends they were; others were introducing themselves to those they barely knew or had not bothered to meet in August. The process of socializing was underway.

Cardinal Krol watched as a flock of young priests and other seminarians scurried around with lists detailing who stood where in the procession and who sat where in the square. The cardinals actually had three ranks: cardinal bishops, cardinal priests, and cardinal deacons. The distinctions between the three were largely ceremonial with little practical difference, but they were important inside the Vatican. Krol oversaw a large archdiocese, so he was a cardinal priest, although younger than some others who were cardinal deacons in the curia. But rank had its privileges, so Krol had already started his mission and was making the rounds, getting initial soundings and dropping subtle hints.

He glimpsed Cardinal Leo Suenens of Belgium, the archbishop of Brussels, standing alone, gazing up at the great dome, and decided to stroll over to him. Suenens was a true power among the cardinals, especially those from Northern Europe, and any time speaking with him was always well spent. The Belgian saw him coming and opened his arms wide, inviting an embrace, which Krol accommodated.

"Your Eminence," Krol softly said as they touched cheeks. "It's very good to see you."

"And you," Suenens replied.

"Quite the day, quite tragic, but we must accept God's will and move forward."

"Yes, we must, and I am sure we will."

The two cardinals fell silent for a few moments, Suenens reflecting, Krol calculating.

Sensing that it was clear to continue, Krol turned to Suenens. "Leo, do you have any thoughts on how we should move forward? To where? With whom?"

The Brussels archbishop glanced at Krol and then slowly walked away from the gathering formation of cardinals. Krol followed. They stopped about twenty feet away, standing among the temporary pews and well out of earshot.

"John, are you asking who I plan to support in the conclave?"

"No, Leo. I'm asking your thoughts about your own possibilities. You had some support the last time. And I sensed it was quite solid."

"Well, perhaps," Suenens responded, a bit shyly. "But not solid enough. And most of our conservative brothers in the curia feel I'm some sort of radical. They'll push Siri hard this time, so Benelli and I will try and hold together the coalition of moderates that succeeded for us in August. I think that will mean a non-Italian pope—finally. But that only works if we can get support from those from the so-called 'third world,' which means we'll need help from Aloísio Lorscheider…again."

Krol stepped a bit closer to Suenens, looking around to ensure they were not being overheard. "There are many who feel Lorscheider should be given serious consideration. He's quite impressive, and I know Luciani thought very highly of him. So…"

Suenens cut him off. "John, he's not the one. If we're going to get a non-Italian, it will have to be a European. Our fellow cardinals are not prepared to go any further given who they are. And besides, although I don't believe it's widely known, Aloísio had heart surgery last year and I think still has some lingering health issues. That's probably why he's not here yet. Given the unexpected death of the Holy Father, I think we'll need someone who is vigorous and without any significant health issues."

Krol paused again. "I was not aware of that, Leo. Is he OK?"

"As far as I know. At least, that's what I hear. But that'll be enough for the curia to start a whispering campaign against him. So, true or not, we need to look elsewhere. And I suspect we are chatting because you have someone in mind, right, John?"

Krol hesitated, looking around to ensure they were still alone. "Perhaps I do. We can discuss it later at the general congregations. But, when we do, I'd like you to give my thoughts some serious consideration. And if you find what I suggest appealing, I'd like you to help me. You have great influence, Leo, whether you admit it or not—among nearly all of our European brothers as well as others from around the world."

Suenens smiled. "I am pleased you think so. And I know this, John—any thoughts of yours are certainly worth serious consideration."

"Your Eminences."

The two cardinals turned to see that one of the young priests had quietly approached them.

"Your Eminences, we need you to take your place for the procession into the square. It is time to start the funeral Mass."

"Thank you, young man," Suenens answered and then placed his large hand on Krol's shoulder. "Thank you for your confidence, John. We'll talk some more. The prattiche of this conclave will be most interesting, won't they?"

Krol nodded, and the two princes of the church followed the young priest to their place in line.

CHAPTER 10

# Wednesday Afternoon, October 4, 1978
# US Embassy, Rome

• • •

A SMALL RED FIAT CAB pulled by in front of the US embassy on Via Vittorio Veneto, but it had barely stopped when the rear door on the passenger's side flew open. Katherine O'Connor popped out, her heels hitting the pavement with the force of several G's. She slammed the door shut and walked around to the cab's front, stopping to watch as a much calmer and more collected Carter Caldwell emerged from the rear driver's side. Carter handed the cabbie several thousand lira, hoping that this was roughly what the tab had been. Understanding the highly inflated Italian currency was a challenge for anyone, but the cabbie nodded and quickly pulled away, the grin on his face suggesting he had been nicely overpaid.

Carter casually strolled over to Kath, who was standing on the curb with folded arms.

"Carter, this is simply not going to work! We're going to be working on this together, perhaps day and night, and it's not going to work!"

"Katherine, we don't have a choice. We'll have to make it work. And it won't be so bad. You just acknowledged we'll be working pretty hard on our little project."

"Carter, I don't want to share a hotel room with you! I hardly know you!"

"Really, well, you've seen files on me—no matter what you say. So if someone here doesn't really know someone, I'm the one who hardly knows you! Maybe I'm the one whose virtue is at risk!"

Kath glared at Carter, who tried his best to glare back, not sure how or when this particular confrontation would end. Fortunately for him, her face slowly turned into a rather broad, blushing grin. "That was pretty good, Carter. Pretty good. Files. Virtue. That was pretty good, I must admit."

Carter smiled and tossed his head slightly away, so as not to indicate that he was gloating at his momentary victory. He then turned his gaze back to her, something he was enjoying more and more. "Kath, we're both adults. We have a serious mission to accomplish. We'll make it work out. So...when we get back to the Russie, I'll check with them again and see if there is some sort of alternative they can provide. OK?"

Kath nodded and then looked up. It was starting to sprinkle. Carter took her arm lightly by the elbow.

"Come on; let's get inside and catch up with Bruce and his people. I hope this rain is passing through quickly. The funeral Mass should be underway by now, and I'd hate for this to disrupt it."

## The Soviet Embassy, Rome

Dimitry had gone to his attic room, freshened up a bit, caught about an hour's nap, and was headed back to Myshkin's office to see what new instructions might have come in since his arrival. He reached the office, opened the door, and walked inside. Myshkin was alone, standing behind his desk and puffing on another of his barely tolerable cigarettes. He looked up as Dimitry entered.

"Get a few minutes to rest and clean up? Feeling better?"

Dimitry walked over and grabbed the chair next to the KGB station chief's desk and plopped into it, indicating that he was still a bit fatigued. "*Da*, shaved and took a quick nap. Anything new since my arrival?"

"Well, we have these." Myshkin tossed a group of pictures held together with a large paper clip into Dimitry's lap.

"What are these?"

"Pictures of the American delegation arriving at Fiumicino. You said you wanted to look at them when they were developed."

Dimitry removed the clip and began slowly and carefully examining the pictures. There was Lillian Carter, Senator Eagleton, and numerous other aides and lesser dignitaries he recognized but did not know. He slowly examined the pictures one at a time. As he got to the last one, his eyes fixed on the three people at the top of the stairs. "Are these pictures in the order by which they debarked the plane?"

Myshkin nodded. "Yes, there's a number written on the back in pencil. That's the order in which the pictures were taken. Why?"

Dimitry tossed the last picture on Viktor's desk. "See these last two men? The two coming down the stairs with the blond woman between them."

Myshkin lifted the picture to examine it. "Sure. What of it? Who are they? They can't be all that important if they were sitting in the back of the plane. And they must have been if they got off last."

Dimitry gave Viktor a pensive look. "The last man is Bruce Harrison. He's the deputy director for operations of the CIA. At Lubyanka, we know him quite well. He's a legend in our world. So why is he here?"

Myshkin looked at the picture again. "Well, he is a senior US government official. Maybe he's Catholic. Maybe he wanted to come to the funeral."

Dimitry shook his head. "He didn't come to the last one. And Paul had been pope for fifteen years. So why is he here at this one for a fellow who was pope for thirty-three days?"

Myshkin scanned the picture again. "Good question. I guess we should see if we can find the answer to that. Know who the woman is? She's quite a beauty."

"No idea. Perhaps an assistant to Harrison. But the fellow in front of her is the one who really intrigues me."

"Why? Who's he?"

"He's a fellow named Carter Caldwell. An American army officer assigned to the White House NSC. He's close to Scowcroft. I don't recall why, but I do recall that he is. And he works primarily on the

SALT negotiations—also some European and NATO stuff, but mainly SALT."

"OK. So?"

"The SALT II negotiations are reaching a critical phase. Their chief negotiator, a guy named Warnke, will be announcing in a couple of days that he's headed to Moscow to put the finishing touches on the draft agreement. We hope to have Carter—that's President Carter—and General Secretary Brezhnev sign it in the spring. So, with all of that going on, why is Caldwell here? At a funeral? I would have expected he would be down at the State Department, slaving away on the SALT draft. And I'm sure that's him. I've seen him a few times before."

"Maybe he's going from here to Moscow to meet up with Warnke and the others," Myshkin gently suggested, impressed with Dimitry's knowledge and recall.

"*Nyet.* I saw the SALT delegation list, and he's not on it. So again… why is he here? And who is the woman who seems to be with him and Harrison? These are extra pieces on the chessboard, and it worries me." Dimitry thought for a few moments more and then turned back to Myshkin. "Get me a coded message form. I'm sending a note back to Kornilov. We'll need to look into this. I just don't like it."

Myshkin handed Dimitry the requested form and then leaned back in his chair and took another deep drag on his cigarette, while his younger colleague feverishly drafted a message on the prescribed code sheet. This was, after all, the KGB, and everything had to be in a prescribed format.

## Fiumicino Airport

The gentle rain falling in St. Peter's Square had forced the aides and seminarians to rush out with umbrellas to shield the ninety-two cardinals seated around John Paul's funeral bier, while others carried out a much larger, more elaborate covering to protect the altar and Cardinal Carlo Confalonieri, the dean of the college of cardinals, who was delivering the eulogy. But at Fiumicino airport, as he stepped from his Air

Austria flight, Cardinal Jedar Katic of Zadar was completely indifferent. He looked up at the drizzling skies and thought to himself that he was more than pleased he had arranged to miss the funeral of the Venetian pope, despite the blunt note he had received from Villot.

Katic was dressed in civilian attire. He had his clerical collar in place but had worn a scarf to conceal it, along with some worn khaki pants and an old sports coat. He was not all that much into clothes, which made his choice of profession additionally fortuitous, and his current garb made his arrival go unnoticed. Even the customs official who almost unconsciously stamped his Yugoslav passport paid scant attention. The Yugoslav embassy had hired a cab to take him to his residence at one of the small parish churches scattered throughout Rome. Katic quickly located the driver holding the paper sign with his misspelled name on it, jumped into the rear seat of the cab, and was off to the city.

Each cardinal of the church was appointed by the Vatican to honorary *governance* over one of Rome's parish churches that were then designated as titular churches. Whenever cardinals visited Rome, they were encouraged to minister to the local parishioners at their titular church, as if they were, indeed, the local parish priest. In real terms, this duty literally was only titular, but it did establish a connection that afforded a place to stay. Most of the cardinals stayed at seminaries, universities, religious order houses, or—for some—in apartments provided by friends. But Katic had no friends, had never attended a seminary or university in Rome, and had no established connection to any resident order. Katic's titular church was Santa Chiara a Vigna Clara, an unusually shaped round church near the center of Rome, and that was where he was headed.

"A beautiful country, even in rain," Katic thought as the miles rolled past. "Too bad it is occupied by Italians. And my role here is to do my part to ensure the college elects yet another one. I think I'd prefer we chose a Byzantine Greek monk." Katic exhaled deeply, his head sinking down so that his chin was nearly resting on his chest. "I'll do what I can. But I hope they don't have to do what they say they will. That would be terrible. I don't want violence. I really don't want violence. I've seen more than enough in my life."

He had mumbled the last sentence aloud, causing the cabdriver to look up into the rearview mirror at his seemingly agitated passenger. "Monsignor Katic, did you say something? Is everything all right? Do we need to stop?"

Katic waved his hand, indicating there was no need to stop. And if the cabdriver felt he was a monsignor, so much the better. "No, I'm fine. I'm just tired. Just get me to the church. I'll be fine after a little rest."

The cabdriver turned his eyes back to the road and pushed a bit harder on the accelerator.

## THE APOSTOLIC PALACE

The funeral Mass was over, and the body of John Paul had been carried into St. Peter's where it was being interred in the crypt beneath the great church. Now that the event was over, many of the cardinals had gathered in the Sala Clementina, one of the large reception halls of the palace, to enjoy some coffee and have the opportunity to greet one another, a normal pleasantry that few had yet engaged in as many had arrived just before the funeral itself. It presented the first chance for a well-attended prattiche, and Cardinal Krol intended to take advantage of it.

The Philadelphian filled his coffee cup, added a bit of sugar, and stepped away from the table, surveying the red-capped landscape around him. Looking to a far corner of the room, he spotted Cardinal John Carberry of St. Louis, chatting with his old friend Cardinal Terence Cooke of New York. "May as well start with my own countrymen," Krol whispered to himself as he slowly strolled over to the two Americans.

"John, good to see you," Cardinal Cooke said as he saw Krol approaching. "Seems as if we see each other in Rome more often than at home. At least over the past two months—unfortunately."

"Yes, most unfortunately," Krol replied, gently shaking Cooke's hand. "And also good to see you, Cardinal Carberry. I trust you had a good flight over."

Carberry chuckled. "Well, I don't travel well at my age, but at least I didn't have Cardinal Cody's problems."

"What happened to Cody?" Krol asked, listening for the answer while continuing to survey the room.

"Oh, you didn't hear?" Carberry replied with a tinge of excitement in his voice. "About an hour out of Chicago, they got some report that there was a terrorist bomb on board, so they turned back to O'Hare. Quite a mess. That's why he's not here yet. I think he'll be in this evening in time for the general congregation in the morning."

Krol shook his head and returned his focus to Carberry and Cooke. "Well, poor Cody. He certainly has a lot of trouble swirling around him at the moment, with all the questions that have come up about his archdiocese's finances. I hope there's nothing to them, and I'm sure there's nothing that involves him directly, but for the moment, trouble seems to follow him wherever he goes—whether to Mayor Daley's office or to the pope's funeral."

Neither Carberry nor Cooke replied. Krol didn't really expect them to, which offered him the chance to get to the topic most on his mind. "Well, I must confess to you both that I am a bit flummoxed over who we might pick next to be the Holy Father. Do either of you have any thoughts that might guide me a bit on this enormous decision?"

Carberry rubbed his fingers across his chin. "Not really, John. I think we'll have to look for guidance again from the Holy Spirit. Luciani was a wonderful choice, and the people of the church embraced him even faster than we did. So, I go into it with an open mind."

"And you, Terence?"

Cooke was taking a sip of his coffee, his eyes looking across the top edge of the cup. Krol and Carberry turned their heads to see what the New York cardinal was eyeing so intently. "See over there?" Cooke said, slightly flipping his head toward the far side of the room where Cardinals Siri, Benelli, and Villot were engaged in what appeared to be an animated conversation. "They're already starting their campaigns. Siri will be for Siri. Benelli will be for Benelli. And Villot will be for whichever of them seems to be gathering the most strength, despite the fact that he rather strongly dislikes them both. He thinks Siri is too conservative and was inadequately supportive of Pope Paul, and he feels Benelli undercut him when he was in the curia. So, that leaves him in a tough spot. In August, we found Luciani—largely because Benelli pointed him out to us—when it seemed there was not enough support for any of our other Italian brothers. This time…well, I just don't know."

The three Americans silently watched the discussion across the room continue. After allowing time for the scene to settle down, Krol made his move. "Perhaps, Your Eminences, we should look for someone who isn't Italian. We've had Italian popes for nearly five hundred years, and there were reasons—most of them quite practical, in my view—that may no longer be so important and relevant. Would you agree?"

Cooke and Carberry briefly glanced at each other, but neither replied, leaving an awkward void of silence.

"Well, it's just a thought," Krol added.

"But an interesting thought," Cooke suddenly replied. "Have anyone in mind, John?"

Krol tried his best to make his answer seem spontaneous rather than rehearsed. "Off the top of my head, I would say…let's see, perhaps Willebrands? Maybe Franz Koenig? Maybe Aloísio Lorscheider? Perhaps Wyszynski? Perhaps…Karol Wojtyla? Perhaps…well, perhaps you, Terence?"

Cardinal Cooke almost choked on his coffee. "Excuse me, John. Sorry. Me? Please, let's not get frivolous. We're talking about breaking a five-hundred-year tradition. And trust me; it won't be broken by an American. Besides, I'm fifty-seven; I'm too young."

Krol countered Cooke's comments immediately. "Terence, OK… you're fifty-seven, but given what just happened requiring us to be here, I would say that's a good thing. Wouldn't you?"

"Maybe. We might want to take a close look at age." Cooke again glanced over to where Siri, Benelli, and Villot were still engaged in their increasingly lively discussion. "Siri is clearly too old, in my opinion. It's his fourth one of these, and I sense that he feels he's now somehow owed the white robes. Benelli is much younger but very smart. I hear he was treated like a rock star at the sermon he gave last week in France. Who is the other Pole you mentioned? Wojtyla? How old is he? I don't know him well. Do you?"

"I believe he is fifty-eight or so. And yes, I do know him well. We were elevated at the same consistory. Take some time over the next week and chat with him. I think you'll be impressed. But, look—there are nine of us in the college who are American, assuming Cardinal Wright is well enough to participate, and I hear he is. And there are also the three Canadians led by Cardinal Flahiff of Winnipeg. That makes twelve. That's actually a pretty significant number, especially if the Italians will be split between Benelli and Siri."

The three Americans looked back over toward the corner where Siri now stood with his arms folded across his chest, as Benelli seemed to lecture him, while Villot watched like a nervous uncle.

"Well, we all agree that at seventy-four I'm too old," Carberry chimed in with a wide grin. "But I'll talk to the ones you mentioned. And I'll make time to meet Wojtyla. If you like him, John, I'm sure meeting him would be worthwhile."

"OK. Good," Krol replied. "Now, if the two of you will excuse me, I need to go say hello to Cardinal Lopez from Mexico. I look forward to seeing you in the morning at the congregation." With that, Cardinal Krol continued on his way. He was slowly shifting into high gear.

## US Embassy, Rome

"Look if the two guys you wanted us to meet aren't here, I think we should just go back to the hotel and get some rest," Carter snapped.

He and Kath had been sitting in a small office for well over an hour, glaring at Bruce Harrison. They were supposed to meet two of the operatives the CIA had working in the Vatican, but both had been no-shows. Carter did not like wasting time, and he saw this as a monumental waste. The CIA did not operate like the army, he had now learned that, but this—in his mind—was ridiculous. If Bruce was the number-three man at the Agency, this would be like foot soldiers not coming to a scheduled meeting with the army deputy chief of staff for operations. And no one in the army would stand up the DCSOPS.

"Calm down, Carter," Kath objected, her voice still carrying a degree of unease. "I don't know about you, but I'm in no big rush to get back to the hotel."

Carter shook his head. "Come on, Kath. Get over it, will you? It is what it is, and we'll make it work. OK?"

Harrison looked from Kath to Carter and back again. "What are we talking about here?" he asked, his face a puzzle.

"Nothing," Carter answered, with a degree of extra emphasis on the *thing*. "Forget about it. We'll work it out."

The phone rang on the bare table in the middle of the room. Harrison grabbed the receiver. "Yes. Right. Send him up. He the only one? I'm expecting one more. Right, the other name I left you. When… *if* he gets here, send him up too." He dropped the receiver back onto the cradle. "The first fellow is coming up…the guy with the media contacts. He's worked with us a long time. Well connected. Always seems to know what's going on."

The three of them went quiet again while they waited. Carter was irritated with Bruce; Bruce was irritated with Kath; Kath was irritated with Carter. It was a triangle of irritation that discouraged small talk. After a few awkwardly quiet moments, there was a rap on the door and it swung open. In walked Avery Dugan. Bruce and Carter stood to greet him. Kath remained in her chair—stone-faced.

"Avery, good to see you again. And this is Carter Caldwell from the White House."

Dugan shook hands with the two men, introducing himself to Carter. "Hello. Avery Dugan. Pleasure to meet you. White House, eh? Strange place."

Bruce then pointed to Katherine. "And, Avery, this is Katherine O'Connor, who works with me at the Agency."

Avery's and Katherine's eyes locked, but neither said anything for several seconds as Carter and Bruce exchanged baffled glances.

Finally, Kath ended the awkward standoff—without leaving her chair. "Avery…it's been a long time. How are you?"

Dugan slightly nodded in reply. "Good, Kath…and good to see you."

The room then went quiet again as Carter and Bruce tried to figure out what precisely they were in the middle of.

"So…I guess you two know each other?" Carter said, commenting on the obvious.

"We do," Kath answered, without further elaboration.

Carter turned and looked at Avery, but he also had nothing further to offer, at least on this topic, so the room again fell silent.

"OK…might I suggest we get down to business," Bruce firmly interjected, breaking the verbal stalemate.

The three men took seats at the table, Avery facing Kath and Bruce facing Carter.

Avery hung his backpack on the back of his chair and placed his hands on the table. He glanced over at Bruce. "What's our play, and what do you need me to do?"

The operations chief paused for a moment before answering, watching as Avery briefly turned his eyes toward Kath, who continued to sit impassively in her chair. "Avery, we need you to use all your access and contacts within the Vatican over the next ten days to give us as full a picture as possible on what is going on within the college of cardinals—who's chatting with whom, when, about what, so that—"

Avery interrupted. "Bruce, you realize that's quite a tall order. There's no more closed-mouthed and secretive group in the world than the cardinals of the Catholic church. You believe you keep secrets safe for the United States; well, they believe they keep secrets safe for God. The large majority of them do anyway. But I have contacts throughout the place, so I'll see what I can do. But in what regard? What are you looking for? There must be some topic? Some slant?"

Bruce looked at Carter and then at Kath. "Avery, we have determined that it is important for the United States and its allies that this conclave elect a non-Italian as pope, preferably an East European. So we want to do what we can—as Carter delicately puts it—to *encourage* that outcome. We have some other people assisting us with this, and I think it best not to tell you who they are, at least not right now."

"Jesus, Bruce!" Avery exclaimed. "Why don't you do something easier? Such as 'encourage' the election of a Marxist as governor of Texas! This is the most opaque process, run by the most opaque organization, having the most opaque electorate on the planet, maybe with the exception of the Soviet and Chinese Communist Party central committees, but I'm not even sure about that. But…Jesus, Bruce!"

"Avery, it's a long shot. We know that. And it's a double or triple bank shot, no doubt about it. But we have good reasons for believing we have to make an effort."

"Such as?"

"We believe if we don't, the Soviets are going to crack down in Poland and Czechoslovakia. The Polish economy is tanking, workers are growing restive, and the Gierek government is losing it. There could be a revolt against the communists. If there is, we want it to unfold gently, encouraged and mediated by the church, rather than harshly, in which case the Red Army could move in. At worst, that will set up a major confrontation with the West and NATO. At best, that would mean we will lose the chance to crack the Warsaw Pact for decades."

Avery leaned back in his chair. "So, your supposition is that a non-Italian pope can stop that? That he'll be more inclined to stand up to the Soviets and make it harder for them to move, correct?"

"Precisely," Carter answered, deciding it was time for him to weigh in. "So, all we need is as much insight as we can get on the direction in which the cardinals are leaning; then we'll see what we can do to get them to lean another way."

Dugan again glanced briefly toward Kath, but the expression she had worn since he walked into the room remained fixed. The reporter moved his gaze back to Carter. "OK, as the old saying goes, I'm yours to command. I'll see what I can come up with. The Italian reporters are a very chatty group. Were I you, I'd never tell them anything unless you wanted it leaked. Their ability to keep a secret is the same as a cooked piece of spaghetti to stand erect. And the Vatican Press Office is such a mess right now that they're leaking without even knowing they're leaking. Plus, I have some good contacts at the lower levels of the curia. As you might imagine, they are quite interested in who their new boss might be, so I'll—"

The phone on the desk rang, and Bruce quickly grabbed it. "Harrison here. Yes. Right. Send him up." He again lowered the phone back onto the receiver. "Sorry for the interruption, Avery. Our other contact is here. He's coming up. I'd like you to meet him."

Dugan scowled slightly. "Your 'other' contact. Tell me that this fellow and me aren't all we have working this, Bruce."

Harrison shrugged his shoulders. "Well, Avery, you're not *all* we have, but you may be the *best* we have—if I can put it that way. Sorry."

"Shit, Bruce. You and I were a two-man operation when you had me nosing around the Church Committee in 1975. If you had thrown some more assets at it maybe their damn report on the CIA might have been a bit less harsh."

"It worked out OK, Avery. Sometimes a small team can have as much impact as a big one."

There was a soft knock at the door, which quickly opened. The foursome around the table looked up as an average-sized man with dark hair, a matching dark mustache, and a dark complexion stepped in to join them. Harrison immediately stood to greet him, while Avery, Carter, and Kath looked at each other to see if any of them knew who he was.

"Good to see you," Bruce said, shaking the man's hand. "Avery, Carter, Katherine, this is the other solid source we'll have working for us in the Vatican. Meet Matteo Ferrari."

CHAPTER 11

## Thursday, October 5, 1978
## Hotel De Russie, Rome

• • •

Carter had not slept well. He had known there was little chance he would. In the cab ride back from the embassy the afternoon before, he and Kath had hardly spoken. She was clearly deep in thought about something, and he was deep in thought about what it was. It obviously had something to do with Avery Dugan, but what? When they arrived at the De Russie, she had headed straight to their room without making a single comment as he headed to the front desk to see what arrangements could be made for him.

The good news was the concierge had come up with a solution; the bad news was the solution he came up with. The head of the hotel's housekeeping crew actually lived in a small room on the top floor, and he was gone for a few days to visit his family in northern Italy. So, that room was assigned to Carter, but it was not much of a room—a small twin bed, a small closet, a suitcase rack, and a sink. The toilet and shower were a shared facility down the hall, very "old Europe." But Carter didn't see any alternative, nor did he feel any further discussion with Kath was worthwhile. At least the hotel staff delivered his bags to the room; that was helpful, as the elevator didn't go to the top floor.

The bed proved to be as uncomfortable as it looked and even less comfortable than he expected. That, combined with the fact that his body had yet to adjust to the time change, made for a miserable night. He awoke early, shaved at the small sink, dressed, and went to the outdoor breakfast area the minute it opened. He needed some food and a considerable amount of coffee. He had just started on an omelet when he saw Katherine walking through the lobby door and heading straight toward his table.

"Good morning," she said as she arrived at the table, her voice flat and cool.

Carter rose, pulled out her chair, and then sat back down. "So, did you sleep well last night, Carter? I assume they found you a room?"

Carter stared at her for a moment as he chewed his eggs. "They had a room in the attic. That's it right up there," he said, pointing to the small dormer window in the roof above them. "It's *very* nice. A bed, a closet, and just for additional elegance—a sink. I couldn't ask for more." Carter tried to match Kath's flat, cool tone. "How about you? Sleep OK?"

"Yeah, fine."

The waiter arrived, and Katherine ordered a small continental breakfast with a cup of tea. She looked up at the terraced restaurant with its lush foliage but said nothing more.

They sat in silence until Carter finished his plate and refilled his coffee cup. "So, are you planning to tell me what that was all about yesterday at the embassy?" he asked, attempting nonchalance. "Given what we're doing here, I'd like to know what was the problem you had with Dugan?"

"None of your business. Forget it. Nothing relevant."

Carter paused for a moment, mentally debating whether to let it go at that. He decided not to. "Well, I think it's relevant, given we are here to penetrate the Vatican, break five hundred years of Catholic tradition, frustrate Soviet desires, and all we have to work with at the moment is Avery Dugan, whom you don't seem to like all that much. So, I think—"

"OK. Avery and I used to live together," Katherine snarled through clenched teeth.

Carter hadn't seen that one coming. "What do you mean 'lived together'?" he asked, somewhat against his better judgment. "Do you mean you shared an apartment as roommates to cut expenses? Or do you mean you…well, you *lived* together'?"

"The latter, OK!" Katherine's reply was short and harsh. "That's more than you need to know, and that's all I'm going to say." She paused for a moment, the fire in her eyes dimming a bit, but then she went on, "I met him at a dinner in DC. I recruited him to the Agency. We moved in together. He went on a couple of assignments for us. After one of them, he came back and said he thought we should see other people. Of course, what that always means is that *he* already was. End of story!"

"Bruce know about this?"

"No. It was before his time. I never said anything about it, and I assume Avery didn't either. Plus, I was in analysis and he was in operations, so our paths never crossed…until yesterday, that is. Anyway, whomever he was seeing apparently didn't like his lifestyle and schedule either. So there it is. Let's drop it."

Carter pondered what to say for a few seconds. "Well, you know what they say: Washington is the world's largest small village. And I guess that extends to Rome."

Kath sat and stared as if she hadn't heard him…briefly. "You know what they also say, Carter? Good Catholic girls, like me, don't live with guys. And you know what? *They* are right." She then calmed a bit, having gotten what passed for a confession off her chest. "Well, it's old history, if three years ago means old. But it's over and we have to do what we have to do now—history or no history."

Carter decided to change the subject. "OK, so…what else do you know about Ferrari? I must say, he has a really cool name. But why's he here? Is he all Bruce says he is?"

Katherine was suddenly more animated. "Oh, he definitely is. I've never met him before, but I've certainly heard of him. He's the best bugger in the business. Certainly the best one we have."

"Bugger?"

"Yeah, he plants bugs. Listening devices. Communications systems. He's a genius at it. We use him all over the world. It just so happens—by wild coincidence—that he lives here and works in the Vatican. He's a native Roman, loves the city, wanted to stay here, got the job over there. So, here we are."

"Great, here we are with exactly two moles in the Vatican to help us pull this thing off, one a wandering journalist and the other a 'bugger,' masquerading as a maintenance man! It's as much as in the bag!" Carter gulped down his last bit of coffee.

"Well," Katherine replied, seemingly back in usual form, "we actually do have one more, in case you'd forgotten."

# THE VATICAN

As Carter and Katherine were finishing their breakfast at the De Russie, John Krol was entering the small chapel off the Vatican Museum that had been set up as the temporary dining room for the cardinals. The sisters who had prepared the morning meal were busy setting it out on two long tables. It was buffet-style, and the few cardinals already there were lined up and selecting what best satisfied their varied tastes.

After picking up his plate, Krol got into line behind another cardinal whom he did not recognize at first. But after filling his plate with eggs, he peeked ahead and recognized the figure in front of him, the prelate of Yugoslavia, Cardinal Jedar Katic, and Krol followed Katic to one of the several tables scattered around the room. He did not know Katic well, but he felt the Yugoslav could be a useful ally.

"Guten Morgen, Your Eminence. May I join you?" Krol innocently asked in German, as he approached the table where Katic was already seated. Krol had heard that outside of Yugoslavia, Katic preferred to converse in German, but the Yugoslav neither replied nor raised his eyes from his plate, merely motioning toward the empty seat beside him. Krol quickly positioned his plate and pushed his large frame into the uncomfortably small seat. "*Danke*, Jedar. Good to see you. I don't believe I saw you at the Holy Father's funeral service."

"I wasn't there," Katic coldly replied, taking a bite from a breakfast sausage. "Had trouble with my clearance papers from Belgrade, so didn't get here in time to attend. As usual."

Krol had always heard that Katic was rather cold and distant, but this was truly Arctic. Nonetheless, he pushed on through the ice. "Well,

Jedar, at least you are here now. And your views will be important as we engage in our deliberations."

"Yes. I presume they might be," Katic replied, slowly picking through the food on his plate. "Who do you think the Italians will rally behind this time?"

"Hard to say, Jedar. Maybe they don't have anyone to rally behind."

"Oh, they'll find someone; they always do," Katic dismissively replied.

Krol was surprised by the attitude that Katic was so openly displaying. It wasn't exactly rude, but it was certainly a close approximation. He dropped the subject and focused on his own eggs, which looked surprisingly appealing.

"Your Eminence."

Krol looked up to see a nun standing next to his seat. "Yes, Sister. How are you today?"

Sister Cummings smiled. "Very good, Eminence. I'm Sister Cummings; we met in Cardinal Villot's office on Tuesday. I'm in charge of the meals for the next two weeks."

Krol turned slightly in his chair. "Yes, I remember, Sister, and thank you for what you're doing. I recognize that it's no easy task, feeding so many having such different tastes. My eggs, by the way, are very good. Thank you."

"Well, thank you, Eminence," Cummings shyly replied, her red face suddenly a match for her red hair. "I just wanted to say hello, and as I mentioned, I have relatives in Philadelphia who speak very highly of you."

Krol showed no outward signs of emotion or heightened interest, but inside he felt it. "Really. I'm quite flattered. Are there many there?"

"About twenty," Cummings continued. "We're a pretty large Irish-Catholic family—nothing unusual about that. I correspond with them often and hope one of these days to get back to Philadelphia for another visit. It's a lovely city, and I love that it has so much history. I've toured it from one end to the other. But I have a question for you."

"Certainly," Krol replied, continuing with his eggs. "Hopefully I know the answer."

Cummings smiled at him. "Well, I'm hoping you do, Eminence. I have a small bet on this with an American friend. As I recall, while in Philly—as you Americans call it—I believe I heard on a tour that Benjamin Franklin was actually born in Boston. Is that true?" The sister's face was covered with a mask of conjured curiosity.

Krol paused for a moment, trying to sustain an aura of nonchalance. "Well, actually it is true," he replied with a slight laugh. "Not many people know that, and—"

"Sister, might you bring me some more coffee?" Katic interrupted, his voice making no effort to be other than rude. After all, from his perspective, who cared where this fellow Franklin was born? He needed coffee and didn't care to wait for it.

"Certainly, Your Eminence," Sister Cummings replied. She looked back at Krol, gave him a most subtle nod, and walked away toward the coffeepot placed in the far corner of the ornate room.

Katic glanced at Krol. "Sorry to interrupt, but I need to get back to my room for my morning prayers."

Krol shrugged his broad shoulders and grinned. "It's OK, Jedar. I understand. I actually need to get going myself. I have to get to the American embassy for an appointment."

This struck Katic as curious. "Why? I believe we have our first meeting with Villot in a couple of hours. Do you have time? What's requiring you to go to the embassy? I thought you Americans had this odd idea about separating church and state."

Krol smiled slightly. "Very good, Jedar. And we do. However, I have misplaced my passport and they are expediting me a new one. But I still have to go there personally to get a photo and sign papers. You know, the usual 'state' stuff."

"*Ja*," Katic replied. "I know the 'state stuff' well. Trust me. I'll see you later in that case." With that, Krol got up to leave as Sister Cummings arrived with the Yugoslav's coffee. Katic saw the Irish nun and the American cardinal exchange a very brief glance as Krol turned to walk toward the door. "There's something going on here," he thought, as he watched the tall American head off in one direction while the Irish nun returned to freshen up the buffet line. Katic fingered his coffee cup, his mind shifting into its calculating mode. "Yes, there is something going on," he thought, "but what?"

## SOVIET EMBASSY, ROME

Viktor Myshkin was puffing on a cigarette when Dimitry burst into the room. The younger KGB man looked at the older one, who had hardly moved to acknowledge Dimitry's presence and who continued to exhale large volumes of acrid tobacco smoke.

"I got your message that you had received new information from Moscow," Dimitry said, walking over to the Rome KGB chief and pulling out a chair.

Myshkin nodded, reached into the bottom drawer of his desk, and pulled out an envelope that he tossed across his coffee-stained desk pad. "Here. Read. Carter Caldwell wasn't with the Warnke SALT group in Moscow. But we didn't have anyone at the airport able to observe the departure of the American delegation after the pope's funeral. So, we don't know if he's still in Rome, if that indeed was him getting off the plane. But from the pictures we sent, Lubyanka believes it's him." Myshin exhaled another cloud of smelly smoke. "*Vwe ponamayetya.* So, it seems he was here, but we don't know where he is now."

"Or maybe," Dimitry inserted, glancing through the memo he had pulled from the envelope, "he's still here and he's working on something that the White House feels is more important than nuclear weapons."

"Nothing is more important than nuclear weapons," Myshkin countered.

"*Da*! Normally! But this may not be normal. Nuclear weapons can kill us all quickly. There would be no winner and enormous damage to us both. But if one was to find a way to defeat us slowly, with no human deaths and little physical damage, wouldn't that be quite appealing?"

The two KGB men stared at each other, digesting the thought that was hanging in the air.

"Give me another coded message form," Dimitry demanded.

Myshkin sat still momentarily, not wanting to leave the impression that this young pup Zhukov could order him around, but he slowly reached into his desk, pulled out a form, and tossed it across the table to the younger man. Dimitry could see that their relationship was moving from chilly to cold, and he was growing increasingly annoyed with Myshkin, but for now, he grabbed a pencil and began quickly scribbling another message for Lubyanka. Once finished, he pushed it across the table to Myshkin.

"Get this to the communications room right away. We need verification on where Caldwell is."

Myshkin glanced briefly at the draft message and then pushed it back across the table. "Why don't you take it there yourself, Comrade Zhukov? I'm rather busy right now."

Dimitry sat in his chair for a few seconds, then rose and slowly moved around the table toward his fellow KGB agent. Reaching a point directly behind Myshkin, he reached across his seated comrade's shoulder and picked up the message, while Myshkin casually took another long drag of his cigarette. He barely heard Dimitry inhale a lungful of air.

*Whack!* The violence of the slap to the back of Myshkin's head from Dimitry's powerful forearm drove his face into the desktop! The KGB chief felt the bridge of his nose cracking as the sweet taste of blood seeped into his mouth. Dimitry quickly grabbed a fistful of Myshkin's thick hair and jerked his head back before slamming it once again onto the table! *Whack!*

Myshkin struggled to get out of the chair, but the pain in his face was too distracting and he felt himself being wrenched from the chair by his collar and then flung across the room, landing in a heap beneath the window. Before he could react, Dimitry was on top of him, pulling Myshkin's bloodied face toward his own.

"Listen to me, Myshkin. I *am* in charge of this operation. Andropov and Kornilov sent me here to run it, and I *am* going to run it! Don't mess with me, Comrade. You may be older and an operator, and you think of me only as an analyst, but I'm also a Zhukov! And never forget it!" Dimitry shook Myshkin hard as he reminded him of his family name. "My grandfather shot Beria. And if you challenge me…I'll shoot you! So remember this: I am from Lubyanka, I work for Andropov, and I am a Zhukov. Now take this message to the communications center before I give you a broken arm to match your broken nose. *Ponamayetya*!"

Myshkin nodded, slowly rose to his feet, grabbed the message form, and stumbled toward the door, reaching into his back pocket for a handkerchief to place over his bleeding nose. He stopped momentarily and glared at Dimitry but said nothing. He would deal with this young punk from headquarters but later, when the time was right.

## US Embassy, Rome

The small cab pulled up to the embassy entrance, and John Krol quickly stepped from the car. He was wearing no hat, and his priestly clothing was concealed beneath a light raincoat that was buttoned up to the collar. He quickly walked to the front door where an embassy official was waiting with an extended hand. "Right on time, Your Eminence," the official said, greeting his important guest and quickly ushering him through the door.

"Thank you," Krol replied, hurrying through the door and then following his escort up the stairs. On the second floor, they walked briskly down the hall before stepping through an unmarked door that could just as easily have been a janitor's closet, but once inside, Krol quickly recognized his two young visitors to Philadelphia from the week before. "Katherine, Carter, how are you?"

"We're fine, Your Eminence," Katherine answered.

"You mean, 'We're fine, *John*,' correct?" Krol replied with a grin. By then, he had noticed two other people in the room, and Carter quickly stepped in to make introductions.

"John, this is Bruce Harrison and this is Matteo Ferrari." Krol pulled off his coat, shook hands with both men, starting with Bruce, whom he correctly sensed was the more important, and sat down in one of the chairs at the round table occupying most of the room.

After making himself comfortable, the cardinal looked to Harrison. "So, I presume you are with the Agency?" he asked, more or less rhetorically.

"No," Harrison causally lied. "I'm with the State Department, here in Rome on a temporary assignment."

Krol leaned back in his chair and paused briefly while leaving his gaze fixed on Bruce. "Do you want my help in this conclave or not, young man?"

Harrison looked nervously over toward Kath and Carter. "Well, Cardinal Krol, if you put it so directly, yes…we want some advice and guidance."

"Actually you want a lot more, Mr. Harrison. So let's not to be coy with each other, as I don't find it appropriate given the subject of this meeting. Stan Turner is a friend of mine. He runs the CIA. Everyone knows that. So, allow me to rephrase the question. Do you work for Stan Turner?"

Harrison had harbored suspicions about Krol and any role he might play, but he liked this no-nonsense approach. "Very well, Eminence. Yes, I work for Admiral Turner, as does Matteo here."

Krol chuckled. "Great. I'm glad we cleared that up, as I didn't want to be in the wrong place chatting with the wrong people. So, I'm John Krol, I work for God, and he's temporarily loaned me out to Stan Turner. Let's leave it at that. So, what do we do?"

"Well," Harrison began, "the key to this—as it pertains to you— will be getting timely information on how the vote is trending in the conclave after you are all sequestered in the Sistine Chapel. Obviously any voice communications are out for three reasons. First, they might be overheard. Second, getting to a place where they won't be overheard would likely make any information untimely. And, of course, lastly, you are not supposed to say anything about what's going on, but we're assuming coded messages don't count as saying anything."

Harrison motioned to Matteo Ferrari who slid around the table and took the open seat next to Krol. "I appreciate your effort to cover my theological flank," Krol replied, "but I think any communications will open me to criticism, and possible excommunication. So, let's operate on the presumption that your first two considerations are the more relevant and let me deal with the third. That's between me and God. But I'm not a cryptographer, so how would I send coded messages and—I guess more importantly—learn how to send coded messages by next Saturday?"

"Your Eminence," Ferrari interjected, "we have a system…at least we think we have a system, and it'll be as simple as possible. You'll only need to learn a few very basic codes that can be sent using a very small device that will fit under your robes. It will have a very small keyboard, kind of like a very tiny typewriter, but with only a few keys—no more than ten."

"Do you have it here?"

"Not yet, we should have it in a couple of days. There's still some testing to be done."

The cardinal rubbed his hands together and sat pensively for a few moments. "I'm not good at learning new things at this point in my life. I can't even type normally on a real keyboard. I do hunt and peck. I'm not sure I can master such a thing in a short time. Can't we just use Sister Cummings?"

The others in the room exchanged glances, until Harrison spoke. "You've made contact with Sister Cummings?"

Krol looked over at Kath. "I have. She asked me if I knew where Benjamin Franklin was born. That was the contact conversation you told me to expect, was it not?"

"Uh…yes, that was it," Harrison answered, "but I had thought she would identify herself to you a bit closer to the conclave, so as to keep her identify covered as long as possible. If she becomes too visible too soon, there's always the chance of a compromise. Was anyone else there when she approached you?"

"Just another cardinal. He's a rather detached fellow and somewhat self-absorbed. I'm sure he thought nothing of it."

Carter waited for Harrison to ask the identity of the other cardinal, but he didn't. This struck the NSC staffer as odd, as it seemed this would be an item the CIA man would pursue, but since Harrison didn't ask, Carter didn't either. It was a mistake.

Harrison continued, "Cardinal Krol, I—"

"Bruce, please call me John. I'm increasingly of the view that in these circumstances, 'John' is more appropriate."

"Very well…John, I think that Sister Cummings is a secondary line of communications that we can use leading up to the conclave, but after it begins, we'll need timely input on how the voting is proceeding. I don't see any alternative to the coded communications device described by Matteo. Do you agree?"

Krol leaned back in his chair and looked at the faces in the room. "Well, I suppose. But is that all you need me to do? Keep the scorecard?"

"No, far from it," Kath quickly inserted. "You agree with us that we need to encourage the election of a non-Italian pope. You are one of the voters for the election and a very important one. We'll need you to plant the seeds and cultivate the view that it's time for a change."

The Philadelphian slowly rubbed his hands together. "OK. Got it. Will you need me to come again and get trained on this thing?"

"I think so," Matteo replied, relieved that Krol had agreed to try his device.

"Meanwhile," Harrison added, "talk up Koenig and Wyszynski."

"Yes, leave that to me," Krol answered. "Leave that one to me."

The Americans smiled, unaware that the cardinal was only willing to follow their secular orders to a point.

CHAPTER 12

# Friday, October 6, 1978
# Camp Peary

• • •

LARRY AND CHRIS HAD BEEN hard at work for the past four days. It was time for a real test. They had labored nearly nonstop, using various designs and experimenting with several configurations, trying to make Chris's device fit into the thermal box that Professor Ames had delivered days earlier. It was a tight fit, but then they knew it would be. The device was turning out to be quite a Rube Goldberg affair, pulled together using pieces of different systems, none of them intended for this type of use. Integrating them into a workable system was a significant challenge, but dealing with significant challenges was the daily routine throughout the CIA.

"Ready to give it a try?"

Chris looked up from her cluttered desk and saw Larry approaching. She was exhausted after a third long night of designing and testing. Her degree was in electrical engineering, and she loved what she did, but she preferred to have more time in which to do it. "I think so, Larry. Let me gather it all up, and let's head down to the lab. Peter will help carry the thing. He's had some invaluable suggestions on pulling it all together."

Larry nodded, looking around the cramped cubicle. "Where is he?"

"Here," came a voice to their right, as Chris's young assistant Peter White hustled over. "Sorry, but nature was calling. I'll get the Prick-68 items," he innocently said to Chris. "You grab the LIB."

Both of the young scientist-engineers carefully placed a series of parts on a wheeled lab table and then started heading toward the far end of the room with Larry walking ahead, the three of them wearing starched lab coats with breast-pocket liners stuffed with pens, the telltale sign that they all had engineering degrees.

They wound their way across the laboratory until they reached a large set of locked double doors. Larry walked up and swiped his ID card through a card reader, and the doors unlocked with a slight click, allowing the three of them to enter. Inside, off to their right, was a coated thermal chamber, a room actually, about the size of the walk-in freezer at a restaurant but designed to generate extreme heat rather than extreme cold. All four sides of the chamber had rectangular glass observation windows, allowing those on the outside to watch what was going on inside. Again, Larry led the way up and opened the chamber's door as Chris and Peter rolled the two carts inside. On a solid stand in the middle of the chamber was the thermal box Professor Ames had delivered days earlier.

For the next half hour, Larry worked outside the chamber, arranging several instruments, setting various gauges, and connecting a simple but large butane bottle to a valve attached to a hose running to cylindrical burners mounted on three of the chambers' interior walls. While Larry attended to the exterior duties, Peter and Chris were busily hooking up several items inside and gently sliding them into Ames's thermal box, whose interior had been configured with several mounts designed to house the pieces of the unwieldy contraption.

"No...not there. That lead goes here," Chris said several times as Peter fed small wires to her.

"I know," he often replied, "but we have to get this one to go under that node. No! Not that node, this node."

To an outsider, this discussion would sound like a conversation heavy with annoyance, but in actuality, it was the way this group of highly skilled inventors routinely communicated. Watching from outside, Larry grinned and slowly shook his head while running his hand through his hair, the feel of which reminded him that once this experiment was over, he seriously needed a shower. After about a half hour, the two engineers bolted the top of the thermal box into place, and Chris turned and looked through the window at Larry, giving him the thumbs-up sign. She and Peter walked out of the chamber, closing and tightly latching the door behind them.

"All set?" Larry asked.

His two colleagues nodded.

"OK. So before we light this thing off, let's go over it one more time. Now tell me again what we have in there, what should happen, and what I should see on the receiver over there." He pointed to a table a few feet away with a large green box sitting on it attached to a teletype machine and surrounded with numerous electrical meters. "Oh, and I'm dying to know what the hell a 'Prick-68' is?"

"I'll start," Peter said, his voice full of excitement. "The 'Prick-68' is a small radio made by Magnavox. The army is beginning to field them as the modern-day version of the old walkie-talkie. It's a small, individual radio that can fit into a pocket or a backpack. The formal army designation is the AN/PRC-68...so, the troops just call it a Prick-68."

"I'm sure they do," Larry answered, his grin insufficient to mask his fatigue. "Go on."

"Well, the 68 is an R/T—a receiver transmitter. It both receives and transmits, which we needed, of course. And it's solid state and small, which we also needed. But we don't need it to operate in a voice mode; we just need it to relay short signal bursts from the transmitter you designed, so we were able to reconfigure it for sending data as opposed to voice. That saved some space, but more importantly, it also reduced our power needs. And we reduced the power needs even further because it only needs to transmit about a thousand feet. But I wasn't able to reduce power as much as I had hoped because the antenna, as you know, is quite long. Still, I got the power demand down from fifteen volts, which the army uses, to four volts while still providing an RF output of half a watt."

"Half a watt enough?" Larry asked, a bit concerned at such a small number.

"Worked on the wiring table."

"Yeah, I'm sure it did, but how far did you transmit?"

"Well, just to the other end of the lab. Maybe 150 feet. But it came through quite strongly. I think we're fine on distance. But I am concerned about the temperature."

"Why?"

Chris jumped into the discussion. "Because of the impact on the battery. In order to get the small size needed, we're going with a relatively new power source, a LIB."

"Which is?" Larry inquired.

"A lithium-ion battery…LIB. It's a whole new idea for powering small devices, pioneered by a scientist working for Exxon, of all places—they want it for undersea exploration. I heard about it while getting my degree at Binghamton University. It'll give us the four volts we need, and it should last for at least three days, but a lot of that will depend on how well Professor Ames's box works. If it allows much heat inside, then the battery life will drop considerably."

"What does 'considerably' mean, Chris…in real terms?"

"Maybe as short as a day. We're not sure."

"Well, they say we need three days. How'd you get a LIB?"

"Had a colleague at Binghamton call the fellow at Exxon and ask for a few prototypes. We have the professor at Binghamton on our payroll, basically the same arrangement you have with Ames. He coughed up a few. I have them all here."

"Good work, Chris. Anything else?"

"Yeah, one thing. We designed and installed a small vent in the box that will allow the external heat in when we want."

Larry's face conveyed considerable surprise. "Why, I thought keeping the heat outside was important for the functioning of the system."

"It is," Chris quickly answered. "But when we're done, if the vent is opened a little bit, enough heat will get inside to cause the LIB to experience a thermal runaway."

"A what?"

"A thermal runaway...meaning it will explode. Not a big explosion, mind you, but enough to destroy the LIB and the 68. Kinda like those tapes used to burn up on *Mission Impossible* after Peter Graves got his mission."

Chris grinned at the last comment. Larry did not. He was too tired. "OK," he said. "Well, let's turn on the heat and see what happens. This thing better work, or we'll all be getting pink slips signed by Admiral Turner himself. The transmitter ready to broadcast?"

Peter nodded his head while throwing a small toggle switch. Their heads simultaneously turned to a series of meters mounted on the table alongside the receiver, relieved as the needles on all meters immediately jumped to the vertical.

"Great," Larry softly said, turning toward Peter, "now hit some random buttons of the Nagra and let's see what happens."

Peter picked up a small keyboard he had built from various components and began to push a series of buttons in slow sequence. As he did, the meters on the table began to fluctuate. The three exchanged excited glances. It was working! The transmitter was broadcasting, the LIB was providing power, the Prick-68 was relaying the signals to the large, green receiver, and the teletype machine started printing the random gibberish being sent.

"OK, now for the acid test," Larry whispered, pushing another button, sending electrical power to a glow plug inside the chamber. Within a few seconds, the burners mounted on the chamber walls burst into flames, and the three of them peered through the window as the thermometer inside began to show the heat rapidly rising. Soon, the temperature around Professor Ames's thermal box was showing 200 degrees. Larry looked at Peter. "OK, send some more signals."

Peter nodded and again began pushing random buttons on each of the keys of the small keyboard. The three of them nervously turned their eyes once more to the needles near the green receiver. They continued to indicate that the system was working, and the teletype kept spitting out paper. For the next eight hours, this small squad of Camp Peary scientists repeated this sequence, sending signals, igniting the burners in the thermal chamber, and then turning them off. Through it all, the system worked exactly as hoped. Larry was tempted to test the thermal runaway feature by sending the signal opening the small vent in the box but decided not to. The thing was doing what they wanted it to, so he thought it imprudent to destroy their only working model. He decided to cool down the chamber and pack the whole thing up. It was a job well done, and—most important—it was done.

Leaving Peter and Chris to get the systems ready for shipment, Larry returned to his office and called the technology office at Langley. The usual person answered the phone. Larry didn't know his name, but he knew his voice, and this voice was the only one he ever heard at the other end of this particular phone line. "Yes, Larry at the Farm. It's all set. We ran a complete set of tests, and it worked as expected. What do you want me to do with it now?"

The Langley voice was brief as always. "Fabulous. A courier will come by and get it tomorrow, about 10:00 a.m. He'll have ticket ID 60."

"Got it," Larry flatly responded. "ID 60. We'll have it ready to go." He hung up the phone. His job was finished. He had no idea whom he had just spoken with, who would show up the following morning at 10:00 with ticket ID 60, where this device was going, or what it was for. It didn't matter. He didn't have a need-to-know any of that. His part of this mission was over. That was what he did on the Farm, working for the Agency. He smiled to himself. "A 'Prick-68.' Who the hell ever thought that up?"

# THE VATICAN

The cardinals' daily general congregation had ended, and they were slowly filing out of the Pope Paul VI Audience Hall. The cavernous hall, mostly in Vatican City with a small piece in Italy, could hold over six thousand people for large papal audiences. Given the tight quarters that they occupied, the cardinals were more than pleased by the decision to hold some of the general congregations in the spacious hall as opposed to the relatively cramped Pauline Chapel.

Today's meeting had been rather perfunctory, as there were no big issues to be decided and the details of conducting the conclave were of little dispute. After all, the cardinals had just been through one six weeks before. Much of the time was taken up with Villot's administrative announcements, followed by prayers and meditations led by Cardinal Pericle Felici, the senior cardinal deacon. Whoever was elected pope, Felici would have the honor of making the announcement from the main Vatican balcony, just as he had in August, informing the world of the selection of Cardinal Luciani. But now, with the congregation finished for the day, it was time for the morning prattiche, the Vatican's version of politicking in its smokeless "smoke-filled rooms." Cardinal Jedar Katic hated the entire ritual.

Coffee and pastries had been placed on tables at the rear of the hall by Sister Cummings and her staff, and the cardinals began slowly moving in that direction, usually in groups of two or three, discussing the congregation or dropping subtle, and occasionally not so subtle, hints and inquiries about who among them might best fit the white robes. Katic tried to stay alone. He had his reasons for doing so, but upon arriving at one of the linen-covered tables with the coffee pots, he heard a familiar voice call his name. "Jedar, how are you today? All rested up?"

Katic recognized the voice and turned again to the smiling face of Cardinal John Krol. "I'm very well today, Your Eminence. Thank you. And were you successful in getting your passport problems resolved at your embassy."

"Well, not completely," Krol answered, stirring a cube of sugar into his coffee. "They took a new picture of me—and a pretty bad one, I must say—but evidently the passport itself has to come from Washington for some reason. So, I'll have to go back."

Katic took a sip of his coffee. This delay struck him as odd, normal for Belgrade perhaps, but it seemed odd for Washington. "I see.

I'm sorry for your inconvenience, John, but all bureaucracies have their rules, as we well know, having just heard our own from Villot and his minions."

Krol's eyes had wandered across the room. "Jedar, have you ever met Cardinal Flahiff from Canada? That's him standing over by the pastry table. Would you care to meet him? He's a delightful chap."

Katic glanced over in the direction Krol had indicated and saw Cardinal Flahiff, who was just being joined by his fellow Canadian cardinals, Maurice Roy and Paul-Emile Leger. "I don't know them," he softly replied. "Why don't you go talk with them, and I'll just get some more coffee? Luciani was right: getting a good cup of coffee in the Vatican is a challenge."

Krol grinned, pleased to have solicited some levity from the dour Yugoslav, but disappointed at his refusal to mingle with others. He nodded politely to Katic and then headed over toward the Canadians, leaving Katic alone—that is, until Sister Cummings appeared beside him with a fresh pot of coffee. "May I freshen up your cup, Your Eminence?"

"Yes, you may," Katic answered, extending his cup downward toward the diminutive Irish nun, who quickly refilled it. "So, did I understand you have family in Philadelphia, where Cardinal Krol is from?"

"Yes, Your Eminence. Quite a few," Cummings answered, smiling.

"Been there to visit them?"

"Yes, Your Eminence. A few times. Have you been to Philadelphia?"

"Once. Had an old friend who moved there from Zagreb. Started a small business. He invited me, so I took a vacation and spent a few days there."

"Very nice, Your Eminence."

An awkward pause came between the cardinal and the nun, which he finally ended after some long seconds fingering his coffee cup.

"What I was most impressed with, Sister, was the magnificent city hall in the center of the city. It is quite a stunning building. And the dome they put on it reminded me of the one here on Saint Peter's, although much smaller, obviously."

"I agree," Sister Cummings replied. "I felt very much the same. It is quite beautiful." Another awkward silence. "Please excuse me, Your Eminence, but I need to check the pastries."

Katic nodded and displayed a rare smile. "Of course, thank you." And with that, Sister Cummings scurried away, leaving the archbishop of Zadar alone with his thoughts, which were rapidly running through his calculating mind. "Hmmm…I see," he said softly to himself, as he placed his cup and saucer on one of the small tables scattered about the hall.

Katic had never been to Philadelphia and had no businessman friend there. But he loved architecture, always had, and had once admired a picture of the Philadelphia City Hall. He knew from the photo that it was not crowned with a dome but something more like a Florentine bell tower, one rising high above an ornate building reflecting a Second Empire design style, similar to the executive office building next to the American White House. So it was now clear to him: Cummings had never been to Philadelphia either and probably had no family there. Something about her was suspiciously phony—very suspicious and very phony.

Katic glanced across the hall. Cummings was over pouring coffee for Krol and the three Canadian cardinals. Katic began doing more mental math. "Something is happening here," he thought. "There are twenty-five Italian cardinals split between Siri and Benelli, so each has about thirteen votes. The nine Americans plus the three Canadians make twelve. Add in the two UK cardinals, and that makes fourteen. Then add maybe half of the twenty or so other West European cardinals, and you are up to nearly twenty votes, a significant bloc, almost equal to the Italians. And Krol is seemingly working them and the South Americans hard; plus he has some odd connection with this phony nun."

It was math that added up to Katic. He clasped his hands behind his back and strolled out of the great hall. He needed to make a few phone calls and then get back to snoop around the other prattiches that would be bubbling up throughout the day.

## The Spanish Steps, Piazza di Spagna, Rome

It was midafternoon when a cab pulled to the curb at the intersection of the Via dei Condotti with the Piazza di Spagna. The two passengers in the rear of the cab paused for a moment to enjoy the view through the windshield framing one of Rome's best-known landmarks, the Spanish Steps. But the moment was over quickly, and Kath exited the cab while Carter paid the fare. On trips to the hotel, they had decided to return to different spots around the De Russie so as not to become a regular fixture at the front door. The narrow street that the hotel was located on made it easy to be surveilled by unfriendly eyes, and a more open area, such as Piazza di Spagna, was harder to watch. The walk was easy, as the hotel was just three blocks away on the Via del Babuino, the main street exiting the north side of the historic square.

The cab departed, and Carter walked over to Kath, who was enjoying the view of the Trinita dei Monti Church, which stood at the top of the 135 Spanish Steps. The piazza was filled with people, as it always was, and there was an air of excitement as the next conclave approached, mixed with some lingering sadness over the need for it.

"Beautiful, isn't it?" Carter asked, looking up at the church and all the people just sitting on the steps enjoying the afternoon sun. "Want a gelato?"

"A what?" Kath asked, surprised at the question.

"An Italian ice cream. They make a very nice, light ice cream here. And there's a vender right over there." Carter pointed across the square. "I'm going to get one, and I'd be happy to get you one as well."

"Sure," Kath replied.

Carter took off, picking his way to the ice cream stand, and returned in a few moments, handing a small cup to her.

"Here you go. Vanilla for you; chocolate for me."

Kath reached for the cup, her face flashing a sly smile. "How'd you know I like vanilla?"

"You told me."

"I did? When?"

"On the train back from Philly, when we rode back after our meeting with Krol."

She had no recollection of that part of the discussion. "If you say so. It's quite good," she said, putting some ice cream in her mouth using the small wooden spoon. "Let's get back to the hotel. I'm quite tired and want to enjoy a warm bath."

"Sounds good," Carter replied as they began walking toward the Via del Babuino. "I could use one myself, but…I don't have a bathroom. Still, I'm sure my elegant communal shower will work fine."

She caught a glimpse of his mischievous grin as they walked along, enjoying their ice cream cups. "Let's talk about it when we get to the hotel," Kath said, offering no further elaboration.

"Well, OK," Carter answered, not sure what she was talking about or what he should actually say about it.

● ● ●

As they exited the square, another cab pulled up to the intersection with the Via dei Condotti. A large man in an ill-fitted suit got out carrying a briefcase and slowly began pushing through the crowd toward the Spanish Steps. Arriving at the bottom, he climbed up precisely forty steps, as he had been instructed, and took a seat along the stone railing. He waited but not for long.

After about five minutes, a second man wearing a dark jacket and blue jeans arrived in the square. He looked up at the crowd seated on the steps and mentally counted up forty steps. Several people were seated on the fortieth step, but he had no problem picking out the one he had come to see. He walked up the steps and then casually squeezed past a few people seated near his contact before plopping down onto the hard stones next to the man with the briefcase. Neither acknowledged the other for a few seconds.

"Vladimir?" the man in the dark jacket finally asked.

"*Da*," came the softly mouthed reply. "Are you Brachi?"

"Yes," Bruno Brachi replied, slowly watching those around them to see if anyone was taking note. "This it?" Bruno asked, throwing a quick glance at the briefcase.

"*Da*."

"You want me to just deliver it to Petrov?"

"*Da*."

"Anything else?"

"*Nyet*. He'll know what to do with it."

Bruno again looked around the crowd on the steps and those going up and down. "You work directly for Myshkin?" he asked.

Vladimir nodded.

"Been there very long?"

Vladimir briefly shook his head but offered no further elaboration.

"A bit of advice, Comrade. Watch your back. I've never trusted Myshkin, and I suggest you don't either."

Vladimir gave Bruno a long, cold look. "Comrade Brachi, I do not believe you should speak like this. Myshkin is the head of our operations here in Rome."

Bruno again looked over the crowd near them before turning his gaze back to Vladimir. "Only some of them, Comrade. Only some of them. There's another superior to him. So, just some friendly advice, be careful."

Vladimir stared at Bruno, the expression on his face frozen. "*Korosho*. Thanks for the advice. Anything else?"

Bruno sat still for a moment. "Nyet. Ochen Korosho. Dasvidanya."

With that, he took the briefcase and began making his way down the steps back to the piazza. Vladimir watched him go, keeping his place on the fortieth step, casually lighting a cigarette. He saw Brachi cross the square and grab a cab on the corner of the Via dei Condotti and then watched as it sped away.

"What the hell was that all about?" he wondered. He had done both things that Myshkin had ordered, even though the first seemed strange to him. Why do that? It didn't seem to make any sense to him. But he was supposed to follow orders, so he did what he was told, no need to think about it. Nonetheless, he was starting to think, and he was distantly worried. He crushed his cigarette on the steps and started down to the square. It was a nice day, so he decided to walk back to the embassy.

## NEAR PIRNA, EAST GERMANY

Captain Belikov's GAZ-69 truck, the Soviet version of the US Army's famous jeep, was driving at top speed down a windy East German road just west of the small town of Pirna. The GAZ was an old vehicle, and it handled poorly as Belikov's driver wove in and out of the numerous trucks and tanks parked along the road, their crews standing outside their vehicles, smoking and exchanging views about why their large convoy had stopped. Belikov leaned out the window and wildly waved for those in the road to get out of the way. He knew why the convoy was stopped, and he also knew it could mean career-threatening trouble—for him.

The radio mounted behind him blared another loud, scratchy, difficult-to-understand communication. "Krasnaya 6, this is Krasnaya 12, where are you?"

Belikov recognized the voice of Sergeant Petrov and reached for the hand microphone anchored on the GAZ's dashboard. "This is Krasnaya 6, I'm about five minutes away. Any change in the situation?"

"*Nyet*, no change," came the reply.

Belikov reached across the seat and slapped his driver's shoulder. "Step on it!"

The GAZ sped up, its horn blaring, as soldiers in field uniforms and tanker suits jumped out of the way. Within five minutes, Belikov arrived at the site causing all the trouble. The driver hit the brakes hard, and the GAZ skidded to a stop, with Belikov jumping from the vehicle and running over to where he could see Sergeant Petrov standing, pistol drawn, pointing it at an officer wearing US Army fatigues. Petrov awkwardly saluted, keeping the pistol pointed at the American.

Belikov looked over to the side of the road where he could see the rear of a green Opel Admiral, the type of car used by the US Military

Liaison Mission (USMLM), and he immediately recognized the distinctive yellow license tags issued to this treaty-protected spy unit of the US Army, Europe. The Soviets had their own unit based in Frankfurt, West Germany, which was equipped with similar yellow tags.

The left side of the Opel was badly damaged, its front wheel all but ripped off, and deep scratches ran the length of the vehicle.

"What happened?" Belikov asked, looking at Petrov.

"I'll tell you exactly what happened, Captain," the American officer, a major, shouted at Belikov in perfect Russian. "My driver and I were driving down this road on a routine observation when this tank, number C-12, swerved into our path, crushed our front fender, and forced us into the ditch!" The American stomped his foot, pointing at Pasha, his voice rising. "And now this soldier has pulled a weapon on me, which you certainly know is not allowed by the military liaison agreement."

"Shut up!" Belikov yelled back, pointing as threateningly as he could at the American. "This is a restricted area. You are not authorized to be here, so if there is an agreement violation, it is yours."

"*Nyet,*" the American major loudly and immediately responded. "It is yours! This is not a restricted area. I have the most recently provided map from GSFG, and this area is not shown as restricted. Look for yourself."

"Stay where you are," Belikov firmly replied as the American started to step forward, map in hand. "As I said, you have no reason to be here."

"Nor do you," the American sharply replied. "The Red Army never conducts exercises in this area. So, why are you here? I'll show you where we are on the map. Maybe you and your unit are lost." The major again started to step toward Belikov.

"I said stay where you are!" Belikov repeated, louder than before.

The American stopped where he was, and Belikov turned his back to him, facing Sergeant Petrov. "What happened?" he whispered.

Pasha slowly slid his pistol back into its shoulder holster and nodded toward another Red Army soldier to keep the American covered. "We came around this curve, and Rostov saw a deer jump out of the woods. He swerved the tank into the center of the road and struck the

American vehicle, which was coming around in the opposite direction. I don't think Rostov ever saw it. When the car went off the road into the ditch, I could see the license plate and knew it was an American spy vehicle. So, we detained the American officer and his driver and radioed you." Pasha paused. "Is this a restricted area?"

Belikov looked back over at the American. "Damned if I know, Sergeant. But it's best to tell the Americans it is—given the circumstances. I'm sure that's what army headquarters will say when this incident gets to Zossen. But the damage is done. They know we're here."

Petrov looked at Captain Belikov, a puzzled expression on his face. "What do you mean by that, Captain—'They know we're here'? The Americans know? This is East Germany. They know the Red Army is in East Germany. So what do they know that's anything new, and why do we care?"

Belikov looked at his sergeant but said nothing for a few moments as he contemplated how to report this incident to his tank regiment's headquarters. A run-in with the American liaison mission—especially here—would not be welcome news. "Keep them here and watch them," he ordered. "I'll get back to you within the hour." With that, Belikov jumped back into his GAZ, turned around, and roared off down the road, leaving Pasha and the American officer silently watching as he left, each thinking his own thoughts about what had just occurred.

CHAPTER 13

# Saturday, October 7, 1978
# Hotel De Russie

• • •

KATHERINE O'CONNOR ALWAYS HAD DIFFICULTY adjusting to travel, and although she had been at the De Russie for three nights, she was still waking up about 4:00 a.m. She had hoped that staying up late the night before and reading Herman Wouk's just-released novel *War and Remembrance* would put her biological clock in the right time zone. She had loved Wouk's first novel about the lead-up to World War II, *Winds of War*, and the romantic in her was interested to see where the obvious relationship between Byron Henry and Natalie Jastrow would go in the sequel. Plus so much of the original story had been set in prewar Italy, and now here she was, in a luxurious room in gorgeous Rome. Still, despite reading several chapters before turning in, she was still awake before 5:00 a.m. Conceding defeat to the clock, she had decided to get up and shower and was now standing in front of the bathroom mirror when she heard a soft knock at the door.

CIA people don't like surprises, and an unexpected early morning knock at the door was a surprise. Kath grabbed the belt on the wonderfully lush bathrobe provided by the hotel, pulled it tighter around her waist and then gently stepped over to her suitcase on the rack under the window. She unzipped a compartment in the suitcase lining, reached in, and pulled out a Beretta 418 pistol. She then reached into her purse and pulled out a seven-round magazine, slapped it into the pistol's receiver, and chambered a round. The soft knocking continued.

Kath walked to the door, the loaded revolver in the hand behind her. "Who is it?"

"Carter," came the reply.

Kath checked to ensure the door chain was in place, paused for a moment, placed her foot firmly on the carpet, and unlocked the door. She opened it slightly, just enough to confirm that the unexpected morning guest was indeed a sweat-suit-clad Carter Caldwell.

"Why are you knocking on my door at this hour?" she asked in an annoyed voice, most of it genuine.

"Can I come in?" was the whispered reply.

Kath hesitated a minute for some reason but concluded she had no excuse to leave her colleague in the hallway. She unhooked the chain, and Carter quickly stepped through the door. Kath looked down the hallway in both directions. Empty. She closed the door and locked it behind them. "To what do I owe this great honor?" she asked, setting the Beretta on the dresser and flipping the safety on.

"You're armed!" Carter exclaimed, looking wide-eyed at the pistol.

"Well, I do work for the CIA," Kath replied, surprised that he seemed to be surprised. "What do you expect, especially when someone is knocking on your door just after dawn!"

Carter stared at the pistol. "Isn't that a Model 418, like the one James Bond initially carried, before they made him switch to the Walther PPK?"

"I guess," Kath replied in an indifferent manner. "I never was much of a James Bond fan."

"Really? You work for the CIA…and you're not a James Bond fan?"

Katherine placed her hands on her hips and rolled her large eyes. "News flash, Carter! James Bond is fiction! Now why are you here at this absurd hour?"

"We need to get to the embassy," Carter replied, his eyes switching back and forth between Katherine and the Beretta.

"Why? Bruce didn't say anything about a meeting when we left yesterday."

"Not sure, but he said to get down there as soon as we could."

"How do you know that? Did he call you? Why would he call you rather than me? I'm the one with the Agency."

"I don't know, Kath. He had the embassy switchboard call me about fifteen minutes ago. Maybe they didn't want to wake you. Who knows?"

Katherine pondered this for a moment. It was some form of sexism, calling him instead of her. She wasn't clear quite what form, but she didn't care for it. "OK. I'll get dressed and meet you in the lobby."

Carter paused before replying, weighing what to say. "Well, I need a favor before meeting you in the lobby."

"What?"

"I need to use your bathroom to clean up."

Kath's eyes widened a bit. "Why? What's wrong with your 'communal bath'?"

"There's no water. They shut it off last night because of a leak in the toilet."

Katherine stared at him without commenting.

"Look, I need to shave and clean up before we go. Goodness, what are you worried about? You're the one with the gun! I'm just another unarmed army officer sleeping on a lumpy cot."

"All right, already," Katherine answered, unsure if she was annoyed. "Get your clothes and toiletries and come down in about twenty minutes."

"Twenty minutes! Harrison said we should get to the embassy right away."

"Twenty minutes is 'right away' for me, Carter. Now get your stuff and come back in twenty minutes, OK?"

"Fine," Carter replied, a bit exasperated. "See you in twenty minutes." He left and took the backstairs up to his room, where he gathered his shaving kit and a fresh change of clothes. He waited for his Omega watch to tick off precisely twenty minutes and then headed back to Katherine's room. Arriving again, he tapped once more on the door. This time, it quickly opened. Katherine was standing there in a gorgeous pale-blue dress, one that was perfectly cut in all the right ways, subtly but clearly accentuating her natural beauty. Carter didn't say anything, but his eyes showed that the twenty-minute wait had been worth the time.

"Here's the key," Kath stated, rather matter-of-factly. "There's another set of fresh towels on the bed. I'll see you in the lobby when you're done." With that, she stepped past him and headed down the hall. He watched her go until she disappeared around the corner. Then as fast as possible, he jumped in the shower and started getting presentable.

Katherine walked into the large lounge to the right of the hotel's reception area, fixed a cup of English breakfast tea, made herself comfortable in a large winged-back chair, and relaxed for a moment. She had only taken her second sip of tea when she heard a male voice.

"Ready to go?"

She looked up to see Carter standing beside her, looking quite dapper in khaki pants and a tailored Brooks Brothers sport coat, clean-cut and clean-shaven as always. Simultaneously he looked at her, admiring the blue dress hemmed to reveal an interesting portion of her long, athletic legs. For a few seconds, nothing was said, so Carter repeated the question. "I said, are you ready to go?"

Kath paused again. "Uh…yes. How…how did you get dressed so quickly?"

"It's something they teach you at West Point, getting up and out quickly in the right uniform. It seemed like just more harassment at the time, but it's a useful skill later in life." Carter smiled and enjoyed admiring her for a second longer. "I'll have the doorman get us a cab." She watched him head toward the front door, smiled, and took another sip of tea.

## The US Embassy, Rome

Arriving at the embassy, Carter and Katherine were again met at the front door and whisked to the small office where they had met with Cardinal Krol two days earlier. Shortly after they had taken their seats, Bruce Harrison walked in. As usual, he was all business.

"Morning, thanks for coming in so early. But we have something that might be an important development that we need to discuss."

"What sort of development?" Kath asked.

"Not really sure yet," the CIA operations chief replied, "but I got a call about it from Dugan saying we needed to meet. He should be here any minute."

Katherine tossed her head back. "Oh, great! Avery…again! How exciting! I get dragged down here at dawn to talk with Avery. Wonderful. Absolutely wonderful!"

Harrison looked over at Carter and then back to Katherine. "Have I missed something here?" Harrison asked. Nothing was said in reply. Bruce was accustomed to having his questions answered quickly, particularly by relatively junior Agency officers. He placed his hands on the table and leaned toward Katherine. "O'Connor, is there something going on here I need to know about?"

Carter butted in. "Katherine, you need to answer Bruce's question. Or should I?" He instantly regretted adding the last phrase, and it drew a very stern look from Kath, before she exhaled a deep breath and flashed her eyes to Bruce.

"OK…" She paused to compose the words she wanted to present. "Avery Dugan and I have…a history. We lived together for a couple of years and had a rather nasty breakup three years ago. I thought we had a serious relationship, and I think we did for most of the time we were together, but he started seeing someone else. I found out about it, and we ended our…shall we say, our living arrangement."

There was quiet in the room as Bruce mentally debated what to say next, if anything, and what to do next, if anything. He glanced over to Carter, who merely hunched his shoulders and said nothing further, so he glanced back to Kath, who was blankly staring at the wall across from her chair. "I see," Bruce slowly began. "What do you mean 'lived together'? Do you mean you shared an apartment? Or do you mean you…'lived together'?"

"My God! You guys are all the same! That's almost the same thing he asked!" she shouted, gesturing toward Carter. "The latter, OK!" She roughly crossed her arms across her chest and returned her gaze to the blank wall, allowing a few awkward moments to replace further awkward discussion.

"Katherine," Bruce gingerly continued, "I'm sorry about the past, but is any of it a reason why you can't work on this effort with us, if it includes Avery? And I'm sure it will include Avery."

Katherine cut her eyes up to Bruce, paused, and shook her head.

"All right, then," Bruce replied, "let's not dwell on it. We have to get a plan together, and given that Avery is about all we have to work with, so far as I can see, you need to just forget it and move on. OK?"

Kath's gaze continued to drill a hole between Bruce's eyes.

"Bruce," Carter said, deciding he needed to cool things down, "she's as much a professional as either of us, maybe even more so. She's a team player…on any team. Trust me. It won't be a problem."

The phone on the table rang, and Bruce reached for it while giving Carter a quizzical look, unsure why he was standing up so firmly for Katherine. "Harrison, here…Yes, he's here…Sure, will do." He replaced the phone in the receiver and turned to Carter. "The communications center says they have a call for you from the White House. Better get down there. It's down the hall to the right, third door on the left."

Carter looked quickly to Katherine and decided she was getting over the earlier discussion, so he excused himself, opened the door, and walked quickly to the embassy's communications center. He had expected to have to show credentials, but he was met at the door and quickly ushered into a small room reserved for private discussions—a sparse room having only a chair, a table, an elaborate secure communications phone called a STU-1, a pad of paper, and a pencil for taking notes. He pulled up the chair and lifted the receiver on the STU. "Carter Caldwell speaking." He immediately recognized the voice on the other end.

"Carter, Zbig Brzezinski here. Good morning."

Carter stiffened a bit. "Good morning, sir. Must be very early morning where you are?"

"Quite early. About 3:07 in the morning, according to the clock on the wall. I'm in the White House situation room. Many of us have been here since last evening. I'm with Stan Turner. Carter, the reason I'm calling is to let you know we've verified numerous movements by Soviet ground forces. It looks like about ten Soviet tank divisions in the Western Military District are moving toward the Polish border, and as many as ten more within GSFG have left their garrisons in East Germany, also moving toward the Polish border. We've had an incident involving a Soviet tank unit and a USMLM tour vehicle. In other words, it looks like they're positioning forces to invade Poland with a very heavy armored force from both directions. We placed some overhead assets to watch for this after we were alerted by Cosmos."

"Who's Cosmos?" Carter interrupted.

"Sorry, that's the code name of our most senior source in the Kremlin. The one I mentioned to you last week."

"OK. I don't think you mentioned a name to me then."

"I probably didn't, and given the look I am getting from Stan, I sense I probably shouldn't have mentioned it now. But anyway, they seem to be moving in the directions we'd feared. This puts us in a very awkward situation: do we say anything or not? Stan feels if we go public with what we know, it might prompt them to move right away, which we want to avoid. We don't want to deal with a fait accompli. On the other hand, if we ignore it, they may get the idea they'll get away with it whenever they move…as they did in Czechoslovakia ten years ago."

Carter was both intrigued and puzzled. "So, why are you calling me with this, sir?"

"We wanted to let you know the stakes were rising. Meaning that whatever you have working regarding the conclave is growing more important by the hour. We are increasingly convinced it'll take the election of either Koenig or Wyszynski to stop them. I know we agreed on pushing Koenig, but we may have to push Wyszynski. What's the plan right now?"

Carter paused, a grimace coming across his face. He didn't want to say what he was about to say to the national security advisor. "Zbig, I don't think we have one just yet. But that's why we're all here this morning. We're working on it." There was silence at the other end of the line. "Zbig? You still there?"

"Yes, Carter. I'm still here. Look, you have to come up with something. Harrison has to come up with something. Somebody has to come up with something. I know this is hard. It's not like some third-rate South American country where we can just buy off a few people. I think we all know that. But this is getting rather dicey. So, you have to make something work! Put your heads together and figure it out!"

"Zbig," Carter firmly replied, "we have good people here and we're doing the best we can. We think we've got something developing right now that may be promising." Carter paused for a moment, hoping Brzezinski wouldn't ask what it was he was talking about, as Carter didn't know, but since there was no request for additional details on the other end of the line, he decided to push ahead before some came through. "Sir, does Harrison know about these troop movements?" Carter could hear Brzezinski and Turner conferring.

"No, he doesn't, and Stan says don't tell him. It's not worth widening the circle by bringing him in. He's an operator, so push him to…well, push him to operate."

"Very well, sir. Anything else?"

"No, I think that's it. Check every afternoon with the embassy switch. We'll leave a note with them if we need you to check in sooner. And, Carter…the other Carter in my life, the one in the Oval Office, is more than casually interested in this. Do I make myself clear?"

"Very clear, sir. I'll be in touch."

With that, the STU clicked off and Carter hurried back to the small meeting room to join the others. He opened the door to what seemed like a meat locker. Avery had arrived and was seated across the table from Kath. Bruce was standing in the corner, cross-legged, his hands in his pockets. Carter could see from his expression that he was glad to have someone else in the room to run interference.

"Anything up that we should know about?" Harrison asked, not really expecting much in the way of information.

"Nope," Carter answered. "Dr. Brzezinski just wanted an update on where we were."

"And you gave him a full briefing of our plans, I presume."

"Right."

"Which means you told him nothing since that's basically what we have…nothing."

"Right again."

"And how did that go down?"

"Well…" Carter paused for some dramatic effect. "Let's just say that they want some action and at the end they want either Koenig or Wyszynski standing on the balcony."

"Great! Nothing to it!" Harrison let out a deep breath and then looked over to Avery Dugan. "So, Avery, we're all here. Now what's up that you're dying to tell us about?"

Avery's eyes were fixed on Katherine, whose eyes were wandering to everything but him. He answered in a very matter-of-fact voice. "I have it on very good authority that Cardinal Siri has conducted a pre-conclave interview that is not to be published until after the conclave concludes."

Kath looked up. "Really? An interview with whom?"

Dugan looked at her briefly and then shifted his eyes to Carter. "Not clear just yet, but I'll bet it's with Gianni Lecheri from the *Gazzetta del Popolo*."

"Which is?" Bruce asked, a bit unsure why any of them should care.

"It's an Italian newspaper that covers the Vatican. And I've known Gianni for some time. He's become a good friend, and he's a hell of a reporter. He has incredible access to almost everyone in the Vatican, which is why I've worked pretty hard to make him into a good friend."

Carter was not yet sufficiently impressed to understand why an interview merited an early-morning rush to the embassy. "So, if there is an interview, what does Siri say, and why do we care?" he asked.

Dugan's expression turned serious. "If what I've heard is true, it'll be dynamite within the church."

"How?" Harrison asked. "I assume Siri doesn't announce that he's a closet Protestant!"

"Actually, that might go down easier. He apparently raises serious questions about the Vatican II reforms."

"Which ones?" Katherine asked, looking at Dugan with an expression suggesting that her professional interest had pushed aside her personal feelings.

"I hear pretty much all of them. He doesn't like Mass being said in local languages, he doesn't believe in collegiality and any further empowerment or power sharing with the bishops, he comes down very firmly in favor of *Humanae Vitae*, and he seems to say that future popes are not necessarily bound by the pronouncements of past popes. He really throws down the gauntlet to the progressive elements of the church, and I'm sure it'll land with a loud thud at the feet of Benelli and his supporters…if there's anything to this."

Katherine leaned forward toward Avery. "So, if this is true, Avery, it sounds like Siri thinks he's going to be the next pope, and when he's in office, the interview will come out, which will send a strong message to the so-called progressives that he plans to turn back the church clock, dismiss Vatican II—along with the whole papacy of John XXIII—and he won't tolerate any sort of dissent when he does."

"That's how I read it, Kath. But he certainly doesn't want to create the next big schism, which explains why I'm hearing that he's been talking with Benelli and has offered to make him Vatican secretary of state, as long as he's loyal, and then when he passes on, Benelli will be well positioned to succeed him."

"I don't get that," Carter interrupted. "If Siri and Benelli are, as we all know and agree, the two most likely Italian candidates, and if they have very different philosophical views, why would Siri want to set up Benelli to succeed him so he could reverse all he had done."

Dugan nodded. "Yeah, I know what you mean. But there are rumors going around that despite appearances, Siri is actually much healthier than Benelli, despite being fourteen years older. There are whispers that Benelli has some cardiac issues."

Carter looked at Kath to see if she would agree with the summary he was about to offer. "So, the Siri plan would be, therefore, to make a deal with Benelli, get his supporters to vote for Siri, bring Benelli back seemingly positioned to be the next pope, yet bet on outliving him, making the deal moot. Meanwhile, after the conclave, the interview comes out revealing how conservative Siri intends to be, but at that point, he's an autocratic pope so the opposition, including Benelli, will have no choice but to fall in line."

"I think, in a nutshell, that's it, Carter."

"It has a logic to it," Kath added, "but if such an overture were made, I don't see Benelli taking it. It would be a real risk for him if he wants to be the next pope, and I think he would lose a lot of credibility with his supporters, whoever they actually are. He's in a good position now. One would expect that those who voted for Luciani last time would be likely to back Benelli this time. So, I see this Siri interview as something of a desperate move."

Bruce took a seat at the table and looked at the others in the room. "Well, desperate or whatever it is, if there's an interview out there, what would we do with it?"

"It's pretty obvious to me," Kath quickly answered. "The first thing we need to do is have Avery meet with Lecheri and see what he actually has, if anything. And if there is an interview and it says what Avery has heard…then we leak it."

"Leak it how?" Carter asked.

"Leak it when?" Avery chimed in. "And we can't just leak it. If it's Lecheri's interview, just leaking it would ruin him. It can't be the usual sort of leak. It's got to have some distance from him."

Bruce Harrison's operational passions suddenly came to the front. "OK, we'll have to think this through. Meanwhile, Avery, get hold of Lecheri; see if there's anything to this, and if there is…get us copy. We'll have to have a copy! Then we'll put our heads together and see what we do with it—if anything." The operations chief let out a long sigh. "Hell of a thin reed, trying to pull something like this off and all we have to work with is a rumor about an interview arguing Mass should be said in a dead language!" He then paused for a moment before changing gears and turning his gaze to Kath and Avery. "Would you two mind stepping outside so Carter and I can have a private conversation?"

It was obviously an awkward request. Avery and Kath glared at each other briefly.

"Sure," Kath said. "I need to go to the ladies' room anyway."

"And I think I need to go find Gianni Lecheri," Avery replied as indifferently as possible.

With that, they both stood up. Avery opened the door, and they stepped into the hall and turned in opposite directions. Bruce closed the door behind them and turned to Carter.

"Carter, you and I are going to have to work tightly together to pull this off, agree?"

"Sure, of course," Carter answered, not quite sure where this discussion was headed.

"OK," Bruce continued. "So what was the White House call about? Carter, we can't have any secrets between us. I trust you, and you'll have to trust me. Now let me guess. Brzezinski had something to tell you that came from Cosmos, right? Some big-picture thing, I'd guess?"

"He did," Carter replied, leaving Bruce waiting for more detail, but none was forthcoming.

"OK, Carter. I'll go first. We have it from Cosmos that if the conclave selects someone the Soviets don't like, he won't live through his first night. They have means, and they'll take him out. Brzezinski tell you that?"

"No, that he didn't mention. Who told you that?"

"Admiral Turner."

"Well, you Agency guys operate in odd ways. Turner was there while I was speaking to Brzezinski, but he didn't mention killing the next pope if the Kremlin doesn't like him."

Harrison tossed his head back and chuckled. "Oh, come on, Carter. Who the fuck knows what guys like Turner and Brzezinski are thinking when they do the things they do? It's way above my pay grade, and my pay grade is pretty fucking high. OK, so stipulated…we're kinda weird. A lot of people have that view. But I only care about one fucking thing at the moment, raising our odds for success on this wild thing from 10 percent to…say, 20 percent! And to get the odds that good, we've got to really be tight with each other and trust each other. So, the call…what the hell was it about?"

Carter thought for a minute. He knew that Harrison was basically correct. And he knew the twenty percent number was likely the upper boundary right now. "OK. They have a message from Cosmos, whoever he is, that the Soviets are moving forces so they can be in position to invade Poland. And they've confirmed it with overhead. Maybe as large as twenty tank divisions, which I believe was the force they sent into Czechoslovakia in 1968. So they seem to be following their old SOP. I took it from the conversation that they didn't think the Red Army was set enough to invade right away, but we probably have no more than two weeks, which means…"

"Which means until just after the end of the conclave," Harrison inserted, finishing the thought.

"About how I see it," Carter answered with a sigh.

"All right, Carter. Do we have a deal? Tell me what you know, and I'll do the same, OK? Brzezinski and Turner can play their game; we'll play ours."

"Deal," Carter answered and then paused for a few seconds while he and Harrison shook hands. "Bruce, ten percent? Do you really think we're at 10 percent?"

Harrison smiled. "Nah, I exaggerated. Closer to five."

## THE VATICAN

It was early afternoon as Bruno Brachi walked through the catacombs under the Vatican Museum with the briefcase he had been given at the Spanish Steps concealed in a plastic shopping bag. There was still a lot of activity going on as workers scurried about, toiling on the reconstruction of the remaining rooms for the cardinals. Brachi was making this particular walk around appear as routine as possible, so he was somewhat relieved to run into Gianluca Giordano, although not fully given their testy relationship.

"How are we doing with the rooms?" Brachi asked, as he approached Gianluca's work crew.

"Getting there, Bruno," came the brief reply.

"Well, get there quicker. We're going to be out of time soon. Seems like it went quicker in August."

"It did, Bruno." Again, Gianluca was as brief as possible, hoping Bruno would pass by as quickly as possible. But his eyes rolled when one of his crew, for some reason, decided to be friendly with their boss.

"What's in the bag, Mr. Brachi? Something for the wife?"

Bruno stopped, a look of annoyance slowly yielding to a smile. He hadn't expected anyone to ask about the bag, but now he was being handed an innocent-sounding cover story. "Yes, in fact it is. Her birthday is tomorrow so I slipped out after lunch to do a little shopping."

"Anything new from the camerlengo?" Gianluca asked, wanting to change the subject to something that would encourage Bruno to move on to the next stop on his useless supervisory tour.

"Nothing. He just wants you to finish the construction of the rooms for the cardinal electors as soon as you can. I have told him he can count on us to have them ready. So keep up the good work." With that, Bruno continued on down the dimly lit hallway of the museum's lowest subterranean level. The others on the work crew returned to sawing and hammering, but Gianluca watched as Brachi slowly moved away, stopping every few feet, making the pretense of inspecting something until he disappeared around a corner.

"Something isn't quite right here," Gianluca thought to himself. "Why would he have a shopping bag down here? Why wouldn't he have left it in his office?" Gianluca looked over to his crew. "Excuse me for a minute. I had something I forgot to ask Mr. Brachi. I'll be right back."

With that, Gianluca headed down the hallway, trying to step as lightly as possible, and to cling to the side of the hall where the shadows were darkest. Arriving at the corner Brachi had disappeared around, he stopped to peek down the dark hall. No one was there. He quickly and quietly scurried to the next corner just a few feet away and stopped again to peek around the wall. About twenty feet away, he could now see Brachi with someone else, dressed in dark clothes, but he could not make out who the shadowy figure was. He watched for a few moments, certain that he was unseen from where he stood. Brachi and the other man were having a whispered discussion, and then Brachi handed over the shopping bag to the dark-clad figure, nodded a couple of times, seeming to acknowledge some unheard instructions, gave a slight wave of the hand, and turned to head back in Gianluca's direction.

Giordano pulled back from the corner and quickly and softly headed back toward his crew. He was the rabbit; Brachi was the turtle. He knew he would easily get back to the men before his boss would. Approaching the men, he said nothing, hoping that Brachi would just walk past them when he reached their location. He did. Nothing was said. But something was up. And Gianluca knew he had best try to find out what it was.

## Hotel De Russie

It was midafternoon before Kath and Carter emerged from their cab and stepped again into the Piazza di Spagna. They hurried down the Via del Babuino to the De Russie, walking crisply without seeming to hurry, Katherine leading the way along the narrow sidewalk. Reaching the hotel, she walked through the entrance and straight through to the courtyard, taking a seat at one of the round coffee tables. Carter followed her. A waiter quickly appeared, and Kath immediately ordered cups of coffee for them, leaned back in her chair, and fixed her eyes on Carter, who fixed his eyes on her in return. The visual standoff lasted for nearly a minute.

"Thanks," Katherine finally said, breaking the strained silence.

"For what?" Carter replied, uncertain if this was a sincere comment or the prologue to something else.

"For sticking up for me with Harrison like you did. I appreciate it. It's not the easiest thing you can do being a woman—working for the Agency, I mean."

"I'm sure it's not. But I just stated the obvious. You're a real pro. That's all I said."

The coffee arrived. "I know. It wasn't much to you, but it meant a lot to me. I appreciated it. I really did. Working on this with Avery is difficult for me. But I'll do what a professional does. I'll handle it."

Carter smiled. "I'm sure you will." With that, the two of them just relaxed, finishing their coffee without saying anything further. They left the table and headed toward the elevator, which opened and carried them up to Katherine's floor. They both walked down the hall toward her door. After a few steps, Kath stopped. "Carter, where are you going?"

Carter's look was one of puzzled bemusement. "I'm escorting you to your room."

"Why are you doing that?"

"It's what a gentleman does…or so I was taught. Once you're there, I'll continue on to the end of the hall and climb the stairs to my place in the attic. I think we both need a little rest."

They stopped in front of Katherine's door, and she started digging in her purse for the large, ornate key common to European hotels but soon abandoned the search. "OK, Carter. Show me your room."

"What?"

"Show me your room. Is it up those stairs?" Without waiting for a reply, Katherine took off for the door at the end of the hall with the stairwell marking on it. She pushed it open and climbed up one level, with Carter close behind. Arriving at the attic landing, she turned to her army colleague. "Which one is it?"

He led her down three doors, reached into his pocket for his small, nonornate key, and opened the door to the small room. Katherine stepped inside, immediately turned on her heels, and stepped back out.

"Carter, this is terrible! You can't stay in this! Get your bags and come with me. We'll share the room."

"Well, how will that work?" Carter replied, his question delivered with genuine surprise. "It only has one bed—as you've pointed out a time or two."

"True," Katherine answered, "but it does have that big oversized chair with a large ottoman. I think that will be an improvement over that horrible cot!" She shook her head as she looked at Carter's room. "And, the bathroom is quite spacious. I'm sure we can schedule that in a suitable way…especially since you get dressed as quickly as you do."

Carter thought the right thing to do here was to graciously compliment her for the offer but to chivalrously stay where he was. That would certainly be the more proper approach. He looked at her for a moment. "Kath, thanks for the offer, but…I'll need a few minutes to gather my things. Can you carry my hanging bag down?"

CHAPTER 14

## Sunday, October 8, 1978
## Soviet Embassy, Rome

• • •

Dimitry and Myshkin sat in the latter's embassy office. The morning light was just beginning to illuminate the room. Being in the same space was uncomfortable for both of them, more so for Myshkin, who now had a large bandage across the bridge of his nose. But it was uncomfortable for Dimitry as well because Vladimir was sitting with them. Dimitry was not sure what, if anything, Vladimir knew about Viktor's broken nose. He doubted Myshkin would have told his muscleman what actually happened; it would have been discrediting for him, but he was sure that Vladimir had received some instructions to watch out for the analyst from Lubyanka and to intervene if he did anything rash.

Dimitry and Myshkin had copies of a coded message that had come back from Lubyanka in response to Zhukov's Thursday request. They were trying to digest it and decide what to do next. It was both interesting and intriguing.

Dimitry dropped his copy on the table and leaned back in his chair. "So, Lubyanka feels the White House is directly working something here to get the conclave to elect a non-Italian pope. They have it on good authority. This is highly unusual. The White House doesn't normally run operations…in fact, so far as I know, it never has. It has to be that fellow Caldwell from the NSC staff." Dimitry looked over at Myshkin. "Did we see him leave Rome with the official delegation after the funeral?"

"As I told you, no," Myshkin brusquely replied, offering no elaboration.

Dimitry thought for a few moments. "I think we have to assume Caldwell is still in Rome and doing something regarding the conclave. And I'm sure I know what it is. But let's make one more effort to verify that before we burn time running down the wrong alley. Give me another message form."

Myshkin briefly glared across the table but then grudgingly reached into his drawer and slid the message pad across the table. Dimitry slapped his hand on the pad, stopping it in place, and wordlessly returned Myshkin's cold stare. "I'll craft a message, Viktor; then let's go to our meeting. I don't want to be late."

## Hotel De Russie

The phone was ringing. Carter slowly pulled himself up in his cushioned chair, throwing an elbow across the chair arm, and fumbling for the phone on the dresser beside him. His first effort only knocked the old-style European receiver from the cradle, but his second grab was successful. "Caldwell," he answered firmly, clearing any sound in his voice that might suggest he had just awakened.

For a few seconds, there was silence on the other end before a male voice softly spoke through the earpiece. "Uh…who's this I'm speaking to?"

Carter sat up a bit straighter and looked across the room at the bed where he could see Katherine was beginning to stir. "This is Mr. Carter Caldwell," he repeated, adding a slight edge to his voice. There was another long pause. "And to whom am I speaking?"

"Ah, yes…Carter, of course, this is Avery Dugan. Good morning."

Carter was suddenly fully alert, glancing a bit apprehensively across the room where the bedcovers continued rustling. "Yes, good morning to you. What's up?"

"That discussion we had yesterday about that really fascinating artifact you were interested in…"

"Yes, the artifact. I recall the discussion."

"Well," Avery continued, "as it turns out, the artifact exists and I've obtained a copy of it. And it's every bit as intriguing as we thought it would be. Do you have time to meet me later to take a look at it? Perhaps around noon?"

"Sure," Carter answered. "Should we meet at the same place as yesterday?"

"I'd rather not," came the quick reply. "I think I've been there a bit too often lately, and I'm not sure the proprietors actually like me all that much. How about at the Nova coffee shop, on the corner of the second block up from the Emanuel Bridge? It's right on the Via della Conciliazione; you can't miss it. And you can walk it from the hotel if you like. Noon work?"

"Yeah, noon…sure. See you there."

As Carter hung up the phone, he saw Katherine sit up in the bed and push the covers down, before recalling her agreement to accept a temporary male roommate. When she did, she slowly pulled the sheets back up to her neck. "Who was on the phone, Carter?"

Carter's head was now fully clear, and he really dreaded answering the question, but he didn't see he had a choice. "Uh, that was Avery."

Kath's eyes widened to their full dimensions as she rose to a sitting position. "Avery! Avery! Avery called here? To my room? Early in the morning! And you answered the phone! *Oh my God*! Why did you answer the phone? What were you thinking?"

"Well, I answered it because it was ringing and it was next to my chair…and I had no idea who it was! And I certainly had no idea it was Avery! And I'm kinda conditioned to answering the phone when it rings at odd hours! Where I work, I get a lot of early-morning and late-night calls, OK?"

"My God, Carter!" Kath quickly calmed herself, concerned that her excited voice might be heard in an adjacent room. "Carter, he's going to think we're…that we're…"

"Living together?" Carter finished the thought.

"Yes! He'll think we're involved! He'll think we're shacked up!"

Carter sat in his chair for a moment and thought carefully about what his next comment would be. "Katherine, can I ask you a simple question?"

Kath kept her eyes fixed on him, the covers still pulled up around her neck. "OK. I guess."

"Why do you care? I admit it, and I'll guarantee you…*he* certainly cares. Why? Because he had a great thing going with you, and he blew it. Out-and-out blew it. And now you've moved on, and I'm sure he has as well. If he hasn't, he should, especially since I don't get the impression that you have any residual feelings for him. Correct? Or am I reading that wrong?"

Kath's eyes stayed on him while her analyst's mind processed his observation and question. "No, you're reading it correctly. He's history." She paused and thought about her next words. She wanted to get them right. "But he's part of *my* history," she continued, "and it's just embarrassing."

"Why? Why shouldn't he be the one who's embarrassed?"

"Well, maybe he is. But that doesn't matter. What if he says something when we meet?"

"He won't."

"How do you know he won't?"

"For two reasons. One, what could he possibly say that wouldn't make him look like an ass? And second, if he says anything about it, I think he knows I'll put him on his ass."

Kath smiled. She tried not to, but she did. Carter's double use of "ass" was clever. Smart guy this army fellow. No wonder the NSC had borrowed him. Carter slightly smiled as well, keeping his eyes on her lovely face. It was a pastime he was enjoying more and more, but they had things to discuss and things to do, so he made it brief. "Kath," he continued, as she sat further forward in the bed to better hear his words and perhaps to get a better look at him, which she was also getting accustomed to, "Call room service and have them deliver us some coffee. I'll jump in the shower and get cleaned up, and then I'll go grab us a table for breakfast downstairs while you get ready. OK? We need to get going."

Katherine nodded as he handed her the phone, its long cord stretching across the bed. He then grabbed his shaving kit, pulled on the bathrobe he had strategically placed by his chair, stepped into the bathroom, and closed the door. Kath took a deep breath, thinking for a moment before ordering the coffee and then—after calling room service—slowly slid down under the covers to get more comfortable and wait until he emerged from the bathroom. He really was a very nice guy. And the more she thought about it, kind of cute too.

## Sico Moro Café

Bruno Brachi was seated at a small table inside the Sico Moro Café on the Piazza Pia across from the Castel Sant'Angelo, a picturesque old fortress on the Tiber River a mile east of the Vatican. He had been waiting for a half hour, and he was getting uneasy. He did not like meetings such this in a public place, even though the café wasn't officially open and wouldn't be for another hour. At some point, he had to decide if those he had come to meet were no-shows and if he should just return to work. He took another sip of coffee and a small bite from a muffin.

"Signor Brachi." The waiter's voice startled him slightly, causing him to spill some coffee on the freshly ironed linen tablecloth.

"Yes."

The waiter motioned for Bruno to follow him and to bring his cup. The two of them headed toward the rear of the café and through an arched doorway into its attached restaurant. The restaurant's dining booths were quite unique, as each one was shrouded with dark curtains. At night, they allowed diners to enjoy their meals in complete privacy, making them a favorite of the Banda della Magliana, one of Rome's most notorious crime families. But this meeting was with another type of family. The waiter pulled back the curtain of the third booth, and Bruno looked in to see the humorless faces of Dimitry Zhukov and Viktor Myshkin.

Dimitry motioned to Bruno with crisp hand gestures. "Come into the booth, and pull the curtain. Quickly!" Bruno did as directed and slid into the seat next to Viktor, whom he knew much better. He didn't know Zhukov at all, but he accurately guessed who he was and where he was from. As usual, there were no pleasantries and no names. Dimitry got straight to business, his words more grunted than spoken. "What do you have for us?"

Bruno fidgeted in his seat. "Katic thinks that there is something going on involving the American cardinal from Philadelphia…Cardinal Krol."

"Why? What's he doing?" Myshkin asked as he fumbled to get a cigarette from the pack he had placed on the table.

Bruno quickly produced a lighter and handed it to him.

"*Ya ne znaiyu*," Bruno answered in the mother tongue he rarely used. "But he says that Krol is lobbying the other cardinals pretty hard at the prattiche after the general congregations."

"Lobbying for whom?" Dimitry asked.

"Not quite clear, but Katic did overhear a cardinal that Krol had just spoken with talking to another one about 'the Pole.'"

Dimitry pursed his lips into a thin line, responding through tightly clenched teeth. "Of course. Krol is of Polish descent and he's pushing for Wyszynski. So, the Americans have enlisted Krol to do their dirty work inside the conclave. They are counting on him being persuasive. But it's a long shot. Krol's a relatively junior cardinal; I can't see many of them being swayed by him, especially the older Italian cardinals in the curia. Persuasion alone won't cut it, so the Americans must be supporting him in some concrete way, but how? And how are they communicating with him?"

Bruno's face broke into a small smirk. "I think we know. Krol seems to have become quite friendly with the woman I brought in to supervise the meals before and during the conclave. She's an Irish nun—Sister Cummings. She and Krol seem to chat frequently during the course of the day, and she seems to talk more to Krol than the others. In fact, so far as I've seen, she only talks to Krol about anything other than food."

Viktor took a deep drag on his cigarette. "So, you think this nun is the one who is the communications link between Krol and some American agent? Presumably someone in the CIA?"

"Or someone from the White House," Zhukov inserted, increasingly convinced that Carter Caldwell was involved in all this.

"We don't know that," Myshkin countered, attempting to show Bruno that he was still the head KGB man in Rome. Dimitry shot him a hard stare but said nothing, at least for the moment. A brief silence settled on the table, making Bruno uncomfortable and leaving him with the feeling he was caught between the proverbial rock and hard place, in this instance a place very rocky and another very hard.

"What are you two talking about?" Bruno asked nervously.

"Nothing of concern to you," Dimitry answered, the edge on his words sharp and cutting.

Bruno awkwardly nodded his head and leaned back in his seat, putting more distance between himself and Zhukov.

Dimitry was unsure what to do next. This was one of those reasons why he had objected when Andropov said he was sending him on this mission. This was operational stuff. He hated to do it and knew it was probably a mistake, especially after the incident at the embassy, but he turned his eyes to Myshkin and slowly formed his question. "What do you think we should do, Viktor?"

Viktor looked up at Dimitry, his eyes as cold as the Siberian tundra where he was born. "So, the kid from Lubyanka finally realizes he is out of his element," he thought, keeping his eyes fixed on Dimitry, setting up something of a childish contest to see which one would blink first. He slowly inhaled another mouthful of smoke before crushing out the cigarette in the hard plastic ashtray on the table. "It's pretty obvious to me, Comrade." He turned his gaze to the Vatican facilities chief seated beside him. "Bruno must eliminate Sister Cummings, and we'll eliminate Cardinal Krol."

Now it was Bruno's turn to be uncomfortable, and his words became slightly stuttered. "What are you saying?" he blabbered to Myshkin. "You want me to kill a nun? A Catholic nun! Right in the Vatican! I can't do *that*!"

Myshkin fully focused his Siberian temperament on Brachi. "We don't know that she's actually a nun. If she's talking to Krol, as you describe and if we think he is working to elect Wyszynski and if that's the American objective, then she's probably CIA."

"No, she's not!" Bruno objected, beginning to feel the drops of perspiration forming on his brow. "We've used her before! She's a nun…a real Irish-Catholic nun! One who cooks!"

"Oh, sure she is," Viktor replied, "and you're a trained facilities manager from Rivanna." Viktor's hand suddenly moved like a flash, shooting up and grabbing Bruno by the throat, locking his fingers around the Italian's windpipe in a strong vice. Bruno initially struggled but quickly decided to end any resistance under the hope that Viktor would shortly release him. The perspiration was now running down his forehead in streams, and he felt fingernails digging into the skin below his jaw.

"Let him go, Viktor."

Myshkin looked across the table in the direction of the soft voice he had just heard. Once again, he and Zhukov locked eyes, but after a few seconds, Myshkin released his grip on Bruno's throat, leaving the Italian gasping for air as he struggled to regain his composure. Zhukov folded his arms and placed them on the table, leaning toward the increasingly frightened Bruno Brachi. "As Viktor just said, you eliminate Cummings, and we'll take care of Krol. And have it done by Tuesday, understand?"

Bruno nodded. "OK. But why Tuesday?"

"Mainly, because I said so. But since you asked, Tuesday will be half a week before the conclave convenes, and I don't want to leave the Americans any more than a few days to figure out something else. They love gadgets, but since they're using this nun they obviously don't have anything helpful for this effort, and I don't want them to have the time to put anything—or anyone else—in place. You follow?"

Bruno's head slowly moved north and south. "Sure. OK. "

"*Ochen korosho*," Dimitry replied. "Now go. Get on with it. And send us a message when it's done. And…we don't want to read about it in the newspapers."

Bruno nodded again, pulled back the curtain, and rose to leave. As he exited the booth, he stopped for a moment and looked at Viktor.

"By the way, that package was delivered and I checked the change you directed."

Myshkin was enormously irritated that Bruno had said anything in front of Zhukov about the briefcase, but he limited his reaction to a slight smile and a nod of the head, and then he motioned for Bruno to leave. Brachi quickly headed toward the front entrance of the café, leaving Dimitry and Victor alone.

Dimitry waited a few seconds and then looked toward Myshkin. "What was that about? What package? What change?"

"It's nothing," Myshkin dismissively replied. "Just some routine administrative stuff…bribes, payoffs, that sort of thing. Some money for him to spread around the building."

Dimitry didn't know why, but he didn't like this vague answer. For a moment, he thought about delving deeper into it, but he decided not to. He didn't like administrative minutia, which was one reason he had become an analyst to begin with.

## Café Nova

Bruno stepped out of the Sico Moro and turned right, heading up the street toward the Vatican. He could see the great dome straight ahead at the end of the Via della Conciliazione. He stopped briefly at the next corner and took a deep breath, trying to regain his composure. He was never sure if Myshkin valued him or merely tolerated him, and the uncertainty was more than a bit frightening at times. As he stood there, a young couple walked past him. He briefly nodded his head at them as they passed and watched them walk toward the entrance to the Café Nova. Other than that mindless pleasantry, he paid no attention. He had his own issues to deal with. He crossed the street and continued on his way.

Carter and Kath took no notice of Bruno either, focusing instead on finding a seat at one of the small sidewalk tables that would be comfortable, look uninterestingly normal, and offer a degree of seclusion. They settled into one farthest away from the wide boulevard leading to the Vatican, deciding that it would have the fewest people passing by and was the least visible from the main thoroughfare. The server appeared quickly, and just as quickly, Carter ordered two cups of cappuccino. Then, they waited.

"He'll be late," Kath said, offering a prediction based on past patterns. "He's always late…to everything."

"That's OK," Carter replied. "We're in no hurry. He'll be here, or else he wouldn't have called."

"Oh yeah, the call…which you answered, in *my* room. He'll have something to say about that for sure." Kath slouched down a bit in her chair and looked away.

"Katherine, drop it, will you? He won't say anything, and if he does…so what? As I said, why does it matter? We have bigger things to worry about."

The cappuccinos arrived. They sat in silence for several minutes, watching the noisy Italian traffic going by. Horn blowing in Italy was either a driving requirement or a national pastime, and they both smiled at the policeman in the middle of the street frantically signaling to the drivers who, without exception, completely ignored him.

"Hello."

Kath and Carter turned toward the voice approaching from behind them. Avery had arrived. Stepping over the low-slung rope marking the café's sidewalk area, he pulled up a chair and joined them. "Sorry, I'm a bit late."

"No problem," Carter replied, glancing at Kath, who offered no greeting. "So, what do we have, Avery?"

"Well," the reporter answered, drawing out the word as he reached into his backpack and pulled out a folder, "we have this. And be careful how you handle it because…it's explosive!"

"How'd you get it?" Kath asked, wide-eyed.

"Don't ask?"

"From Licheri?"

"No," Avery answered as he pulled copies from the folder and handed one to Kath and another to Carter. The two of them started to read.

Avery had already translated it into English, and Katherine's eyebrows arched as she read. Carter skimmed through his copy, not sure he would have the background to catch all of the nuances, preferring to wait for Kath's reactions. It was a short wait.

"Good grief!" Katherine exclaimed. "Frankly, I didn't believe it when you mentioned it the other day. But…*this* is dynamite!"

"It certainly is," Avery gently responded. "I can't believe Siri gave the interview to begin with, much less understand why he would wander into touchy areas with such a harsh tone. I doubt even the most strident of his conservative supporters could be comfortable that he would be a wise and kind pope after this."

Kath continued reading the article, continually shaking her head. "My goodness! He all but calls John Paul incompetent, implicitly criticizes John XXIII over the Vatican Council reforms, basically says the bishops are too stupid to be included in any sort of collegiality arrangement, and all but states the church was adrift during the last years of Paul VI. Unbelievable! This would be like running for president of the United States and giving an interview just before the election saying George Washington was an idiot, Abraham Lincoln was a country bumpkin, and Congress is a bunch of intellectual retards!"

Carter grinned. "Well, a lot of voters might agree with that last one."

Katherine chuckled slightly, reaching for her cappuccino. "Come on, Carter. You know what I mean." Kath scanned over the transcript once more, still slowly shaking her head. She finally put the paper down and looked at the two men with her. "So, what now? What do we do with it?"

After a brief pause, Avery spoke; after all, he would be the one needing to take action. "OK, here are my thoughts. First, we can't be seen as having anything to do with this, agreed?" Carter and Kath nodded in agreement. "So, we want at least two degrees of separation on this. And we need to do something to get a buzz going about it just as the conclave convenes. If it's out too soon, that'll give Siri time to renounce the interview, explain it—spin it, as they say—or turn it to his advantage by accusing others of distributing it, generating a sympathy vote. So, we can't give him any time to react to it. It's got to hit just before they start singing the "Litany of the Saints" and parading into the Sistine Chapel."

"And if we get it leaked just ahead of the conclave," Carter added, "Siri only has time to cry foul in some way, which will make it look like it was leaked by someone out to discredit him."

"In short, by Benelli…or someone in his camp," Katherine inserted, finishing the thought. "So that will leave the two Italian heavyweights at odds with each other, even more than they already are, forcing the cardinals to look for another Italian as a compromise candidate, meaning we now have that block split in three ways, maybe four."

Carter leaned back and thought for a moment. "There's something else we have to do, and I don't know exactly what it is. Splitting up the Italians and diminishing the stature of Benelli and Siri is fine, but we can't let this be only an intramural game among the Italian cardinals. We have to make sure the others in the conclave know what's going on. I mean, let's say this thing comes out early in an Italian newspaper; how many of the cardinals speak Italian or read Italian newspapers?"

"Oh, the word will get out," Katherine countered. "This will spread quickly."

"But maybe not if they're already in the conclave," Carter replied.

Avery leaned forward in his chair. "Carter's right. We have to do more than just try and leak it through the media. I think I may have an idea on that. Meanwhile, we have just six days before the conclave starts, so we need to get moving. I'll call Paolo Garda right away and ask for a meeting."

"Who's he?" Carter asked.

"He's the senior reporter covering the Vatican for the main English paper around here, *Corriere della Sera*. We've worked together quite a few times. And he owes me a couple of big favors."

"What are you going to ask him to do?"

Avery rubbed his chin and then glanced over to Carter. "I'll ask him if he's heard about the story, wait a couple of days, then go see him with a copy and ask him to pulse Licheri about it…which will scare *Gazetta* into running it early, hopefully on the thirteenth, just before the conclave starts. And I'll go to a friend of mine at the university here and see about getting a hundred or so copies printed in half a dozen different languages."

Carter looked at Katherine, who rubbed her hands together as a soft smile appeared across her face. "Ah, I get it," she said. "That's very clever, and it just might work. And if it does what we expect, it could make Krol's job a little easier."

Avery smiled. "And I think we'll need a little additional help from Matteo."

Carter leaned back in his rickety metal chair and reached for his cup of coffee. For the first time, he saw a plan coming together. "I'm sure Matteo will figure out what to do. You know, this just might work." He paused and repeated the thought to himself. "It just might."

CHAPTER 15

# Monday, October 9, 1978
# Washington, DC

• • •

It was a quiet Monday morning in Washington, DC, especially along the row of townhomes comprising Fourth Street Southeast just off Pennsylvania Avenue, Carter Caldwell's neighborhood. A bright sun was up, and a few people were still heading off to work, walking in small groups of twos and threes toward the Eastern Market Metro stop. Everyone was jovial with the talk dominated by one topic: the Redskins had beaten Detroit the previous day and were now undefeated. In no small way, the mood in Washington rose and fell with the record of the Redskins. Sure, things were brewing in Washington as always, but those were secondary concerns—the Redskins were undefeated! Several of the groups walking down the street were singing, "Hail to the Redskins!" It was a good DC day.

And because it was so good, no one paid any attention to the white van that slowly drove down the street and pulled to a stop in front of Carter Caldwell's town house. The sign painted on the van's side read "T&J's Plumbing and Heating." A refugee named Juan from Nicaragua, who had come to the United States a few months earlier to escape the civil war boiling in Central America, usually drove this particular van. But not today. Juan was dead. His lifeless body was lying not far away in a wooded area along the Anacostia River. The DC police would not likely find him for a month. Today, the van was being driven by Alexei Tereshkov, the KGB's most experienced hit man in Washington, operating from the Soviet Embassy on Sixteenth Street.

Alexei placed the van in park and emerged from the front seat, wearing white coveralls, his face unshaven, his boots scuffed and slightly muddy. He nonchalantly went to the back of the van, opened the door, grabbed a rusty toolbox, and headed up to the front porch. This would be so simple; the lock was almost an antique, operated with a skeleton key. It probably was backed up with a dead bolt, but Alexei was skilled at quickly defeating those as well. Reaching the door, he looked down the street. Three young men strolled by, like those walking just ahead, also singing "Hail to the Redskins." They waved up to him as they passed, and he waved back, giving them a thumbs-up for good measure. He opened the toolbox and made the appearance of repairing the porch light next to the door, making sure no one was watching, and then quickly picked the two locks and walked inside.

All he knew about Carter Caldwell was that he worked in the EOB next to the White House and that he was a bachelor. He and a colleague had watched the EOB over the past few days and saw no one going into any of the building's staff doors fitting Carter's description. He believed he was out of town, but there was only one way to know for sure. Bachelors all lived the same, and if Caldwell were home, there would be considerable evidence from the weekend.

Tereshkov closed the door behind him and headed to the kitchen. It was unusually orderly. There were no dishes in the sink, no pizza boxes or other residue from a fast-food dinner in the trashcan. There was a box of Cheerios on the counter but no bowl, nor was there any milk in the refrigerator. Alexei headed up to the second floor and easily determined which of two choices was the master bedroom, not that they were all that different. "That's unusual," he thought upon seeing the neatly made bed. He opened the closet door. There were several empty wire coat hangers dangling on the clothing rod beside two nicer wooden hangars labeled "Britches of Georgetown." There was one small suitcase on the floor next to an empty spot that undoubtedly was the normal location of its larger companion.

The agent next went into the bathroom, opened the medicine cabinet, and then looked under the sink. There was no shaving cream, no razor, and no signs of anything looking like a toiletry travel kit. A toothbrush holder was on the sink, but it was holding no toothbrush, and there was no toothpaste anywhere to be seen.

Tereshkov went back downstairs and returned to the kitchen. He unlocked the door leading out to the garage behind the house. The garage had a small window along the walkway, and the KGB spy stopped to look inside. He held his hands up to cut the glare and tried to focus his eyes. "Ah, case closed," he murmured to himself. He could see the definitive outline of a dark-blue Corvette inside. "*Korosho*," he murmured again. "No suitcase, no clothes, no toothbrush, no razor, no mess, no man, but a car. He's not here, and he took a cab somewhere to fly out of town."

The old spy turned and headed back into the house. He relocked the kitchen door, gathered up his things, and exited out to the front porch, closing the door behind him and pulling the white hat a bit lower on his head.

"Hail to the Redskins! Hail victory! Braves on the warpath! Fight… for old…DC!" Another group of young men went by waving to him. He flashed another thumbs-up and then trotted down the steps, very casually got into the van, and pulled away from Carter's town house. He'd park the van in a neighborhood near Catholic University in northeast Washington where an embassy colleague would pick him up. There was so much crime in DC that the police would take days to notice the van and would find it completely clean of evidence when they investigated it, and it would slowly sink to the bottom of the paper pile, as there were always plenty of local homicides to investigate. A missing Nicaraguan illegal named Juan would be a low priority. Meanwhile, Alexei needed to get his report back to Lubyanka. Major Carter Caldwell was not in Washington, DC.

## Santa Maria della Vittoria Church, Rome

The phone was ringing on the desk where Mario Grone was temporarily conducting business for Cardinal Siri. Santa Maria della Vittoria was Siri's titular church in Rome, and it provided more than adequate office space for the respected old cardinal to use when needed. And over the past two months, it had been needed quite a bit.

Grone reached for the phone. "Good afternoon. This is Monsignor Grone. May I help you?"

A brief pause followed. "Good afternoon, Monsignor. Are you the secretary for Cardinal Siri of Genoa?"

Grone was getting quite a few such calls as the conclave approached, and even as they grew more tedious, he always handled them with proper pleasantry. "Yes, I am the secretary and personal assistant for His Eminence. With whom am I speaking, please?"

Another brief pause.

"Monsignor, my name is Paolo Garda. I am an assistant editor and—even at my age—still a part-time reporter *for Corriere della Sera*. Do you have a couple of moments so that we might speak? I have something I would like to discuss."

Grone was immediately nervous. His instincts told him what the questions likely related to: either comments about Siri's chances of being the next pope or possibly the interview he had given to Licheri a week before. So far, all seemed fine, but Grone remained uneasy with the comments his superior had made in the interview, and he was even more uneasy about the possibility of a premature leak. The next words he heard through the earpiece heightened his discomfort.

"Monsignor, I have heard from a couple of sources that Cardinal Siri may have given an interview some days ago to another of the Italian newspapers. Given the importance of the next few days, I feel it only fair that *Della Sera* also be given an interview or, at the very least, given access to what he said previously to one of our sister publications. I'm sure you would agree that is quite reasonable. So, can you help me? Was there such an interview?"

Grone paused, his mind rapidly processing multiple equations. "Well, Mr. Garda, His Eminence has given numerous interviews as of late. Nearly all have been rather mundane and brief."

"You say 'nearly all,'" Garda responded. "So does that mean some, or even one, is lengthier and more comprehensive?"

"Well, that would depend on what you consider to be 'comprehensive,' would it not? What paper do you feel was allowed such an interview with His Eminence?"

"I hear it was *Gazetta del Popolo*."

Grone's heart sank. The word was out. Licheri or someone else at the *Gazetta* was talking. Even if they were only talking in vague generalities or just engaging in some professional bragging, someone was talking. Siri's deal withholding publication until after the conclave was breaking, if not already fully shattered. It was against his principles, but this was not a moment where he could stand on principle. He had to lie. "Mr. Garda, I really don't know what you could be referring to. So far as I can recall, His Eminence gave no such interview to anyone at the *Gazetta*." Grone drew a deep breath. He certainly wanted no more of this conversation. "I'm sorry, Mr. Garda, but we're very busy here and I really must go. Thank you for calling." With that, Grone slammed down the receiver.

It rang again, almost immediately. Grone considered ignoring it but decided to answer.

"Hello, Monsignor Grone."

The voice at the other end of the phone was familiar to him.

"Mario, it's Cardinal Siri. I'm still at the Vatican. There's been considerable chitchat at the general congregation and the prattiche today. Benelli is quite subtle, but those in his camp are working hard for him. You can tell they fear they may be in a weak position as I've had more than a few drop hints that I should bring him back to replace Villot. I have, of course, dismissed that. It's a foolish suggestion. We'd never get along, and at some point, it would show. Anything new happening?"

Grone took a deep breath. "Perhaps, Your Eminence. I just had a call from an editor at the *Della Sera*. I think they know about the interview with Licheri."

Siri's reply was quick. "Why do you think that? What did they say? What have they heard?"

"Somehow, Eminence, it's out that you gave a lengthy and rather detailed interview to *Gazetta*, meaning Licheri, of course. I don't know how much of this is just others fishing around based on rumors or whether Licheri has said something. But the request from *Corriere della Sera* was for an interview of their own or for a copy of what you discussed with Licheri." There was a quiet on the other end of the phone. "Your Eminence, did you hear me?"

"Yes, Mario, I heard you. Licheri would never publish the interview early. He knows there could be very serious consequences for him and his paper if he did, especially if the conclave goes in the direction I expect. What did you say to the fellow who called?"

Grone sighed and his shoulders dropped. "I lied, Your Eminence. I lied. I told him there was no such interview...but I doubt that will be the end of it. I'm sure they will keep searching. No newspaper can stand being on the losing side of a major scoop—as they call it."

"Don't worry about it, Mario," came Siri's quick reply. "The conclave starts in five days. For all the other papers, it will take them at least that much time to sort it out and do all that would be necessary to publish early. Don't worry about it. Let's focus on the conclave. Give me names of some other cardinal electors I need to chat with. As I said, it's obvious Benelli is attempting to influence them, and I must do the same. OK?"

Grone nodded his head. It was clearly not "OK" with him, but he saw nothing that could be done. The die might not be set, but it was clearly cast.

## The Vatican

Cardinal Villot had already had a most busy day, and it was only midafternoon. Nonetheless, he was close to exhaustion as he sat slumped in the chair behind his desk. All of his days since finding John Paul dead had been long, but somehow they kept growing longer. He lowered his head into his hands and momentarily dozed off.

"Your Eminence? Your Eminence?"

Villot raised his head to see Monsignor Petar Sarac standing before him, leaning down across the cardinal's desk to check on him. "Are you all right, Your Eminence?"

Villot sat up straight in his leather chair. "Yes. Yes, of course. Why do you ask?"

Sarac smiled slightly. "Well, Your Eminence, it's been a rather trying few days, and we have several more to go. You look tired, and that is because…well, because you are tired. You need to go to your apartment early tonight and get some sleep. Will you agree to do that?"

Villot pushed his glasses up to his forehead and rubbed his eyes. "We'll see. Maybe. I still have a lot to do. Every time we have a congregation, it generates a pile of things the attending cardinals feel should be done—now, of course—and a second pile of issues they feel the new pope should address immediately. I require that these items be submitted in writing, which slows the train down a bit, but look at the stack of papers on the corner of my desk! I'm sorting through them individually, as I've promised those who wrote them I would, and I'm putting the ones with merit in the briefcase." Villot reached under his desk, but his wriggling fingers found nothing but empty air. "Where's the briefcase!" he barked, pushing his chair back and looking under the desk.

"It's over there," Sarac calmly answered, pointing over Villot's shoulder, "next to the file cabinet by the window.

Villot spun around in his chair and let out a sigh of relief. "Oh, thank goodness. Why is it over there? I always keep it here."

"I moved it so you would stop bumping your feet against it. You needed more room for your legs to stretch out or else your knee will stiffen again, making it awkward for you to walk, which—"

"I know," Villot responded in agreement, "which will make my hip hurt. Getting old is not for the meek."

Sarac paused for a moment. "Perhaps, Your Eminence, I should keep the suitcase in my apartment; in that way—"

"No!" Villot barked, cutting his secretary off in midsentence. "It needs to stay here with me. In a way, it's become something of its own file cabinet. But as soon as we have a new pope, I want you to come here and immediately take the briefcase to the papal apartment, as we have discussed. Usually, elections happen rather late in the day, and I want the important items the new pontiff must see present in his apartment right away. Their presence will give him something to do; he'll certainly be too emotionally charged to sleep."

"But if you are putting sensitive papers in it, shouldn't I keep the briefcase in my room? The briefcase has very crude locks on it, and I have the small safe we installed in my apartment for such things." Sarac waited as Villot considered the proposal.

"No, let's keep it here," Villot answered. "The office is safe, and I want to have it here so I can put papers in it, or at least appear to, when anyone brings more in. It's safe enough. There's a guard outside my office."

"But only when you are in it," Sarac protested.

"Then, Monsignor, put one out there all the time until we have white smoke," Villot adamantly answered.

Sarac could see his boss was tired and even more irritable than usual. He dropped the issue. Once Villot had made up his mind on something, it was set in stone. Sometimes that quality served him well, sometimes less well—as was painfully visible after Pope John Paul's death. But further discussion was invariably futile. "Very well, Your Eminence," Sarac dutifully replied, although puzzled as to why the camerlengo was so personally possessive of the briefcase.

Villot thought for a few moments. "I think that will be all for now, Petar. How about checking on the progress of the living quarters? I'm still quite uneasy about them, and we'll be moving into them in five days. No one is looking forward to it; trust me. But, the Holy Fathers for some time have tried to make this a trying experience to encourage a quick selection. This is a time for decision more than deliberation, and I am concerned that many are considering a radical choice."

"Radical?" Sarac responded, curious as to exactly what Villot was referencing.

"Well, yes...perhaps a big change. I am opposed to it, of course, and I think cooler heads will prevail. Still, there are some serious problems being caused by Siri's supporters who don't like Benelli, and Benelli's supporters who don't like Siri. I'm trying to craft a compromise, but so far this seems more a political campaign than a Papal election. All we're missing are posters and banners hanging from the front of the basilica."

"What sort of compromise are you referring to," Sarac asked, feeling the need to pursue the conversation further.

Villot snapped at him. "Never mind, Monsignor Sarac, it's none of your business, and I've probably said too much already. Please go and check the rooms. That's all for now." With that Sarac offered a slight bow and left the office, closing the door behind him. Villot paused for a moment, then looked over at the briefcase, unsure as to why Sarac seemed so interested in it. But, it did hold very important papers, Sarac knew that, and it was important to get them to the Papal Apartment quickly when the time came, so the thought quickly exited Villot's mind. He had more than enough to worry about, starting with the increasingly unseemly competition between Siri and Benelli.

## VIA DEI FEINILI – ROME

It was late afternoon when the tall man in dark clothes rounded the corner onto the *Via dei Feinili* and headed towards the main entrance of the large apartment building on the left. This area was not far from the famous Rome Coliseum, and he had walked from there after being dropped off by a cab. A black fedora was pulled down on his forehead somewhat shielding his face, and the lapel on his black coat was pulled up snuggly concealing the collar around his neck. He walked up to the apartment entrance, scanned the numbers and pushed the buzzer next to number 16, one of the apartments on the top floor.

A voice quickly answered through the speaker box. "*Buon pomeriggio.* Good afternoon."

The man at the door quietly answered. "*Ciao, mi chiamo, Ben.*"

There was a brief pause before another voice answered, "Yes. I'll buzz you in. Come to the top floor, the apartment on your right."

The front door buzzed, and the lock released, allowing the visitor to enter and climb the stairs as directed. Reaching the top landing, he gently tapped on the door to apartment 16. The door opened, and the visitor quickly and quietly stepped inside, while his host stepped outside, looked around, and then closed the door and turned toward his guest, who was removing his coat. "Cardinal Krol, thanks for coming. I hope the drive over was easy. Do you think anyone saw you?"

Krol hung his coat on a hook behind the door. "I don't think so, Matteo. I'm not trained at this as you are, but I didn't see anyone. I got out near the Coliseum and walked once around the block, but no one seemed to pay me any attention."

Matteo Ferrari nodded. "That should be fine. I have a couple of people watching the building so if anyone did follow you or is observing the front door, we'll see them. Tea?"

"No, thanks," Krol replied. "I need to get back to the church as soon as possible. As we get closer to the conclave, it's harder to sneak away. And the prattiche are becoming more important—and interesting. If I'm not there for them, then our odds of success will be lower. So what do you have?"

Matteo got right to business, leading the cardinal over to a small kitchen table. "We still don't have the final device I'm afraid. We may get it in another day or two, but I do have a prototype for you to familiarize yourself with and practice on."

Approaching the table, Krol saw a slightly oversized, hardbound Italian Bible placed in the center. The two men took seats, and Matteo reached over to release a small, seemingly decorative latch on the top cover that locked the Bible together. He opened the book, revealing that it was far from Holy Scripture. On the inside was a rectangular device looking something like a keypad. Along the sides were six small, cylindrical slots—each empty.

Krol's eyes narrowed as he looked at what was before him, and then he turned to Matteo. "So, this is what Q has devised?"

Matteo grinned. "More or less. There's another piece that is separate, but we'll take care of that. This is all you need to master. The empty slots are for batteries to power the device. You'll have six, as you see; each will only last for half a day. So after the morning session of the conclave, you have to get back to your room and change the battery. Be careful not to turn the device on until needed, as the batteries won't last long."

"So, since I have six," Krol interrupted, pointing to the empty holes. "You feel the election will be done in three days?"

"That's our guess," Matteo answered. "Do you feel it could go longer?"

Krol paused, shaking his head. "No, I'm sure it won't. No one can stand living in Villot's cells longer than that. God help us if it goes longer. So, what does this thing do?"

"Essentially," the Italian began, "it's a scoreboard. It will send a brief message on what were the results of each scrutiny—who got how many votes. See the buttons along the top?"

Krol adjusted his glasses and looked closely at the device. "Yes, these here?" he replied, pointing.

"Yes, those. Note that they are for the letters B, C, K, P, S, and W, and then the two at the end are I and N. Below that are three buttons with 1, 2, and the letter X. See those?" Krol nodded, and Matteo continued, "As I said, a very crude scoreboard. The numbers across the top relate to those we feel are the likely *papabili*—'B' for Benelli, 'C' for Colombo, 'K' for Koenig, 'P' for Poletti, 'S' for Siri, and 'W' for Wyszynski. Since there may be others, the 'I' and the 'N' will help us figure it out—they stand for Italian and non-Italian, a total score. Then the number buttons are how you enter the number of votes each received. They must be entered in specific sequence. I'll show you how in a minute. We made it as simple as possible."

"What's this button here in the corner, the one with the 'V'?"

"Don't touch that one until the conclave is over," Matteo sternly answered. "When it is done and the final ballots are being burned, push it. But not before. Be careful, OK?"

Krol grinned. "So, it's a 'V' for 'Victory'?"

"Yes, something like that."

Krol's eyes scanned the device again before turning back to Matteo. "What if someone other than the ones associated with the buttons gets votes? How do I indicate that?"

"You don't," Ferrari replied. "The next pope will be one of those. And if it's not one of those, then it will be a surprise to everyone and a worthless effort, won't it?"

Krol paused for a moment, his eyes still fixed on Matteo. "Well, Luciani was a surprise, as was Cardinal Roncalli in 1958. This thing rarely goes as planned, you know? But…well, OK. I'll do the best I can. But this requires me to keep a lot of numbers in my head."

Matteo grinned. "Anyone who speaks ten languages can remember seven numbers, Your Eminence."

Krol grinned. "That seems logical, my friend. Unfortunately my experience indicates that the part of the brain that handles words is not connected to the part that handles numbers, which is why I never balance my own checkbook. How do I do this so no one notices?"

"It'll fit under your red robes. Here's a roll of surgical tape. Just tape it to your side, reach inside, and push the buttons. If anyone asks, just say your tummy itches. The message will go to a broadcast station and from there be retransmitted to a van in the square. The messages will be processed through a computer algorithm that can make sense of it all, which is why we need the Italian and non-Italian votes in total. The computer is a smaller variant of an advanced American army artillery computer called TacFire. We adjusted it for this mission."

"Seriously?" Krol replied. "You modified an army artillery computer for this? Well, whatever you say. Where's the rebroadcast station, or whatever you called it?"

"A secret. We decided it's best you don't know. In any event, its location is irrelevant to you. You push the buttons, and the info will pop up in the van and be washed through the computer."

Krol nervously rubbed his hands together. "So what then? What do you do with the vote tallies? It's not like you can stuff the ballot box."

"True. And in all honesty, I don't know what will be done with the vote tallies. But I'm sure we'll review them and then decide what avenues, if any, we might pursue to encourage an outcome. Frankly, Eminence, I think we'll be depending more on you than you'll be depending on us. In my world, the technology is great, but it can't substitute for the human dimension."

"Same in my world," Krol replied with a grin. "So, what do I do with this thing now?"

"Take it back to your room at the Catholic Conference and try and practice. You'll need to memorize where the buttons are in sequence, as you certainly won't be able to look at them. So, just practice until you are sure you're pushing the right buttons in the right sequence the correct number of times."

"And when do you think the real one will be here?"

"Hopefully tomorrow, maybe Wednesday…no later than Wednesday certainly. We'll have to test it. I'm sorry to say that we haven't been able to do what we call 'system integration.' In other words, this system has been cobbled together from various parts that should work together… in theory, but we haven't rigorously tested them as a unit. So, cross your fingers."

"And if it doesn't work?" Krol asked.

"Well," Matteo replied, "then we'll have to come up with some way to communicate through Sister Cummings. But I'm afraid you two will have to figure that out."

Krol slowly shook his head. "Seems like many unknowns in this operation, Signor Ferrari."

Matteo nodded. "A generous assessment, Eminence. A most generous assessment. So, let's practice."

CHAPTER 16

# Tuesday, October 10, 1978
# The Vatican

• • •

It was barely 5:00 a.m., and Sister Cummings was alone in the kitchen beneath the Vatican Museum, already at work checking the supplies for the day's meals and snacks. So far, it had all gone well. The cardinals had lodged only a few complaints about the food, and those who had were well-known dietary complainers anyway. Moreover, most of them were from the Vatican curia and had tired of the Vatican's food long ago. They were like students in a boarding school; even the most varied and tasteful menu was certain to be the topic of derision born of repetition.

Cummings was removing cans of supplies from one of the large storage cabinets when she heard the creaking of the door from the main passageway. The room was dark, as this this subterranean area had no windows, and she had turned on few lights, as they hung from bare wires crudely attached to the cave-like ceiling, creating stark shadows and adding to the usually uncomfortable heat. Sister Cummings looked down the long table running nearly the length of the room, peering into the darkness toward the door, where she could make out a figure in dark clothing. "Yes...who's there?" she quietly asked. There was no reply.

The dark figure stepped gingerly around the table, slowly being illuminated by the farthest light bulb. Sister Cummings squinted through the brightness as the figure slowly came into full view. She now could see that his face was covered with a dark ski mask and his hands with black leather gloves.

"Who are you?" she asked again, and again there was no reply. The dark figure continued to move methodically toward her. His right hand reached rearward, and Cummings heard a sharp click. The light reflected off the sharp edge of a shining stiletto switchblade. Now she knew what was happening.

Cummings slowly retreated toward the end of the table and reached underneath it. Her eyes remained fixed on the intruder as she carefully pulled up a large carving knife from the shelf under the table, rotating it slightly so that he could see the reflection from her blade as clearly as she could see his. He stopped briefly, his eyes focusing on her, slowly assuming a slightly crouched position, moving his hands outward, improving his balance, now fully aware that she was not going down without a fight.

As he moved down one side of the table, Cummings slid in the opposite direction along the other. His posture and movements, as well as the way he held his weapon, showed he was experienced in this, but the nun mirrored his actions, silently communicating to him that she was no novice either. He stabbed at her across the table, but she stepped back, deftly avoiding the attack. He realized she was moving toward the door to attempt an escape, so he reversed direction. As he did, Cummings bolted for the door, and the intruder bolted after her.

*Thud*! Cummings crashed into the door, frantically grabbing for the handle. As it started to open, she saw a large hand slap the door slightly above her head, slamming it shut. She instinctively ducked and slipped away, hearing the *thwack* as the stiletto struck the wooden door, briefly sticking in it.

She turned toward her attacker, pointing the carving knife at him and beginning a slow retreat alongside the table and back into the room. "*Who* are you?" she angrily snarled, hoping to get some clue but not really expecting one. She was surprised.

"Someone who has been sent to end your treachery," came the low, male voice. "Someone who will make you pay for what you have done…for what you are doing!" The last word was accompanied with a lunge toward her, aiming to stick the knife in her chest. But Cummings was quicker than expected, jumping back a couple of feet to avoid the attempt. She then swung the carving knife toward the arm holding the knife, barely missing it.

"So, you have had some training," the attacker sneered, the words slipping between the knitting of the dark ski mask covering his face. "Of course you have. I should have known."

Cummings switched the knife to her other hand and quickly lunged again, this time catching the intruder's forearm before he could react. "Ahhhh!" The loud cry told the nun that she had made a painful cut, and as she continued backing away, she saw small drops of blood falling to the kitchen floor. But her attacker seemed largely unfazed, and he continued cautiously moving toward her, lunging again with his knife, which she again dodged, countering with her own wide swipe that missed. She quickly retreated again to the opposite side of the table.

They faced each other for a few moments. A large bowl of flour was on the table, and Cummings subtly slid her hand toward it. Then, with catlike speed, she grabbed the bowl and hurled the flour at the black-clad figure. He turned his face away as the white powder filled the air, momentarily providing a culinary smoke screen. Cummings again dashed for the door, grasped the handle and pulled it open.

She bolted through the opening, hoping desperately to find someone standing in the hallway, but it was eerily empty. Cummings came to a dead stop, debating which way to run, but almost immediately a hard tackle jolted her body from behind. Her head snapped rearward, and both she and her attacker collapsed to the floor in a heap of twisting humanity. She glimpsed the stiletto and instinctively reached to grab the wrist of the hand holding it, while attempting to plunge her own knife into her assailant's back, but his large frame and her short arms prevented her from getting the attack angle she needed. A large hand grabbed her throat, and she felt warm droplets of blood trickling onto her neck from the cut she had inflicted on his arm. With her free hand, she pushed her open palm up against the intruder's nose, pushing… pushing…pushing, as the two of them struggled against one another.

She took a breath, struggling to draw air down her constricted windpipe and again shoved her hand hard against his nose, a fingernail catching the knitting of the ski mask and pushing it off his face. She froze, and momentarily, he did too. "*You*! *You*! What are you doing? How could this be *you*? How you? *How*?"

They were her last words. She felt a sharp pain spreading from her chest as the stiletto entered between her ribs. Instinctively, she started to scream as the pain spread, but his hand quickly moved from her throat to her mouth, trapping her scream behind her lips.

Her body shook violently as the long knife went in again, sliding between her ribs and penetrating her heart. She exhaled her last breath and went limp. The struggle was over. Her killer sat up, his body straddling her legs. He was exhausted; it wasn't supposed to have been this hard. She was a small woman, but she had obviously been instructed in hand-to-hand fighting. His arm hurt, and he rolled up the sleeve to look at it. The cut was more serious than he had thought, and the blood was oozing out. She had not cut an artery, but it was still a serious wound. He started to go into the kitchen to get a cloth for a bandage, but he heard steps coming down the hallway. He pulled a handkerchief from his pocket and quickly dressed the cut, picked up the knife and his mask, and then slipped away into the darkness, leaving Sister Cummings's body on the floor where the Swiss Guard making his rounds soon found her.

## Soviet Embassy, Rome

Dimitry Zhukov was sitting in Viktor Myshkin's office reading over the various intelligence reports that had come into the message center during the past several hours. Most had nothing to do with his immediate mission in Rome, but he felt it prudent to skim through them anyway, certain that continued advancement in the KGB required a broad awareness of events going on throughout the world and a sophisticated analysis of what they meant to the Soviet Union.

The message volume today was unusually thick. The leadership in Kenya was about to change, creating uncertain prospects for continued

Soviet inroads into southern Africa; the civil war in Lebanon was still raging, presenting Moscow with both risks and opportunities while complicating its relations with Syria, but most significantly, there were indications and suspicions that the Carter administration was engaging in serious background discussions with China, seemingly aimed at a mutual recognition and the establishment of diplomatic relations. This was a very unnerving prospect in the Kremlin, where any improvement in the relations between Washington and Beijing was viewed as enormously threatening.

Zhukov dropped the heavy message pack on the desk and began to mentally consider what analysis of the US-Chinese *rapprochement* he might offer to Comrade Andropov. That would certainly be a major development, dwarfing his current assignment, or so it would seem.

"Comrade Zhukov."

Deep in thought, Dimitry at first did not hear the voice calling his name. "Excuse me, Comrade Zhukov."

He turned to see Vladimir, Myshkin's muscleman, standing in the partially opened office door and extending a small folder in his huge hand.

Dimitry turned his head and reached for the folder. "*Spasiba*," he said to Vladimir, more in acknowledgment than appreciation. He waved his hand, signaling for Vladimir to close the door and leave. But the hulking Soviet stood there, glaring at the young man from Lubyanka, the chill between them threatening to trip the thermostat and turn on the heating system.

"*Da?*" Dimitry dismissively asked. "Is there something else?"

"The nun—she's dead," came the flat reply.

A slight tingle went through Dimitry's body. He wasn't sure if the information caused it or if it was the matter-of-fact way in which it was delivered. "Why should I care? Why should I have this emotion?" he thought. "After all, I was the one who had ordered her elimination. Maybe I'm bothered because…I've never ordered such a thing before." He kept his eyes fixed on Vladimir's dispassionate face, hoping none of his inner feelings were visible. But they were, and he knew it. "Are you sure?" he asked.

"Of course I'm sure," was the icy reply. "How could I not be sure?"

Dimitry nodded and again motioned for Vladimir to leave. As the door creaked shut, he tore the envelope open and pulled out the three papers inside, the top being only a cover sheet with routing instructions, but the other two contained the report he had been awaiting. He read it quickly, his eyes widening. He had been correct. Carter Caldwell was not in Washington. The agents who watched the entrances to the Executive Office Building had not seen him in several days, and his home was empty with no signs that he had been there over the past week. "He's here," Zhukov softly said to himself. "Yes, he's certainly here. That was him getting off the plane, and he's not gone home, so he's here. The Americans are up to something, and the White House is directing it. I knew it."

Zhukov started to draft another message but after scribbling only a few words dropped his pencil. "No, I'll handle this from here," he thought. "I've already told Lubyanka all they need to know, and I've known all along the Americans were doing something in Rome with tentacles reaching back to the White House. I've already directed steps to frustrate them, and I've eliminated their first agent. And we'll silence the other one soon. We'll get the result we want, and I'm sure Comrade Andropov and the entire Politburo will be very pleased." He tossed his head back and looked at the ceiling. "And my grandfather would be very pleased. Yes…very pleased."

## THE VATICAN

Cardinal Jean Villot's large body once more slumped heavily into his chair, the ashes from his cigarette falling onto his red sash, his face a mask of pain and disbelief. He stared at Monsignor Sarac, who stood before him. "What did you just say?" Villot groaned, crushing the stump of the cigarette into his ashtray.

Sarac cleared his throat. "I said, Your Eminence, that...Sister Cummings, the Irish nun, has...been found on the floor in the hallway outside the cellar kitchen...dead."

"Dead? Dead?" Villot's eyes widened behind his large spectacles. "Dead how?"

Sarac took another deep breath. "It appears she has been stabbed to death."

Villot gasped, placed his hand over his heart, and then removed it to make the sign of the cross, lowering his head and whispering a brief prayer before turning back to Sarac. "Stabbed! You mean she was... murdered?"

Sarac nodded. "It would seem so, Eminence. Sergeant Bruhlmann of the Guards found her there. He was making his routine rounds when he came across her body on the floor. There was fresh blood on the floor, and she was still warm, so evidently her murder had just occurred. But he didn't see anyone or hear anyone in the hallway."

Villot's big hands went to his head, his face now completely pale. "But who would have done such a thing? Who would want to do such a thing? Why? Why would someone want to murder Sister Cummings? A simple nun! Why?" He knew Sarac did not have any answers, and none were forthcoming. But the initial human shock was now gone, replaced by the management perspective of the camerlengo, who knew again that the church must be protected and the solemn duty of the cardinals continued. "Where is her body, Petar? Has she been moved, the crime scene disturbed?"

"Yes, Your Eminence. I ordered her body taken to the clinic in the palace. I also had Sergeant Bruhlmann get another guard and clean up the blood before anyone else saw it."

"What?" Villot exclaimed, before downshifting to a whisper. "You ordered tampering with a crime scene! We've destroyed the evidence of a crime scene! How will we find who did it and why?"

Sarac placed his hands on Villot's desk and leaned toward the old cardinal. "Eminence," he firmly replied, his voice matching the camerlengo's whispered tone, "first, we are an independent country; we can't allow an outside entity, such as the Polizia di Stato, into the Vatican to investigate a murder, especially right now with the conclave approaching. And second, we don't have anyone on staff, even among the Swiss Guards, qualified to conduct a murder investigation."

"So what are you saying?" Villot interrupted. "We're just going to let someone get away with murder? Someone who has access to the inside areas of the Vatican! While all of the princes of the church are gathered here! How do we know this animal might not attack one of the cardinals? Or me? I live here, you know?" Villot took a deep breath and slumped further into his chair. No camerlengo had ever had to deal with anything like this, and he was fighting the sensation of being overwhelmed. But he knew he couldn't let that happen. There was too much going on and too much yet to be done. He had to control his emotions and focus his mind. He looked up to Sarac. "Come with me," he said, rising from his chair.

"Where to?" Sarac asked.

"To the Sala Clemintina. Most of the cardinals are still there. We must inform them what has happened."

"Why?" Sarac protested. "What can they do other than worry? And what will you tell them?"

"I don't know," Villot snapped, heading briskly toward his office door. "I'll figure that out when I get there."

## The Sala Clemintina, The Clemintine Hall

Most of the cardinals were sitting in small clusters in the Sala Clemintina, another of the Apostolic Palace's ornate audience areas. The morning's general congregation had been routine and was quickly adjourned following a brief sermon by one of the curial prefects. The cardinals were now engaged in what was the more useful investment of their time, the prattiches. And Cardinals Franz Koenig and John Krol were using the time well. They sat huddled in a far corner of the hall with Cardinal Lauren Rugambwa of Tanzania and Cardinal Mario Casareigo y Acevedo of Guatemala, continuing to focus their attention on the cardinals of the third world, who they thought might eventually decide the identity of the next pope. They were engaged in an intense conversation and trying to keep it quiet, a serious challenge given Cardinal Casareigo's poor hearing.

"No! It's out of the questions, and I won't discuss it any further!"

Krol and the other three cardinals with him turned their attention to a large group of their colleagues seated around a small table about twenty feet away. The stern voice was that of Cardinal Siri, who had risen to his feet and was glaring at the others in his group, all of them Italian red hats.

Krol turned his eyes to Koenig. "Looks like some more friction in the Italian camp."

Koenig shifted in his chair and craned his neck to get a better look. "So it seems. And look at who's there—Samore, Pignedolli, Baggio, Corneliano, and Ciappi, all from the curia—the head of the papal household, the in-house theologian, the head administrator—even the Vatican librarian who controls the secret archives. They obviously are still trying to find some sort of accommodation between Siri and Benelli."

"What did you say?" asked Cardinal Casareigo, his face a puzzle.

Koenig turned to the Guatemalan, leaning in close to his right ear, which seemed to be the better of the two. "We were just commenting on the gathering over there." He pointed to the Italians, whose faces showed considerable concern. Koenig then leaned toward Krol. "Look. As Siri walks out, Benelli walks in."

Cardinal Rugambwa was also watching the developing scene and nodded in agreement as the archbishop of Florence slowly crossed the floor toward the group of obviously flustered Italians, who rose and cordially greeted him.

"They're clearly trying to build a bridge across a wide divide," Krol commented.

"What did you say?" Casareigo asked again, extending his body in Krol's direction. "Did you say something about crossing a bridge?"

Koenig and Krol exchanged a brief glance and then, along with Rugambwa, turned their full attention back to the Guatemalan, all leaning in close to him and offering him thoughts for conclave consideration. After a few moments, Casareigo sat up straight in his chair, commenting in a loud voice, "Who is this Cardinal Bottiglia you're talking about? I don't know any Cardinal Bottiglia!"

Krol grinned at Koenig, who started to explain when a loud voice boomed from the main hall entrance. "Your Eminences, might we gather together so I can speak with you about an important matter." All eyes turned to see Cardinal Villot enter with Monsignor Sarac. The camerlengo walked quickly past the various groups, his eyes fixed sternly on the center of the historic hall. The cardinals scattered around the room ended their discussions and did as requested, creating a tide of red robes moving toward Villot. Within a few moments, those present were gathered in a semicircle while Villot nervously paced in front of them, all eyes focused on his clearly pained face.

"Your Eminences," Villot began slowly, "I have some very sad news to report to you all. Our dear Sister Cummings has been found dead in the Vatican kitchen."

The cardinals looked from one to another, and a murmur immediately filled the room. Villot knew the obvious question that was coming, if he waited for one. He didn't wait. "She evidently died from…a heart attack."

Sarac looked at his boss, surprised that Villot had decided to lie to his colleagues about Cummings's death. He had advised Villot to do so, to avoid creating additional concern and distracting from the serious matter of the conclave, but Villot had said he would not be dishonest with his peers. But, he had obviously changed his mind.

Krol stumbled slightly, stunned. The murmur began to grow louder around him, and his mind was whirring, but he could not speak. He watched silently as Villot and Sarac exchanged nervous glances, and he wondered why. Something was going on; something was not quite right. But his immediate concern was Sister Cummings. She seemed quite healthy and vivacious the few times he had met with her. Of course, one could never know for sure. After all, six weeks ago, Luciani had seemed healthy and vivacious. But Cummings was younger and had not borne the heavy burdens of great responsibility. However, she had borne the burden of the heavy secret the two of them were sharing. Was that the burden that had strained her heart? Or was there something else? Had someone discovered what the two of them were engaged in?

"I appreciate your concerns, but we shall continue with our solemn responsibility."

Krol refocused his attention on Villot, who was concluding his sad announcement but was offering no further details about Sister Cummings. "Let me suggest for now that you all return to your respective quarters or to one of the chapels and offer prayer and thanks for the service of Sister Cummings to the holy church."

With that, Villot departed, striding quickly out of the hall, the other cardinals slowly following him, their discussions echoing in the staircase outside. Krol remained, moving to a chair in the now largely vacant hall and taking a seat, still stunned. This would make things much harder for him, as he no longer had the connection to Carter and Kath that had been the more comfortable one. Now he'd have to use the clumsy device they had provided, and he didn't like it—he didn't fully trust it. But it was all he had left. He felt a hand softly tap his shoulder. He looked up to see Koenig standing beside him.

"John, I know you were fond of Sister Cummings," the Austrian said, using his best pastoral diction, "but she's now at peace. Go and pray as Villot suggested, and try to relax. We have much left to do, and I'll need your full assistance." With that, Koenig turned and left the hall, taking Cardinal Casareigo with him, filling in some of the words that Casareigo had not heard from Villot's announcement.

Krol looked around the area where he was seated. Across the room, he spotted Cardinal Katic, sitting alone, his face quite impassive. He seemed in no great hurry to leave for prayer, and he seemed unmoved by the news they had just heard. Katic turned his head in Krol's direction, and their eyes met briefly. Then Katic looked away with no acknowledgment of Krol's presence. "Katic is such a loner," the Philadelphian thought, "but even loners should have emotions. Yet he's always so distant, so detached, so cold."

Krol stood, shaking his head slightly, and headed toward the door, looking behind momentarily at Katic, who was now the only person left in the room. As he reached the exit door, Krol heard his name softly called. "Cardinal Krol." He stopped and looked to his left. "Over here, Eminence." Krol turned his head the other way and saw a figure standing in the shadows created by the small arch above the hallway leading to a service area. He slowly stepped over and into the shadows.

"Matteo. What are you doing here?" Krol was surprised to see Ferrari standing in the dark corner.

Ferrari looked around to ensure they were alone. "Your Eminence, you must be very careful from now on. And I do mean *very* careful."

Krol also looked around momentarily, alarmed at the warning. "Why, Matteo? Careful of what? What are you saying?"

"Your Eminence," Mateo whispered, "Sister Cummings was murdered. She was stabbed to death. There was no heart attack."

The words hit Krol even harder than Villot's original announcement. He felt his spine stiffen and the blood drain from his face. "Murdered! Murdered by whom? And why? And why would Villot not tell us this?"

Ferrari scanned the immediate area once again. "Your Eminence, they must have known she was working with you…with us. So they eliminated her. We had warned you to be careful and watchful, but now you must be always on guard. Always! Be careful what you say, where you go, what you do! You may be in great danger."

"Who are the 'they' you refer to?"

"Eminence, it has to be the KGB. Someone in the Vatican is a KGB operative."

Krol's eyes widened, forcing him to push his glasses up on his nose. "Certainly you're not suspecting the camerlengo?"

"No, we don't think so," Matteo replied. "That would be too obvious, and I think too hard. I think he's only trying to protect the church by keeping this quiet, at least as quiet as he can—for now. He must convene the conclave in four days. That's the most important thing to him at the moment. But the KGB has someone here, maybe more, so you must be very careful and watchful. I have to go now. I'll be watching out for you as best I can, but please keep your own eyes open."

With that admonition, Matteo quickly and quietly slipped away down the service hallway, leaving the tall cardinal alone with his thoughts and, for the first time, fears.

## The US Embassy, Rome

As Katherine and Carter approached the small embassy room they had been using for their meetings, its door opened and Bruce Harrison motioned for them to quickly step inside. After they had entered, he closed and locked the door behind them. "We have a very serious problem," he snapped.

Carter looked to Kath and then back to Bruce. "OK. I assume you'll tell us what it is."

Harrison shook his head. "Sister Cummings—she was found dead in the hallway outside her kitchen this morning. Stabbed to death. A messy scene. Looks like she put up a fight, but she was a slight woman. Obviously didn't have a chance against a pro, and it looks like this was done by a pro."

Carter looked at Katherine again, who had raised her hand to cover her mouth. "How'd you get that information?"

"One of our assets inside the Vatican."

"Is he sure?"

Harrison tossed his head back slightly. "Oh, he's sure. Quite sure." Bruce paused for a minute. "Damn it. I was afraid something like this would happen. She moved too fast. She contacted Krol too soon, and someone somehow figured it out. So now she's dead and our best channel to Krol is gone. But worse than that, this means there's someone in there—probably KGB—who's a real danger…to Krol…and maybe others. They're worried; the Lubyanka boys are really worried, and this tells us they're not going to fuck around. Sorry, Kath." Harrison looked to Katherine, who waved her hand at him.

"It's OK, Bruce. I've heard the phrase. And I've heard worse—often from you."

Carter sat down at the small table. "Do we have the signal device yet?"

Harrison nodded. "Yeah, it's here. Came in this morning. Both pieces."

"Have we tested it yet?"

"No, and probably won't. There's no time. We know it works in a lab, but we don't know if it'll work in the expected conditions, or over the distances we need, or if the weather gets bad. At this point, it doesn't matter. It's all we've got. We have to get it to Krol right away so he can get familiar with it. I hope he's been practicing with the mock-up, 'cause we'll really need it now. Anyway, I'll need you two to get it to him tomorrow. I'll set up a time and place."

"Shouldn't Matteo get it to him?" Kath asked, a bit uncomfortable at being handed this assignment.

"No, can't risk it. He needs to stay inside and lay low. We'll be in real deep shit if they figure him out. Besides, he's got his own piece of this thing to install, and it may be a bit tricky." Harrison paused briefly, his thoughts returning to the dead nun. "Damn, she should have been more careful. Well…it is what it is. Hear anything new from Dugan?"

"Yeah, he called this morning," Katherine replied. "Paolo Garda, his contact at *Della Sera*, called Siri's secretary, Monsignor Grone, and asked about the interview. He said Grone became quite nervous and evasive. Garda then called Licheri at the *Gazetta* and told him Grone had confirmed the story."

"Did Grone actually confirm it?" Harrison asked, suddenly feeling a bit better.

"No," Kath continued, "he actually denied it. Situational ethics apply to Catholic priests as well, I suppose. But Licheri and *Gazetta* will now have to decide whether to publish early or risk having their own story scooped by *Della Sera*. It's the worst thing that can happen in journalism, when your own scoop gets scooped."

"Does Avery think *Gazetta* will print it before the conclave?"

"Oh, he's pretty sure they will, but if they don't, *Della Sera* probably will—after all, they have no agreement with Siri on anything. But if they don't publish it either, we have one more thing ready to go."

"Which is?"

Katherine smiled. "Avery has 111 copies printed in a half dozen different languages."

"Why 111?"

"Because there are 111 voting cardinals in the conclave, and each one will get a copy."

"How?"

Katherine paused for effect. "Well, Bruce, I was rather hoping you could handle that part. You're the operator here."

Harrison scowled momentarily, before his face broke into a wide grin. "*Touché*, Katherine. Good work. Fair enough, I'll arrange for the paper boys."

There was a knock on the door, and it cracked open. A young embassy officer stepped partly inside. "Mr. Caldwell, there's a call for you in the message center."

Carter looked at Harrison and then stood up, looking at the embassy officer. "Sure. I'll come with you."

"And remember our deal, Carter," Harrison said, pointing his finger in Carter's direction as the NSC staffer headed off to the message center.

Once there, Carter stepped over to the desk with the STU-1 telephone, pushed the blinking button, and lifted the receiver. "Carter Caldwell here."

The accent on the other end was the one he expected.

"Carter, Zbig here, I wanted to give you an update, and I'm afraid it's not good."

Carter settled into a chair. "Go ahead, sir."

"Carter, the Soviets have moved nearly all their divisions into what you army fellows would call 'attack positions.' It looks like they are poised to move on short notice on both fronts. We think the East German–based forces will secure the Baltic coast and the southern mountains. It looks like most of the Soviet-based divisions will head straight to Warsaw. And we have some new information from the senior source."

"Cosmos?" Carter asked.

"Yes, Cosmos," Brzezinski replied. "They have moved several *Spetsnaz* units forward. So we can expect those units to fan out and round up the key Poles who might rally a resistance. I really fear this could be another Katyn Forest."

Carter knew the Spetsnaz well. They were Soviet special forces units with a reputation for efficiency and brutality. If the Soviets intended to eliminate all of the potential opposition, the Spetsnaz would be their preferred tool. "I understand your concern," Carter added, knowing this was a particular fear of Brzezinski's.

"One last thing, Carter," Brzezinski continued, "they plan to attack next week, on the Wednesday the eighteenth, at 0800 local time."

"Why then, Zbig?"

"It's pretty clear to me," the national security advisor continued. "The two people in Poland most likely to oppose them and incite a resistance are in Rome."

Carter sat up straighter in his chair. "Of course! Wyszynski and the other cardinal, the one from Kraków."

"Precisely," Brzezinski answered, his verbal tone reflecting both concern and exasperation. "So, you better get one of the non-Italians elected, or we'll have a serious mess on our hands—which we may have anyway! That's all I have. Good luck."

Carter heard the phone click off at the other end. The countdown was on for the Soviet invasion, and it was moving in tandem with the countdown to the conclave. And all they had to stop it were Bruce, Katherine, himself, a couple of operatives—one of whom was now dead—and some communications contraption that had never been fully tested and might not work. "Great!" Carter thought. "Just another twenty-five-footer from the corner with no time on the clock and Bobby Knight yelling at you!" He rose from the table and headed back to the meeting room to give Bruce and Kath his cheery news.

CHAPTER 17

# Wednesday, October 11, 1978
# The Café Vaticano

• • •

It was slightly past noon when Carter and Kath exited their cab two blocks from the Vatican Museum and proceeded south along the Via Tunisi toward a small café across the street from the museum entrance. It was a lovely day in Rome, and as Via Tunisi's pavement changed into a pedestrian-only cobblestone stairway, they were treated to a wonderful view of the north wall of Vatican City. They casually headed toward their destination, seemingly just another American couple enjoying a trip to Rome during a special time. Carter was wearing jeans, a light jacket, and a pair of worn docksider shoes, while Katherine was in khaki pants, a blue knit sweater with a stylish cowl-neck collar, and leather boots. Carter thought she looked fabulous and decided if he got the chance later, he might try to slip away for some shopping to spruce up his own wardrobe.

The steps were damp as they began their ascent to the Viale Vaticano, the narrow two-lane road bordering the Vatican. Katherine was carrying an annoyingly heavy shopping bag in one hand and with her purse thrown over the opposite shoulder, keeping her balance was a challenge. As she stepped on one of the cobblestones, her boot slipped. "Oh my God!" she yelled, feeling herself falling backward, flailing her arms to regain her balance while trying not to drop the shopping bag and its important contents. "Oh...my...God!"

Carter was walking about a step behind and quickly lunged in her direction, catching her in his arms before she completely tumbled backward. Instinctively she reached up and grabbed his neck with her free arm, leaving the two of them clinging to each other in an awkwardly posed position, their faces close.

"Goodness, Carter." Kath sighed after a pause. "Thank you. I think my bottom was about to bounce off the stones like a basketball."

Carter smiled at her. "Well, I guess we're both lucky that I'm experienced at catching basketballs."

They stayed as they were for a few more seconds, until Carter gently set her upright on her feet. "Come on; it's just a few more steps up to the café." He extended his arm to her, and without any delay or hesitation, she took it and they continued up the slight incline. He tried not to look at her, but his mind was spinning. "That was easily the best catch I've ever made," he thought.

The Café Vaticano's sidewalk seating area was surprisingly empty for this time of day, and they moved to a table in the corner, one offering a view of the exit from the Vatican Museum as well as some slight concealment from observation by those walking along the sidewalk to their right. A server quickly arrived, and Carter ordered two cups of coffee and two pastry rolls and then pushed one of the other chairs at the small table away, leaving only one empty seat across from them. Katherine set the shopping bag down behind her in a small nook in the limestone building. "Do you think he got the message to meet us?" she asked, carefully scanning the area around them.

"Let's hope so," Carter replied, intently watching the cars and pedestrians passing by. "If he didn't and doesn't show, then I think we're basically out of options for this escapade."

"That'd be my conclusion," Kath replied, and they both fell silent, carefully watching everything going on around them, as fifteen minutes turned into thirty, thirty turned into an hour, and—still nothing.

Carter was about to ask whether they should leave when he heard a familiar voice from behind his chair. "Are you two waiting for someone? Or just enjoying the autumn air?"

The couple's heads snapped to their left in perfect unison. "Your Eminence!" Kath exclaimed and then quickly covered her mouth, realizing she had been a bit too loud given the circumstances. "We were about to decide you weren't going to make it."

Cardinal John Krol smirked. He was dressed in a plain black suit with a poorly knotted dark tie over a wrinkled white shirt. A brown hat was pulled low, its brim partly covering his face. "Well, given all that's been going on, sneaking out of the Vatican is getting a bit more challenging. But your man on the inside knows the place well, so I was able to sneak out through an old tunnel that comes out down the hill from here, in fact on the other side of this building. I'm turning into a seasoned spy—moving around through secret passages and sneaking up on…well, professional spies. I mean seriously, neither of you saw me coming through the café?"

"Well, I certainly didn't," Kath chuckled. "So, Matteo helped you get out?"

Krol shook his head. "No, the other one…Gianluca. I think he's Matteo's uncle or something. I don't know how you got him on the team, but he sure knows every light and dark corner of the place."

Katherine chuckled again. "It seems to me, John, that maybe you're in the wrong profession. I don't even know who Gianluca is."

"In that case, I suspect I shouldn't have told you," Krol replied, picking up his coffee and moving over to Carter and Kath's table. "So there, I'm not as good at this as I thought." Krol paused and took a deep breath. "I presume you've heard about Sister Cummings."

Carter and Kath nodded.

"It was a great shock to me," Krol continued. "It shows again that even in a place of the greatest sanctity, somehow evil can seep in and exist comfortably alongside good and can even masquerade as good while never revealing the smallest shred of its dark character. Churchill once described Nazism as a 'monstrous tyranny, never surpassed in the dark, lamentable catalogue of human crime.' I've never personally been so close to that dark, lamentable catalogue, and it was chilling…very chilling."

The cardinal's head briefly dropped to his chest, and he let out a deep sigh. Carter and Kath looked at each other, trying to decide what they might say.

"John," Carter softly whispered, "is this too much for you? Are we asking you to take risks that are too great and to cross boundaries that are too firm, ones that you are already uncomfortably close to?"

Krol looked up, reached across the table, and placed his large hand on Carter's shoulder. "I am uncomfortable, Carter. And I am about to take an oath that I will be following only by stretching its meaning to extreme limits. Arguing later that I have respected it will be quibbling, plain and simple. But the church is led by real men…human beings, and we live in troubled times, and there are times when human beings have to reflect on what those times demand. Are the rules eternally applicable, or are there moments when getting the best outcome, indeed the necessary outcome, requires some degree of compromise? I could never compromise with evil, and over the past two days, we have become aware how near evil can be. But there are times when one good must compromise with another good, when we have to ask ourselves, 'What is the greater good?' I believe, for me, this is one of those times. As I told you when we met in Philadelphia, I do what I do because I believe it is best for the church, and if doing what is best for the church coincides with what is best for others, even those not in the church, I feel that is a path I must walk. So, now…what do you have for me?"

Kath and Carter were moved and took a moment to allow Krol's wisdom to settle in. Then Kath reached behind her seat and lifted up the shopping bag. She removed an ornate wooden case from it with a small locked latch holding its halves together. She removed a tiny key from her pocket and released the latch, opening the case and exposing an equally ornate Bible.

Krol's eyebrows arched into his forehead. "Goodness, how beautiful!" he exclaimed. "You people seem to like to package things in Bibles. I recognize the work on this one. Lebanese wood with inlaid mother-of-pearl, correct?"

Katherine nodded. "Correct," she replied, impressed by his familiarity with the cover. "But it's only partially a Bible." She opened the cover, showing that most of the chapters after Genesis had been carved out;

sitting inside was the transmitter Krol had been awaiting. He gazed at it and then turned his eyes back to hers. She then opened the Bible to the New Testament, showing that six cylindrical plugs had been cut out of the book of John. Inside each of the six round holes was a silver wafer.

"What are these?" Krol asked.

"Batteries. They're a new type of battery that's just coming out. Each will last about half a day. So assuming you'll take a break for lunch during the conclave, you'll need to change the battery out."

"So, since there are six, that suggests, as Matteo indicated, that you still think we'll have a new pope within three days after the conclave starts. I'm no longer so sure it will go that fast," Krol continued, rubbing his chin. "What if I need more?"

"Well," Kath replied, "then I guess we'll have to get you some more… somehow. Either through Matteo, or this other fellow—Gianluca."

"That won't work," Krol answered, a twinkle in his eye. "You don't know Gianluca, remember?"

"A good point," Kath responded, smiling, "but I presume somebody in our Rome station does. We'll cross that bridge when and if we get to it. One more thing, in Revelation, I've stuck five small envelopes, each containing a three-by-five card."

"Crib sheets?" Krol asked with a chuckle.

"No, Your Eminence. They're some brief notes on the five Italian cardinals other than Siri and Benelli, who we believe might be a compromise candidate."

"What sort of notes, Katherine?"

"Don't get angry with us, John, but they have some information, all very sketchy, that you might use to—shall we say—'discourage' them from consideration."

An uneasy expression crossed Krol's face. "Katherine, do you mean some sort of dirt?"

Kath shook her head. "No, not dirt exactly, nothing salacious or anything like that but just a couple of items that might get more public visibility should one of them become pope—you know, things that might be uncomfortable for them or their families. As I said, something you can use if you feel necessary—and appropriate."

Krol thought for a few moments. "Well, we'll see. I'm comfortable advocating for someone, but I'm uncomfortable colluding against anyone. I'm not sure I could—or would—do that, but…I'll think about it."

While Kath and Krol were going over the contents of the Bible, Carter had been watching a small white Fiat slowly move along the street and then stop momentarily at the curb about ten feet from their table. The passenger side window rolled down but then quickly rolled back up, and the car speedily pulled away. He hadn't thought much of it until he noticed the same car return, slowly going back down the Viale Vaticano in the opposite direction, this time with the driver's side window mostly down, giving him a good look at a tough-looking man with a sharp nose and thin, receding hair. Carter had started to interrupt Katherine's discussion with Krol but decided not to.

While they were discussing the batteries, he had gotten up from the table and walked closer to the curb, giving him a clear view down the street to the east, the direction in which he had last seen the car traveling. He stood and stared. Suddenly, he saw the Fiat appear a third time. It rounded the corner about two blocks away and turned in his direction. It began picking up speed. Carter took a couple of hasty steps back toward the table where Kath and Krol were still talking. He looked again. The Fiat was still coming, and the passenger window was opening. He saw the man in the passenger seat partially stick his head out the window. He was holding something in front of his face. Carter squinted in the noon sunlight to get a clear view. A gun! It was a gun! And the man holding it was now looking straight at him!

"*Down!*" Carter yelled as he dashed toward the table.

Krol and Katherine looked up, but did not move.

"Down! *Get down!*" Carter yelled again, diving for the table just as the Fiat screeched to a halt at the curb.

It all happened in an instant! *Bap*! It was a pistol! He hadn't been able to get a clear view of what type, but whatever it was, he instantly started counting the shots; there should be at least seven left. He hit the table, knocking Kath and Krol back against the building wall of the café as the first bullet hit the limestone above the table, filling the air with a powdery smell as bits of limestone flew about. The old army saying was true: the first shots are always high!

*Bap*! The second bullet made a loud, metallic *thwack* as it ricocheted off the table!

*Bap*! *Bap*! *Bap*! *Bap*! Four other shots—two hit the café's sliding glass door behind them, shattering it, throwing shards of glass everywhere, splashing them across the sidewalk, while two more hit the coffee bar! Six shots! There couldn't be more than two left.

"*Mafiosi*! *Mafiosi*!" the sidewalk waitress screamed, tossing her tray to the ground and darting away toward Via Tunisi. Carter looked up as the Fiat, wheels squealing, started to pull away, but as it did, it struck a man on a bicycle who was furiously pedaling, trying to get past it, knocking him into the other lane. A taxi heading down the street in the opposite direction swerved to avoid the bicyclist and crashed head-on into the Fiat. The Fiat driver's head hit the windshield hard, knocking him out. The gunman leaped from the car and looked at Carter, raising his pistol, taking aim directly at him.

*Bam*! The gunman slumped back against the Fiat, reaching for his left shoulder, the shirt around it slowly turning red. Carter's head snapped to his left to see where that shot came from, recognizing from the sound it was from a different weapon. When he did, he saw Katherine lying across Krol, her right arm raised and smoke trailing from the barrel of her Beretta. "He's getting away! Go get him!" she yelled, tossing the gun to Carter, who caught it in his right hand.

"Are you both OK?" he shouted above the noisy confusion of people swirling around the café and on the sidewalk.

"Yeah! We're fine! We're OK! Go! Go!" Kath shouted.

Carter turned his eyes toward the gunman, who was running up the street, holding his left shoulder, the pistol still gripped in his right hand. Carter took off after him. "Shit!" he thought, running in a slight crouch. "What am I going to do if I catch the guy? Shoot him? Great! An American army officer, working for the White House, guns down some hit man on the streets of Rome! Outside the Vatican! With a pistol borrowed from the CIA agent he's sharing a hotel room with! This will be so fucking *great*! Brzezinski will love visiting me in my Italian jail!"

As he finished this line of jolly reflection, Carter came to a rapid halt. The gunman had stopped and turned to face him. He saw the pistol come up into firing position. *Bap*! Carter dove behind a trash can placed by a set of steps. Clang! The bullet hit the can, ripping away the top corner, as the gunman again turned and fled.

"Close one!" Carter said to himself as he jumped back to his feet. "Probably has only one bullet left. He won't want to waste it." Carter dashed up to the next corner and stopped to peek around the edge, pressing his back against the wall. It was another cobblestoned pedestrian way with steps descending to the next block. The gunman was already down on the third level of steps where he stopped again, turned toward Carter, and once more raised his pistol. But he was seriously wounded, and the loss of blood and shock were starting to take a toll. He stumbled a bit. Carter jumped out from the corner and assumed the firing posture he had first learned on the pistol range at Camp Buckner, West Point's summer training area. "Drop it!" he yelled, quickly realizing he had no idea whether this fellow even understood English. The gunman aimed the pistol with his trembling hand.

*Bam*! Carter's shot was deadly. He caught his attacker square in the chest, and he watched as he dropped like a sack of flour. Carter paused for just a moment, then dashed over to the assailant's body. He could see when he arrived that the man was already dead. Again, his army training kicked in. He quickly went through the man's pockets, searching for whatever information or identity might be there. Surprisingly, in the back pocket was a wallet. He took it out and without looking further tucked it inside his shirt.

In the distance, he could hear the characteristic sounds of Italian police car sirens. People were scurrying all about, some running down the steps, others running up, none—strangely enough—seemed focused on him. He quickly tucked the Beretta into his belt, pulled out just enough of his shirttail to cover it, and started walking down the steps. After a few feet, he ducked into an alley on his right, hoping it would connect with the next street over. It did. He then turned left and crisply walked to the next main street, Via Candia, all the while debating what he should do and where he should go—and where Katherine and Cardinal Krol might be. They had not planned for anything like this and had no prearranged rally points. The police sirens were getting closer now, but they seemed to be up the hill on Viale Vaticano. He was sure they would find the body of the gunman soon and then start fanning out to find him. He saw a trash can and quickly removed his light jacket. He wadded it up and pushed it as deep into the can as he could before continuing on.

"The embassy," he thought. He would have to go to the embassy. He'd need diplomatic cover and immunity if this shooting were traced to either him or Katherine. They might have to be sneaked out of the country—maybe to Austria, maybe to France.

He turned right onto Via Candia and started walking a bit faster but decided that might look suspicious so he slowed his pace. Suddenly, the sounds of a car engine cranking out extra RPMs caught his attention. He kept walking but glanced up the street behind him as a car careened in his direction and screeched to a stop next to him. He was sure it was undercover police and he was about to be arrested.

"Get in! Quick!" It was Katherine's voice. He looked to his left and saw the car's door fly open. He jumped in, and the car sped away. "You OK?" she asked as he exhaled the deep breath that seemed to have been trapped in his throat forever and then took a quick glance out the rear window.

"Yeah. Yeah. I'm fine. You? Krol? Where's Cardinal Krol?"

"Back in the Vatican," Kath replied. "When you took off, we left the café and headed down the hill to the secret tunnel he mentioned. The thing looks like just another apartment door entrance. He had a key. Wow, was he great. Cool as could be. He's back inside...with the Bible!"

"How'd you know where to find me?"

"Just guessed. I had looked at a map this morning and figured whether you got the guy or not, you'd head away from the Vatican and try to backtrack to where we met Krol. Via Candia was the most likely spot in my mind."

Carter shook his head in disbelief. "You looked at a map? You, who don't know north from south, looked at a map and guessed where I would be. Impressive…very impressive. I must be rubbing off on you."

Katherine smiled. "Well, maybe you are. I hope you still have the Beretta?"

Carter reached behind him and produced the pistol, handing it to Katherine, who stuck it back in her purse. "How many shots did you fire at him?"

"One."

"And?"

"He's dead. I have his wallet."

"He had a wallet! Really? I'm shocked. You wouldn't think a fellow in his line of work would carry a wallet. I'm sure it doesn't have anything useful in it."

Carter was now fully calm and turned his head to Kath. "Should we be talking about this?" he whispered, motioning toward the driver.

"It's not a problem," Katherine replied. "He's with the Agency. Works for Bruce's station chief. He's their usual driver. Knows his way around Rome like the back of his hand."

"OK," Carter said, "so how'd he happen to be here ready to pick us up?"

"I asked Bruce to arrange it. I thought we should have someone nearby just in case."

"I thought you were an analyst. This sounds like operational stuff."

"Well," Katherine answered with a smile, "we have to always be learning new skills, don't we?"

Carter laughed. "Well, if you say so. So where are we headed now?"

"To the embassy. We'll need a lot of help from them to sort this out. We've got to find out who tried to take out Krol and how anyone knew where he was or that he was meeting with us. This thing will get out of control if this sort of stuff continues. We've already got a dead nun, and we were close to having a dead cardinal. Obviously the stakes are going up."

Carter knew clearly why the stakes were going up, but he didn't indicate to her that he did.

## US Embassy, Rome

The car with Carter and Kath pulled straight through the embassy gates and into the building's underground garage. A consular officer met them there and took them directly to the meeting room where Bruce Harrison was waiting. As they walked in, Carter was surprised to see a wide grin covering Harrison's face. Given that their cover was likely blown, that they had been the targets of an attempted hit, and that he had gunned a man down on the streets of Rome, he had expected a rocky reception.

"Rough afternoon, eh, guys?" Harrison asked, in a surprisingly jovial voice.

Carter and Kath looked at each other. "I guess you might say that," Carter answered, unsure of what was making this a lighter-than-expected moment with the CIA operations chief.

Harrison sat down in one of the chairs. "Quite a coup you pulled off there, Carter. Quite a coup."

"What do you mean, Bruce?"

"The guy you blew away this afternoon…his name was Vladimir Kuznetzov. He was the KGB's designated thug for Rome. Worked directly for their station chief, Viktor Myshkin. Actually, they're both thugs. And worse than that, they're dumb thugs. The two of them can screw up ball bearings. A competent operative would have killed all three of you and gotten away with no one even noticing. But not this clown. He misses everybody he was supposed to kill, wounds a little Italian grandmother pushing a baby, hits another car, and finally—the coup de grace—gets his dumb ass dropped with one shot. And, Carter…

damn man! One shot! You army guys are good. And I thought you could only handle a forty-five!"

Carter was still not sure how to react to Bruce's discourse. "Well, thanks…I guess. If you know who he was, I guess you won't need this." He tossed Kuznetzov's wallet on the table.

Bruce gave the wallet a quick gaze. "Doubt anything in there is useful, but we'll look."

"So what does that mean going forward?" Carter asked. "I'm sure the Italian police will be investigating what happened, won't they?"

"Nah, forget it. They checked in with us already. How do you think we knew who it was so fast? They're glad you wasted the asshole. They're going through the motions, but it'll be case closed. They'll take the body to the Soviet embassy and tell them they won't make any noise or lodge a diplomatic complaint if they'll just send the remains home and not say anything about it. The Soviets will be happy with that deal. That's not our problem."

"Yeah, I agree with that. Our problem is that they obviously have a mole inside the Vatican who knew we were meeting with Krol. It's probably the same guy who killed Sister Cummings."

Harrison nodded. "Yup, you're right; that's clearly our problem. In fact, I suspect they have more than one mole in there. So, we have to have our guys find out who they are, keep a close eye on Krol, and see if there's some way we can neutralize their agent—or agents. Given that we don't have much of a footprint in there, that'll be no easy task in itself."

"Who's Gianluca?" Kath asked, immediately catching Harrison's attention.

"Where'd you hear about him?" Bruce replied, a bit gruffly.

"From Krol. He said 'Gianluca' showed him how to get out of the Vatican."

"Bruce," Carter interrupted, "remember our deal? Perhaps it'd be best if you let us in on exactly who you have in there."

"Why?"

"Well, for one thing, I'd sure hate to gun him down by mistake. I mean, who knew I was taking out a KGB hit man this afternoon!"

Harrison thought for a few moments before offering a sober reply. "No, sorry, I don't think so. This is a professional call, but I just don't see where either of you have a need to know. And with no NTK—no identity…at least for now."

"I see," Carter answered, his words a bit icy. "So, in your world, I need to tell you everything I know, but it doesn't work the other way, right?"

Bruce grinned slightly, holding his hands open with palms up. "Well, I hate to say it, but…yeah, something like that."

"I don't like unbalanced deals," Carter responded, the displeasure clear in his voice.

"We'll *balance* it if we need to," Bruce replied. "As for now, I'd suggest the two of you go back to the hotel and relax. You've had a rough day."

"Should we continue to stay at the De Russie? I mean, after today, they know who we are, don't they?"

Bruce shook his head. "I don't think they have either of you made yet. They were following Krol, not looking for you. That's why Kuznetzov drove by twice before he tried the hit. What a dumb shit! I guess Andropov left him and Myshkin here, thinking there was nothing much in Rome they could fuck up…sorry, Kath!"

Kath waved her hand. By now, she was getting used to Bruce's linguistic habits.

"Krol got the device, right?"

"Yes, he got it. And I think he'll master it well enough. When will the other part be in place?"

Bruce smiled. "The central station in the van is here and assembled. The transmitting and relay station will go in tomorrow."

"Where is it being placed?" Carter asked.

"Sorry, Carter. No NTK!"

"OK, but how's it going to be put in place now so that nobody will notice it, especially given all the activity going on in the Vatican?"

"Sorry, Carter. No—"

"I got it. No NTK."

Bruce smiled again. "Correct. But I'll tell you this. It'll be installed and hidden in plain sight."

Carter and Kath exchanged glances. They were tired, and it was time to get to the hotel and rest. The coming days hopefully wouldn't be this exciting, but they would certainly be long.

Bruce paused momentarily and rubbed his hands together. "You know, I can't say this thing will get the result we want, but we'll at least know what the result is before anyone other than the cardinals do—for whatever that's worth. You think they bet on conclaves in Vegas? We might have time to put some money down!"

CHAPTER 18

## Thursday, October 12, 1978
## Hotel De Russie

● ● ●

*Grrrrring! Grrrrring! Grrrrring!* European telephones, even those in a hotel as elegant as the De Russie, had a very sharp, annoying ring. And inevitably they were several decibel levels louder than needed. Katherine jumped up from the chair that had been serving as Carter's bed and bolted across the room, motivated by both professional curiosity about who was calling and an immediate need to end the phone's irritating sound.

"Good morning," she softly uttered into the receiver. There was no reply. "Hello? Who's this?" she asked.

"Katherine," came the voice on the other end. "It's Avery. Sorry, I guess I was expecting Carter to answer the phone."

"He's in the shower," Kath replied, a bit more curtly than she had intended. "What do you need, Avery?"

Avery paused for a moment before continuing, "I just wanted to check in and let you know that I have the printed material we discussed. My contacts at the university came through splendidly. I'm taking them to the Vatican this morning to get them positioned for distribution to those we want to read them, hopefully by tomorrow. Their big meeting is just two days away, so the clock is really ticking now."

Kath switched into a more professional mode. "Great. That was good work getting that done. I guess we'll see what happens. If anything."

"Well, the other aspect will kick off today as well. Garda is going to call Licheri and tell him *Della Sera* has the interview and is going to publish it tomorrow. That's bound to panic the editors at the *Gazetta*. I'd be shocked if they don't have the thing on the street tomorrow morning."

"Did you actually give *Della Sera* a copy?"

"Yeah, I did. As I said, Paolo owed me a favor, but I thought it best to give him one so he had extra leverage if needed. He was evidently quite convincing with Grone, so I'm sure when he calls Licheri to tell him he has the interview, *Gazetta*'s presses will start running within ten minutes."

Kath smiled. Avery had delivered. "Thanks, Avery. Great job." There was a long pause as she debated how to end the conversation.

"Kath," Avery's voice continued, "can I tell you something?"

"I guess," she replied softly.

There was another long pause on his end of the line. "Kath, I'm so sorry for everything. I really am. It was my fault, all of it. But, you know, things tend to work out. I wish you and I had worked out differently, but…well, Carter strikes me as a really great guy. Really great."

"Avery," Kath whispered into the phone. "There's nothing going on between Carter and me. We're here on a job, and we're sharing a room because of a screw-up by the embassy staff. That's all there is to it. OK?"

"OK, sure, of course," Avery sheepishly replied, concerned that his effort to be helpful might be producing the opposite effect. "I'm just saying…he's a great guy, Kath. That's all. No suggestions. No inferences. No judgments. I know guys, and I'd say this one is pretty special. That's my only point. Do with it what you will. It's just input from… well, from an old friend."

Kath paused for a moment, pleased that Avery could not see the smile coming across her face. "Thanks, Avery. I appreciate your input. Catch you later." With that, she slowly lowered the receiver into its cradle, reflecting briefly on Avery's comments before her mind switched back to the business at hand. The job was still a long shot, and all things considered, it was a flimsy plan, but flimsy or not, the wheels were turning. She stuffed a few more things into her suitcase and latched it shut.

# The Soviet Embassy

"What the fuck do you mean Vladimir's *dead*?" Dimitry Zhukov was in a rage. Viktor had just informed him that the body of his hit man had been returned to the embassy by the Carabinieri. "Vladimir is fucking *dead*? We sent him out on a simple hit, and the guy we wanted dead is alive and Vladimir is *dead*?"

"It was bad luck!" Myshkin awkwardly replied. "Some guy spotted the car and interfered. Then this fellow on a bicycle caused an accident with another car."

"*Excuses*!" Zhukov shouted, the veins on his forehead and neck bulging. "Do you think Andropov cares about some fellow on a bicycle? We're the KGB! We kill heads of state. And you clowns can't take out an old priest!" Zhukov slapped his hands on his head and tried to calm himself. "What happened to our driver?"

"The Carabinieri brought him back, too," Viktor said, his voice reduced to a low mumble.

"Well," Dimitry growled, his teeth clenched. "Did he say what happened?"

Myshkin exhaled a mouthful of cigarette smoke. "He said they were coming up to the café to make the hit when a tall man at the table, where the cardinal was sitting with a young woman, started shouting. The man yelled for the woman and the cardinal to get down and then tossed a couple of tables on top of them. Vladimir got off a couple of shots—"

"And he obviously couldn't shoot any better than he could think," Dimitry interrupted.

Myshkin continued, ignoring the comment, "That missed. As they were speeding away, they were hit by another car. Myshkin jumped out of the car and was evidently shot by the woman, who then tossed her gun to the tall man."

"Wait a minute," Dimitry said, cutting off the description. "You mean the woman sitting with the cardinal had a gun? How many women sitting in cafés outside the Vatican Museum have guns? And she tossed it to the tall fellow! Meaning they were working together!" Dimitry threw his head back. "*Dermo*! It's Caldwell! Shit…it was Caldwell! And the woman was obviously the one we saw getting off the plane with him. They're clearly CIA, and they're here working with Krol. Somehow they're rigging the election of the pope. I don't know how, but somehow they intend to do it. I need to call Andropov right away."

"You're going to call Comrade Andropov directly, without going through Comrade Kornilov? Can you do that?" Myshkin asked, stunned.

Dimitry stared at Myshkin, slowly shaking his head. "Viktor, you are such an imbecile. Yes, I can call him directly. And when I do, one of the things we'll discuss is your next assignment in Novosibersk!" Dimitry jumped to his feet. "Go find out where Caldwell is staying, and take him out! And the woman too! Now! Today! I want them dead. Or is that also too hard for you and your fellow bumblers, like everything else you clowns attempt?"

With that, Dimitry headed toward the message center, leaving Myshkin seething. To him this whole thing was nonsense anyway. And if Zhukov thought he would become a favorite of Andropov's with this scheme, well…not if Myshkin had anything to do with it. If somebody was going to Siberia, it wasn't going to be him.

## OFFICES OF *GAZETTA DEL POPOLO*, ROME

Gianni Licheri had just sat down at his desk with a hot cup of tea. He had spent most of the morning working with his editor on the final version of his story about the interview with Cardinal Siri. He was still a bit puzzled as to why Siri had asked him to Genoa and was still trying to determine why the cardinal's comments in the interview had been so blunt, so candid, so harshly critical. But it was no longer all that relevant, as the article was finished, it had been reviewed, and the *Gazetta*'s senior editors had decided to run it on Saturday after the cardinals had gone behind the closed doors of the conclave. That had been the agreement with Siri, and they were going to keep it. After all, when Siri became the next pope both Licheri and the *Gazetta* could expect considerable access to the new pontiff, who would certainly use them to state his views without the filter of the Vatican Press Office. It was all falling nicely into place, and Licheri leaned back in his chair to enjoy a few moments of daydreaming about what should be his newfound prominence. He was so lost in his thoughts that he didn't hear the phone on his desk until its third ring.

"Buongiorno, Licheri here. How may I help you?"

The voice at the other end got right to the point. "Buongiorno, Gianni. It's Paolo Garda from *Della Sera*. I think we need to talk. Do you have a few minutes?"

"Of course," Licheri replied, casually leaning forward toward his desk, not yet aware that all casualness was about to leave the room. "What have you got, old friend?"

"What I have, Gianni, is an interview that you conducted with Cardinal Siri in Genoa Tuesday before last. And I must say, it's quite interesting…fascinating even."

Licheri's muscles tensed throughout his body. "I'm not sure I know what you're talking about, Paolo."

There was brief laughter at the other end of the line. "Gianni, don't play games with me. I know you conducted the interview, and being a good reporter I have verified it with Cardinal Siri's household staff."

"Verified it with whom…exactly?"

"Monsignor Grone."

"Grone verified that there was an interview?" Licheri was not sure whether to be shocked or angered. How could Grone do such a thing? The whole agreement had been to keep the interview secret. Why would Grone even agree to take a call from *Della Sera*? Licheri decided to play dumb. "Well, I really don't know what you're talking about, Paolo. If you have such an interview, what does it say?"

"Oh, it says a great many interesting things," Garda replied. "Let me read you something of what it says regarding Siri's views about the Vatican II reforms." Garda started reading from the copy Avery had provided, as Licheri slumped ever deeper into his chair, his free hand landing heavily on the top of his head.

"Paolo, stop, OK? All right, there was an interview that I conducted with Siri in his office in Genoa on October 2d. You obviously have some version of it…I don't know how, but you have something. So what are you going to do with it?"

"Well, dear friend," Garda responded, "I think that very much depends on what you are going to do with it. What plans does *Gazetta* have?"

"My agreement with Siri was that we would not publish the interview until the conclave convenes…on Saturday. I have just gone over the story and interview with the senior editors here, and that remains our plan. We'll run my story and publish the interview on Saturday." Licheri waited for a reply from Garda, but none was forthcoming. "Paolo, are you there?"

"Yes, Gianni, I'm here."

"Did you hear me? We'll publish Saturday. What are you thinking?"

A few more seconds passed. "Well, Gianni, frankly we had planned to run the interview without any comment tomorrow. We'll let the readers, whoever they may be, make of it what they will."

"You can't do that!" Licheri snarled into the phone. "It's my interview. It was exclusive to me. And I have an agreement with Siri not to publish until the conclave is in session, which will be Saturday!"

"Well, then," Garda quickly answered, "I guess you're stuck with Saturday. But I don't have any such agreement with Siri. And given that I have a copy, it seems your interview is not as exclusive as you once thought."

"*You can't do that, Paolo!*" Licheri shouted.

"Actually, I think we can, and I'm quite certain we will. But I thought you should know about it…as a professional courtesy. *A presto!*"

With that, Licheri heard the phone click off. He immediately slammed a hand on his desk, a finger catching the edge of his saucer, sending a spray of tea through the air, drenching the papers scattered in front of him. He leaped out of his seat and darted toward his editor's office. This would change everything. There was only one option—*Gazetta del*

*Popolo* would have to run the story tomorrow. They would have to take their chances with the future pope, who could very well be angry with *Gazetta* in general, and Licheri in specific, perhaps for years. Licheri arrived at his superior's door and slammed it behind him, enclosing the two of them in the glass office. Those in the newsroom could hear the glass rattling as their editor's booming voice erupted.

## THE VATICAN PRESS OFFICE

As Licheri and his editor screamed at one another, Avery Dugan walked into the Vatican Press Office, a package wrapped in plain brown paper under his arm. He was a familiar sight in the office, so almost no one paid any attention to his presence, and those who did merely looked at him and smiled, a few offering brief greetings. The conclave was starting in two days, and they were all very busy replying to the numerous press inquiries that had descended on them like an Alpine avalanche.

Avery passed through the cramped outer office and sauntered back to the small room occupied by the head of the print shop. All of the functional offices in the Vatican were small and tight, an obvious condition given the size of the city-state itself, which made all space a precious commodity. The tight space allotted to the press office reflected its rather minor standing with the Vatican hierarchy.

As Avery stepped into the small, windowless room, the head printer in the corner looked up from his compact standing desk. "Here they are," Avery said, dropping his package on the empty chair that served more as a doorstop than a seat. The printer in the corner nodded but said nothing. Over the past couple of years, Avery had learned that he understood English perfectly, but was not comfortable speaking it and rarely did.

"You know what to do?" Avery asked, slowly looking at the busy scene out in the main room.

The printer nodded again.

"Friday night, agreed?"

Another nod.

"Any questions at all?"

A slight shake of the head.

"Any copies that are left about or that turn out to be extra, destroy them, OK?"

Yet another nod.

Avery waved his hand to signal their meeting was over, stepped back into the main press room, and worked his way across it to the door where he had entered. The printer watched him go and then stepped over to grab the package. He placed it safely beneath his desk before returning to his day job.

## The Sala Clemintina Hall

As Avery was making his way out of the Vatican, Cardinals Krol, Koenig, Willebrands, and Tomášek were huddled around a table in the Sala Clemintina, chatting with a group of Latin American colleagues who had been brought to them by Cardinal Lorscheider. In addition to the four other Brazilian cardinals, Lorscheider had included in this prattiche the cardinals from the western coast of South America, extending from Colombia down to Chile.

Cardinal Juan Ricketts, the archbishop of Lima, leaned toward Krol and Koenig. "You make excellent points," he said, smiling at the others gathered around the table, "and I will pray and give your observations great consideration, and given your persuasive presentation—very serious thought. As you know, I believe the traditions of the church are important, even more so in a small and poor country such as mine, but I can see you have given this matter enormous consideration and I, for one, appreciate your insights."

Lorscheider waved his hand toward his fellow Brazilians, all of whom nodded, either in agreement or merely in an effort to appear to be in agreement. A quiet settled in for a few moments until Cardinal Maurer from Bolivia, leaning toward Koenig and keeping his voice low, broke it. "Your Eminence," he said in Spanish, "I understand your concerns about the threat posed by communist ideology, and we all agree it is not only irreligious in concept but in practice hostile to the church. In Bolivia, we have been directly threatened by a communist revolution in the not-too-distant past, and Che is still revered by many in the far reaches of our small country. But is this the right time to make such a bold departure?"

Koenig, ever the skilled diplomat, reached toward the Bolivian's hand. "Time is infinite for God," the Austrian stated with a smile, "but for those of us who are mortal, it is quite finite. It runs out. There are moments when it is left for us to decide how time is best used, to decide what time is right for action, and to decide times that are intolerant of inaction. I believe we are living such a moment. God trusts those of us who have gathered here to express His will, and I believe we will do so, but we must open our minds to consider fully what His will actually is. That is all we ask—that we all open our minds to the possibility of being vehicles of the future rather than captives of the past."

Maurer gently pulled his hand away from Koenig's, placed both his hands together, indicating prayerful reflection, and smiled at the Austrian. As he did, he saw Krol rising from his chair, his arms spreading wide. "Your Eminences, how good to see you both." All those gathered with Krol and Koenig turned to see the two Polish cardinals approaching, Cardinal Wyszynski walking about two paces ahead of his younger colleague, Cardinal Wojtyla.

"And good to see you as well," Wyszynski replied, reaching out for Krol's extended hand. "This seems like a serious discussion you're having."

"An interesting and perhaps enlightening one," Cardinal Maurer answered, his eyes moving from Wyszynski's face to Wojtyla's, where they were suddenly fixed and focused. "I have heard, Cardinal Wojtyla, that you have always had a great interest in the conditions of those around the world who wrestle daily with the burdens of poverty and despair. I recognize, of course, that in Poland, you and the prelate have your own serious challenges, but it has been a comfort to us that many, such as you, realize the difficulties of others who are far away from Europe."

Wojtyla smiled. "Your Eminence, my dear friend from Bolivia, wherever people are suffering, wherever they are humiliated by poverty or injustice, and wherever a mockery is made of their rights, we of the church must make it our task to serve them."

Maurer's gaze turned toward Krol and Koenig and then returned to Wojtyla where it remained as the others paused to reflect, subtly nodding in agreement at the archbishop of Kraków's comment.

Krol recognized the potential for an awkward moment and smoothly stepped in. "I'm sure Cardinal Wyzsynski is well known to all of you, but I'm glad you have had this chance to briefly meet and hear Cardinal Wojtyla."

"Thank you, John," Wojtyla replied, reaching past Krol for Ricketts's hand before briefly embracing Tomášek. "This is a true pleasure for one best known as 'the other Polish cardinal.'"

"I doubt that happens all that much anymore," Wyszynski inserted with a laugh, "especially after the last conclave."

As the others greeted Wojtyla, the Polish prelate turned and looked across the room to a spot where Cardinals Villot and Benelli were chatting; then he stepped nearer to Koenig. "It seems that the camerlengo is still trying to establish some degree of cohesion between those who support Siri and those supporting Benelli," Wyszynski commented with a sly smile. "I saw him with Siri just a few minutes ago. I guess by Saturday afternoon, we'll have a sense on where his efforts and, of course, our individual prayers have led us." Wyszynski then turned toward his younger compatriot. "I guess you are still with Benelli, Karol?"

Cardinal Wojtyla smiled but said nothing.

"I saw Villot earlier today speaking with Cardinal Colombo," Koenig interjected, being both informative and inquisitive, as he was never quite sure where Wyszynski stood on papal selection issues. "I interpreted that to mean he may be trying to encourage Colombo as an alternative. And he could be a suitable alternative, perhaps another Luciani."

Krol's eyes cut over to Koenig as he thought about the three-by-five cards Katherine had stuffed in the Bible she had given him. One had information on Cardinal Colombo that he did not want to use. "Well, perhaps," Krol said, "but I don't see Colombo as another Luciani. The differences are far greater than the similarities."

As they spoke, they saw Cardinal Villot being approached by Monsignor Sarac, who interrupted his conversation and whispered something in the camerlengo's ear, prompting him to end his discussion with Benelli. Villot and Sarac quickly departed the hall with Villot offering pleasantries and smiles to his college colleagues as he walked toward the door.

Koenig watched them depart and then turned to the group gathered around him. "These prattiche are quite interesting events, are they not?" he observed, his expression showing the irony he was clearly trying to convey. "Yes, they are most interesting…as well as educational and informative." His eyes looked directly at Cardinal Wojtyla, who nodded his head in seeming agreement but again said nothing further as the two Poles turned and wandered away.

"John, Franz."

Krol and Koenig turned to see Belgian Cardinal Leo Suenens approaching.

"May I have a word with you?"

The three cardinals stepped away from the group.

"Would the two of you be available for a discussion later today at the Pontifical Belgium College where I'm staying?" Suenens inquired.

"Certainly I'm available," Krol quickly replied, as Koenig also nodded an acceptance of the invitation.

"I think your presence would be very helpful," Suenens continued. "I think I've managed to attract a rather influential group to the meeting."

"Such as whom?" Koenig asked.

"Well, Aloísio will be there. He's had most productive discussions with many from Latin America—as you have just seen—and I am something of an intermediary between him and Benelli."

"Will Benelli be there?" Krol inquired, feeling Benelli's presence would be awkward.

"No, he's not been invited. But I expect Tarancón and Jubany from Spain, along with Willebrands and Alfrink from Holland, Marty from Paris, and Ratzinger and Höffner from Germany. I understand Volk has another commitment. As I said, Aloísio is coming and bringing his Brazilian colleague Arns. With the two of you, I believe we will have… well, quite an interesting discussion."

Krol's mouth dropped slightly open. This was a powerful meeting, almost a conclave before the conclave. All of the attendees Suenens had rounded up were true heavyweights within the College of Cardinals, and Krol was quietly thrilled to be included. He looked at Koenig, whose expression was emotionless. The Austrian, like Suenens, operated in the upper stratosphere of church politics, so he was not surprised that the Belgian had been able to orchestrate such a gathering. Koenig smiled and without even looking at Krol, replied simply, "Yes, we'll be there."

## The Sistine Chapel

Workmen from the Vatican facilities office were scurrying everywhere, placing the finishing touches on the small cells that the cardinals would occupy once the conclave began. A few of the younger red hats had already moved in to the Spartan accommodations, but the older ones were putting off the inevitable discomfort as long as they could.

"Please, step aside and give us some room," Gianluca Giordano shouted as he and another man dragged a heavy four-wheeled dolly down the central hallway leading from the museum to the chapel. On the dolly was a large object covered with a tarp. Gianluca guided the trip by maneuvering the handle attached to the dolly's front wheels, moving as quickly as possible while avoiding the risk of turning too fast and tipping the contents over. He pulled hard to his left as he moved his awkward load across the threshold and into the famous chapel, glancing up as he always did to glimpse the magnificent fresco painted on the ceiling centuries before by Michelangelo, indisputably one of the most famous pieces of art ever created. He then returned to pulling the load toward the far right corner of the chapel where other workmen were waiting beneath a scaffold of aluminum piping extending up to the ceiling, a haphazard pile of copper pipes and metal fittings scattered around their feet. Two of the men dashed over to assist Gianluca in dragging the dolly the last few steps of the journey.

"Grazie!" Gianluca shouted to his crew, while wiping some sweat from his forehead. He then reached over and pulled the tarp off the load, revealing the most famous stove in the world, a gray cylinder, slightly tapered on the sides and rounded on the top, standing about five feet tall. It had been used for every conclave since 1939, the one that elected Pope Pius XII. Its history was engraved on its top, and after only a month of rest, it was being installed again.

"Gather around, please," Gianluca ordered. "You three place the base on the floor there, where I have marked it with white chalk. Then Matteo will install the special adapter. Part of it will have to be placed inside the chimney, so someone will have to climb the scaffold to lower down the components."

A couple of the men looked at each other. "What special adapter?" one asked. "We didn't have a special adapter last time."

"Yes, I know," Gianluca quickly replied. "This is a new piece we had made by the university to ensure we get the right color *fumata*. There was some confusion before about whether the smoke was black or white. This new device will make sure that it is clearly either black or white, understand?"

"How does it do that?" another worker asked.

"I have no idea!" Gianluca snapped. "And I don't care. Matteo has been instructed on it. He knows how to put it together. That's all I know...and all you need to know. Now let's get moving! We still have much work left to do on the cardinals' quarters. So go! *Go!*"

The workers all scrambled. Two grabbed the base and placed it where Gianluca had directed, while Matteo carried over a metal container and opened it. Inside was a box, which he removed and lugged over to the base. He gently set it inside. It was a perfect fit. It was supposed to be.

Next came the stove, which with some effort slipped down snuggly over the base.

"*Buono!*" Gianluca shouted. "Now start assembling the copper pipes to make the chimney." His crew began slipping the copper sections together, and the chimney quickly started to come together. Two men climbed the scaffold as each section was mated and rose toward the ceiling, securing the sections temporarily to the scaffold with thin metal banding that would later be removed. When the chimney had reached the level of the windows running along the top of the chapel, Matteo reached into the metal box and grabbed a set of small-diameter sectional tubing; then he quickly climbed the scaffold. Once at the level where the pipes ended, he began snapping the tubing together and lowering it back down the chimney. Gianluca waited at the bottom until the tubing appeared, opened the door of the stove, reached inside, and snapped it securely into the box nestled in the base.

Up on the scaffold, one of the workmen installed a piece of the copper joint that turned the chimney ninety degrees so that it could be routed through the window where another angled piece allowed it to continue up the roof. From there, its exterior portion would be secured and capped. As these pieces were installed, Matteo added more tubing to them and then scurried down the scaffolding and raced outside with the last few pieces of tube that would have to go in the part of the chimney outside the chapel.

"Very good!" Gianluca shouted, clapping his hands together and smiling at his crew as the complicated assembly neared completion. "Now let's get this all cleaned up and out of here. Then we'll run a test." The dolly was quickly loaded with unused and unneeded parts, and the crew began to sweep and clean the area. After about twenty minutes, Matteo returned, running up to Gianluca and giving him a thumbs-up.

"Does it work?"

Gianluca turned toward the voice he had just heard and found himself facing Cardinal Villot and Monsignor Sarac. "Your Eminence, how good to see you," he said, thankful that the camerlengo's unexpected arrival had not happened a half hour earlier. "We haven't tested it yet, but I am confident it will work."

Gianluca saw one of the workmen coming over toward them, doubtlessly so Villot could see him and observe personally how hard he was working. "Your Eminence," the workman exuded, "it will work fine. And with the new device, the color of the smoke will be clear this time."

Villot looked at the workman and then turned his eyes back to Gianluca. "What device is he talking about?"

Gianluca could be cool, and he knew when he had to be. This was obviously one of those times. "Eminence," he confidently replied, "he means the device we got from the university. It allows a slight chemical mixture to seep inside, which will make the white smoke clearly be seen by everyone in the square as white smoke…no more confusion."

"How is it controlled?" Sarac asked, his face reflecting clear puzzlement. "I don't think any of the cardinals have been instructed on how to make white smoke in some new way…at least not that I am aware of."

Gianluca was at a loss as to how to answer that particular question. "It's quite simple, Father."

Sarac turned to see Matteo approaching.

"All you do is turn this knob so that it's aligned with this scribe line." Matteo reached down to the base of the stove and twisted a knob that controlled the flue feeding air to the fire. "If you want black smoke, turn the knob all the way; if white smoke, then only to this line. The device will do the rest."

Cardinal Villot looked at the knob for a few moments before his face broke into a smile. "That's fabulous!" he exclaimed. "We've had trouble in the past with the color of the *fumata*. So I guess I'll have to instruct the scrutineers on what to do after they have counted the votes and we burn the ballots and other notes, correct?"

"Yes, Your Eminence," Matteo replied. "We had thought that would work best as you will, of course, be here in the chapel. This valve controls the flue. You put the ballots in, light them with a match, and close the small door. Black smoke, turn it to here; white smoke, turn to there—and add the straw."

"Fabulous," Villot exclaimed, excited and fully unaware that the setting on the line had nothing to do with the color of the chimney's smoke. "Just fabulous! Another problem solved! One less thing they can complain about." With that, Villot turned and strolled away.

"Who are you, by the way?" Gianluca and Matteo turned to see Sarac intently eyeing them.

"Well, Father, this is my cousin Matteo Ferrari," Gianluca answered, a bit haltingly. "You met him last week. Remember?"

Sarac turned his face to Matteo, eyeing him carefully, his face intent. "How long have you worked here?"

"About six months," Matteo replied.

Sarac continued to stare and then slowly turned on his heels and strolled away to catch up with his boss, who was examining the tables where the cardinals would sit to fill out their ballots, stopping briefly to again scribble in his notepad, "Matteo Ferrari—facilities?" He had not bothered to check out Matteo the last time he had written down his name, but this time, he would. Something about him was bothersome—something.

Gianluca and Matteo stood at the stove until Villot and Sarac had exited the chapel and then let out a sigh of relief. After that, Matteo walked over to the stove and checked his watch. There were five minutes left until his planned test. Gianluca watched Villot and Sarac as they continued their inspection of the chapel's preparations, noting that Sarac looked over at him on occasion. He was concerned as to why.

Matteo's watch showed that it was exactly 5:00 p.m. He opened the door of the stove and reached inside, feeling around for a small butterfly switch. When his finger located it, he pushed it down and then quickly checked his watch. They had to save as much power as possible, so the test would last only three minutes. He reached under his vest for his transmitter, randomly pushed buttons, and then watched the sweep hand on his watch go by three times before reaching once more into the stove and flipping the switch off.

● ● ●

In a white van parked across St. Peter's Square the crew in the back exchanged excited smiles and then high fives. Their various instruments and nixie tubes had jumped to life with needles fluctuating and tubes glowing, recording the gibberish being sent. It had worked. Now they would have to await the literal "trial by fire."

## Hotel De Russie

He was known only as *Ombra*, Italian for "Shadow." He worked alone—always, and his usual client was the Mafia. They gave him steady work, because he was the best; he was quick, quiet, and efficient, and he never failed—ever. But this job was somewhat more challenging. The client was not the Mafia, and he had been called in on very short notice. Still, it seemed pretty straightforward.

He had slipped into the lobby of the De Russie unnoticed, a task made easier by the simple circumstance that he stopped in there for dinner on occasion. He loved the terraced garden restaurant, and the food was always fabulous. His dress, as usual, was impeccable—a well-tailored dark suit, a personalized fedora with a brim slightly larger than usual to partially conceal his eyes, a silk tie with a matching pocket splash, diamond-encrusted cuff links, and an expensive Rolex. He looked just like all the other well-heeled guests who were the common backdrop of the hotel lobby.

He knew the room number. Even in a hotel as ritzy as the De Russie, there was always someone who could be bribed for necessary information. In this case, it was the head of housekeeping. Ombra had bribed him before, a few years earlier, when a Sicilian-based Mafiosi family wanted Luxemburg's finance minister taken out. But in that case, he had time to plan the job down to the smallest detail; for this hit, he had only been given a couple of hours to decide how to "execute the execution," as Ombra always described it. That meant it was riskier and would also be messier—and, accordingly, would cost the client three times the customary price. There wasn't time to arrange anything clever or subtle. This one would be a simple hit, but Ombra had mastered that approach early in his career. In his trade, you progressed from brutality to subtlety, never the opposite.

Ombra arrived just before darkness, enjoyed a couple of drinks at the bar, and charged the expense to a room he was not occupying, but one where the housekeeper had given him the guest's name. A couple of drinks helped him relax, not that he needed relaxing, but they were calming anyway, and he was one of those who could consume a large amount of alcohol before it had any physical effect. He waited until the bar was nearly empty and the restaurant staff was fully engaged with clearing the tables and starting the reset process for the morning breakfast. He downed the last gulp of his large martini and headed toward the courtyard entrance to the hotel's east stairwell, avoiding the elevator bank near the lobby.

He went down one level and made sure the exit door into the service alley was unlocked. It was. He then started up the stairs, heading toward the top floor, walking slowly, his rubber-soled shoes muffling any sound. Arriving at the top floor, he stepped into the hallway. It was empty. He walked down the hallway's long oriental runner, carefully removing the light bulbs from the three sconces closest to the stairwell and the last room, darkening that end of the hallway. He turned and walked softly over to the door of the target room. He pressed his body against the wall beside it, reaching inside his coat and removing his own nine-millimeter Beretta. He quietly attached a silencer to its barrel. From his pants pocket, he removed the key to the room, inserted it into the lock, and turned, taking care to minimize the sounds of the tumblers. Ombra slowly and cautiously pushed the door open, checking to see if the inside security chain was attached. It wasn't. That made it easier; at least no brute force would be necessary on the door.

He paused and listened. He heard nothing from inside the room, and the hallway was still empty and quiet—deadly quiet. Ombra took a deep breath and then quickly flung the door open. Very little light from the hallway spilled into the room, but there was just enough to make the outline of the bed visible. In one quick motion, Ombra raised his Beretta and aimed, his finger reflexively squeezing the trigger.

*Phut! Phut! Phut! Phut!*

Two shots hit each side of the bed. Ombra paused, his eyes concerned about what he had neither seen nor heard. There were no groans of anguish and no involuntary muscle reflexes as the bullets penetrated flesh, no blankets flying to the floor, no creaking of the bed springs, no flailing arms and legs. Just quiet. Ombra fired twice more, again placing bullets on each side of the bed.

*Phut! Phut!*

Still nothing. More silence. He reached up and flipped the light switch by the door. Ombra stiffened. The room was empty. A few feathers from shredded pillows floated through the air, drifting slowly down onto the duvet covering the bed. He reached behind the door and jerked the closet door open. Empty! Nothing! Immediately, he unscrewed the silencer from the Beretta and stuffed both beneath his coat; then he turned the lights off and quickly shut the door. He was instantly back in the stairwell and bounding downward, making it from landing to landing in only three hops, his shoes once more deadening the sound of his steps. In less than forty seconds, he reached the basement level and charged through the door. Then he downshifted to a brisk walk as he headed toward the Via del Babuino where he turned right toward the Piazza del Popolo. His cousin Luis was waiting there in an aged Fiat 1500. Reaching the car, Ombra jumped in, and the car sped away. It was his first failed hit, and he was very pissed. The Russians were idiots! Absolute idiots!

CHAPTER 19

# Friday, October 13, 1978
# The Vatican

● ● ●

Cardinal Krol had been correct—learning new tricks was difficult for old dogs, and evidently even more so for old cardinals. But he was determined to master his device and had worked to devise ways to attach it under his robes so that it was unobtrusive, if still uncomfortable. He had not discovered a comfortable configuration and so had abandoned the effort.

Krol had moved into his cell in the Apostolic Palace, as had a handful of other cardinals. He had decided to get it over with, as the conclave formally began with a Mass the next morning, and he was pleased to see his space was not far from cell number 91, Cardinal Wojtyla's. Krol had placed his special Bible on the table by his bed and piled some other theological readings he had brought along on top of it. He was humored to learn that Wojtyla had brought along a book on Marxist philosophy, evidently continuing his efforts to learn ways to confront the numerous communist contradictions. But for the time being, he was focused on mastering the transmitter Katherine had given him along with Matteo's codes.

"Your Eminence."

Krol turned toward the simple plywood door serving as the entrance to his cell. Standing there was Gianluca Giordano, looking to the left and right, trying to ensure they were not being observed. "Eminence, are you ready to give it a try? We're going to test the stove to make sure the chimney works. There's a lot going on, so no one will notice you."

Krol nodded. "I guess, Gianluca," he softly replied in Italian. "Hopefully I won't be sending them numbers having no relationship to anything going on. But OK…let's give it a try."

The two of them walked down the halls toward the Sistine Chapel, passing and often stepping around Gianluca's workmen, who were busily hammering and sawing, feverishly trying to get the remaining cells finished. A couple of them took notice of the tall American cardinal, but most stayed focused on the tasks at hand. Gianluca suddenly reached over, his arm across Krol's chest. "Stop here for a moment, Your Eminence."

Krol came to a halt. "What's happening, Gianluca?"

"It's my boss," Gianluca answered. "He's down the way a bit, yelling at one of my crew, confusing everyone as usual. But I'd just as soon he doesn't see us. I don't like or trust him. We're taking care of him later." Gianluca held the cardinal in place for nearly a minute while Bruno Brachi shouted orders at the men, who seemed to be savvy enough to ignore him. Finally, Brachi turned away and headed off to some other location that needed his special brand of useless supervision. As soon as he was gone, Gianluca motioned for Krol to follow him. They strode quickly down the marble hallways toward the Sistine Chapel.

Inside the historic sanctuary, other carpenters were still frantically emplacing the tables where the cardinals would sit during their deliberations and while voting. Like the August conclave, the October conclave required some special work, as the chapel had never had so many electors crowded inside, and each had to have enough space to sit at his designated place and mark his ballot with enough separation from those on his left and right to maintain the desired degree of secrecy. Once again, only a handful of those present took any note as Gianluca strolled in with his tall, distinguished guest.

In the far corner of the magnificent room, Matteo stood next to the stove, seemingly making adjustments to the joint connecting it to the copper chimney. He exchanged glances with Gianluca and then opened the door of the stove, reached inside, threw the switch, tossed in a handful of papers, and then lit them with a match, nodding toward the cardinal, indicating it was time to give it a try. Cardinal Krol pretended to be looking around the room and evaluating the arrangements as he reached beneath his robe and began pressing buttons. Still, no one noticed.

## St. Peter's Square

In the far corner of the square sat a white van, marked with the black, eye-shaped logo of America's CBS broadcast network. Inside were Carter and Katherine, along with Matteo's crew of three technicians. They were all looking at the nixie tube display on the front of the van, showing both local and Washington time.

One of the technicians, named Steve, started the countdown, as Carter and Kath looked over his shoulder. "Five…four…three…two…one—activate!" The three technicians all instantly flipped several switches, and the electronic bank of gauges and tubes along the inside of the van came to life.

"It's hot!" one of them snapped.

"Check here. I'm hot too," the other replied.

"OK," Steve answered, his eyes fixed on his own set of instruments. "Here we go."

Carter and Kath exchanged glances, not fully sure what they were watching or even what success might look like. The technicians seemed a bit tense, so they copied their worried demeanor, keeping their eyes focused on the display in front of Steve. The nixie tubes on his main control panel all read zero. "Come on, baby," Steve whispered through clenched teeth, trying to coax the nixie tubes to show numbers other than zero, their default setting. "Come on, baby! Show us some damn numerals! I'm tired of seeing doughnuts!"

Still, they waited. Nothing was happening. Each person suffered a moment of despair, and then the nixie tubes started to twinkle.

"Ah! There it is! There it is! They're coming through! Bradley, look outside!"

The technician nearest the rear of the van opened its door and glanced across the square and up at the chimney perched atop the Sistine Chapel. He saw it bellowing black smoke! "*Fumata*, boss!" he yelled to Steve, grinning widely as he closed the door and latched it shut. "No doubt! Black fumata!"

The head technician continued to gaze at the nixie tubes for several long seconds and then grabbed a pencil. "OK, we've got B at 30, C at 31, K at 40, P at 41, S at 80, W at 10, I at 160, and N at 20. Push compute… and let's see what the TacFire tells us."

The computer lights began to twinkle, and in a few more seconds, the electronic line printer connected to the computer came alive, slapping numbers on a wide piece of lined paper and spooling it out onto the floor. When the printer came to a halt, Steve ripped the paper from the spool and handed it to Carter.

"Well, Carter, it looks like it worked."

"Maybe," Carter answered, scanning the ream of paper. "What's this code mean here at the bottom?" He pointed to the last line of the printout, which read, "XXXX—No solution."

Steve turned in his roller chair and leaned in. "Hmmmm. Not sure," he answered, his face reflecting confusion and concern.

Katherine peeked over Carter's shoulder and smiled. "Well, I'm no computer expert, but my guess would be that the numbers don't add up. There's only 111 of them voting, and only twenty-five are Italian, so the 'I' entry can't be 160, and when added to the 'N' he sent, that equals 180, so my guess is that the computer couldn't reach a conclusion because the numbers are outside the limits you loaded. But, hey, I'm just a girl. What do I know?"

Carter grinned at Kath while Steve threw up his hands and chuckled. "Well, girl or not, I think you nailed that one, Katherine. As they say, 'Garbage in, garbage out.' And the computer was telling us it had 'garbage in.'"

Katherine laughed. "And Krol's also played a little joke on us. If Siri gets eighty votes, he's the new pope, which would be our least favored outcome. So, I think the cardinal was just jerking our chain."

"Let's hope you're right," Carter added. "If not, then the other possibility is he hasn't really mastered the keypad, and if he hasn't, we'll be getting a lot more garbage and really flying in the dark…if we can fly at all."

All their heads turned toward the door upon hearing a slight tapping from the outside. Steve nodded to Bradley, who cracked the door slightly and then pushed it fully open, allowing Avery Dugan to step into the crowded van, a small bundle of papers tucked under his arm. "Morning, everyone," he said, shaking the slight chill from his jacket. "Brrr. A bit nippy out there." He turned his gaze toward Carter and Kath. "I thought you'd be interested in these. They're advance copies. The newsstands will have them in about an hour." He handed each a copy of the day's edition of *Gazetta del Popolo* and *Corriere della Sera*. Neither Carter nor Kath read Italian, but a glance at the headlines above the pictures of Cardinal Siri were sufficient to convey the message. The Siri interview was now public, a day before the conclave, just as they had hoped.

"What's it say?" Kath asked, impressed that Avery had pulled it off.

"What we thought it would. Both have an article and a transcript of the Licheri interview. A bunch of us from the press have been invited to a meeting with Monsignor Grone, Siri's aide, around noon. Grone has already released a statement. He's clearly in damage-control mode."

"What'd the statement say?" Carter asked, flipping through the *Gazetta*.

"What you'd expect it to say. 'The cardinal's comments have been misrepresented, the articles do not fully reflect his thinking, they've been taken out of context, and this is all an effort to embarrass him just before the conclave.' He used all the usual stuff; plus, he all but blames Benelli for it."

Katherine shook her head. "The 'out of context' part will be a tough sell given that they printed the transcript. As for Benelli, well…I guess we'll just have to see how that plays. But this should drive a large wedge between the two Italian camps."

"It should," Avery agreed. "Now we'll just have to see if it creates a surge toward one of the other Italians—Ursi, Colombo, maybe Poletti. If it does, I think Colombo will be the more likely."

Kath turned her attention back to the computer, and Avery leaned over toward Carter, whispering in his ear, "Did you guys move out of the De Russie, as I suggested?"

"Yeah," Carter replied. "Bruce got us in to the Excelsior on Via Venetto. It's a bit further away from where the action's been—at least so far—and it's embarrassingly nice. Close to opulent."

"You have separate rooms now?"

Carter paused momentarily, deciding how to answer that question and mentally debating whether to answer it at all. It briefly entered his mind that "none of your fucking business" might be a sufficiently direct response, but he decided there was no point in getting adversarial with Avery at this particular moment, so he went with calm and flat. "Nope, no options. Still sharing one. They were fully booked, like everyone else."

Avery accurately sensed he had ventured onto touchy terrain. Carter's voice was cool, but his eyes were hot. "Well…good. That's good. I feel better knowing you're watching over her…especially after the other day at the café. This thing is getting dangerous."

Carter thought for a moment before replying. "Yeah, OK…I agree. I'm watching out for her. And, of course, she's watching out for me, which is probably more important. After all, she's the one with the gun."

## The Sala Regio, The Royal Hall
### of the Apostolic Palace

Cardinal Koenig was busy making his rounds. He had come over to the Apostolic Palace to find the cell he would be assigned when the conclave opened. Being seventy-three years old, he wanted to make sure that there were at least the basic amenities he would need if the conclave lasted more than a couple of days. He also had a second mission: he was placing beside his bed several copies of a 1976 writing, *Segno di Contraddizione* (*Signs of Contradiction*), a thoughtful piece that had been the source of much discussion at the Lenten Retreat two years before. Koenig, along with many others, had been impressed by it, and now he wanted to encourage a selected audience to reflect back on it and give some thought to its theological message and, of course, its author.

The Austrian had placed himself in the Sala Regio, the Royal Hall, outside the Sistine Chapel, guessing that many other cardinals would be wandering about after the morning's general congregation and he could simply give them a copy, asking that they reflect on its observations. He had—quite innocently, of course—already succeeded in giving out a few copies when he saw Cardinal Willebrands, the archbishop of Utrecht, approaching, smiling at the sight of the elderly Austrian standing with books wedged under both arms.

"Franz, what are you doing?" the Dutchman asked with a smile. "This is a strange place to be peddling books."

Koenig smiled. "Well, Johannes, one never knows. I found this particular paper quite insightful, and I thought as we begin our deliberations, everyone should review it, as it is most thoughtful and raises numerous points worthy of consideration during our reflections over the coming days."

Willebrands took the book and gazed at the cover. "I've read it, Franz. And it *is* very insightful, well reasoned, well argued, and quite well written. So, are you encouraging us to review the book's arguments and observations, or are you reminding us of the author who wrote it? With whom, I should say, I am already quite impressed."

Koenig smiled slightly. "In my humble view, Johannes, there is certainly nothing wrong with doing both. I'm certain there is great benefit to the church in both reflection and awareness, would you not agree?"

"Yes, I think I'd very much agree. So, thank you for calling this to my attention. I'll, as you say, reflect on it, and, of course, pray about it." With that, the Dutchman continued down the hall toward the chapel. As he did, Koenig saw another red-clad figure slowly coming in his direction, with a slightly unsteady walk.

Koenig opened his arms in greeting. "Guten Tag, Kardinal Katic. Wie geht es Ihnen?"

Katic walked up to Koenig and stopped. "I am well Cardinal Koenig. Quite well, thank you."

Koenig had not seen much of Katic over the past two days, and he was somewhat concerned by his appearance. Katic's forehead was slightly damp with perspiration, and his expression suggested a degree of discomfort, as did his stance, slowly if subtly swaying from side to side. "Your Eminence," Koenig said, looking closely at Katic's face and using the formal titular address, acknowledging that they were not well acquainted, "you do not seem well to me. Are you running a slight fever? Perhaps with all of the travel and changing accommodations, you are a bit out of sorts. Have you seen a doctor? If not, I would be pleased to summon one for you. My regular doctor has actually made the trip from Vienna with me; he's always concerned about the well-being of the humble old priest he attends to."

Katic smiled. He was obviously somewhat feverish and, as usual, ill at ease and awkward with his colleagues, especially one as respected and distinguished as Koenig. "Thank you, Your Eminence, but I'm well. I'll try and get some rest this evening, and I'm sure I'll feel much better in the morning. I see you have some reading material you are offering for us to pass the time tonight and, perhaps, during the ballot counting."

"Yes, I do," Koenig answered, still a bit bothered by Katic's appearance. "It's a short thesis written for a Lenten retreat a couple of years ago, titled *Segno di Contraddizione*, which I think is worthy of some consideration and reflection. It raises many useful theological issues that should be seriously considered by the modern church."

Katic took the book and scanned the cover, his eyes then rising to meet Koenig's. "Very well, Your Eminence, I will use it for my bedtime reading…and give it the consideration it merits. I always value your views on such topics. *Wiedersehen*."

With that, Katic sauntered away, leaving Koenig wondering whether he should take it upon himself to call for a doctor, as the Yugoslav was clearly not well. But he decided such an intrusion would not be appreciated, so he merely watched as Katic disappeared in the direction of the basilica. His attention quickly returned to his mission of the moment as he spied a group of three other cardinals coming in his direction. He reached down to the bench next to him and grabbed three more copies of *Segno di Contraddizione*.

As the group approached him, Cardinal Gordon Gray of Scotland extended a hand, holding what Koenig thought where some new curial instructions. "Franz," Gray asked, handing him the papers, which unrolled from his hand, "have you seen this?"

Koenig reached out, his eyes widening as he looked at the screaming headlines across the front page of the *Gazetta del Popolo*.

"And how about this one?"

Koenig looked over toward Cardinal Tomášek, who was handing him a large piece of paper, which was a copy of the Siri interview. "And how convenient that mine's in Czech. Quite impressive as I'm the only Czech cardinal."

"And mine is in French," added Cardinal François Marty, the archbishop of Paris, waving his copy. "Someone went to considerable effort."

Koenig took Marty's copy and looked over it. "Where did you get these?"

"They were put in our rooms, if you can call Villot's cells rooms," Tomášek answered. "Have you looked in your cell? I'm sure you'll find one. Of course, given your linguistic skills, I'd be fascinated to see which language they felt most useful for you."

"Well, so am I," Koenig replied. "So am I."

## SAINT PETER'S BASILICA

The great basilica was largely empty except for the facilities crew, who were busily scurrying about preparing it for the Mass and Holy Communion to be held for the cardinal electors the following morning.

Workers were everywhere, carrying chairs, setting up rope barriers, and mopping the floor. With all this activity, no one paid much attention when one of the red-robed cardinals entered the front of the church and walked down its central aisle toward the altar.

Despite its central place in the Catholic faith and its legal position as the capital of a tiny city-state, Saint Peter's served another basic function—it was a church. Accordingly, a row of confession booths was tucked away in the far corner behind its huge, ornate altar. The cardinal strode slowly down the central aisle and around the altar, heading toward the rightmost booth, the one that was the most heavily shadowed from the morning sun. He pulled back the red curtain across the right entrance, stepped inside, and fell heavily into its seat, reaching up to pull the curtain closed. He was breathing heavily.

"Are you feeling well, Your Eminence?" The disembodied, flat voice came from the shadowy figure on the other side of the booth's screen, which separated priest from penitent.

"Yes, I'm fine," Cardinal Katic replied, pulling a handkerchief from under his robes and wiping his damp forehead. "I'm just a bit winded from the long walk."

"The walk is not that far, and you seem more than a bit winded."

"It's nothing. I'm fine. What do you want?"

There was a brief pause from the other side of the screen, but Katic waited patiently.

"I just wanted to get your thoughts on how things have been going in the prattiche and in the other discussions you have heard." There was another pause. "And have you heard about the interview with Cardinal Siri that appeared in the *Gazetta* today?"

Katic wiped his forehead again. "I think by now everyone's heard about it. There was a copy delivered to each of our cells this morning. And now I'm seeing others walking around with copies of the paper itself. So, yes, I think we're all fully aware of it."

The voice on the other side of the screen remained flat and unemotional but became a bit firmer and more deliberate, indicating a simmering anger. "Did you say that copies had been delivered to the cells? By whom?"

"I don't know by whom. They were just there. And they were printed in about a half dozen different languages. You got one in the language you commonly used. Mine was in German. I'm sure most believe that they were distributed by friends of Benelli, which rules out the curia as the source...for the most part. Siri is, of course, furious. He said many critical things in this interview, but the most damaging comments were about the Holy Father. It's never good to speak ill of the dead." Another pause followed, one lasting long enough that Katic finally tapped lightly on the screen. "Did you hear me?"

"Yes...I heard you. This is very disturbing. Everyone will now be suspicious of everyone else. But what is more disturbing is how these copies got into the palace in the first place. Someone has penetrated it."

Katic coughed and then cleared his throat. "Well, why not? After all, I have. And you have. But it makes everything quite uncertain. Koenig badly wants a non-Italian, European elected, and he is campaigning hard for one."

"Such as whom?"

"He speaks favorably of many in all the prattiche where I have had a seat or been able to overhear his comments. He would be happy with Willebrands, Tomášek, Wyszynski, even Wojtyla. He speaks highly of them all. And many are listening to him. He is very influential and highly respected. As you know."

"Yes, I know," came the reply. "We could probably tolerate Willebrands or Tomášek, but certainly not the Poles. Fortunately, neither is likely. One is too old, the other too young. But it's irrelevant as we will not accept a non-Italian."

Katic adjusted his body, trying to get more comfortable. "How can we just not accept someone? The conclave will elect whomever it elects. The days of secular interference in a conclave are long past."

"Maybe, maybe not. But...for the next two days, your job is to see how the winds are blowing after the Siri interview. And assuming it results in insufficient support for either Siri or Benelli, we want you to start speaking favorably of Cardinal Colombo as a compromise candidate. Others in the curia will join with you, but it is important to have the support of those who are, like you, cardinal priests from outside Rome."

Katic thought for a moment. "I like Cardinal Colombo, certainly as well as any of the Italians, so I'll do what I can to advocate for him. But I don't believe my voice is often heard on such matters or my views respected. At least not like Koenig's. So what happens if they elect a non-Italian?"

Even for Katic, the reply was chilling. "Your job, Comrade Cardinal—as you well know—is to ensure that doesn't happen. But if it does, then my job is to step in and stop it. If the conclave elects a non-Italian as pope, he'll never get off the balcony."

"What do you mean…'he'll never get off the balcony'?"

"I mean what I said. He'll never get off the balcony. His reign will make John Paul's look like Leo XIII's. Your job is to make sure it doesn't come to that. But if it does, you'll have to get the word to me as soon as someone has seventy-five votes. I'll take it from there. Understood?"

Now it was Katic's turn to pause. He had not signed up for this. And he had already done more than he should have. Plus, for his personal reasons, he hated the Italians and did not really want another Italian pope. This challenged him with another contradiction, among the many with which he constantly struggled. But he knew he had to follow orders, as he always had, despite his growing sense of regret. "Yes, understood," he meekly mumbled. "But I won't do this again. Do you hear me? I won't do it again."

"Of course, Eminence. So, don't fail. But if you do, well…we'll do what we have to do. *Guten Tag.*"

Katic quickly reached up and pulled the red curtain open, grabbed the side of the booth, and pulled himself from the seat. He almost fell negotiating the one step down to the floor but retained his balance and slowly moved away. He stopped briefly and looked back at the booth, but its center door remained closed. There was nothing to see. He knew there wouldn't be, and he didn't really want to see anything or anyone anyway. He turned and headed toward the front of the basilica, disturbed about what he was doing, but still committed to doing it. As before, no one under the great dome paid him much attention, except for a Swiss Guard standing in one of the naves in the center of the church. His job was to watch Katic, and he was now doing it very nearly full-time.

CHAPTER 20

# Saturday, October 14, 1978
# Saint Peter's Basilica

● ● ●

THE PRINCES OF THE CATHOLIC church were filing out of Saint Peter's following the morning Mass, "Pro Eligendo Romano Pontifice" (For the Election of the Roman Pontiff), a sermon by Cardinal Carlo Confalonieri, the dean of the College of Cardinals, on the qualities needed by the church in its supreme leader. The Mass completed, they strolled toward the Apostolic Palace, some talking casually with one another, while many others were talking but not casually. The final discussions between the 111 cardinal electors were in full gear, yet being conducted in the subtle manner that only this unique electorate could muster. But even this subtlety was less evident than it had been in the past, leading one Italian newspaper to comment that the current papal election was more like a political campaign than any before, perhaps an inevitability of the media age.

Cardinals Siri and Benelli had been busily making the rounds since the previous evening, and both continued their efforts as the cardinals left the great basilica, with Benelli expressing his serious concern about the *Gazetta* interview and Siri downplaying and dismissing it. The net result of their efforts was that the Italian cardinals were more puzzled and divided than ever. History was on their side, but that was about all. They had neither a consensus candidate nor an obvious compromise. In August, they had quickly found a suitable nominee they could rally around and had only taken two days to elect him, but he was now buried beneath the basilica. As they headed toward their lunch in the palace, the Italian cardinals from the curia chatted about how to elect Siri, while the noncurial cardinals chatted about how to block him and pondered whether Benelli had enough clout to do it.

Cardinals Krol and Koenig watched the red procession from the basilica steps and wondered if they had done enough and if not, how much more they would need to do—and how they could know in any event.

Koenig looked at the Philadelphian with a twinkle in his eye, as he watched three of the Italian red caps arguing. "Well, John, I don't know if we have managed to get the ball rolling toward anyone, but I think it's clearly rolling away from Siri and Benelli."

Krol nodded in agreement. "So, it seems," he answered. "I think we'll have to just lay low for a couple of votes and then see what sort of momentum we can generate for a much different type of compromise. My guess is that if it looks like a stalemate is emerging, they'll move toward Ursi or Colombo. That's our main threat."

Koenig arched his eyebrows and canted his head. "Well, certainly no one will be elected today. There's never been anyone in modern times chosen on the first day or even the first scrutiny. Pacelli was the clear choice and favorite in 1939, and it still took three votes and two days to elect him Pius XII. I wasn't yet a cardinal for the 1958 conclave that chose John XXIII—he elevated me shortly afterward—but that one took eleven votes and four days. I think this one may have much in common with that conclave—including Siri as a contender, yet again."

"Well, Your Eminence, let's hope the similarities aren't too great," Krol answered with a grin. "I'm not sure my sore back can stand four nights on the cot Villot put in my cell. As for Siri, I'm confident the outcome will be much the same for him. And as for John XXIII, there's certainly no one like him among our Italian brothers."

As Krol and Koenig stood on the steps, Cardinal Katic slowly walked past them, the last to leave the basilica. Koenig turned to watch him, once more concerned by his appearance and slow movement. "Cardinal Katic," he called out, "are you well? Can I assist you?"

Katic paused and glared at the Austrian. "No, Your Eminence. As I said yesterday, I'm fine. Certainly you could better invest your concerns in someone else and other matters."

Koenig glanced at Krol and then back to Katic. "My apologies, Cardinal Katic, I did not mean to be intrusive or presumptuous."

Katic's shoulders slumped a bit, and his expression softened. "And my apologies to you, Cardinal Koenig. I thank you for your concerns." Katic started to walk away but halted after a couple of steps and turned. "Also, thank you for the book you gave me yesterday. It was most enlightening."

Koenig nodded in acknowledgment and then watched as Katic slowly moved away toward the palace.

Koenig and Krol stood silently for a few more seconds, each lost in thought, and then started down the steps themselves, walking quickly to catch up with the others heading to the Apostolic Palace for lunch and the inevitable discussions to follow. Afterward, all would retire briefly to their cells for a few minutes of prayer and for Cardinal Krol to open his specially equipped Lebanese Bible, remove its contents, tape it into place under his red robes, and then head off to the Pauline Chapel where the ritual of the conclave would begin.

## SAINT PETER'S SQUARE

In the van in Saint Peter's Square, Steve and his crew were running through a checklist, ensuring that all was ready on their end. Bradley was working his way through a set of diagnostic tests on the computer after loading the line printer with fresh paper and rolling the gears back and forth a few times to ensure they were aligned. It was nearly 2:00 p.m. when the door opened and Carter and Kath stepped inside.

"Oh, good, you're here," Steve said in greeting. "It looks like everything is working, but we'll know in a few minutes. Meanwhile, here… take these." He handed Carter and Kath two small walkie-talkie devices.

"Goodness," Carter replied, giving his an admiring examination. "I've never seen any commo gear this small. Where'd you get these? From Captain Kirk and Star Fleet?"

"Specially made," Steve answered, laughing at the allusion to *Star Trek*. "They'll work here within the square and maybe as much as a half mile away. Matteo has placed some electronic relays in various places around the top of the Bernini Colonnades, mostly tucked against the statues up there, and there are some more of them in the basilica's bell tower and a couple of others inside the palace."

"So, what do these things do?" Kath asked.

"They allow us to communicate. Just turn it on, and talk. Not even a push-to-talk button. Very simple. They're just like a phone."

"Who all has these?"

"You two, me, Matteo, and a few others inside the Vatican."

"Inside the Vatican? Such as?" Carter probed, not yet comfortable in not knowing who all was out there and supposedly on his side.

Steve smiled. "Sorry, Carter. NTK, man. Strictly NTK."

"Steve, look!" Bradley had leaned over his boss's shoulder and was pointing at the computer console. "It's on!"

"What's on?" Carter asked.

"The transmitter," Steve answered. "And right on time. That means Matteo has gone into the Sistine Chapel and thrown the switch. Now, let's just hope the thing has enough juice to last through the voting. What's the longest a conclave has ever lasted?"

"Three years," Kath replied to this frequently asked question.

Steve's head snapped around. "Three years! When the hell did that happen?"

"Between 1268 and 1271," Kath replied with a grin. "But don't worry. That's why they lock them up in a conclave and make it a bit uncomfortable. It encourages a decision. So, I think we're looking at four days—max."

"Well, that's good," Steve replied. "'Cause nobody has a battery that can last three years."

## The Vatican Museum Entrance

Bruno Brachi knew it was a special day, but he had made no special effort to get to work early. All the details he had to address were under control, and Gianluca would handle those that weren't. He always did. So, why get there any earlier than usual, especially with all the crowds milling around? And because of the crowds, he had parked his small Fiat far from the Vatican and walked, figuring it would ease his trip home at the end of the day.

Bruno had just reached the Vatican Museum door, to which he had a special access key, when two Carabinieri police cars screamed to a stop behind him. Bruno watched as the police leaped from the car and started running toward him. "Signor Brachi?" shouted the one who seemed to be in charge.

"Si," Bruno sheepishly replied.

"Please come with us, signor." The policemen grabbed Bruno by the elbows.

"Why? To where?"

"To headquarters. We'll explain when we get there. Please come with us."

By then, Bruno had three officers around him and he saw no alternative to doing as he was asked.

"But there must be some mistake," he complained, as the officers basically carried him along, scuffing the toes of his shoes on the sidewalk as they went. "I haven't done anything. I'm an important Vatican official!"

Arriving at one of the cars, the officers stuffed Bruno into the backseat and then jumped in with him, one on each side. The cars sped away, leaving those sitting outside the Café Vaticano watching with some curiosity, but otherwise uninterested. Things liked this happened in Rome.

## The Pauline Chapel

It was time to begin. Lunch was over, prayers had been rendered, and the cardinals of the Catholic church had gathered in the Pauline Chapel to begin the process of electing a new pope. The procedures they would follow had been tightly prescribed over the years and made even tighter during the reign of Pope Paul VI. The cardinals were seated and awaited the dean of the college, Cardinal Confalonieri, to start the proceedings. Confalonieri would only participate to a point, as he was over eighty and no longer eligible to vote, but he initiated the proceedings. Getting the sign to begin from the master of papal liturgical celebrations, Cardinal Confalonieri began the slow procession from the Pauline Chapel, through the Royal Hall, and into the Sistine Chapel.

The cardinals slowly peeled off from their positions in the chapel, formed two lines, and began singing the "Litany of the Saints," symbolically summoning the saints to inspire their thoughts and actions. Accompanied by over eighty priests, nuns, and choir members, the long line of red moved at a slow pace toward its destination, each cardinal in deep reflection about how to vote and hoping that as a body they would make the decision that would be best for the church and its millions of congregants. A few, of course, had other thoughts regarding their own status and aspirations, but those thoughts were kept as private as possible, consistent with the old adage that "he who enters the conclave as a pope, emerges as a cardinal."

Entering the Sistine Chapel, many cardinals looked up from their hymnals at the great fresco above, contemplating its timeless depiction of the relationship of God to man, considering its broader message, and reflecting on those who had for centuries sat beneath this same ceiling to exercise this same heavy responsibility. They filed behind the benches and long tables, ones that had been erected by Gianluca's crew and then covered with tapestries to give them an elegant appearance commensurate with the occasion. After all were in place, they began to sing "Veni Creator Spiritus" (Come Creator Spirit), once more summoning the Holy Spirit into their presence. The whole procession was highly structured and scripted, intended to create a sense of continuity, seriousness, and solemnity—although little was needed.

Once the hymns were finished, Cardinal Villot asked all to sit and another sermon was delivered about the responsibilities the electors had to each other, the church, and the Almighty. Throughout the sermon, Cardinal Krol sat uncomfortably, recognizing that he was not fully within the letter of the law and that he would shortly be taking an oath that in some ways he would immediately violate but hoping that his actions were consistent with the true objective of the conclave, which was, after all, to find the right man to lead the church through the challenges of the modern world. Krol was sure he knew who that man was. His role was now to guide the others to the same awareness. He had known this since he first heard the news of John Paul's death, and it had become clearer when Carter Caldwell and Katherine O'Connor had appeared on his Philadelphia doorstep.

The sermon was over. Cardinal Krol could not recall a word. Almost immediately, the vice dean read the lengthy oath to be sworn individually by each cardinal, pledging to keep the proceedings of the conclave secret. This time, Krol listened to every syllable, thinking one last time about who he was and what he was pledging. Once the dean had finished the lengthy reading, the cardinals were called forward one at a time to acknowledge it. Krol awaited the calling of his name, and when it came, he paused for a moment, said a silent prayer as he rose from his desk, walked down to the front of the chapel, and placed his hand on the gospel laid out before him. He looked briefly at the vice dean, paused to reflect one last time, and then opened his mouth: "Et ego, Johannes, Cardinalis Krol, spondeo, voveo, ac iuro. Sic me Deus adiuvet et haec Sancta Dei Evangelia, quae manu mea tango."

He placed his hands together and returned to his seat. It was done. He had taken the oath. He prayed God would give him consideration and, if deemed necessary, forgiveness. His mind brought forward several comforting thoughts: "Let he who is without sin cast the first stone," and "Here on earth, God's work must truly be our own." He was at peace. He was ready. His focus returned.

The meeting organized by Cardinal Suenens two days ago had been useful. They had a plan, or so they believed. The curial cardinals always had the advantage. They lived there, had offices with telephones, knew one another well, saw each other frequently, and even knew where all the bathrooms were. If there was any useful organization in this process, they had it. It was a game of catch-up for those who had to fly in. Had they caught up? They'd soon know.

The oath was finished, and the electors had been reminded of the rules. At last, it was time. The master of papal celebrations, Monsignor Virgilio Noè, walked to the entrance of the chapel and turned to face the assemblage. "*Extra omnes!*" he shouted in a commanding voice, the order for everyone other than the electors and a few designated aides to leave the chapel. The extras quickly filed out. After they did so, the door was closed and locked. *Cum clave!* With a key! The conclave had begun.

## Saint Peter's Square

In the van at the edge of the square, Steve and his crew waited with Carter and Kath. The hours passed slowly, and there was still no twinkling of nixie tubes or whirring of paper spinning through the printer. It was the routine torture of any operation, whether intelligence or military. After the planning and the careful placement of all the pieces on the chessboard, there came that time when you just had to wait, when others had to act, when the reality of success or failure was in someone else's hands and perhaps beyond anyone's influence. The old saying was being practiced once again: "Hurry up and wait." And in this case, the amount of waiting was in the hands of 111 elderly men who actually knew very little about one another and who were making a fateful decision using a process rooted in past historical and technological eras. But it was what it was, and those in the van had to let it play out, hoping that the one thin connection they had inside the historic building across the square would be workable and useful. And it was unclear it would be either.

"Anything happening?" The group in the van looked to the door as Bruce Harrison stepped inside to join them.

"Nothing yet," Steve answered, slumping back in his chair as his fingers nervously tapped the edge of the keyboard in front of him.

"Well, we got one thing done today to increase our chances," Bruce responded with a sly smile. "The Carabinieri picked up the KGB's Vatican insider this morning while he was heading to work. Whatever they're doing, that should really fuck it up…Sorry, Kath."

Katherine grinned and waved her hand. Bruce's language had become far too common to be noticeable, much less offensive. "How'd you get them to do that?" she asked. "What are they charging him with?"

"Who knows? They'll cook something up that will keep him out of circulation for a few days and then release him, claiming it was all a mistake. The mayor of Rome may be a communist, but the Carabinieri aren't. They owe us a few favors for the tips we've given them on the Red Brigades." Bruce unzipped his jacket and looked over to Kath. "So, what do you think the Vatican's 'Red Brigade' is doing over in the Sistine?"

"Hard to say." Kath sighed. "Under the rules of the conclave, they can take a vote today, but they don't have to. They have a lot of, shall I say, *administrative* things to do. There are sermons, another review of the rules, checking the chapel to make sure all the doors and windows are locked, a head count to make sure everyone is present, they have to each take an oath about the election, and they have to choose the scrutineers."

"The what?" Harrison asked.

"The scrutineers—the three cardinals chosen by lot who will count and record the votes. It's all very, very detailed and derives from instructions prepared by Pope Paul back in 1976, which modified some of the past procedures."

"In what ways?"

"Basically he made the conclave more secret and less transparent and took the vote away from any cardinal over eighty years of age. All of those who were close to eighty were quite unhappy about that one, many arguing it was an effort by Paul to ensure his successor would be someone more like him and committed to continuing the Vatican II reforms."

Bruce shook his head. "Well, it's hard for me to see how anything could possibly make this show any less transparent, so I'll take your word for it. But given they just did this six weeks ago, you'd think they'd have the basic process down."

"You'd think," Kath replied. "But if it goes a bit slow today, that's actually good for us, Bruce."

"Why?"

"Because it means they have no one who is an obvious choice, which means neither Siri nor Benelli have the votes to make it on the first ballot. I think we won't see a vote until tomorrow."

"How many tomorrow?"

"Two in the morning and, if needed, two more in the afternoon. Four per day until we get *fumata bianca*—white smoke!"

Bruce rolled his eyes and chuckled. "Anybody ever told these people about the telephone being invented! Jesus! Watching for smoke from a fucking stove...Sorry, Kath."

"I'm with you, Bruce," Steve replied, still tapping on his keyboard. "Somebody ought to clue them in. It'd have been a lot easier to tap a phone than build that contraption Matteo's stuck up their chimney."

"Amen to that," Bruce answered. "Amen to that."

They waited for several hours. Inside the van, they could hear two things: the steady hum on the small generator powering the receiver and computer and the muffled sounds of the crowd gathering in St. Peter's Square, hoping to be there when the great moment arrived, most evidently unaware that the odds were against them on the first day. It was getting dark, and the chill expected on an October evening began to descend, but inside the van, it was growing stuffy.

Carter reached over and tapped Kath on the shoulder. "Katherine, let's step outside. Get some fresh air. See what's going on out there...if anything."

She nodded.

They slipped past the others, opened the door, and walked down the aluminum steps. The sun had set, and it seemed that the crowd roaming the square was smaller than they had expected, maybe only a few hundred. They walked to the center near the obelisk and looked up at the roof of the Sistine Chapel and then over to the Apostolic Palace. There had been no smoke from the chimney, and the palace's windows below the top floor were nearly all lit. As they watched, a few lights switched off and a few others switched on. There was activity swirling within its walls, but what was it?

"You know, this would be a great place to come for a vacation someday," Carter said, seemingly directing his observation to no one, while clearly directing it to Kath.

She looked away, smiling slightly, before replacing it with a neutral expression and looking back toward him. "Yes...it would be a wonderful place for a vacation...someday," she answered, her voice as flatly objective as she could make it.

## Outside Loebau, East Germany

"Why do you think that?" Sergeant Petrov asked his driver, Igor Rostov, as they sat eating their dinner under a fir tree, enduring the discomfort of a chilly evening drizzle. Both were wet and cold and quite tired of this unexpectedly long field exercise.

"Because I came over here once with some friends from back home in Gorky," Rostov answered, wiping the rain from his brow, trying to keep it from further watering down his already thin soup. "They're with a motorized rifle regiment in Dresden. We bought a bunch of German beer and came out here into the woods and had a party. Lasted most of the night. I remember this town. It's where we got the beer. And one of the people at the local brewery told me it's a stone's throw from Poland."

Petrov's eyes narrowed. "Why would we march our whole tank regiment to the Polish border? It doesn't make any sense. The Poles are an ally."

"I'm just a lowly Red Army private who drives a tank," Rostov answered, downing the remainder of his soup from his tin cup. "So, don't ask me why we're here. But I do know where we are, and I'm telling you—it's about five kilometers from the Polish border. Hopefully we're not here because Captain Belikov took another wrong turn."

"I think that'll be enough, Rostov," came a stern voice from behind them. Petrov and his driver jumped to their feet, recognizing the humorless voice of Captain Belikov, who was sloshing toward them through the thickening mud of the forest. "Sergeant Petrov, come with me. Rostov, return to your tank."

"Yes, sir," Pasha replied, motioning for Rostov to leave and get back to tank C-12 as rapidly as possible. The private quickly gathered up the pieces of his mess kit, saluted the captain, and quickly disappeared into the night.

"Over here," Belikov ordered, pointing to a relatively dry spot under a large tree.

Pasha followed the captain as the two of them awkwardly walked through the mud created by the nearly one hundred T-72 tanks that had entered and then dispersed in the forest, their heavy tracks churning up the wet soil. Nothing generated thick mud as quickly as armored vehicles, especially tanks.

"Sergeant Petrov," Belikov began when they arrived under the tree, "tell your stupid driver that if he knows what's good for him, he'd better keep his mouth shut and his opinions to himself. That would include his views about what we are doing and where we are, *ponamayetya*?"

"*Ponamayu*, Comrade Captain," Pasha nervously replied.

Belikov paused briefly before continuing. "Petrov, I've never mentioned it before, but my father is a senior officer at Group Soviet Forces headquarters in Zossen. I'm sure you weren't aware of that?"

"No, Comrade Captain, I had no idea," Pasha lied, since the truth was Belikov told anyone who would listen about his father and his numerous family connections in the Communist Party. It was among the major reasons he was so disliked by officers and enlisted soldiers alike.

"Well, my father is quite senior," Belikov continued. "So, I know our mission. Even the regimental commander doesn't know it yet. So,

I'm going to let you in on it…not the whole operation, but just a bit of it, *ponamayetya?*"

Pasha nodded.

"We're going to invade Poland in the next forty-eight hours. The country is falling prey to antisocialist and anticommunist instigators, so we will be going in to eliminate them and restore socialist order. No one is sure right now…It may be easy, or it may be rough. But we'll do whatever must be done."

Pasha paused for a moment, unsure what to think and less sure what to say. "Very well, sir. Understood." It wasn't much of a response, but it was all he could muster under the circumstances. He understood fighting NATO forces; he was trained for that, especially the American Third Armored Division, which his unit faced across the border in its sector, but the prospect of fighting civilians bothered him and always had.

"Now, Sergeant, return to your platoon and tell your soldiers that they'll have orders soon enough. Meanwhile, tell them to end idle speculation about where we are and what we are doing. I don't want to hear any further discussion about it from anyone in your unit, especially that drunk Rostov."

Pasha saluted. "Yes, sir."

Belikov returned the salute, then turned and walked away into the darkness. After a few moments, Pasha did the same, heading back to his tank, which was parked in a wood line, its front crudely concealed by a tangle of broken tree limbs Rostov had tossed across it.

As he approached the tank, he could see the telltale signature of a lit cigarette, its oscillating glow verifying that Rostov was standing by the tank smoking, never a good idea with so much ammunition and fuel on board. Assuming the shadowy figure he saw approaching was his tank commander, Rostov quickly dropped the cigarette into the mud and pushed it into the muck with his boot.

"Have another cigarette?" Pasha asked upon reaching the tank.

"I thought you didn't smoke," Rostov replied, digging into his pants pocket. "And I thought you were going to give me the usual lecture on how far an enemy observation post can see a lit cigarette at night."

"Not tonight," Pasha answered, pulling a cigarette from the pack his driver handed him. Rostov produced a lighter and lit another cigarette for himself, and the two of them leaned back against C-12 and started puffing away, staring off into the darkness.

"So, what did Belikov have to say?" Rostov asked.

Pasha paused briefly. "He says we're invading Poland in the next forty-eight hours, but I'm not supposed to tell you that."

"Well, I thought it would be something like that," Rostov replied. "My brother went into Czechoslovakia in 1968. He told me it started out like this. A strange alert, heading off to someplace they usually didn't go. Back then, he was an infantry BRDM driver."

"He say what happened when they went in?"

"*Da*, spoke of it many times. But I'm not sure what was truth and what was bullshit. Not always easy to distinguish the two with my brother. According to him, entering Prague was like entering Berlin in 1945. I'm sure most of it was just blocking roads and looking mean. But…some of it sounded rough."

"Like what?"

Rostov inhaled another mouthful from his cigarette. "Well, he said on the way into Prague, they were confronted by a large group of Czechs who blocked the way to the train station in the center of town, which was his unit's objective. So, they machine-gunned them. He said there were women and children there, many of them evidently thinking we'd never fire on women and children. But…as I said, who knows? My brother likes a good story."

Pasha thought for a second. "I've heard similar stories. I think some of them are true, which is why I can't do it."

Rostov turned toward Pasha, not sure if he had heard him correctly. "Why you can't do what, Sergeant Petrov? If we're ordered to go into

Poland, we'll have to go in. You can't just say you won't go. You'd be shot. So, what is it you're saying you can't do?"

"I won't kill helpless civilians, especially women and children. Blocking a road is one thing, aiming a machine gun at unarmed civilians and pulling the trigger…that's something else."

Rostov took one last drag of his smoke and dropped the butt into the mud with the previous one. "Why this reservation, Sergeant? Worried about a bad conscience or something?"

Pasha also finished his cigarette and dropped it to the ground. He then grabbed his tanker suit collar, pulled the zipper down a few inches, reached inside, and lifted out something on a chain around his neck. "This answer your question, Private?"

Rostov leaned in closely to get a good look. He'd never known a Red Army tank commander who wore a crucifix under his battle gear.

CHAPTER 21

## Sunday, October 15, 1978
## Outside the Sistine Chapel

● ● ●

THE PRINCES OF THE CHURCH were heading toward the Sistine Chapel. There had been much ritual and some discussion the day before, but now it was time to begin voting, and an air of excitement and nervousness coexisted in the air, emotions that each cardinal elector sensed and some carried with great weight. Looking down the hallway leading to the chapel, Cardinal Leo Suenens spotted his old friend Cardinal Koenig and waved to him. Koenig stopped and then as casually as possible walked over to where Suenens was standing in a corner of the large hallway.

"Do you think we're ready, Franz?" Suenens asked, looking straight into the Austrian's eyes, his expression serious.

"As much as we can be, dear friend," Koenig replied. "I think our meeting Thursday may turn out to be historic. Of course, it won't be known history, since none of us can ever talk about it or even acknowledge it happened. But I thank you, Leo, for showing such initiative and courage."

Before Suenens could reply, the two European cardinals' private miniconclave was interrupted.

"My dear friends, how are we this morning?"

Suenens and Koenig turned to see Cardinal Lorscheider coming toward them, his hands placed together. "I saw you standing over here, so thought I would wish you—or shall I say *us*—well today. I've gone around this morning to as many of my third-world brothers as I could find and gave them all a gentle nudge. Something of a *pep talk*, as the Americans call it."

Suenens and Koenig chuckled at the Brazilian's expression. Then Koenig threw his arm around him, and the three of them entered the chapel.

Once inside, all of the cardinals took their assigned seats, prayers were offered again, and the papal master of ceremonies and his assistant went to each table and handed out paper ballots, whose upper half said simply: "Eligo in summan pontificem" (I choose as supreme pontiff). When the ballots were distributed, each elector grabbed a pencil and attempting to disguise even his handwriting, as Paul VI had instructed, wrote the name of his preferred choice and folded the paper in half, and then in half again.

At the front of the chapel, the three scrutineers had taken their position near the altar. They began to call the roll of the college in order of service, starting with the cardinal bishops, then the cardinal priests, and lastly the cardinal deacons. As his name was called, each elector rose from his seat, held his ballot up for all others to see, and walked to the altar, where he placed his folded ballot on a silver plate atop a large chalice. After a brief prayer, each announced, "I call to witness Christ, the Lord, who will be my judge that my vote is given to the one who, before God, I consider should be elected." Then the plate was tilted, and the ballot dropped into the chalice. This ritual was repeated 111 times.

After the last vote, the scrutineers shook the chalice, placed it on their table in front of the altar, and began withdrawing the ballots. To begin the electoral process, the ballots were counted to ensure exactly 111 had been cast, and then the first scrutineer opened the first ballot before him, noted the name written on it, and passed it to his right. The second scrutineer did the same and then passed the ballot on to his right. The third scrutineer noted the name, recorded it on his sheet, and announced whose name it contained before inserting a needle with thread through the word *eligo* on the ballot. The process continued until all the votes were announced and recorded. The senior scrutineer then stood to inform the others of the tally. At this point, the cardinals stopped what they were individually doing and paid close attention. Cardinal Carberry of St. Louis put away his chocolate bars, and Cardinal Wojtyla of Kraków lowered his book on Marxism. The results were then announced.

## US EMBASSY, ROME

The communications specialist was waiting when Carter walked into the message center. The NSC staffer had been into the tightly secured room so often that the US ambassador had ordered that he be given an access badge to avoid all of the usual clearance procedures.

"Morning, sir," the specialist said, as he stood to greet Carter, using usual military etiquette as he was now aware that Carter was actually an army officer.

"Morning, Specialist Smith," Carter answered. "Ready to make the call?"

"Yes, sir," came the crisp reply, as the specialist grabbed the STU and began dialing the number he had been given. It rang twice. "Hello, White House? Yes, this is the US embassy in Rome. Major Carter is here. Very well." The specialist handed the receiver to Carter, leaned back in his swivel chair, and tried to appear disinterested.

"Hello, Carter?" came the crisp voice from Washington.

"Yes, Dr. Brzezinski, this is Carter."

The president's national security advisor got right down to business. "Carter, I just have a few minutes but wanted to bring you up-to-date. It appears the Soviets are all set for the invasion, and their senior commanders want to go in late Tuesday evening. Apparently there is bad weather predicted starting on Wednesday the eighteenth, so they want to get going before the roads get bad. I suspect the Spetsnaz will go in first…as soon as it's dark."

"OK," Carter responded, "but what does that mean for us here? We can't hurry up the papal voting process. It is what it is. And there doesn't seem to have been a vote taken yesterday."

"So I presumed," Brzezinski answered. "There was nothing about it in the news here—broadcast or print. But as soon as you have white smoke let us know who's been elected, and then we'll have Ambassador Wagner go straight to the Vatican with transportation and get the Polish cardinals back to Warsaw as quickly as we can, unless Krol has been persuasive enough to have Wyszynski elected, in which case, we'll hope to get by with the other fellow. What's his name again?"

"Wojtyla. Cardinal Wojtyla."

"Right. Wojtyla. But if it's Koenig or Wyszynski or even Willebrands, we'll ask them to issue a strong statement after their election. How long do you think it will take? Have any insights?"

Carter sighed slightly. "Not really, Zbig. Katherine, the CIA agent with me, thinks it'll be done tomorrow. If they get in a tight deadlock over this…well, who knows?"

"What's the longest it's ever taken?"

"The longest conclave, Zbig? Three years."

There was a pause on the end of the line before Brzezinski replied, "Well, Carter, we have three days. So hurry them along, or kiss Poland as we know it good-bye!"

## Saint Peter's Square

The agents and technicians in the van were growing tired. Despite the small ventilator and air-conditioning unit, the inside air was again growing stale, and it was starting to give Katherine a headache, as was Steve's incessant tapping on his computer keyboard. Katherine glared as Steve sheepishly looked away, adjusting a couple of knobs attached to the system's receiver. Nothing. No one said anything, but each wondered what was going on. There should have been a vote and tally by then. Had the device failed? Had Krol decided not to use it? Worse, had someone found him out? Boredom became tension, and tension made Kath's headache grow worse. Then the nixie tubes started to crackle and twinkle.

Steve instantly leaned forward in his swivel chair. "Here it comes!" he said, his voice quiet but intense. He reached over to ensure the

TacFire was working and powered up the line printer, which shortly afterward began clacking out paper. When the paper spooled out, indicating the transmission was complete, Steve reached up and tore off the sheet, handing it to Katherine. "So, what have we got? I assume no pope since they didn't light the stove yet."

Katherine scanned the printout. "No pope, but about what I expected."

"Meaning?" Steve asked, wanting to get some understanding about what the numbers meant.

Before Kath could reply, the door to the van opened and Avery Dugan jumped inside, slamming the door behind him. "Got a tally yet? How'd the first scrutiny go? Or do we know?"

Kath nodded. "It seems Krol did a good job. I think this makes sense. Looks like Siri got thirty-seven votes and Benelli twenty-two. Then Colombo with nine, Koenig with seven, Poletti with eight, and…" Kath's eyes widened a bit. "Wyzsynski with five! Italian cardinals got eighty-nine votes, meaning Ursi and Felici probably got a few, perhaps others for Baggio and Pappalardo. The non-Italians got twenty-two. It adds up: eighty-nine plus twenty-two is 111, so Krol is working the transmitter correctly."

"What does it take to win?" Steve asked.

Kath continued to look over the sheet, turned to grab a pencil, and continued making notes. "Seventy-five votes, which is two-thirds plus one."

Avery looked over at Kath's pencil calculations. "So, that means Siri is halfway there, doesn't it?"

"It does. And if the information we got after the August conclave was correct, this would be more votes than he got on the first scrutiny then. But I don't think that's anything to worry about."

"Why not?"

Kath put the computer paper down and rubbed her hands together. "Because at this point, they're basically all stalking horses for each other. I'm sure there are many who promised Siri—and Benelli also—that they'd vote for them. So now they can say they did. What concerns me is that there are four times more votes for the Italians than the possible non-Italians. That really worries me. It may mean that as a group they're still not comfortable with a non-Italian pope. But, this vote was largely a beauty contest. The second scrutiny will be more useful. We'll be able to see some trends once we see those numbers."

## Moscow, KGB Headquarters, Lubyanka Square

Sergei Kornilov bounded up the stairs leading to the KGB chairman's office, slowing only to flash his ID card to the two security guards at the door before rushing inside, immediately coming face to face with the always imposing General Korilenko, CCO himself. Kornilov expected to be waved in to Andropov's office right away, and Korilenko did exactly that. Sergei took a deep breath, pulled down on the door latch, and stepped inside.

As always, the room was dark, but he could see the back of the chairman's large chair and heard a slight cough coming from its far side. "Is that you, Kornilov?" The chair slowly rotated around, bringing Sergei face to face with the KGB chief.

"Yes, Comrade Chairman. I was told you wanted to see me immediately."

Andropov pointed to one of the chairs in front of his desk, and Sergei stepped over and gently sat down.

As usual, there was a pause before any words were spoken. Andropov's cold eyes were staring, glaring at Sergei with an intensity so great Sergei felt he might get frostbite. "Comrade Kornilov, a few days ago, I authorized the elimination of the American White House staff officer who seems to be orchestrating something to elect a new pope, one who might threaten the interests of the Soviet Union. That would be the second elimination that I have personally ordered for this operation. I do not like ordering people killed, Kornilov, but do you know what I like even less?"

"No, Comrade," Sergei answered nervously.

"What I like even less, Kornilov, is ordering someone to be killed and then the effort fails!" As Andropov's voice began to rise, Sergei sank deeper into his chair, hoping it might offer some cover as the chairman became more agitated. "In both instances, these eliminations failed! Both failed! We are the KGB...and we evidently can't even take out an old priest and a young staff aide to Brzezinski! I am beginning to worry about this operation, Kornilov! And I don't have time to be worried about this! With the American peace initiative between Egypt and Israel, our influence is eroding in the Middle East. We are under considerable pressure to conclude a new SALT agreement that benefits us and hurts the Americans. Afghanistan is going down the drain, and many in the Politburo feel we should invade it after we're done with Poland! We seem to have many who feel the answer to every challenge is to invade some bordering country! But as big as it is, the Red Army doesn't have enough troops to invade everyone! And that's where we supposedly come in... Kornilov! We shape things surreptitiously so invasions aren't necessary! But in this case, there's going to be one and it has to be successful! And I certainly don't need fifty million Poles fighting us on orders from Rome issued by that ass Wyszynski!" Andropov coughed again, forcing a pause in his diatribe.

Sergei took advantage of the momentary quiet. "Comrade Chairman, the chances of getting a non-Italian elected as pope are one in a thousand. The chances of them electing Wyszynski are one in a million. The elimination efforts were not intended to increase our odds but to keep them where they are, and they are still good. It appears there has been some unflattering coverage in the Italian media about Cardinal Siri and he may no longer be a contender, so we're starting the whispering campaign to encourage Colombo or Poletti—as we had discussed with you."

Andropov leaned forward, his forearms on his desk. "Very well, Kornilov. But you had better be right about the odds. Because if you are wrong, we'll have to take steps that no one will view as subtle or surreptitious. There's nothing subtle about killing a world leader in public. Everybody will notice...and everybody will immediately conclude we did it. But that will be our only choice if you're wrong! So, given that those fools at our Rome station have shown themselves to be even more incompetent than I suspected, are you confident our inside agent can do the job…if we have to order him to do it?"

Sergei dug deep to find the calmness he needed. "Comrade Chairman, he is well trained, committed, and easily capable of doing it." Sergei paused for a moment, unsure he should add the next comment, but he did. "And, Comrade Chairman, you have already ordered him to do it if necessary. You already sent that order to Zhukov, sir."

Andropov slumped back into his large leather chair, removed his glasses, and rubbed his eyes. "Yes. You are correct. I have already ordered it. But I am holding you and Zhukov responsible to make sure it won't be necessary. Do you understand me?" Sergei nodded, stood up from his chair, and walked out of the chairman's office, hoping with each step that he had quoted Andropov accurate odds.

"Kornilov!" Sergei stopped at the door and turned to face Andropov's desk. "Have they voted yet?"

"They probably have, Comrade Chairman. But we don't have any results yet."

"When will we have results?"

"Probably when they break for lunch, Comrade Chairman."

There was a long pause. Sergei was about to leave when Andropov's chair spun around. "Kornilov, bring me the numbers when you get them."

"Yes, Comrade Chairman." With that, Sergei Kornilov quickly walked past CCO and rushed back to his office.

## Saint Peter's Square

It was nearing noon, and everyone inside the van was bored. Steve was doodling on a pad of paper, Bradley was working a crossword puzzle, and Katherine was mentally running over the various possibilities for the second scrutiny and what each might mean. All their heads turned toward the sound of the van door opening.

"Where have you been?" Katherine asked Carter as he stepped inside. "I thought you said you'd just be gone a few minutes, and that was three hours ago!"

"Sorry," Carter answered. "I had to go to the embassy and take a phone call in the message center."

"Brzezinski?"

"Yup."

"Trouble?"

"Yup."

"Gonna tell us what it is?"

"Nope. As you people always say to me…NTK."

As Carter fell into the one open seat, a low murmur began to fill the square. As the seconds passed, it grew louder; clearly those gathered outside were reacting to something. Bradley walked through the van, opened the door, and stepped outside but within seconds jumped back inside, slamming the door behind him and pulling down the locking latch. "Black smoke! There's black smoke!"

Steve turned to look at his nixie tubes, adjusting a couple of the knobs along the side of the receiver. "Are you sure?"

"Yeah. Quite sure," Bradley answered, reaching up to ensure the printer was on. "It's definitely black. Looks like they at least solved their smoke color problem."

"So why don't we…" Before Steve had finished the sentence, the nixie tubes started twinkling and the printer came to life. Kath and Carter stepped over to watch the printout as it began to roll out of the awkward machine. When the computer had processed the last data burst, the printer spun the wide piece of paper into Katherine's hands. She quickly tore the printout from the printer and started examining the numbers, as Carter looked on over her shoulder.

"This is pretty good," she said. "At least I think it is."

"How do you figure?" Carter asked, squinting to see the numbers himself in the dim light.

"Siri has dropped three votes, and Benelli has picked up fifteen, so he now leads thirty-seven to thirty-four. Colombo has also gained and now has fourteen. Koenig has dropped back to three—that's not good—but Wyszynski has dropped to one and that's even worse. The Italians have ninety-nine votes and the non-Italians twelve. So, that's bad and good."

"How so?" Carter probed, struggling to make sense of it.

Katherine laid the paper across Steve's small table and grabbed a pencil to add some numbers and circle others. "It's good because I think this means Siri is done," she started circling Siri's thirty-four votes. "He's topped out. Some who voted for him the first time have reconsidered, probably influenced by Avery's newspaper article. I don't see him getting more votes going forward—he'll keep going down. Bad because it looks like a lot of votes moved to Benelli and a few to Colombo, meaning that Benelli is the new favorite and has momentum—maybe a lot. But if he can't get thirty-eight more votes, then Colombo is emerging as an acceptable compromise. And also bad because the non-Italian vote was only twelve, ten lower than last time, so we only know that Koenig and Wyszynski got any, which leaves eight out there that are unaccounted for. That means that few of the third-world cardinals find any of the non-Italians appealing, and they're probably throwing their votes to Benelli, Colombo, and Poletti...maybe even Felici and Baggio."

"Do we think Benelli can get thirty-eight more votes?" Carter asked. "And if things start moving in his direction, what do we do?"

Katherine looked up at him with a sly smile. "Well, Carter, we're in Saint Peter's Square. We can pray."

## OUTSIDE THE SISTINE CHAPEL

Monsignor Sarac and Sergeant Bruhlmann were standing outside the doors of the Sistine Chapel, sharing the burdens of guard duty. They had been there for nearly four hours, and their ankles and knees were beginning to ache. Bruhlmann was impressed by Sarac's fortitude. After all, Swiss Guards were accustomed to such duties, but executive assistants to the camerlengo weren't. Throughout their time at the door, neither had said a word, only communicating with an occasional side glance.

Bruhlmann was about to ask Sarac how much longer he expected they would have to stand there on the hard marble when he heard the clacking of an old key being inserted into the door from the other side, followed by the clicking of old tumblers. They stepped aside as the doors of the chapel slowly opened and the cardinals of the church began filing past them and into the Royal Hall. Both watched as the Italian curial cardinals, along with several others, scurried across the marble floor and gathered in a group, speaking softly but gesturing excitedly. As other cardinals began to emerge, the Italian group quickly headed outside into a small Vatican courtyard as a second, much smaller group, emerged trailing Cardinals Koenig and Suenens. The second group slowly strolled toward the museum windows, looking out on the courtyard, their hands clasped leisurely behind their backs, slight grins on their faces.

"They're panicking," Suenens said, looking intently out the window.

"Yes, I think they are," Koenig replied. "They're in a tough spot now. Siri is no longer viable, and Benelli is gaining momentum. He's their worst nightmare. If he ran over them as a bishop while Paul's undersecretary of state, imagine how he'll treat them as pope. They're trying to find one among them who's an acceptable alternative."

"So who would that be? Colombo?" Koenig and Suenens turned to see Cardinal Krol approaching them with Lorscheider, Willebrands, and Tarancón walking close behind.

"Probably," Koenig answered, turning his eyes back to the courtyard scene outside.

"Do you think Benelli has enough momentum to get another forty or so votes?" Tarancón asked, looking over Koenig's shoulder to the courtyard gathering, which seemed to be increasing in verbal intensity.

"I don't see it," Willebrands answered. "I just don't see where the votes…" He paused in midsentence and looked down the hall. They all turned to see Cardinal Benelli approaching.

"Your Eminences," Benelli said, greeting them with a smile that to Suenens was somewhat reminiscent of Luciani's. "A most interesting morning."

"Very," Suenens replied with a nod.

"I believe it may be even more interesting this afternoon." Benelli's eyes looked past Koenig to the courtyard scene outside and then shifted back to the Austrian. "A most fascinating gathering out there."

"I hadn't noticed, Your Eminence," Koenig replied with a sly expression, showing considerable deference to the much more junior Benelli, who after all, had received the largest vote in the latest scrutiny and could yet become pope. "I wonder what they're discussing."

Benelli smiled without commenting and then moved away to exchange pleasantries with others who stood in the hall waiting for the lunch to be served. When he was beyond earshot of the others, Koenig turned to the small group standing with him. "Your Eminences, I believe we should spread out and engage in some discussion with our colleagues. I'm going to guess at who has been voting for me and request they look elsewhere, as I will not accept election. Aloísio, I believe it would be helpful if you offered some advice for your Latin American contingent, and, John, the same for you with the North Americans. Leo, perhaps you and I should converse with our friends from Northern Europe. No arm twisting, mind you, just a gentle observation that it's unlikely an Italian can get the necessary votes, so they should look elsewhere. Agreed?"

"*Ja*," Krol replied in German with a mischievous grin. They all shared a brief chuckle at this successful effort to lower the emotions of a tense moment, then scattered to perform their assigned tasks.

Koenig himself lingered for another few moments, watching the courtyard meeting before noticing Cardinal Katic sitting alone on a padded bench a few feet away. Katic still did not look good. His appearance suggested he was feverish, and his complexion was now ashen. Koenig had been concerned watching him walk unsteadily to the scrutineers' table to cast his ballots during the morning session. He was tempted again to go check on him but decided against it, as all his previous efforts had been rebuffed. Koenig decided he needed to go conduct his share of the *miniprattiche* encounters he had just directed. He turned and walked away, leaving the Croatian alone in his discomfort.

## Saint Peter's Square

The nixie tubes had twinkled again at midafternoon, and Kath was again speculating at what the third scrutiny meant. Benelli had picked up more votes, moving up to forty-five, and Siri had lost more ground falling back to twenty-four. Clearly his fourth candidacy was going to end as the previous three had, with the Genoan wearing red robes. What disturbed Katherine was that some votes being lost by Siri were evidently moving to Colombo, who was the biggest gainer in the third vote. Moreover, there were now 102 votes for Italian cardinals and only nine for non-Italians, all being cast for a candidate, or candidates, who remained unknown. Were the cardinals from outside Italy incapable of finding a candidate? Would Benelli's bandwagon continue to roll? Was there anything they could do? The van was once more growing hot and stuffy, for more than one reason.

Inside the van, they began to hear the same murmur they had heard hours earlier, starting slowly and then building in volume. Once again, Bradley popped the door open and looked out. "Black smoke," he announced for the second time that day, his voice reflecting fatigue as he closed the door.

"OK, here we go again—I hope." Steve once more made a couple of adjustments, and the computer again came to life, receiving the latest data feed from Krol's waistband. This one took a bit more time, suggesting that it had likely been a long day for Krol as well. Kath waited by the printer as the latest results were slapped on the lined paper. When the printing was done, she again tore the paper off along the metal guide and inspected it, wide-eyed.

"Benelli now has forty-eight. He picked up three more. But Colombo now has thirty-four, so he picked up eight. Siri is down to fifteen, so he's clearly toast. I'd guess only the hard-core curialists are still hanging with him. Poletti got a couple, but he's not a serious alternative. But... there's only twelve non-Italian votes. Koenig must have passed the order at lunch not to vote for him, because he's been zero ever since. Overall, the Italian vote seems to have peaked; it's three less than last time." Kath laid the printout down in front of Steve and leaned back against the van's wall, reflecting for a moment. "Guys, I think we're gonna make it! I think it's downhill for the Italians from here. They couldn't get the votes for either Benelli or Siri, and I can't see them electing Colombo. How would they explain to the church electing a guy who has more years and less charisma than Luciani?"

Carter looked at the numbers. "Well, could be, Kath. But forty-eight plus thirty-four is eighty-two, which is bigger than seventy-five. So what if all Colombo's votes go to Benelli in the morning? Or the other way around, if Benelli's all go to Colombo?"

Kath looked up to Carter. "A possibility. We gave Krol some information on Colombo if needed, so I guess we'll see if he uses it."

## Outside the Sistine Chapel

Again, the cardinals filed out of the Sistine Chapel, the Italian curial contingent wearing pained expressions, and those walking with Krol and Koenig wearing more obvious smiles. Many were clustered around Benelli as he emerged, and a similar number had gathered around Colombo.

Krol and Koenig again stopped near the courtyard window as they had earlier, watching the unfolding scene in the hall but not speaking. They were encouraged but still uncertain of the outcome. Like the Americans in the van, they too could add forty-eight and thirty-four.

"Excuse me, Your Eminence," Krol said to Koenig, bending down to whisper in the older man's ear. "I think I'll have a word with Cardinal Colombo." Koenig looked on with a puzzled face as Krol walked away and then watched as he stepped into the group surrounding the latest candidate with clear momentum. Koenig could see Colombo nod and then follow Krol off to a secluded portion of the hall. Once they were there, he saw Krol whisper in Colombo's ear and Colombo step back, a look of concern sweeping over his face. Krol stepped forward again, whispering something else, something that caused Colombo's shoulders to visibly sink. They spoke for several more minutes, Krol doing all the talking and Colombo doing all the listening. The Italian then reached up and patted Krol's shoulder, gently nodded his head, and appeared to say, "Thank you," as the two separated and walked away, Colombo heading toward the dining area while Krol headed back toward Koenig.

"What was that about, John?" Koenig asked as Krol arrived, his face reflecting puzzlement.

"Nothing," Krol replied. "I just wanted to wish him well tomorrow."

Koenig was clearly skeptical. "That was a long discussion to simply wish him well, John."

"Perhaps, Franz. Perhaps it was. But we'll see what happens tomorrow. Now…shall we dine before turning in? I'm anxious to enjoy another night on my lumpy cot."

Koenig chuckled as the two cardinals walked away, watched closely by Katic, who was again slumped on the window bench, uncomfortable, and breathing heavily. With great effort, he lifted himself to his feet and walked over to Monsignor Sarac, who was still standing by the chapel door, trying to restore the circulation in his feet. Katic and Sarac walked away, leaving Sergeant Bruhlmann at his post. He wasn't certain, but he thought he heard Katic say *"Polnich"* to Sarac. What did that mean?

CHAPTER 22

# Monday, October 16, 1978
# Outside the Sistine Chapel

● ● ●

CARDINALS FRANZ KOENIG AND LEO Stuenens were standing across the hall from the doors to the Sistine Chapel. They had just been joined by Cardinal François Marty, who had collaborated with them the previous evening in discussions with numerous of their Northern European colleagues.

"Have either of you been approached by Cardinal Colombo?" Marty asked in a low voice.

Suenens and Koenig looked briefly at each other and then shook their heads. Marty glanced around before stepping a bit closer to his two colleagues. "He approached me this morning and asked that I not vote for him again, if I had previously done so—which I haven't—and asked that I kindly inform others of his decision that he would decline election as the Holy Father."

"Well, that will certainly make this morning's vote interesting," Koenig observed, his eyes reflecting that his mind was rapidly calculating the implications of this latest news.

They heard a loud voice from several feet away near the dining area. "Who are you talking about?"

Koenig, Suenens, and Marty turned their attention to the other side of the hall where Cardinal Lorscheider was speaking once again with Cardinal Casariego of Guatemala. "I've told you before, I don't know this Cardinal Bottiglia you keep mentioning." Like most suffering from hearing loss, Casariego tended to talk loudly, unaware how annoying his volume could be to others. Out of the corner of his eye, Lorscheider saw Koenig looking at him, smiled back in his direction, shook his head, and continued the discussion, convinced that he was doing the Lord's work.

"Ah, here comes our other conspirator," Suenens commented, pointing to Cardinal Krol, who was walking quickly toward them and fidgeting with the arrangement of his vestments.

"Something wrong with your waistband, John?" Koenig asked as Krol arrived.

"Uh…no, Your Eminence, it just seems to be fitting a bit tighter than usual."

"Perhaps you are eating too much, John. After all, Villot has treated us to a feast at every meal, hasn't he?" Koenig smiled at this culinary sarcasm and then quickly turned serious. "Have you heard that Colombo has passed the word not to vote for him?"

Krol nodded but said nothing.

"Might this have anything to do with the discussion you had with him yesterday evening?"

Krol hunched his shoulders and held out his hands with palms up but again said nothing.

"Come, friends," Marty said to his colleagues, placing his hands on Koenig's and Suenens's shoulders. "I think it's time we went back inside the chapel and took our seats. This will be either a great day in the history of the church or…perhaps merely another day."

Together, they strolled across the hall and walked past Sergeant Bruhlmann and into the chapel.

## SAINT PETER'S SQUARE

Dimitry Zhukov had come to Saint Peter's Square to get a firsthand view of the layout. He had, of course, been there many times before during his student days in Rome, but that had been long ago, in a period where his interests had been more historical and architectural. His interest today was much narrower; in fact, it was brutally operational. He focused his interest on the front balcony of the basilica and then slowly scanned the top of the Bernini Colonnades, which defined the square's northern and southern sides. There were numerous clear sight lines to the balcony above the main entrance to the great church, but he hoped none would have to be used. The newspaper articles the KGB had planted appeared to have had the desired effect, and it seemed that if Benelli didn't make it, then Colombo was the clear alternative. Today would be crucial, and a new supreme pontiff would likely stand on the balcony in white robes by sunset. The important question was who would he be?

As he glanced around the square, something odd caught his eye. Over in the southeast corner, he spotted a white van with the logo of the American CBS broadcast network. "Didn't I see a CBS van tucked away on the north side?" he asked himself. "Certainly, they don't need two." He started to move toward the center of the square to get a better view of the south-side parking location assigned to the Western news networks, but a large group of children escorted by a contingent of nuns cut him off as they scurried into the center of the historic square, expecting to see some history themselves by late afternoon. Dimitry had a lot on his mind, and those other details shoved the second CBS van from his consciousness.

As Dimitry continued his scouting trip, with his eyes focused upward, he bumped head-on into another man whose gaze was also skyward. "*Scusi*," Dimitry said, stepping slightly back.

Bruce Harrison looked at the shorter, stouter man, gently waved his hand in a gesture indicating "No problem," and moved away. Beyond that, neither took any additional notice of the other, continuing with their individual surveys of the colonnades and other elevated spots around the square. They were two ships passing in broad daylight, each on the same course but heading to different harbors.

● ● ●

Bruce circled the square in a counterclockwise direction for several more minutes before he arrived at the door of the CIA's "CBS" van, opened it, and stepped inside. "Carter," Harrison growled, calling to the NSC man who had arrived earlier, tilting his head toward him in a summoning manner, "could we chat outside for a moment?"

Carter squeezed past Kath and Bradley and followed Bruce outside. "Something up, Bruce?" he asked, looking around at the swelling crowd.

"Yeah, just so you know, there'll be Carabinieri on the colonnades as soon as we see white smoke," Bruce replied, his hand sweeping across the square.

"Can you do that?" Carter asked. "I didn't think the Carabinieri had any jurisdiction inside the Vatican."

"They don't."

"Well, how have you gotten clearance to place them there?"

"We haven't, Carter. We just did it. This is far too risky a moment to rely on the Vatican's 'sunshine' soldiers in their Hollywood costumes."

Carter gazed at the colonnades himself. "Do the Swiss Guards know Carabinieri will be there? You sure don't want some confused confrontation breaking out between them."

"Yeah, they know. They don't like it, but they know. Do you know the furthest distance from the balcony to someone sitting on one of the colonnades with a rifle? We checked it: about 350 feet. Do you know how far it was from the School Book Depository in Dallas to Kennedy? About 280 feet...but he was in a moving car."

Carter grimaced. "Bruce, you don't think they'd do something that crude and obvious, do you?"

Bruce's jaw noticeably tightened. "Carter, we never know exactly what they might do. We have to plan for what we think they can do and what we know they want to do—just like you army guys do. And there's a good reason for that. They've shown that they're pretty willing to do just about any fucking thing they believe they have to. And also—so you know—there'll be two black limos parked next to your van shortly. They're to rush the two Poles to the airport and back to Warsaw. Their plane's even getting get an air force fighter escort out of Aviano for as far as they can shadow them. When do we expect the next vote to pop?"

Carter looked at his watch. It was 9:45 a.m. "Could be any time, Bruce. I'd better get back inside. Coming?"

Harrison shook his head. "Nah, I've got other stuff to do. I'll actually be leaving for DC in a couple of hours to tie up a loose end. We're where we are here, and there's nothing more I can do. If there's big news this morning, call me on the cell phone when you know the winner."

"What's a cell phone, Bruce?"

"You know, those walkie-talkie things we gave out. You have one. We call them cell phones. Don't ask me why. The guys at Peary think in a few years damn near everybody will have one. Just use it and call me, unless an Italian wins. In that case, just take Katherine out for a nice dinner and go home in the morning. We'll meet back in DC…and go get our asses chewed out together."

As Harrison turned to walk away, the door to the van cracked open and Bradley's head popped out. "Vote coming in, Carter."

Caldwell turned and stepped into the van, arriving just as the printer came to life. Kath stood in front of it, watching as the paper spooled out yet again. "Well, look at this!" she exclaimed, ripping the paper off and holding it in front of her wide-open eyes. "Benelli seventy, Siri fourteen, and Colombo zero! The Italian total is eighty-eight, and the foreigners have increased to twenty-three. So, none of the other Italian cardinals are getting many votes, and some non-Italians are moving up. So, hey… we're going to have a non-Italian pope! I just can't tell you who he's going to be!"

Carter stepped over to review the numbers. "How can you be sure? Benelli only needs five more votes."

"Yeah, Carter, but they'd all have to come from Siri's supporters, and it looks to me like his supporters have decided to go down with the ship. If they go anywhere, it won't be to Benelli, which means that the next vote will be the really important one."

"Colombo just dropped to zero! From on the rise to zero?" Carter was stunned.

"Well, looks to me like Krol must have had a talk with him last night and used the info we gave him. I'm sure Krol presented it in a very sweet and gentlemanly way."

"What was it anyway?"

"I have no idea. I didn't want to know. I'm sure it was related to his family or something like that."

Carter offered no reply. This was an element of this whole business he found unappealing, and he could see that Kath felt the same way. He looked over toward Bradley. "Any coffee left in the thermos?"

● ● ●

A couple of blocks away, Dimitry Zhukov stepped into a small café on the Via dei Corridori, having finished his reconnaissance of the square. He stepped up to the bar and paused as the proprietor handed him a cup of cappuccino. He had known Dimitry for years, going back to his earlier days in Rome. Dimitry took the small cup and stepped past the bar and through the curtains behind it, leading to a small office. He put the cappuccino on the desk next to the phone and made himself comfortable. He checked his watch: 10:00 a.m. As scheduled, the phone rang, and he reached for the receiver. "*Da?*"

"It's not going well," came the emotionless voice on the other end. "Colombo, Poletti, and Baggio have all dropped out. Benelli only needs a few more votes, but I don't see where he gets them. None of those with Siri will ever vote for him. Koenig and Suenens clearly have a campaign going to elect a non-Italian."

"Who are they pushing?"

"I hear Willebrands, Wyszynski, maybe even Suenens himself. But not Koenig. He passed the word to leave him out. But I don't like the direction of this."

"Nor do I," Dimitry replied, pausing afterward, reluctant to ask the necessary question. "Are you ready?"

The answer was clear and quick. "*Da.*"

"Your escape plan understood?"

"*Da.*"

"*Korosho.* You have clearance for Plan X. Execute as needed. Understood?"

"*Da.*"

Dimitry nodded and hung up the phone. He sat quietly for a few moments, finishing the cappuccino, and then stood and walked back through the curtain, placing his empty cup on the counter. He exchanged a brief glance with the proprietor and then stepped out onto the street. He needed to begin focusing on his own escape plan from Rome, although he was now distressingly certain he would not be getting a hero's welcome back in Moscow.

• • •

"Holy crap! That was fast!" Steve exclaimed as the nixie tubes began twinkling. His eyes turned to the clock at the back of the van. It read 11:15 a.m., only an hour and a half since the last vote. The pace was picking up. Outside in the square what sounded like another large groan began reverberating between the colonnades. Bradley popped open the door to peek outside and then quickly ducked back in. "Black smoke… again."

Katherine took what had become her usual position next to the printer and waited, but nothing happened. She and Steve exchanged a nervous glance as he began to check the equipment. "Oh, shit," the technician mumbled as he reached up toward the top of the TacFire and pulled a cable out with his hand. "The printer cable came loose. Give me a second."

"What about the data feed?" Kath asked. "Did we get it?"

"Should have," Steve answered as he struggled to reattach the cable into the cramped space behind the computer. "It saves all the data. There…that should have it. Katherine, throw the printer switch off then back on."

Katherine did as asked, and the line printer again came to life, spooling out a blank sheet of paper and then immediately beginning its annoying clacking as it printed the most recent data. Katherine scanned it again. "Well, we've survived Benelli," she softly commented. "He just lost thirty-eight votes, over half of what he had. Siri's hard core is hanging with him, same as last time."

"Where'd the votes go?" Carter asked.

"Well, a bunch of them went to non-Italians, who now have sixty-six votes. I assume those are scattered all around. But I can't tell who's getting them. So, the Italians now only have forty-five votes, basically for Benelli and Siri. In tennis terms, the Italians just lost match point. Benelli and Siri won the battle against each other, but they've lost the Italian papacy as a result. Five centuries of historical precedence gone… in one morning." Kath paused momentarily. "I don't know why, but I'm a bit saddened by it."

"That's because you're Catholic," Carter answered. "And it's a big change. No large institution likes a big change…I know, I'm in the army. But the church needed it. We needed it. That's why we're here. And we may have just stopped something terrible."

Katherine looked up at him. "Stopped what, Carter?"

"Uh…nothing," Carter answered, recognizing that he had inadvertently gone too far, momentarily forgetting NTK. "Nothing, really. I was just being a bit…too dramatic."

Katherine didn't pursue the comment, skipping to the issue at hand. "Carter, we're in the dark here. We know there's certainly going to be a non-Italian elected, but we have no idea who. We know it's *not* Koenig or Wyszynski, which was our objective. We need to get someone inside to find out from Krol what's going on."

"How do we do that, right in the middle of the conclave?"

"Not my problem," Katherine answered, turning to her left. "Steve, call Bruce on the cell. This is in his fiefdom!"

## OUTSIDE THE SISTINE CHAPEL

The chapel doors opened again, and Monsignor Sarac watched as the cardinals filed out. Most wore smiles on their faces, and their chatter indicated a sense of excitement, muted excitement—given the group—but excitement nonetheless. Cardinal Benelli, clearly not sharing in the excitement, rapidly walked past Sarac, his face drawn, lost in his own thoughts, whatever they were. After Benelli came Cardinals Koenig and Krol, with about a dozen other cardinals following closely behind. They moved as a group to the spot overlooking the courtyard window that had become their usual meeting place.

Breaking out of the sea of red, Sarac saw Cardinal Villot coming toward him, gesturing for his assistant to follow him over to a corner of the hall. As they moved away, Sergeant Bruhlmann watched closely. The camerlengo was instructing Sarac on something, but Bruhlmann couldn't hear what was being said, nor could he deduce anything from their expressions or behavior, as their backs were to him. All he could see was Sarac pulling his ever-present notepad from beneath his coat, but he did that so often there was nothing noteworthy about it.

● ● ●

"It's about over," Villot whispered matter-of-factly to his assistant. "I think the outcome is becoming obvious. We may have a selection on the next scrutiny, but there will certainly be one today. I don't think anyone wants to drag this out any longer. And I can tell you I certainly don't! I'm tired of all the complaints about the beds and the food. Anyway, have all the materials we have discussed ready to take to the papal apartment this evening after the last vote. I'm sure the new Holy Father will be tired, but he'll also want to ensure he has the draft agenda for tomorrow as well as the plans for the coronation ceremony—which I'm sure he'll change. They always do. It's all in the briefcase, except for the coronation details. You'll have to get those from the files. Questions?"

Sarac looked at his superior, his face reflecting the innocence of a teenaged altar boy. "But the apartment is sealed, Your Eminence.

Certainly you don't want me to break the seals and enter the Holy Father's living area?"

Villot was clearly short tempered. "Oh, for goodness sake!" he exclaimed to his young aide. "You and I both know that the seal on the main door is symbolic. Use the back stairs to get up there! Do I have to do all the thinking around here?"

"No, of course not, Eminence. My apologies for burdening you further." Sarac badly wanted to ask who the likely selection was, but he knew better. He scribbled the last couple of notes. "No more questions, Your Eminence. It will be taken care of."

● ● ●

With that, Villot departed, heading off toward the lunch area, leaving Sarac where he was, standing in the corner of the hall, as if waiting for someone. Soon, Bruhlmann saw Cardinal Katic step over toward him, and another conversation ensued. This time, he could see Sarac's face, which now appeared stern and cold. Katic was obviously no one's favorite, and after a few moments of discussion, he headed over to the padded bench by the window and sat down, once more heavily and clumsily, evidently deciding to skip the lunch. But that was fine with Bruhlmann, for it made his job of watching him a bit easier.

"Excuse me, Sergeant."

Bruhlmann turned to see Gianluca Giordano standing beside him, holding a light bulb. "Can you tell me where the American Cardinal Krol might be?"

Bruhlmann pointed his lance toward the group by the window. "I believe he's over there. Should you be here?"

Gianluca held up the light bulb. "I was told he had a problem with the light in his cell. I thought maybe it's just a dead bulb, but I need to ask him. I didn't want to go there without his knowledge."

Bruhlmann nodded and watched as Giordano walked away, heading toward the window gathering. He saw him pull Krol out of the group, and the two of them moved away toward the far stairwell.

● ● ●

"What do you need, Gianluca?" Krol asked, a bit nervous at this unexpected intrusion.

"I've come to fix the light in your cell that you had asked about," Giordano replied, holding up the bulb as the necessary prop.

Krol quickly caught on to the game. "Oh, yes. Thank you. Yes, of course. Cell 67." A pause followed as the Philadelphia cardinal glanced around. "What do you need?"

"There's concern about what's happening. It seems things are moving toward a new sort of pope, but they can't tell who. Is there any need to worry? Is there anything else we need to do?"

Krol grinned and answered with a voice loud enough for others to hear. "No, the new bulb should be fine, and it looks like it has the correct brightness. That's all I needed. Thanks. I'm sure that'll fix the problem perfectly."

It was rather oblique, but Gianluca felt he had his answer—"Don't worry; we're fine." He immediately left to head toward cell 67 to install the unneeded bulb, being watched as he walked away by both Monsignor Sarac and Sergeant Bruhlmann.

## SAINT PETER'S SQUARE

It had been over three hours since the last scrutiny results had been received, and those in the van were getting restless, not to mention increasingly uncomfortable within their confined space.

"Steve, would you please stop that?" Katherine implored.

"Stop what?"

"Stop that constant pencil tapping on the computer keyboard. It's driving me crazy."

The head technician shrugged, making little effort to conceal his annoyance at the request. It was, after all, his van, the place where he was lord and master. He was inclined to tell the lovely Langley girl to stuff it, but he resisted the temptation. He had done this many times during his career, sitting around and waiting for some sort of message on some sort of machine. He knew people got edgy. "Sure, Kath. Sorry. Anybody hear who won the Redskins game yesterday?"

"Lost to the Eagles…seventeen to ten," Bradley replied.

"So the undefeated season is over, huh?"

"Yup, over. A good start for Jack Pardee as head coach, though."

"Have we ever tried these cell phones?" Carter interrupted, breaking his own sense of boredom, which included the fortunes of the Redskins.

"Sure," Steve answered. "Tested them at Peary. They worked fine. They're really cool. Somebody will make millions on these when they take them commercial."

"Great. But have we tried them here?"

"No, not really."

Carter hopped down from the power box that served as his uncomfortable seat. "How about if I take mine out in the square and see if it works?"

"What if someone sees you?" Steve protested. "The thing is bound to attract attention."

"Who cares?" Carter replied. "There's lots of media out there walking around with all kinds of gadgets. I doubt anyone will pay any attention." With that, Carter grabbed his stylish new jacket, opened the door, and stepped out of the van. The midafternoon scene in the square was extraordinary. It was quickly filling with people. Banners were now flying, vendors were walking around selling food and various souvenirs, and nuns and priests from various orders seemed to be appearing from nowhere.

Carter quickly walked through the crowd toward the southern colonnade and then walked along it to the side closest to the basilica. He found a relatively secluded spot and reached into his jacket pocket, pulled out the small phone, and flipped it open. "Damn, what was Steve's phone number on this thing?" His mind was something of a whirr. "Oh, yeah. One. He's number one. Duh!" Carter pushed the numeral one on the small keypad and waited. Nothing happened. Then, much to his surprise, he heard something that sounded like a dial tone, followed by a phone ringing.

"Steve, here."

Carter smiled. "Damn, Steve. This thing works great. I hear you clear as a bell."

"Told you it would. Now how about getting back here. We may have a problem."

Carter closed the phone, briefly looked at it admiringly, glanced around to see if anyone had noticed him—no one had—stuffed it in his pocket, and headed back toward the van. He made the trip in about three minutes, opened the door, and jumped inside. "What's up?"

"We started to get a vote feed, and then it stopped," Steve reported, shaking his head. "It started and then just went dead."

"Do you know why?" Carter asked, stepping to the keyboard.

"Nope. Everything seems fine here. I just ran an E2 diagnostic test, and it all seems normal."

"Meaning what?"

"Meaning that the problem is either in the stove or with Krol."

Carter slumped back against the wall of the van. "Great. As we say in the army, the technology always craps out on you at the worst possible moment."

## INSIDE THE SISTINE CHAPEL

Cardinal Krol was fumbling with the device strapped inside his waistband. He could tell something had popped loose, but he couldn't tell what. The device was beneath a red jacket, that was beneath a white lace smock, that was beneath a red cape. In other words, it was under three layers of clerical cloth. His fingers felt around as he tried to remember the alignment of the small latch covering the battery compartment. He had changed the batteries in the morning, and perhaps he hadn't seated them correctly. As his fingers probed, he noticed that his efforts were attracting the notice of Cardinal Poma, who was seated to his left. Fortunately, Krol was seated at the end of his table, so only Poma was next to him.

Krol ceased his probing for a moment and tried to concentrate on remembering the vote that had just been announced. It had been dramatic. Benelli was down to nineteen votes while Siri had retained his immovable bloc of thirteen. But the shift had occurred, and it was a historic shift. He debated as to whether it was best to try to fix the device or to ask for a break to go fix it in the bathroom. Was it vital to get this tally out to the van, since no one had won? But it was getting close to the climax, very close.

He decided to try and see if he could find the problem. His fingers continued to probe, as Poma's gaze began to focus on him. "Sorry, to be distracting, Your Eminence," Krol whispered to Poma in Italian, leaning over toward him. "I seem to have a terrible itching today around my waistband."

Poma nodded and turned his attention back toward the scrutineers, who were judiciously preparing for the next vote.

Krol probed some more until his fingers felt one of the small wafer batteries, which had in fact popped out of the battery compartment. It took some effort, but he was eventually able to get two fingers on it, guide it back into place, and snap the battery cover closed. He hoped he had put the battery in right side up, but there was no way he could tell. By then he had forgotten the details of the vote, except for one—the important one. He transmitted that.

## SAINT PETER'S SQUARE

The nixie tubes lit up, cycled through briefly, and then flashed off.

"What the hell is happening?" Steve exclaimed as the printer came to life and printed out only two letters and four numbers: "I 32" and "N 79."

Katherine and Carter stared at the paper and then at each other. "What in the world?" Carter asked to no one in particular.

Katherine ran her fingers through her long blond hair, which she hoped to be washing by the end of the day. "I'm guessing Krol's had some problem with his transmitter," she said. "I don't know what happened, but it looks like he got us the important numbers. The non-Italians are now leading the Italians seventy-nine to thirty-two. Assuming those seventy-nine votes are not scattered between several cardinals, which would seem unlikely at this point, we're about to see history made by someone inside the chapel, but we have no idea who he is."

Steve's cell phone rang. "Yes?" he answered, saying nothing that would offer any clues about the caller's identity. Kath and Carter watched as Steve listened for several seconds before punching the phone off. "Our source inside got to Krol. He says the cardinal said things are 'A-OK.'"

Carter turned his eyes toward Katherine. "Are you at all worried about this? Because I am."

"What do you mean?" Kath replied.

"I mean basically this whole thing is dependent on Krol. About the time the vote moves away from the Italians, his transmitter starts acting funny. We know there are a lot of non-Italian votes; we don't know who they're for, but we know they're not for anyone we had in mind. You don't think he's gaming us somehow, do you?"

"Why would he do that? What would his motivation be?"

"I don't know, Kath. Maybe he's worked out some deal to be the new camerlengo? Maybe the new Vatican secretary of state? Maybe he's made some deal with the Latin Americans? Maybe he's made some deal with…I don't know, the cardinal from Liberia, because they went to seminary together!"

Kath rolled her eyes. "Carter, first of all, there is no cardinal from Liberia. Second, I think Krol recognizes the seriousness of the current world situation, and he sees a way for the church to play a bigger role." Kath paused for a moment and gazed at the printout. "Carter, we have to trust him. I don't know what's going on in there right now any more than anyone else. But I trust him. I do. And besides, what choice do we have…seriously?"

Carter glanced around the van. All eyes were fixed on him. He took a deep breath. "OK. I guess you're right. Krol's the only card in our deck. I just hope he's an ace."

CHAPTER 23

# Monday, October 16, 1978, 4:30 p.m. Inside the Sistine Chapel

● ● ●

CARDINAL JOHN KROL THOUGHT BACK to his discussion with Carter Caldwell and Katherine O'Connor in Philadelphia two weeks before and the metaphor he had used about the Normandy landings. And now here he was, in the Sistine Chapel, waiting for his name to be called for the eighth time, waiting once more to walk down the aisle to the scrutineers' table, to place his ballot on the silver plate and drop it into the chalice, with the same name he had scribbled on it since the first scrutiny yesterday morning. It was D-Day, it was H-Hour, and Krol had none of the concerns that had troubled General Eisenhower thirty-four years before. He had watched the votes grow, watched as more and more of his colleagues had come over, perhaps drawn by the power of persuasion being exercised by Krol, Koenig, Suenens, Lorscheider, and Germany's pedantic Cardinal Ratzinger. Perhaps it was just the collective sense within the College of Cardinals that it was time for a change, or maybe they were just tired of being confined in the old chapel. Whatever the numerous sentiments, it was time.

Krol held his ballot in his hand, folded it in half, and then folded it in half again. He sat ready. For him, it no longer mattered if the transmitter worked. What difference did it make? This was history. He was a part of it and had played a key role in making it, emboldened to do so by the two young Americans who had come to him in his hidden rectory. They had their motivations, and he had his—motivations that were not identical to theirs but still overwhelmingly compatible.

"Cardinalem Krol." Krol heard his name called. The ballot briefly felt heavy. He gazed at it for a moment and then clutched it in his hand, stood from his chair, nodded at Cardinal Poma, and headed down the central aisle, the ballot held over his head for all to see. As he walked toward the scrutineers' table, he could see many of his colleagues smiling at him, as they had at Cardinal Koenig just before. He was confident these were smiles of appreciation—he hoped even to some degree smiles of admiration. Krol placed the ballot on the tray, made the same proclamation as before, and dropped it into the chalice.

## Saint Peter's Square

It started, as before, like a swelling murmur. But this time, it grew quickly, first to an excited buzz, then a rolling shout, and finally a wild cheer. Inside the van, the tired and uneasy crew suddenly stirred to life. Once again, Bradley opened the door and stepped outside, but within seconds, he bolted excitedly back inside, slamming the door behind him. "White smoke! Finally…God-damned white smoke!"

Steve scanned the nixie tubes, and Kath moved to the printer. Carter glanced up at the clock; it read 6:15 p.m. The noise outside grew steadily louder, but nothing was coming through the transmitter, and the printer sat frustratingly quiet. Carter decided to take a look for himself, as much out of curiosity as anything practical. He slipped past Steve, opened the door, and stepped out into the great square, looking off to the distant outline of the roof of the Sistine Chapel. His eyes widened. It seemed clear enough to him! White smoke! He jumped back into the van, his eyes meeting Katherine's as he entered, hers silently informing him there was still nothing coming through the receiver or computer. It had, after all, been three days. Maybe the transmitter in the stove had exhausted its battery. They had no way to know.

As the van crew silently pondered, the nixie tubes started twinkling, and in a matter of seconds, the printer once again came to life—very briefly. The chain drive on the printer's type line made one pass and then stopped. The paper spooled out, and Kath ripped it off.

"What the hell?" she mumbled as Carter stepped up beside her, and the two of them looked at the printout. All it said was "W97."

"What in the world could that mean?" Carter asked, his mind in a full state of confusion. "Wyszynski has been at zero since the second scrutiny, and now all of the sudden, he's got ninety-seven votes and he's been elected pope? Is that possible?"

Kath slowly shook her head. "I don't get it. It just doesn't make any sense. It'd be like some sort of coup taking place in there. I...I just don't know what to say."

As they spoke, the celebration in St. Peter's Square continued and the crowd began to swell. The word of the white smoke was emanating outward into the surrounding Roman neighborhoods, as the smoke from the chimney itself began to grow thin and wispy. Fewer people were paying it much attention, and those who were hardly noticed the brief cough of bright orange flame that erupted from the stack. The device inside the stove had just experienced death by thermal runaway. Its job was done, and like everything else swirling at the moment, it too was now history.

## Outside the Sistine Chapel

It had been nearly an hour since Monsignor Sarac and Sergeant Bruhlmann had heard what seemed to be applause coming from inside the chapel, and now they heard the old skeleton key unlocking its door. They stepped slightly away as the large door cracked open just wide enough for the large frame of Cardinal Jean Villot to squeeze through, his face reflecting a combination of emotions. Sarac looked at his superior, unsure whether the French cardinal was elated, distressed, or simply relieved. The priest and the guard had known for several minutes that something had happened, as they had heard the cheers out in the square, and each had assumed it meant white smoke was bellowing above them, although, as usual, neither spoke a word.

Villot leaned toward Sarac and whispered, "Go. Do as we discussed earlier." With that, he disappeared back inside. Bruhlmann expected

Sarac to leave immediately to do whatever he had been instructed to do by the camerlengo, but surprisingly, Sarac stayed where he was. This seemed odd to the tall Swiss Guard. What was he waiting for? Sarac was always quick to carry out the orders of Cardinal Villot, so why the delay?

The door opened again, and Cardinal Katic appeared, more ashen than usual and evidently struggling to stand. "Can you help me?" he asked, reaching to Sarac.

The monsignor nodded and offered his arm, which Katic quickly grabbed, and the two of them slowly headed toward the cushioned window seat Bruhlmann had seen Katic occupy so many times over the past three days. Sarac seemed to be almost carrying the Croatian, who was now shuffling more than walking toward their destination.

● ● ●

"They won't like this," Katic said to Sarac, his voice low and labored as he sat down on the seat.

Sarac lowered the cardinal down and then occupied the space next to him. "What, Katic? What won't they like?"

"The Pole. They've elected the Pole." Katic reached up and grabbed Sarac's shoulder, searching his face, increasingly distressed as he saw the monsignor's eyes turn cold, his expression intense. "Don't. I ask you—don't," Katic pleaded weakly.

"You know that's not possible," Sarac replied, his hand reaching up and removing Katic's cold hand from his shoulder as he stood up. Sarac looked down at Katic and then briefly glanced across the hall toward Sergeant Bruhlmann, who was watching them. "Thank you, Your Eminence," Sarac continued, in a voice loud enough for Bruhlmann to hear, "but I must go. Cardinal Villot has asked me to take care of certain matters."

Katic slumped back further into his seat as Sarac quickly walked away. The Croatian cardinal reached beneath his robes and pulled a handkerchief from his pocket, wiping the dampness from his forehead, his mind suddenly a mishmash of conflicting thoughts. As he sat there, struggling with his emotions, the door to the Sistine Chapel opened wide, and Cardinal Pericle Felici, the protodeacon of the College of Cardinals, the senior cardinal deacon, emerged. He paused briefly by Sergeant Bruhlmann, waiting for two white-clad priests, who seemingly appeared from nowhere, to join him. Felici looked over at Katic, a puzzled look on his face, no doubt wondering why Katic was seated outside the chapel, but he didn't have time to ask why. There were larger things on his mind. He and his small entourage headed toward the far stairwell that would lead them to the basilica. For the second time in six weeks, Cardinal Felici would have the honor of announcing to the hundred thousand or more people gathering in the square and the millions in the world beyond it that a new pope had been elected.

Katic wanted to call after him. He couldn't let this happen. But he was too weak. He watched as Felici disappeared and then lifted his eyes toward the ceiling. There was little more he could do but pray, asking for forgiveness, certain he would soon need it and uncertain it would be granted.

• • •

As Felici was making his way to the basilica, Sarac was arriving at Villot's office in the Apostolic Palace. It being late in the day, the outer office was empty, making it all the easier for him to slip into and out of the camerlengo's office without being observed. Sarac opened the office door and walked across the dimly lit room toward Villot's large desk, reaching beneath it to retrieve the briefcase that had been sitting there for several days, slowly accumulating papers that would soon have little relevance. Sarac placed the briefcase on the desk and then reached into his pocket and grabbed his small key chain. He fumbled with the keys briefly as he searched for the one he was looking for, the smallest one on the small ring. He inserted it into the briefcase and turned, watching as the small clasp holding the two halves together popped open. He had the right key, and it worked. Sarac then pressed the clasp back into place, grabbed the briefcase, and headed out the door.

There were over a hundred little-known and seldom-used staircases in and around the Vatican complex, and Sarac was familiar with them all. In his position, he had to be, as they allowed him to do his job for Villot, getting around the city-state quickly, and this knowledge was essential for the job he had at the moment—getting quickly and safely out. He had to go down one flight of stairs and then down a hallway to get to the small staircase he wanted, the one that would go up six flights to the rear entrance of the papal apartment. Sarac took his time. He had plenty; there was no need to rush. He had checked his watch when he heard the cheers in the square, indicating white smoke was coming from the chimney, so he knew he had about an hour from that moment, meaning there were about forty-five minutes left. It was proceeding as he had planned it. All was on schedule.

Sarac arrived at the top floor of the palace, set the briefcase down, and again pulled out his key chain. Finding the necessary key was easier this time, as it was larger and he had used it many times before to carry important papal documents to the Holy Father. He twisted the key, and the door opened easily if creakily. He grabbed the briefcase and stepped inside, closing the door behind him but leaving it unlocked.

The papal apartment was dark. The lights had been turned off since John Paul had been found dead nearly three weeks ago, but Sarac was intimately familiar with the layout and there was enough light for him to find his way down the hallway, past the now empty bedrooms of the pope's personal attendants, through the private chapel, and down the hallway past the kitchen to the door of the papal living area itself. The interior doors were all unlocked, allowing Sarac easy access to the small sitting room and through it into the pope's bedroom. His soft-soled shoes made no sound as he crossed the bedroom and placed the briefcase on the bed. He could see the illuminated outline of the window facing the square, as the wooden shutters that opened outwardly were not precisely matched to the windowsill, an imperfection allowing light to seep in around the edges.

Sarac stepped over to the window and carefully twisted the latch, allowing him to pull the large wooden frame slightly open. He then reached through the window and gently pushed open the exterior shutter, cracking it just enough to see outside, verifying it gave him the view he expected of the front of the basilica. He had hoped to be able to work from elsewhere, but because of the orientation of the palace itself, a bit oblique to the square, the bedroom was the only room offering an unobstructed view of the balcony. And he knew it would be empty.

Sarac moved the nightstand from beside the bed to next to the window so that it would provide the needed platform and then went to the bed and was opening the briefcase when he heard a large roar erupt from the crowd below. He stepped to the window and looked toward the balcony just as the large doors behind it swung open. Felici was about to emerge, but Sarac decided he didn't need to stay and observe the formalities of the announcement. He already knew what was about to be said—or so he thought. At the moment, he had a more pressing issue. He'd been standing around for most of the day, and he badly needed to get to the bathroom. He left the papal bedroom and headed toward the attendants' living quarters at the back of the apartment.

● ● ●

Far below and several hundred yards away, Carter and Kath also watched the great doors slowly swing open. By then, having no thoughts on what else to do, they had stepped outside the van and into the square, finding a spot just outside the metal barricades that had been erected by the carabinieri. The Italian police struggled to control the growing crowd while waiting with everyone else to see what was about to happen and what formal announcement was about to be made.

Carter and Kath found themselves in a state of considerable excitement as they waited with growing exhilaration to hear the name Cardinal Felici was about to reveal. Obviously, some sort of historic announcement was coming, that much they knew, but they had no idea about its key component—the name of the new pontiff. The last broadcast from Krol couldn't possibly be right. They hoped that it was, but they couldn't believe it could be. The indications were that their mission in Rome was a success, but was it? They thought the man they wanted had won the vote, but how was that possible? They knew only enough to be baffled by what they didn't know, but one way or another, the old dean of the College of Cardinals was about to settle the issue, enlightening them, along with the rest of the world.

● ● ●

As Katherine and Carter waited attentively in the large crowd and Monsignor Sarac sat quietly in a dark bathroom, Cardinal Felici, along with two assistants from the ceremonial staff, stepped slowly onto the large stone balcony above the central entrance to the basilica. The protodeacon paused, allowing the crowd to roar its welcome and simultaneously allowing himself to settle his old nerves as he absorbed the fact that this was a moment of history, and he was, for the moment, its central figure. Felici cleared his throat as the crowd began a rapid descent from raucous to reverent. The aide on Felici's left held up a large book on which the famous words he was about to utter were printed in large type, while the aide to his right held out a microphone on a long, adjustable wand. Felici pressed his hands together and then opened them wide and began to read his lines from the Latin script.

"Annuntio vobis gaudium magnum."

The crowd once more erupted with a great cheer at the expected introduction, and Felici again waited as the noise died down, which it quickly did. He then uttered the words they had come to hear: "Habemus papam!" Again Felici paused as another loud roar erupted, and those below began to enthusiastically wave white handkerchiefs. It was official; it had been white smoke, and there was a new pope. But who was he? The crowd fell silent once more, eagerly awaiting the next words.

Felici turned his bespectacled eyes back to his script and took another deep breath. "Eminentissimum ac reverendissimum Dominum..."

Standing next to Carter, Katherine listened and mentally translated the Latin into English. "The Most Eminent and Most Reverend Lord..." Like all those standing around them, Katherine and Carter waited for the name and like everyone else in St. Peter's Square, stiffened in surprise when they heard it.

"Dominum Karolum Sanctæ Romanæ Ecclesiæ Cardinalem Wojtyla, qui sibi nomen imposuit Ioannem Paulum II."

"Lord Karol, Cardinal of the Holy Roman Church Wojtyla, who takes to himself the name John Paul II," Katherine translated in her mind.

The one hundred and fifty thousand people now crowded into the square fell briefly silent, slowly absorbing the news. The cardinals had elected a pope from Poland? And it was not even the Polish cardinal they knew! What would this mean for Rome, whose bishop was now from a faraway Slavic country? What would it mean for the church and its teachings? But somewhat slowly, a polite applause started, began to spread, and then grew louder as those in the square recognized that they were witnessing history. They were seeing something that had not been seen in five centuries. All they could do now was wait for the new pontiff to appear, and given past practices and the experience of just a month before, that should happen within the next thirty minutes.

*Cardinalem Wojtyla!* Katherine turned to look at Carter, her eyes and mouth wide open in surprise. "What? Wojtyla! Carter, how did we not see that coming?" Her hands reflexively went to her cheeks. "So, you may have been right. Krol has been on his own agenda, but luckily it matches ours—at least I think it does. This will work! It'll work just as we wanted. Maybe even better!"

Carter turned to face Katherine, but before he could say anything, he got his second major shock of the last thirty seconds. Kath threw both her arms around his neck, pulled him close to her, and lightly kissed his cheek; then realizing what she had done, she sheepishly stepped back. "Oh my goodness! Sorry, Carter! I guess I got a bit carried away."

Carter smiled. "Well, getting carried away like that is fine with me, Katherine. I'm just glad I was the one standing next to you when you did." He reached over and put his arm around her shoulder, and she did the same with him, leaving the two of them in a sort of semiembrace as they listened to the excitement sweeping through the crowd. He thought her grip on his shoulder was growing a bit firmer, while she was convinced his was tightening on her. But neither cared.

● ● ●

Sergeant Bruhlmann stepped back as the doors of the Sistine Chapel opened and the new pope, already wearing the white robes of his office, with a great, embroidered crimson shawl draped across his broad shoulders, emerged with those who an hour earlier had been his colleagues trailing closely behind. Cardinal Wyzsynski, who had been Wojtyla's titular superior and spiritual mentor, was walking beside him as they began the procession to the basilica. Among the last to leave the chapel were Cardinals Koenig and Krol, who stopped just outside the door, grinned, and shook hands, recognizing that their efforts to build a coalition for Wojtyla had worked. They had conceived it, built it, and held it together through eight scrutinies. They spoke briefly and then started to follow the others, but as they headed toward the staircase, Krol spotted Katic sitting alone and slumped on the window bench.

"Franz, go on ahead. I'm going to check on Katic. He's obviously ill. I'll catch up in a moment."

With that, Koenig moved away and Krol walked over to Katic, sitting down next to him. "Jedar, I know you have not wanted any help, but you must let me get a doctor. The conclave is over, and you are clearly ill."

Katic turned his pale face toward Krol. "I'm much sicker than you think, Your Eminence. Much sicker." With that, Katic fell forward from the seat, sprawling across the marble floor, groaning in pain. Krol immediately bent down beside him and began unbuttoning Katic's red cloak and the garments beneath it, as it was obvious that Katic was feverish. As he did so, Sergeant Bruhlmann dashed over to them.

"Can I help, Eminence?" the Swiss Guard asked, bending down to raise Katic enough to allow Krol to remove his upper robes.

"Yes!" Krol shouted. "Go get a doctor! Do you know where to find one?"

"Yes, Eminence, of course." Bruhlmann picked up his ceremonial halberd lance and dashed off down the hallway.

As Krol unbuttoned Katic's shirt, he suddenly saw that there was blood all over the left sleeve of the Croatian's shirt. Krol unbuttoned the cuff and rolled the sleeve up, revealing a nasty, deep cut on the lower arm, a wound that Krol could see was badly infected.

"Jedar! What in the world is this?" Krol exclaimed, as an unpleasant odor began to reach his nostrils.

By now, Katic was gasping for air, his eyes rolling briefly back into his head before returning and locking on Krol's face. "John…Your Eminence…John, you must forgive me. Please forgive me, Father…for I have sinned…I have sinned."

"Jedar, what are you talking about?" Krol grunted as he struggled to remove Katic's shoes and elevate his feet.

The sound of footsteps running down the hall echoed off the walls, and Katic reached up with both hands, grabbing Krol's face and pulling it toward him. "Listen to me, John. Please listen."

Krol pulled away as he saw the doctor and nurse coming toward them. He started to wave for them to hurry, but Katic grabbed at him again, once more pulling him down.

"John, listen, please listen…*bitte!*" He began whispering in Krol's ear.

The doctor and nurse reached them and immediately dropped down to the floor beside the two cardinals.

"Step back!" Krol barked. "Give us a moment, please."

The doctor and nurse stood and backed away, watching as Katic spoke softly into Krol's ear, his body showing signs of convulsion. Krol gently lowered Katic's head to the floor, stood, and turned to the doctor. "Please attend to him. Do what you can." Krol then knelt on the floor, said a quick prayer, and made the sign of the cross before again coming to his feet. Something told him Jedar Katic would not survive much longer.

Krol had to act and quickly, but how? What could he do? He looked over at Sergeant Bruhlmann, who was now standing beside him. "Sergeant, I need some help very quickly, but I'm not certain what to ask for."

Bruhlmann gently took Krol by the elbow and led him across the hall. "Your Eminence," the Swiss Guard whispered, "I'm here to help. I know Benjamin Franklin was born in Boston."

Krol's head snapped instantly toward Bruhlmann, who suddenly had his full attention.

Bruhlmann continued, his face intense, "Eminence, quickly, tell me what Cardinal Katic told you. Quickly!"

Krol steadied himself. He knew he had to concentrate. He grabbed Bruhlmann by the shoulders, whispering excitedly to him, trying to retain a degree of calm. "They're going to try to kill the new pontiff. They plan to kill him right now…tonight! Shortly!"

"Who is?"

"Monsignor Sarac! He works for the KGB! He's here somewhere, and he's been ordered to kill the pontiff."

Bruhlmann pulled Krol into the now-empty Sistine Chapel and closed the door behind them. He reached under his colorful uniform; pulled out a small, rectangular device; and opened its cover, while Krol watched with fascinated puzzlement. Bruhlmann pushed a number on a small keyboard and held the device to his ear. Krol looked at the guard with a baffled expression, as he was sure he was hearing a dial tone followed by ringing and then a click.

"Yes, it's Bruhlmann. I'm here with Cardinal Krol. I don't have time to explain. As we feared, they're going to try their termination plan." Bruhlmann paused. "Yes. It's Sarac. He left about a half hour ago. I don't know where he is or how he plans to do it, but we can't call out the guards or the Carabinieri. Most of the guards are standing at attention in the square, and if the Carabinieri haven't seen him by now, they never will. I could run to the bascilica and try to stop the ceremony, but I'm sure Villot would never listen to me—much less believe me. We have to handle this ourselves. Tell Major Carter to meet me by the guardhouse at the north colonnade. And tell him to hurry; we only have about twenty minutes!"

• • •

Carter and Katherine had returned to the van and were just stepping inside. She was still elated by the election, and he was still elated that she had kissed him. As Carter reached for the door, it flew open and Steve greeted him with a wild-eyed stare. "Carter, it's on. They're going to take him out. Monsignor Sarac is the agent we've been trying to uncover."

"Sarac!" Kath exclaimed. "Villot's secretary! Working for the KGB! Oh my God! He'll know every nook and cranny of the Vatican. How will we ever find him in twenty minutes! That's about all we have… twenty minutes!"

Carter looked excitedly at Steve. "Do you have some sort of reaction force around here?"

"Yeah, Carter, we do! You! The Swiss Guard sergeant wants you to meet him at the guardhouse by the north colonnade immediately! His name is Bruhlmann! Dark hair, about your height!"

Carter looked at Kath. "Do you have the Beretta?"

She nodded and dashed into the van where she grabbed her purse from the shelf above the printer, pulled out the gun, drew back the slide to chamber a round, and flipped it to Carter, who stuck it under his jacket and inside his belt.

"Carter!" she yelled as he began to run away.

"What!"

"Carter…please be careful!"

He smiled, nodded, and took off as fast as he could, picking his way through the growing crowd now crammed into St. Peter's, hoping he could find Bruhlmann in all the chaos. Within a couple of minutes, he had made it to the north colonnade and ran as quickly as he could along the outer row of marble columns. Up ahead, near the center of an opening in the colonnade, he saw a tall, dark-haired Swiss Guard, looking over the crowd, armed only with his ceremonial halberd, a long shaft with a sharp ax-like head on it. Carter ran toward him as fast as he could, momentarily thinking that this was the sort of aggressive defense Bobby Knight would like.

"Bruhlmann!"

The Swiss Guard turned toward the voice. "Caldwell?"

"Yes, what can we do? Do you know where he is?"

"No, but he has to be someplace with a clear view of the balcony! Follow me!" The two men dashed out into the square toward the obelisk with Bruhlmann leading. Given all of the celebration and anticipation, no one paid particular attention to them, but those who did quickly got out of the way at the sight of a tall Swiss Guard with a threatening-looking pole. They stopped near the obelisk and started scanning the square. Carter could see the shadowy figures of the Carabinieri positioned on the top of the colonnades. Certainly no one could be on those.

"He'll have to be on the north side!" Bruhlmann yelled. "There aren't good sight lines on the south."

The two of them turned and began methodically looking at the buildings towering above the north colonnade, including the Apostolic Palace. Bruhlmann's eyes were soon drawn to the papal bedroom, to the same window where he had seen the light on the night Pope John Paul was found dead. There was no light, but he could see that the outside shutter of the pope's bedchamber was now slightly open, whereas it had been latched shut all week after the apartment had been sealed. He took a few steps to his left to increase his vision angle. "Look!" he yelled to Carter, pointing to the window.

Carter immediately understood the concern. "How do we get up there?" he shouted, as the crowd grew ever more excited.

"Follow me!" Bruhlmann yelled, and the two of them took off as quickly as they could. When they reached the colonnade, the crowd again began to cheer. The sergeant stopped and pointed at the balcony. The large doors had opened again, and several men appeared and began draping the huge papal coat of arms from the balcony's stone balusters. "Come quickly!" Bruhlmann shouted again. "The new Holy Father will appear shortly. We only have ten minutes! Maybe less!" Carter nodded, and they sprinted through the gate and past the guardroom.

Bruhlmann barged through the palace door just off the Sixtus V courtyard and raced toward the stairs leading up to the papal apartment. Carter was impressed with Bruhlmann's speed and stamina, and he was working hard to keep up with him as each took the steps three at a time. When they arrived at the top landing, Bruhlmann paused, pointing to the rear door of the apartment, which was unlocked and ajar. Carter reached under his jacket and pulled the Beretta out, slipping the safety off with his thumb, turning his eyes to Bruhlmann in a manner saying, "I've got the gun; I'll go first." The two of them cautiously stepped into the apartment, hugging the walls of the dark corridors as they slowly crept toward the bedroom in the front corner.

● ● ●

Sarac was also busy, now back in the bedroom and diligently disassembling the briefcase, unaware that he was no longer alone in the papal apartment. He lifted Villot's papers from the briefcase and tossed them on the floor. He then pulled the soft padding away from the four interior sides of the briefcase and removed two tubes, a receiver group, a small threaded handle, and a small sniper scope. Next, he pried away the hinge pins and removed the leather handle from the top of the briefcase. Sarac could hear the crowd outside getting restless, but he knew he still had time and he continued carefully and methodically with his task.

He screwed the longer tube into the receiver group, hearing the soft click as it snapped into place. He next attached the shorter tube, which became the weapon's stock, and then snapped the briefcase's leather handle into it, making it into a crude but fully functional shoulder pad.

The scope slid onto the top of the receiver, and the threaded handle screwed into the bolt. Finally, Sarac took one of the handle pins and pushed it snuggly into the bottom of the receiver, where it would serve as the trigger. He then removed two bullets from the briefcase's bottom padding and pulled the handle, opening the bolt. He inserted one bullet into the weapon's chamber and then closed and locked the bolt. Sarac was an expert marksman, and he was confident he would only need one bullet. The other was just in case.

He moved the nightstand slightly and assumed a kneeling position behind it. He twisted the focusing knob on the scope, and the reticle pattern inside quickly and clearly framed the scene at the balcony where the large, maroon papal banner now hung. Sarac sat perfectly still, watching and waiting. His body didn't move as the large doors behind the balcony slowly opened. He pressed his eye to the scope; centered the reticle pattern just above the banner; pulled the stock back, making it firm against his shoulder; and applied a slight pressure to the trigger. The crowd roared loudly as the new pope walked out onto the now floodlit loggia, but for Sarac, it was suddenly an unexpected and puzzling scene.

"What the heck's this?" Sarac thought, removing his finger from the trigger and lifting his eye from the scope. He then quickly pressed his eye back to the lens and looked again at the surprising scene on the balcony. Cardinal Wyszynski was clearly standing there…but still wearing red robes! And Felici was there, also wearing red! But the figure in white with the dark crimson shawl was…who? "Wojtyla? They've elected Wojtyla!"

Sarac again pulled his eye away from the scope and mentally recalculated his task. He had two bullets, so now he could take out both Poles, Wojtyla and Wyszynski! What a coup this would be! Comrade Andropov would be thrilled! He placed his eye back on the riflescope and centered the reticle pattern on the crucifix hanging squarely in the center of the new pope's chest, framed between the two sides of the crimson shawl draped across his shoulders. He let out a slow breath…

and squeezed the trigger. He heard the click from the receiver as the hammer slammed against the bolt...but nothing happened.

"What the hell!" Sarac cursed as he pulled the bolt back, ejecting the unfired bullet. He inserted his finger into the chamber, feeling the front end of the bolt. "What the hell!" he loudly repeated, looking in the chamber, realizing there was no firing pin. He looked back at the balcony where Pope John Paul II stood with raised hands, accepting a warm response from the crowd in the square. Sarac turned to the briefcase on the bed. Had he forgotten something? Was he supposed to have inserted the firing pin? No one had told him that was needed! He was rummaging through the case when the door to the bedroom flew open.

"Drop it, Sarac!" Carter shouted, pointing the Beretta at the priest, unaware the rifle had malfunctioned.

Sarac threw the useless rifle at Carter and reached beneath his jacket, pulling out his own pistol, a Makarov, the standard sidearm of the KGB. Carter dove to the floor just as he heard the shot from Sarac's handgun. The Makarov's bullet hit the wall just above him, and pieces of plaster scattered across the floor. But with his focus on Carter's Beretta, Sarac had ignored Bruhlmann and his halberd and hardly reacted as the tall Swiss Guard rushed toward him, covering the distance across the small room in two steps, the halberd pointing forward. The Swiss Guard expertly swung the grip-end of the ancient weapon at Sarac, knocking the Makarov out of his hand with his first swing and then catching the would-be assassin across the side of his face with the reverse stroke. The force of the second blow threw Sarac onto the bed, blood dribbling from his broken nose, pain circling his head from his shattered zygomatic arch. He bounced off the bed and fell unconscious to the floor.

Carter slowly rose to his feet, the Beretta still pointing at Sarac. He looked over to Bruhlmann in amazement. "Damn, Sergeant, you're pretty good with that thing."

Bruhlmann smiled and shrugged. "Well, believe it or not, sir, we actually do train on how to use them. Don't ask me why, and—so far as I know—none of us ever have...until now. Excuse me a moment."

Bruhlmann reached again for his cell phone and dialed another one-digit number. "Gianluca, I need you to get up to the Holy Father's bedroom in the papal apartment...Yes, I know...Use the back stairs. Bring a tool kit...and some fresh bedding. You'll need to repair some furniture and put new sheets and a fresh blanket on the bed...and some plaster to repair a hole in the wall. Also, call the head of the Carabinieri detachment and ask him to meet us with a car by the guardhouse. We have a prisoner for him."

Bruhlmann closed the phone, and he and Carter stepped briefly over to the window to view the scene below. Both were surprised. The new pope was speaking casually and conversationally in Italian to the huge crowd, and they were listening in rapt attention.

"This has never happened," Bruhlmann said, astonished.

"What?" Carter asked.

"Speaking like this to the crowd in the square after a papal announcement. The new pope is supposed to just wave, offer a blessing, and then wave again. This is really different."

Carter looked at the balcony. "Well, Sergeant, maybe this guy is different in more ways than one."

With that, they grabbed the rifle, closed the briefcase, lifted the unconscious Sarac by his upper arms, and began dragging him through the door and down the hall, on the way passing Gianluca, who rushed past them with a toolbox in one hand and fresh linen in the other.

CHAPTER 24

Monday, October 16, 1978, 1:30 p.m.
The White House

● ● ●

Dr. Zbigniew Brzezinski was dashing through the White House's West Wing. He was one of the few who had open access to the president, although he used this privilege as rarely as possible, normally only to deliver the most important of news on international developments. And clearly, this was a meeting satisfying that criteria.

Brzezinski blew past the president's secretary and opened the door to the Oval Office. As he entered, President Jimmy Carter looked up from the famous Resolute desk, a pile of papers scattered across it, his close aide Hamilton Jordan standing over him, explaining their significance in great detail—Jimmy Carter loved detail.

"What is it, Zbig?" the president asked, somewhat apprehensively, as an unexpected appearance by Dr. Brzezinski often meant bad news was right behind him. But in this case, the president relaxed a bit when he saw the broad smile on Brzezinski's face.

"Mr. President," Brzezinski began, "I have just received word from Rome that the papal conclave has concluded and the new supreme pontiff of the Catholic church has appeared on the balcony."

"OK, Zbig…so who is he?"

"Mr. President, it is…Cardinal Karol Wojtyla."

Carter looked up at Jordan, who stood silently, perplexed at the discussion. "Who's Cardinal Wojtyla, Zbig? Where's he from? Doesn't sound like an Italian name."

Brzezinski's smile widened. "Sir, he's the archbishop of Kraków. We have a Polish pope."

"So, he's the other Polish cardinal? Not Wyszynski?"

"Yes, sir. He is—or should I say—he *was* the other Polish cardinal. He's fifty-eight years old, so he'll be the pope for a long time. He's a firm anticommunist. I'm quite certain Moscow is going batshit as we speak—if you'll excuse the description."

The president's famous toothy grin swept across his face and then receded slightly. "What about the invasion? Any word on what they're doing?"

"General Odom at NSA reports a high volume of message traffic from the Soviet defense ministry to the Red Army headquarters of both the Western Military District and Group Soviet Forces Germany. We don't have a full interpretation of the content just yet, but overhead shows no movements of the divisions they had moved forward. I'm sure they're trying to decide what to do, but my intuition is that they'll call it off. The Polish people will be overjoyed with the news, and an invasion now would certainly be met with exceptionally strong resistance, especially with the strong papal condemnation that would certainly follow."

The president leaned back in his chair. "And he got off the balcony?"

Brzezinski nodded. "Yes, sir. He got off the balcony. I don't know what happened there, but I'll brief you as soon as I have the details."

President Carter smiled again, this time wider than before. "Well, congratulations, Zbig. It worked. You and Major Caldwell pulled it off. When will he be back?"

"Tomorrow, Mr. President. Probably tomorrow."

"Well…get him a ticket in first class for the trip home. He's earned it."

"Yes, Mr. President. Anything else?"

The president leaned back again in his large chair. "Actually, yes…a couple of things. Would you call President Ford for me and brief him. He and I had talked about this, and he thought it was worth a try. So, let him know for me…if you would."

"Yes, Mr. President. I'll be happy to."

"And also, Zbig…call General Scowcroft. I think you should notify your predecessor as well. After all, he recommended that we put Major Caldwell on the staff."

"Yes, sir. I'll be happy to let Brent know."

The president smiled one last time. "As for me, Zbig, I'm going to call Rosalynn and my mother. After all, they each flew all that way to the popes' funerals for us. So, I think they'd like to know it all turned out—shall we say—surprisingly well."

"Of course. Thank you, Mr. President." With that, Brzezinski smiled, turned, and quickly departed the office. He was in high spirits. It wasn't often he was able to barge in on the president with good news.

## Monday, October 16, 1978, 8:30 p.m.
## Warsaw, Poland

Edward Gierek, the first secretary of the Polish Communist Party, was about to adjourn a meeting of the Party Central Committee, when the door to the paneled meeting room flew open and an aide rushed inside. All of the committee members looked on with both surprise and apprehension. It was highly unusual for such a senior group to have its sessions interrupted by a junior assistant. Gierek himself said nothing as the aide hurried over and handed him a folded piece of paper, then turned and departed just as quickly as he had arrived. The committee had been meeting late into the evening to discuss the steps Moscow had instructed Warsaw to take to ensure public calm when Soviet forces crossed its borders the following night. Although assurances had been given, no one in the room was quite sure what would happen to them personally when the Red Army entered Warsaw, and more than a few were seriously concerned about their own safety.

Gierek slowly unfolded the note and reached for his glasses. Then he read slowly, his eyebrows arching as he digested each word. The others in the room watched silently, nervously awaiting whatever was coming next. After a few moments, Gierek removed the glasses from his face, slowly lowered the paper, and tossed it onto the table. He looked around the room as he pulled the microphone closer to his mouth.

"Well, Comrades, I have just been handed some rather disturbing news." He paused and gazed at the nervous faces staring back at him. "It seems that about an hour ago, it was announced in Rome that Cardinal Wojtyla has been elected as the next pope of the Catholic church. He's taken the name John Paul II."

There was stunned silence. Nearly everyone in the room wrestled with conflicted emotions, a sense of pride that was mentally wrestling with a sense of apprehension. Finally, a local commissar seated in the front row slowly stood, looking up at Gierek. "Comrade Chairman, what does this mean?"

"I'm not sure," Gierek replied, his words heavy with the fatigue he felt after so many meetings over the past few days.

There was a pause for a few moments before another commissar, seated further back in the meeting hall, excitedly jumped to his feet. "What does it mean?" he shouted. "How can you be asking such a dumb question as 'What does it mean?' I'll tell you what it means! It means that we're going to have to kiss his ass!"

All eyes turned back toward Gierek, anxious to hear his reply. Gierek again glanced at the note before looking back to the gathering before him. "Comrade Wojiek is correct," the chairman replied. "We'll definitely have to kiss his ass…if he'll let us!"

## Monday, October 16, 1978, 10:30 p.m.
## Headquarters, Group Soviet Forces Germany

General Yevgeni Ivanovski was in the main conference room at his headquarters in Zossen, East Germany, about thirty miles south of Berlin. He had served for six years as the commander of Group Soviet Forces, and he was putting the final touches on what was certain to be the most important effort of his tenure. He had sixteen Red Army mechanized and tank divisions in the field, deployed all along the border between East

Germany and Poland, and all of them were leaning forward in attack positions, awaiting the order to move. Along with the principals of his senior staff, he was leaning over a large map that had been spread on the conference table, unit markers down to the regimental level scattered across it, all illuminated by a large bank of neon lights suspended from the ceiling.

"Comrade General, may I have a word?"

Ivanovski rose from the table and turned toward the familiar voice of his chief of staff, Colonel Valery Belikov. "*Da, shto?*"

"Sir," Belikov continued, "perhaps we should step over here for a moment. I have a message that just came in from Moscow, and I think you need to see it."

Ivanovski glanced at the others leaning on the table. Their eyes were all on him, certain that Belikov had just delivered the strike order that would start the wheels turning on their intricate invasion plan, one coordinated down to the minute with the Red Army forces in Belarus that would simultaneously be attacking from the east. The GSFG commander stepped away from the table and took the message from Belikov, walking over to a small table where he was able to read it more clearly under a desk lamp. He scanned over the short text and then looked up at Belikov. "*Pochemu?*"

Belikov looked at his boss and hunched his shoulders. "We don't know why, sir."

Ivanovski dropped the message on the small desk and slowly walked back to the large map, his subordinates following each step. "Comrades, the invasion has been canceled."

Those gathered around the map looked at each other in surprise. Cancel a major military operation now? When soldiers were in the field? When plans had been drawn up? When orders had been given? When Spetznaz units were already in position at key locations inside Poland? The GSFG operations chief was especially perplexed—and angered, struggling to keep his sense of outrage internal. "Comrade General, why? This is Politburo bullshit! We're ready to go. We can do this. It'll be even easier than Hungary in 1956 and Czechoslovakia in 1968. Why are they calling it off?"

Ivanovski stood for a few moments in silence. "The message doesn't clearly say. But it has something to do with the election of the new pope in Rome."

Another officer chimed in to the discussion. "Why? Who is this new pope?"

"The message didn't say."

"Why do we give a damn who the new pope is?" the operations chief asked, increasingly agitated at the dismissal of his great plan. "Whoever he is, he doesn't have any tank divisions!"

Ivanovski smiled at the comment. He remembered that Stalin had once made a similar statement. "I don't know who he is or what they think he has. But they obviously think he has something."

Colonel Belikov shook his head, slowly looking at the bewildered faces around the room. Like the others, he found this decision incomprehensible, but he suspected his son commanding a tank company would be pleased at receiving the recall order. His unit had been camped out near Loebau for over a week and was no doubt ready to come in from the cold common in the German autumn.

## Tuesday, October 17, 1978, 2:15 a.m.
## KGB Headquarters, Lubyanka Square, Moscow

Sergei Kornilov had been summoned from home some hours earlier. The message he had first seen was bad, the ones that followed were worse. He had failed. The KGB had failed. And now he had been summoned to see Andropov. It was never a good thing to be summoned to see the KGB chairman late at night, especially when you knew the topic of the discussion was an operational failure. Kornilov walked up to Andropov's office, flashed his badge to the uniformed guards, and stepped inside. There was no one standing behind General Korilenko's desk, which was not unusual given the late hour. Sergei was pleased to see that CCO was absent, as his presence and intimidating stare would have made things even more uncomfortable. He walked across the outer office and pulled the latch on the door leading into Andropov's office.

As always, the office was dark, and the back of the large leather desk chair was facing him. "Is that you Kornilov?" The KGB chief's voice was louder than normal, which was certainly not a good omen.

"Yes, Comrade Chairman." Sergei crossed the office and seated himself in one of the chairs facing the KGB chairman's desk. Andropov's chair swung around.

"What happened, Comrade Kornilov? This is an embarrassing failure and has been from the beginning. What happened?" Andropov never shouted or yelled. The fact that his voice level changed little, and his inflections even less, made him all the more intimidating. One never knew for certain how angry he was, as the distinctions between slight unhappiness and enormous rage were barely visible.

"Comrade Chairman, it seems we have had multiple failures. Katic appears to have gone soft on us. He evidently fell ill during the conclave and died just outside the chapel after the final vote had been taken. We don't know for sure, but he may have tipped off someone that we were planning to act if we didn't get a result we found…acceptable. Our sources in the Carabinieri tell us that Monsignor Sarac was apprehended in the papal apartment with the weapon we had provided and has been taken into custody. He evidently got in position for the termination, but the weapon didn't fire."

"What do you mean it did not fire?" Andropov growled. "It's the same weapon we've used many times. The only difference was that we packaged it in a briefcase. How could it not fire?"

"The firing pin had been removed, Comrade Chairman."

"*Shto*! What! Removed by whom?"

Sergei swallowed hard. "Apparently by Viktor Myshkin, Comrade Chairman. From what I have been able to determine, Myshkin resented Zhukov running the operation and did not feel it was advisable or necessary anyway, so he had ordered the firing pin removed."

Andropov slumped back in his chair. "Are you telling me that in an effort to screw Zhukov, Myshkin has screwed us all?"

Sergei took another deep breath. "We have not gathered all the facts yet, Comrade Chairman, but...*da*...this seems to be the case. And it seems that somehow—we don't know how—the Americans were able to influence the vote and had good information on what was going on during the conclave, better than what we had from Katic."

"How? Katic killed the nun!"

"There must have been someone else. We don't know who, and we don't know how."

Andropov leaned back in his chair. "Zhukov? Could it have been Zhukov?"

Kornilov shook his head. "Certainly not, Comrade Chairman. The old suspicions were never real. He's a Zhukov. He would never do anything to betray the Soviet Union. He did the best he could with what he had. There was someone else keeping the Americans a step ahead of us, and we need to find out who."

Andropov rubbed his hand across his chin and then fidgeted with his glasses as he processed what he had just heard. "The invasion of Poland is off," he stated, his voice sounding weary. "I told the Politburo we should go ahead and send the Red Army in anyway, but Kosygin and Gromyko sided against me, and Comrade Brezhnev then sided with them. Such fools! They are all fools! Trust me; this will come back to haunt us. It just delays the inevitable. Meanwhile, they all seem to feel we need to go into Afghanistan! Afghanistan! Afghanistan is crazy because Afghans are crazy! Nothing good will come of it."

Andropov paused, his frustrations bubbling over. Sergei was glad that the discussion had turned to Afghanistan, as it took the focus off Rome – and him. "Comrade Andropov, do you have any orders? Should we do something now?"

Andropov's cold eyes turned back to Sergei, making him immediately uncomfortable and edgy. "Of course we should do something now!" Andropov snapped, his voice reflecting a high measure of agitation. "I want Myshkin eliminated...*now*! Get the Mafia fellow to do it...what was his name?"

"Ombra," Sergei replied, appearing to be making a note on his notepad but actually just trying to avoid the KGB chief's gaze.

"Tell him to kill the bastard! Today! This morning if possible! And throw his body in an Italian garbage dump where it belongs. I don't want his remains anywhere near the sacred soil of the Soviet Union. Is that clear?"

"Yes, Comrade Chairman." Sergei paused. "And what about the new pope? Should we develop another plan to eliminate him? He's certain to make a triumphant visit to Poland soon, and that will certainly encourage those worker organizations that are already agitating against us, especially that antisocialist group in the Gdansk shipyard."

Andropov removed his glasses and rubbed the bridge of his nose. "*Da*, we'll get him, but not now. We have too much going on. And after this failure, they'll be closely guarding him." Andropov thought some more. "Contact the Bulgarians. They're good at this sort of thing. And when they take him out, it'll give us a degree of separation...some extra distance and some deniability. Tell them to develop a plan that can be executed—not now, but on short notice. If this new Polish pope encourages trouble for us in Eastern Europe, or anywhere else, we'll have to remove him. And the next time, we won't fail. The next time, there'll be a firing pin. *Ponymaete*?"

Sergei nodded. The orders were clear and understood. Conduct one execution and plan for a second. He was relieved that neither was his.

## Tuesday, October 17, 1978, 11:30 a.m.
### Dulles International Airport, Washington

The Pan American Airways Boeing 707 hit the runway at Dulles Airport somewhat harder than normal, giving the passengers a bit of a jolting welcome to American soil. Carter Caldwell had been dozing for the past hour, and the shake of the wheels hitting the pavement woke him up. He looked out the window and saw the distinctive Dulles control tower in the distance as the plane slowed to taxi speed. He turned his head back to his right and saw Katherine sitting there smiling at him. "Good morning, Carter. Sleep OK?"

Carter pushed himself up slightly in his comfortable seat and smiled back. "Certainly did. This flying first-class could be habit-forming. It sure beats coach."

"And it sure beats a C-137," Kath replied, referring to the air force version of a 707. They laughed and then leaned back to enjoy a few more comfortable minutes as the plane taxied to a corner of the field reserved for arriving international flights. The 707 soon came to a halt, and Carter looked out the window as three mobile lounges, Dulles's signature ground transportation vehicles, pulled up next to the plane, elevated upward, and pressed against the fuselage. Carter and Kath gathered their carry items and led the other first-class passengers off the plane and into the mobile lounge's sitting area. When the lounge was full, its doors snapped shut and the awkward-looking bus backed away from the plane, headed toward the international arrivals area on the north side of Dulles's main terminal, bouncing slightly as it went, forcing those standing to hold tightly to the aluminum grips hanging from the ceiling.

It was just a few minutes before the vehicle pulled face first into a loading receptacle at the terminal, and its doors opened. The driver grabbed the microphone above his head. "Please watch your step and proceed down the hallway along the yellow line that leads to the customs control area. Have a nice day." Along with everyone else, Carter and Kath shuffled off the vehicle and followed the yellow line, each carrying a small flight bag along with a large purse for Kath and a backpack for Carter. They soon arrived at the customs area where an airport guard directed them into one of the long lines that had formed in front of about twenty passport control booths, each occupied by a badged government official.

"Great," Kath said, turning to Carter, who was standing behind her. "Looks like several international flights have arrived at once. It might be a while before we're through customs. Maybe the C-137 to Andrews was the better option after all."

Carter smiled. "Better than first class on Pan Am?" he replied with a chuckle. "No way."

● ● ●

Seated in a small, windowed room not far away, Bruce Harrison was nervously checking his watch. He had not had any updates for several hours on the person he was meeting at Dulles, and the apprehension was wearing on him. "Did he make it?" he thought. "He should have been on one of the flights that arrived earlier." Harrison paced around the small office, drinking cup after cup of coffee, looking through the glass windows down the long line of custom booths, increasingly concerned something was wrong. Suddenly, the ringing of a phone broke his concentration.

"Sir." Bruce turned to the chief of the customs inspectors who was seated at his small desk, a phone to his ear. "I think he's at booth 7."

Bruce nodded, gulping his last sip of coffee and tossing the Styrofoam cup into a trash can. He opened the door and stepped into the large baggage area, looked down the row of booths, and headed toward the one with "7" stenciled on the back. When he arrived, he rapped on the rear door. The young, blue-uniformed inspector inside turned in his swivel chair and stepped out, a small document in his hand. As he did, Bruce looked through the glass to the front of the booth, where a stocky man in a heavy overcoat was standing, a rumpled hat pulled low on his unshaven face, his eyes looking back through the glass to Bruce.

"This it?" the inspector said, handing Bruce a worn red passport. "He was on the Air Austria flight from Vienna. No visa, of course."

Bruce examined the document and then glanced back through the booth, where the man continued to stare at him, his face calm and expressionless. "Yeah, that's him. Let him through. I'll take it from here."

The customs inspector stepped back into his booth, pushed the passport under the glass, and waved for the man to pass through the turnstile, with his characteristic "Welcome to the United States" greeting. The man stuffed the passport into his pocket and walked through, lifting his head slightly higher, now smiling—extending his hand toward Bruce.

Bruce also smiled and reached out to shake hands. "General Korilenko, sir. Welcome to the United States."

Korilenko smiled broadly, stretching facial muscles he had rarely used in his time as CCO. "Spasiba, Mr. Harrison. I'm sorry to be late, but I had to make some last-minute changes in my arrangements."

"Quite understandable," Harrison replied. "Let's get your bag." With that, they headed toward the baggage rotary, both of them relieved and much more relaxed. Cosmos had arrived safe and sound.

● ● ●

Back in the line, as they inched toward their own passport control official, Kath peered through the gaps between the booths, turned, and tapped Carter on the shoulder. "Isn't that Bruce Harrison?" she asked, pointing.

"Sure looks like him," Carter replied. "Who do you suppose he's with?"

"I have no idea. Must be somebody important for him to be here to meet him."

"Passport please."

Kath was now at the front of her line, and the customs official was uninterested in whatever she was watching. She slipped her passport to him and watched as he examined it.

"Returning from Rome?" he asked.

"Yes."

"Business or pleasure?"

She paused for a moment. "Mostly business," she replied flatly, glancing at Carter standing behind her.

"Welcome home. Next!"

Carter was also quickly through the customs booth, after following an identical ritual. The two of them started walking toward their baggage claim area when Carter stopped, reaching for Katherine's elbow.

"Well, I'll be," he said. "Look over there."

Kath looked toward the adjacent baggage rotary where Carter was pointing. A tall gentleman was standing there watching the carousel as it went around, a black overcoat hung over his arm, a white collar around his neck. The couple walked over to him.

"Cardinal Krol!" Carter said, his voice a mixture of surprise and relief. "Did you just get in? And why are you here in DC?"

"Well, my goodness," Krol replied, turning to give them each a hug. "I had some important affairs I needed to get home to attend to. Alitalia had a convenient flight here, but none to Philly. One of the priests at the archdiocese is meeting me outside, and we'll drive up. It's only a couple of hours at this time of day, assuming no backup at the Baltimore Harbor Tunnel. So, how are you two?"

Kath smiled, a bit uncertain about what to say. "We're just fine, Your Eminence."

"You mean, John, right?"

"Yes, sorry…we're just fine, John. It all turned out quite well, I think. Thanks to you. I'm sure everyone here is thrilled and very appreciative. I don't know how any of us can ever thank you for the efforts you made and the risks you took."

Krol smiled at her. "I really have no idea what you're talking about, Katherine." He paused briefly, looked around, and then turned his eyes back to Kath. "As I said before, I always try to do what is best for the church. Ah, there's my bag."

Krol reached out and pulled his worn suitcase from the carousel. "Well, I'm off. Good seeing the two of you." He paused again, turning toward his young friends. "You want to thank me? Thank me by being good people and living a good life." He stepped over and gave Katherine a hug, shook Carter's hand, and then grabbed his bag and headed toward the exit.

Carter and Kath waved to him as he left and then stepped back over to their own baggage carousel, where there were still no bags on the rotary. They awkwardly stood together in silence, each waiting for the other to say something. Finally, Carter did.

"So, have any plans for the rest of the day?" he asked.

She looked over at him, slightly shifting from one foot to the other. "No. How about you?"

"Not really. Thought I'd catch a cab home, unpack a bit, maybe go out to dinner at this great Italian restaurant I really like in Georgetown."

"OK. That sounds good to me."

Carter's face became a puzzle, with a major piece missing. "What do you mean by 'that sounds good to me'?" he asked, hoping it meant what he thought it did.

She smiled. "It means that I accept your offer to share a cab, go to your place, relax, and then you can take me to dinner at that great Italian restaurant in Georgetown—in that hot car you claim to own. Then you can drive me home...whenever we decide I need to go home. After all, my suitcase is still packed."

The missing piece fell into the puzzle on Carter's face, fitting in perfectly, changing his expression into a broad smile. Perhaps this truly was the beginning of a whole new era. The world now had a Polish pope, and he now had a date with Katherine O'Connor.

## Accolades for *Conclave*

● ● ●

"THE OCTOBER 1978 CONCLAVE WAS historic. The politics of choosing John Paul I's successor were not opaque--factions within the Church struggled while the public awaited the outcome. No one really knows what happens in a conclave, but Tom Davis weaves the circumstances of that decision into a most intriguing and spell-binding novel."

> Tyrus W. Cobb
> Former Special Assistant to the President
> for National Security Affairs

"Tom Davis finally shines a magnificent bright light of international intrigue into a dark Vatican shadow of the Cold War. He is a brilliant author, and his novel is savagely thrilling, breathtaking in its clarity of language and narrative. *Conclave* is that rare intellectual excursion that takes us on a wild ride into could-have-been history, wide-ranging in scope and importance, with telling and compelling imagining. Here it is: a new masterpiece from a gifted master storyteller."

> Michael Pocalyko
> Bestselling Author of *The Navigator*

"A very entertaining novel! Herman Wouk and Tom Clancy would both be proud of its historical context and its blending of the human with the technical. You'll keep turning the pages to see what happens next."

> Patrick Parker,
> Author of *Treasures of the Fourth Reich*
> and *War Merchant*

"*Conclave* is a truly remarkable blend of suspense, international intrigue, domestic politics, and the secrets of a conclave that makes for a gripping historical novel."

> Jerry C. Harrison
> Major General, US Army (Retired)
> Former Chief of Army Legislative Liaison

AUTHOR BIOGRAPHY

• • •

TOM DAVIS IS A RETIRED army officer and corporate executive. In the army, Davis served as military assistant to the Secretary of the Army and oversaw part of the US Army Special Operations program. He graduated from West Point and received a graduate degree in international studies and economics from Harvard University.

Printed in Great Britain
by Amazon